The Second Time Around
When Love is Lovelier

by

Stephen M. DeBock

Gypsy Shadow Publishing LLC

Copyright Page

The Second Time Around
When Love is Lovelier

by Stephen M. DeBock

Gypsy Shadow Publishing, LLC.
Lockhart, TX
www.gypsyshadow.com

Library of Congress Control Number: 2023950731
eBook ISBN: 978-1-61950-701-2
Print ISBN: 978-1-61950-700-5

Published in the United States of America

First eBook Edition: November 17, 2023
First Print Edition: November 25, 2023

Dedication

For Andrew and Colleen, with love

Contents

Bronze Star

I wouldn't have believed it. There I was, sitting in a tony café opposite none other than Sydney Brand. The Sydney Brand, the girl I'd worshiped from afar throughout high school, and the object of my adolescent fantasies. Sydney was by far the most popular girl in school—and also the most unapproachable.

Sydney, as Homer once said of Helen, had a face that could launch a thousand ships. Her eyes were bright blue, her nose classic Roman, her mouth—well, sensuous, although the word might not have occurred to me back then. Her hair was a rich auburn and fell well below her shoulders. As for her figure, the obnoxious guys—that is, the guys who had no chance with her, which happened to be all of them—would remark about her long legs, tight ass, and bodacious boobies. As one who worshiped her from afar, as only the most love-struck teenager can, I refused to join in their jibes and turned a deaf ear. For all intents and purposes, I distanced myself from them whenever the conversation turned to Sydney.

Sydney hung out with Leslie Benson, who painted sets and did make-up for the school plays, and who in the yearbook would be named class artist. In appearance she was the opposite of Sydney, looking something like that little teapot, short and stout. Her clothes were often ratty, and the other loser guys compared her face to that of a toad—with acne. Conventional wisdom among them went that pretty girls hung out with homely ones just to make themselves look even better by comparison. More nuanced wisdom surmised that Sydney was a friend to Leslie because no one else was, and she saw her as a charity case. I'd had no opinion of Leslie, but I preferred to think the two were simply friends, that being more in keeping with my image of Sydney.

As for my own self-esteem, or lack of it, I saw myself socially as a loser with a capital L. I was overweight, had braces on my teeth, and a cowlick that the heaviest application of Brylcreem couldn't keep down. I didn't participate in sports, so I filled my spare time with studies. If the yearbook back then had had a category for class nerd, my photo would've been there for all to see.

Sydney, on the other hand, captained the cheerleading squad; presided over the student council; reigned as homecoming queen; and—the only thing we had in common—took all Advanced Placement courses. While we shared many of the same classes, we never exchanged greetings, never made eye contact, never added to one another's classroom contributions. It wasn't that she consciously ignored me; she probably wasn't even aware that I existed.

But in my dreams? Sydney was at the beach, got herself caught in a rip current, and I saved her from drowning. She kissed me and told me she loved me. Or... Sydney was in an automobile crash, and I pulled her out of the car before it caught fire. She kissed me and told me she loved me. Or... Sydney was being pushed around by a bully whose attentions she'd rejected, and I beat him to the ground. She kissed me and told me she loved me.

At graduation, Sydney gave the valedictory address. She delivered it in a strong Southern accent that attested to her family's roots and made her sound even more charming. They'd moved north from Louisiana the summer before Sydney began her junior year.

After the ceremony, I noticed her leave the bleachers and give her cap and gown to Leslie Benson to turn in for her. Then she walked over to two forty-something couples and a handsome, preppy-looking guy whose ramrod posture and designer attire attested to his affluence and private school pedigree. She kissed her parents, hugged his, and linked her arm with the boy's as she bussed his cheek. I watched them all get into a limousine, and that was the last time I saw Sydney Brand.

The last time, that is, until a certain Friday in July eight years later, when I brought my résumé and application to teach in the middle school I myself had once attended—and to my shock saw Sydney sitting behind a desk in the office, as compellingly beautiful as I'd remembered. She was staring at her computer screen and either hadn't heard me come in or was finishing what she was doing before acknowledging her visitor.

The nameplate on her desk read Ms. Brand, not Mrs. something. I placed my paperwork on the counter, and when I cleared my throat, she looked up.

"May I help you?"

"Yes, please. The board secretary told me to deliver my job application and résumé directly to the middle school office."

She walked over to the counter, her heels clicking on the tile floor, and picked up my papers. She was dressed in a summer-weight skirt and satiny blouse, her hair worn loose. She gave me a perfunctory smile, saw my name, and did a double take. "You're not Matthias Hayes."

"I prefer Matt these days," I said.

"Not the pudge—excuse me—the kid in my AP history class?"

"Among others, yes."

"Well, look at you now." It was the first time I'd been aware Sydney had even noticed me back then. She gave me a quick eyeballing before she picked up my application and résumé. "May I?"

"Of course—please."

She scanned my paperwork and her eyes popped partway down one page. "Marines?" she said.

"Uh huh. The Corps hardened me up a little." I stood six feet tall with a thirty-two-inch waist, my teeth were free from braces, and my cowlick was controlled by my jarhead haircut.

"A little, you say?" Sydney still spoke with that sweet southern drawl. She looked farther down on the résumé. "Purple Heart? What does that mean?" I told her it's for having been wounded in combat. "So that makes you a hero."

I shook my head. "No. I just managed to get myself shot."

"And he's modest too," she said, flashing me a winsome smile. "But you're okay now, right?" I nodded as Sydney noticed my address on the application. "You still live in town? A lot of our teachers don't. They can't afford it."

Before our little hamlet had become a bedroom community for New York executives and self-made millionaires, it was largely a farming region. The house I grew up in was a two-story colonial on a quarter-acre lot in a middle-class neighborhood on the outskirts of town. The only luxury we had was an oversized pool. My parents had been on their college swim teams, and they'd remained aquaholics—their term. Around the time I was in high school, some farmers sold their land to wealthy developers, and before long McMansions sprang up like mushrooms.

"You're telling me the teachers work in town but can't afford to live here?"

"Basically, yes. The property taxes are outrageous. Now, I should caution you, even though you'd get salary credit for your four years of service, putting you on step five of the guide, it still wouldn't be enough to support a single man living alone. You are single and living alone, I take it? I don't see a ring."

"Yes, to both questions." This was not the aloof Sydney I remembered. "I collect partial disability from the Marines, and I get reserve pay, so those would supplement my income. Not counting my chickens, you understand. I might not even get hired."

"Hometown hero, I think you've got a good chance. Hey, listen."

Listen? Sydney could read a Merriam-Webster Dictionary, front to back, and I'd happily lose myself in that honeyed lilt.

I mean, this was Sydney Brand!

"The eighth-grade history teacher left in May to have a baby. She was planning to come back in the fall, but a couple of weeks ago she called to say she's not. The board's looking for someone to replace her. I'd be happy to give you a heads-up for the kind of teacher the administration will be looking for. How about we do lunch tomorrow, my treat? I know this really nice place across town..."

I arrived first, ten minutes early—hurry up and wait, as tradition goes—and Sydney walked in just a few minutes late. Her long red hair was tied back in a ponytail, and she looked stunning in a sleeveless white blouse that stretched taut against her ample curves. The frayed hems of her designer denim shorts revealed legs that would be the envy of a Broadway dancer. Leather sandals showed off her painted toenails, and in one hand she carried a small purse—washed denim, like her shorts. All this I took in during the ten seconds or so it took her to walk to our table. I stood and she offered her cheek for a friendly kiss.

We sat down and Sydney ordered beer and burgers for us both. Over our drafts, we began our get-reacquainted small talk with Sydney, reminiscing first about our high school years. I mentioned how I'd seen her leave graduation with her boyfriend, and she told me she'd married the so-called "college boy with a bright future. He turned out to be a pretentious prick, pardon my southern-accented French. He joined his father's company as VP, lorded it over the other employees, and treated me, especially around his equally pretentious friends, like a trophy wife. I hated it, Matt. I had so much more to offer, and he never acknowledged me as anything more than arm candy." They'd quarreled often, and she said he'd become abusive—verbally at first, then physically. "I showed up at the police station one night, five years into the marriage, with an eye swollen shut, bruises on my face and arms, along with photos I'd taken of other beatings, and that was that. The good news is, Burt had signed a pre-nup that granted me half our combined total assets should we ever divorce; plus, he put himself on the hook for alimony. He told me then it was a sign of his confidence in our everlasting love. His parents objected; but love is blind, right?"

"And that means?"

"Half of what I'd brought to the marriage—which was zip compared to what he had—became his, and half of his—the value of the house, sports car, bank account, IRA, pension—all became mine. I had no regrets about that, believe me, considering the abuse he'd put me through. After the divorce became final, I moved back to the area, bought a really nice town home on the other side of town, mortgage free, and applied for a secretary's job in the school district."

"Huh. I'd have thought you'd have your doctorate by now, teaching in some college."

"Nah. Living with Burt five years put me behind the eight-ball timewise. It'd take me, what, ten years to get my degree going to school nights? That's a lot of time I'm not sure I'm ready to invest right now."

"Hm. Tell me, Sydney, how old will you be in ten years if you go for your degree?"

She gave me a look as if to say duh, we are the same age, you know. "I'll be thirty-six."

"And how old will you be in ten years if you don't go for your degree?"

She paused, shook her head, and laughed. "Thirty-six. How come the same?"

I laughed with her. "If you ever get a lower number, let me know, okay?"

"Point taken. But at least for now I'm happy—free, white, and over twenty-one, as my daddy says. Seriously, one day I might start taking night classes. But right now, well, there's no pressure in my life, and you know what? I kind of like it that way. It's a lot better than all that social primping I had to do when I was married."

I tried to keep my eyes on her face, and Sydney laughed when she caught my surreptitious glance. "AC will do that to a girl; darned things have a mind of their own."

I apologized for noticing, and Sydney laughed it off. Then she turned the conversation to my life. "You said you got shot. How did that go down?"

"It's something I'd really prefer not to talk about," I said.

"Right. I've heard veterans don't like to talk about their time, in—what do you call it—in country?" I nodded. "Maybe later on, when we get to know each other better, you'll tell me. But for now, can you tell me what happened after?"

"Thanks for understanding. After I recovered, I was reassigned to the Pentagon—clerical work, by the way, so you and I have that in common. I performed administrative tasks most days, but on others I'd get to don my dress blues and lead visitors' tours in the building. The best part of that duty, it turned out, was interacting with the youngsters who came with their parents or school groups. My boss observed me at it one day, and he told me that my future as a civilian lay with teaching kids."

"And you took his advice, obviously."

"When my enlistment was up, I transferred to the active reserves, came home to board with my parents, gave them my disability checks as rent, and used the GI Bill for college. Living with them allowed me to attend school full time. So here I am, four years later, with a newly minted bachelor's degree, scouting for a job."

Sydney tilted her head to one side and frowned. "You still live with your folks?"

"No, and I don't blog from the basement in my pajamas either. First place, I don't own pajamas." We laughed, and she leaned closer. "Once I got my BS, my folks informed me that Dad was retiring early and they were headed to Florida—what they called an active adult community, with an Olympic-sized pool—and sold me the home I'd grown up in."

"Really."

"Uh huh—for the princely sum of one dollar US. Plus, they'd invested my rent checks in a mutual fund account in my name without my knowledge."

"Wow. My parents were just the opposite. They were disgusted when I broke off the marriage and said it was my fault it didn't work out. They basically disowned me."

By now we'd finished our lunch, and it was obvious we were taking table space from people waiting, so I suggested we leave.

Sydney called for the check and refused to let me pay. "I still have to prepare you for your interview. Which leads us to the question of the day—your place or mine? Yours is closer, by the way."

We chose mine. In the Marines, every Thursday night was designated, euphemistically, as field day, when we scrubbed the barracks top to bottom for inspection. I'd kept up the tradition by habit—the whole house, not just my room—as a thank you to my parents. Now that they were living the good life in Florida, I continued the routine.

Today, Saturday, the house was still spotless and ready for the white glove treatment. And when Sydney walked in, I could tell that she was impressed. She asked who my maid was, and I told her she was looking at her—him. She laughed and told me to marry her, as in right now.

I got two bottles of sparkling water from the fridge—I'd noticed a bottle of the same brand on her desk at school yesterday and bought a case, just in case—and filled two glasses with ice.

Sydney had brought the school's handbook, published by the board of education and given to each administrator and teacher. She sat next to me at the kitchen table as we went over the district's philosophy—high-sounding generalities, mostly—and more importantly told me what the principal and superintendent wanted to hear from a candidate.

A couple of hours later, my stomach was getting ready to growl, and I asked Sydney if she'd like to stay for dinner. I could offer her chicken Marsala, one of my specialties, and she said, "You cook too? Like I said, marry me, now!"

I'd hopefully anticipated this scenario and prepared the ingredients this morning, before meeting Sydney for lunch. I served it with a nice pinot grigio, and as we ate, I dared to inform Sydney of my high school crush, my insecurity, and even my dream scenarios.

She received them with a sugary smile. "And each dream ended with a kiss? Nothing more?"

"Nothing more," I admitted. "I was pretty shy back then, even in my dreams."

"Or noble. But that would mean I was a love object rather than a lust object, is that right?"

"I suppose so. I never thought to analyze it."

"All right, my turn for full disclosure," she said. "You think I ignored you in class, right? Not so. I knew full well who you were, and frankly you intimidated me."

This I could not believe.

"It's true. Your comments in history class were so, I don't know, insightful that I felt anything I could add would seem, well, either naïve or downright ignorant. As a result, I kept my mouth shut when you spoke up, to save face more than anything else."

"I'm no smarter than you, Sydney. I just enjoy history."

"Matt, listen. Yes, I was in AP classes, but my placement had a lot to do with my looks, my self-confidence, and my Suuuh-thun chaaahm." She undid her ponytail and shook out her auburn mane. "My teachers said I looked like I'd just come up from Tara to visit my Yankee friends. Good grades always came pretty easy to me. You, on the other hand, were the real deal, and to be frank, your grades depended upon your smarts rather than your looks."

"I still think you're selling yourself short."

She stood and leaned across the table toward me. "It's time for me to get going. But before I do, I'm going to give you that kiss you dreamed about back in school," she said, and she briefly pressed her lips to mine. There was no tongue, just the softness of her lips. It was over almost before it had begun.

I asked Sydney before she left if she'd like to come by tomorrow for a swim. I'd grill some burgers and hot dogs later. She giggled as she accepted. "Maybe you can save me from drowning, and then I can kiss you again." She said goodnight with a peck on the cheek.

I stared at the door long after she'd left.

And damn: like a lovestruck teenager, I still had trouble falling asleep.

It was mostly Sydney's angelic face that I'd mooned over in high school. The next day, seeing how she filled out her bikini, I confirmed there was much more to appreciate. I'd put her on a pedestal back then; today I was ready to bow down before her.

All right, what I just wrote was high school level purple prose, but now high school fantasies were about to mature into real life... and then what? Anyone? Bueller?

We swam some laps, drank wine, nibbled on appetizers, and swam some more. At around five o'clock, I put burgers on the grill and doctored the final product with cheese, tomato, pickle, and my own secret sauce, patterned after the famous Hot Shoppes Mighty Mo burger, found only in D.C. and suburban Virginia. After her first bite Sydney once again told me to marry her, as in right now.

Sundown wouldn't come until after eight, so while it was still light, we spent more time in the pool. I climbed out first to dry off, but Sydney said she'd stay in and swim a few more laps. Suddenly, she doubled over, grasping at one leg.

"Cramp!" she cried from the deep end. "Matt!"

I jumped back into the water, wrapped her in a cross-chest carry, and swam to the shallow end of the pool. She was still moaning as I lifted her out and placed her onto a chaise. I massaged her calf as she lay back, breathing heavily, her hands gripping the side of the chaise.

When her breathing returned to normal, Sydney reached her hands to my head and drew me up, so my face was directly above hers. She gave me a sly grin and whispered, "You think maybe I need mouth-to-mouth resuscitation?" Without waiting for a reply, she lifted her lips to mine and thrust her tongue into my mouth.

When we broke the kiss, I smiled down at her and called her a minx.

Sydney didn't deny it. "My hero," she breathed, a dreamy expression on her face. "I love you." We kissed again, and she breathed, "That's one of your fantasies fulfilled." Then she reached behind her, untied a string, and lifted her bikini top up and over her head. I looked down. "See? They do have a mind of their own. Now take me inside and collect your reward."

We made love on my bed, the first time with Sydney beneath and the second with her riding me like a cowgirl. Afterward, we showered and dried each other off with oversized beach towels. Sydney had me stand still, examining my scars, touching the puckers in my flesh. Those indentations hid organ damage that had required multiple surgeries to repair and made me unfit to return to my unit. "Souvenirs," I said simply.

"You're still not going to tell me the story behind these so-called souvenirs?"

"I'm sorry. It would bring up too many memories—and it would end this wonderful night on a powerful downer."

"Okay, then. When am I at least going to see you in your uniform?"

"Probably never," I replied. "The only time I wear it is when I'm on reserve duty. But if you want, you can check my closet. The blues are hanging there inside a garment bag, and the utility uniforms are folded in my lower dresser drawer."

"That's not the same thing. I want to see them on you... my hero."

"Please humor me on this. Sydney."

She pouted. "Oh, all right, honeybunch. I'll take a rain check."

I needed to change the subject. "It's getting late. Do you need to go home tonight, Sydney? Because I'd prefer it if you didn't."

That seemed to brighten her up. "I thought you'd never ask. But I didn't think to pack a sexy nightie in my beach bag."

"Would a pajama top do?"

"You wear pajamas? You said you didn't."

I laughed. "No. When I left the service, my buddies at the Pentagon gave me a pair as a gag gift. Told me now that I was a civilian again, I couldn't sleep in regulation skivvies anymore."

"Oh, now I'm stoked. I'll wear the tops and you'll wear the bottoms. How sexy is that?"

The master bedroom's en suite bathroom was large enough for a vanity, and I looked in and saw Sydney sitting there in my pajama top, appraising herself in the mirror. She took a brush from her purse and began stroking her hair. She saw me studying her and gave me a coy look as she finished with the brush and took out a tube of lipgloss. After applying that, she brushed a trace of eye shadow on her lids and a touch of blush on her cheeks. We weren't going out, yet she was making herself up as if we were. Or, as if she were a courtesan, here to seduce me.

Satisfied with her look, Sydney stood up, and while looking at my reflection in the mirror, she began unbuttoning the pajama top, very slowly, very much aware of my appreciative eye. She slipped out of the top and draped it over the chair. She did a slow, teasing turn and said, "So which are you, Matt Hayes—a boob man, a butt man, or a leg man?"

"Looking at your perfect body, I'd have to say all of the above."

"You silver-tongued devil, you. Why don't you come over here, so you can look closer?" I closed the distance between us and kissed her. Into my open mouth she murmured, "And about that silver tongue..."

Third time, they say, is charm. And it certainly was.

Later, much later, we fell asleep, utterly exhausted.

Thankfully, for the first time in years, I didn't dream.

There were two recurring dreams that triggered my PTSD. The worst was a reliving of the day I got wounded in combat. The other was about the aftermath, when I found myself in the hospital.

Consciousness returned as I lay on a bunk. A single bunk in an air-conditioned room, not a cot in hundred-degree-plus heat. Before cracking open my eyes, I could hear the telltale beep, feel the cannula in my nose, and note the dull discomfort of the IV needle in the crook of my arm. I sensed someone hovering over me and opened my eyes.

"You're in Ramstein, Marine," the corpsman said. "Welcome back to the land of the living."

Ramstein, Germany, where the Humpty Dumptys were treated. If you got to Ramstein, it meant the facilities at the base weren't capable of putting you back together again. And more often than not, it meant permanent reassignment from combat duty.

"No, don't even try to get up," the sailor cautioned me. "What you've been through, you should welcome a long bed rest."

"How's Sergeant Burke?" I asked, my voice weak.

"Ask him yourself," he said. "He's right here."

Standing next to my bed, in a whole leg cast and supported by crutches, was Amos Burke, my platoon sergeant. "Well, if it isn't Corporal Shitbird," he said, grinning, his pearly teeth contrasting with skin the color of tree bark.

"Hey," I croaked. "What are you doing here?"

"Same as you, just not as fucked up."

"You saved my life."

"And that dumbass trick you pulled back there saved a lot of other lives, so we're even."

"We'll never be even. I'll always owe you."

He chuckled. "Considering the circumstances, I guess it's okay if you call me Amos—at least here. But go back to formalities when the troops are around. Wouldn't want them to think you're a kiss-ass or anything."

I nodded. "Thanks, Amos; means a lot."

"Hayes," he said, "I've been talking to the docs, and they say you've got good news and bad news. You're going to be okay; that's the good news. The bad news is you won't be going back to our unit with me. Brass tells me your orders will assign you to the Pentagon as an office pinky until your enlistment runs out. Oh, but the other good news is that when you get there, you'll have another stripe to add to your chevrons."

"I'm a sergeant now?"

"No. Here you're still Corporal Fuckup. But when you get to D.C., you'll be awarded the Purple Heart and given your promotion at the same time. You'll also be issued a set of dress blues for your new assignment."

Amos Burke was a staff sergeant, pay grade E-6. "Will you be promoted to gunny then?"

"Not for me to say. I would appreciate the pay bump, though, considering I have dependents back home."

He reached into the pocket of his hospital gown and showed me a photo of his French wife and their mixed-race daughter. "How did an ugly dude like you snag a beauty like her?" I said.

Amos Burke sighed. "I ask myself that all the time."

"You're going back to the sandbox, then?"

"Affirmative, or that's what they tell me. Soon as my femur mends. There's a metal rod in it now. I'll check in with you before I book out. I'll tell the troops when I get back you're sandbagging your way out of the field."

"*Sand* being the operative word. Listen, Amos. I'm not shitting when I say I owe you. If I could give you an order, it would be this—keep in touch. You're my brother for life."

He showed those pearly whites again. "Yeah, I'll think about it," he said. "You're still a shitbird, you know." Which was as sentimental as Staff Sergeant Amos Burke ever seemed to get.

We stirred. Sydney lay alongside me and propped herself on one elbow. She leaned over my face and kissed me.

"Hello, lover," she said.

"Hello yourself." She brought my hand to her breast.

"How do you like Sydney's love pillows?"

"Pillow talk, this is?"

"Yes, Yoda, pillow talk it is," she said, grinning. I told her I liked them fine. Which happened to be an understatement.

"Sydney, before this goes further, I have a confession to make."

"What? Breaking up with me already?" She pulled back and looked me in the eyes.

"What? No, of course not. But just so you know, if you continue to spend more nights here—which I dearly hope you will—when I reported to the Pentagon, I brought PTSD with me. I spent a lot of time with a therapist whose job was to treat patients like me. He wasn't a quack—he did the best he could—but the nightmares still come back. They're like I'm reliving my experiences rather than dreaming about them."

"This comes from the time you got shot?"

I nodded. "In the dreams I flash back to the sandbox when we were under enemy fire. I wake up with tremors, and sometimes I even scream. So, if it happens, don't be alarmed."

"That must truly suck, honeybunch." She ran her fingertips gently over my scars. "Guess I'll just have to learn to cope."

I sat up, my back against the headboard, and Sydney did the same. I put my arm around her shoulder, and she leaned in, taking my hand and draping it over the rise of her breast. She sighed. "You're so gentle, Matt. I love that about you." I kissed her forehead and brushed a strand of red hair from her half-lidded blue eyes. Sydney asked me to continue my story—what I felt comfortable telling her, that is.

"I was wounded, as you know, and my platoon sergeant, Amos Burke, literally saved my life. Years later, he and I still keep in touch."

"Like a real band of brothers, right?"

"When I was stationed at the Pentagon, Amos's wife and daughter were living in Camp Lejeune; that's in North Carolina, on the coast. He emailed to ask if I might call on them every now and then. Lily met Amos when he was on embassy duty in France, and they fell in love. Now Lily's an American citizen, teaching French, and their daughter

11

Cheri is a heartbreaker in training. Lily likes to joke that she and Amos are like ice cream—vanilla for her and chocolate for him—and their daughter Cheri is coffee."

"Wait." Sydney lifted her head and looked at me. "You're telling me your sergeant friend is black?"

"Dark brown, actually. That wouldn't bother you, right? This is the twenty-first century, after all."

"No—no, not me. Just kind of surprised is all. You know my family moved here from the Deep South, right? My daddy still has a Confederate flag pinned to one wall in the den, and he still believes the KKK is a patriotic group. But that's him, and my mom just seems to go along to get along, you know what I mean? As for me, I wouldn't consider myself prejudiced at all."

I nodded, hoping that the day would never come when Sydney took me home to meet her parents. "Anyway, on my first visit to Lejeune, Lily told me that after he left Ramstein, Amos was promoted to gunnery sergeant and awarded the Bronze Star for heroism. Typical Amos—he never mentioned it to me."

"Huh. What about you? Didn't you get a Bronze Star too?"

"I was only wounded—in retrospect, my own stupid fault. But Amos deliberately exposed himself to heavy fire—took a round just below his hip, which shattered his leg. And that happened while he was dragging me off the battlefield, with bullets whizzing all around him. Even after his injury left him with only one working leg, it didn't stop him. Seriously, if it hadn't been for him..." I let my voice trail off.

"Well, good for him. I still don't think it's fair, though, that he got a medal for bravery and you didn't."

"The Purple Heart and a promotion are nothing to sneeze at, you know."

"Hmph. I've seen your scars, and if anyone deserves a reward for courage, it's you."

"Know what?" I said, changing the subject. "I don't care about rewards—except for one, when you made a nerdy adolescent's high school dreams come true."

Sydney wrapped her arms around me and kissed me. "Oh honeybunch, you certainly know how to make a girl's day."

That September, thanks largely to Sydney's coaching to prepare me for my board interview, I began my new career as a member of a four-party eighth-grade teaching team. My partners, all women, all middle-aged and married, taught English, math, and science; my subject was American history.

Sydney's and my professional relationship remained just that. In school we'd address each other as Ms. Brand and Mr. Hayes, and we only lived together on weekends, as my nights were busy grading papers, planning lessons, preparing tests and quizzes and, as is the case with first-year teachers everywhere, fighting to keep one step ahead of the kids, subject matter-wise. We gave no hint that the principal's secretary and the new history teacher were anything beyond collegial acquaintances.

One weekend, Sydney stumbled into the house with her blouse torn, blood running down her cleavage, more blood from a gash on her forehead, and red and purple bruises on her face. I ran to the door to take her into my arms, and she told me she'd been in an accident on her way over.

I led her to a chair and sat her down, then picked up my phone.

"What are you doing?" she cried.

"Calling 911," I said. And she laughed.

"Silly. This is make-up. Remember your dream of saving me from a car wreck? Well, this is your chance."

I studied her, and a smile spread across my face. Then I picked her up and placed her on our bed. I asked where she hurt the most, and she said, "I'm sure you can find it." And she kissed me, and you can guess the rest.

After our shower, I asked Sydney how she'd done the make-up, and she told me she didn't. "Do you remember Leslie Benson from school? We used to hang together." I told her yes, and she said, "We're still kind of close. She did the make-up for the school plays, and now she's a make-up artist for a community theater company." She grinned as she pinched my cheek. "Gotcha, didn't I?"

I asked how Leslie was doing these days, was she married, and Sydney said she was doing okay, but as for marriage she still hadn't met the right woman.

Another weekend, another fantasy, acting out the dream I'd had of rescuing Sydney from a bully. In high school days I couldn't have done it; today I definitely could. But there are different types of bullying, and Sydney showed up at my door dressed as if she were going to work. She wore a conservative black knee-length skirt, dark blue jacket, pale blue blouse and pearls. Her make-up was perfect. She could have been an executive for a Fortune 500 company.

"I can't take this hostile work environment anymore," she sobbed as she fell into my arms. The women hate me for my looks. They think I get special treatment from the boss. And some of the men will lean over me to look down my blouse or graze their hands along my butt as I walk by their desks. I can't take it anymore!" She sobbed. "Please tell me you love me for who I am, not for my looks."

"I've always loved you for yourself," I said, and she kissed me.

This episode was especially glorious. Sydney made love like a lady whose wounded self-image was miraculously restored to emotional health by my worshipful ministrations. This was the Sydney Brand I'd envisioned in high school. I wanted this fantasy to go on forever.

I wanted to believe it wasn't a fantasy at all.

I sent Christmas cards to two households only, my parents' and Amos's. Lily always sent a card, along with a hand-written personal letter, not a word-processed generic one for the masses. The latest mentioned that after putting in his twenty years, Amos would be retiring that spring, and she would be supplementing his pension by continuing to teach high school French. Moreover, she was looking for a permanent home for their family, one where they could put down roots and where their daughter Cheri would have consistency and continuity in her education—qualities that were lacking by their having to relocate to different duty stations every two or three years. The envelope this year was postmarked Beaufort, South Carolina, the quaint town just outside the gates of the Marine Corps Recruit Depot, Parris Island. It seemed Amos was closing out his enlistment as a drill instructor. I pitied those kids—no, on second thought I envied them. There was no one more qualified to turn soft civilians into hardened young warriors than Amos Burke.

Call it serendipity or call it karma, whichever. Sometimes things just fall into place.

My mom and dad were constantly trying to persuade our next-door neighbors, their best friends for years, to retire and relocate to their community. Their urging paid off, and the couple placed their home on the market. I immediately thought of Amos and Lily. After Christmas break, I did some snooping at the local high school, and it seemed they were seeking to expand their foreign language program to include French. Our school system had a great reputation, so I figured Cheri would thrive here. I emailed Lily and told her to send me her résumé, and I'd forward it to the board. She sent it along with a heartfelt thank you. I delivered her CV to the board secretary, and that was that. I didn't hear anything further from either.

I needn't have worried. The board called Lily for an interview in March, and she flew up from Charleston to meet with them. Had I known she was coming, I'd have offered her my spare bedroom, but she said she didn't want me to get my hopes up, in case she wasn't hired.

Again, I needn't have worried. They hired her on the spot.

Meanwhile, the real estate market was in a slump, and my parents' friends—who had already moved to Florida while waiting for an offer—lowered their asking price.

Lily, still flying under the radar, looked at their house with a real estate agent while I was at school. She signed a contract immediately, with closing on July first, shortly after Amos's official retirement. Again, none of this would I get to know until the second week of summer vacation. As June approached with no word from the Burkes, I emailed Lily to ask if she and Amos had found a place in which he could spend his retirement years. She replied that they'd made a decision but would wait until everything was finalized before telling me; something about not wanting to jinx it.

Sydney and I took the first week after school let out and headed to the shore, where we'd rented a bungalow near the beach. This would be the first time we actually lived together twenty-four/seven for an extended period of time, and when the week ended, we decided that for the duration of the summer Sydney would move in with me, returning to her condo only to collect the mail and pay bills.

When we pulled into my driveway at the end of the trip, the Burkes were standing on the lawn waiting to greet us. This was Amos's peacetime version of shock and awe. And I was appropriately shocked and awed.

Amos and I bear-hugged like the long-lost brothers we were, and Lily was still as lovely as she'd been the first time I visited, some six years ago. Their daughter Cheri, now a bright and sassy thirteen-year-old, would be entering seventh grade in the fall.

"How'd an ugly moke like you snag a prize like this?" Amos groused as he hugged a surprised Sydney, and I reminded him I'd said the same thing to him years ago in Ramstein. Sydney stiffened when he wrapped his beefy arms around her. I attributed it to her discomfort at being hugged by a perfect stranger. She finally returned the hug, weakly, before saying hello to Lily and Cheri.

"You're coming to a reunion barbecue later," Amos said. 'That's an order, Marine. And the other reason is—wait for it—to celebrate Lily's position as the new high school French teacher."

"Surprise!" she said, pronouncing her *r* from the back of the throat the way the French do.

While we congratulated her, Amos said, "I think it was her dynamite looks and that sexy accent that convinced them to hire her."

She cuffed him playfully. "Oh, very nice. You're saying my qualifications didn't count?"

Cheri asked if I'd be her teacher come fall, and I said no, but the next year probably yes. Sydney observed that Cheri too spoke with a slight French accent, and Cheri cracked, "Blame Mom. I can't shake it."

"Credit Mom," I corrected her. "Imagine if you'd turned out talking like your father!" I made a scowly face and mimicked his drill instructor's bark, and she laughed.

After returning home that night, stuffed with Amos's world-renowned ribs, Sydney advised me of something I should have realized earlier. "You know once she gets into school, that girl will be telling her new friends that you're sleeping with the secretary."

"Oh, right. We'll talk to them tomorrow, Cheri and per parents together," I said. "I trust Amos to stress confidentiality to his daughter, and if he runs his home like he ran our platoon, we have nothing to worry about."

"That's good." She began undressing, saying she was going to take a shower. She pecked me on the cheek and headed for the en-suite bathroom. Soon I heard the sound of water running. "Honey-bunch?" I heard from behind the door. "Don't you think you should get in the shower before I use all the hot water?" I grinned and began slipping out of my clothes. "I mean, it's getting awful, awful lonely in here all by little old myself."

That night the nightmare returned. I woke up convulsing and crying, which brought harsh slaps to my face and fists to my chest.

"What's going on? Wake up! Matt, wake up!" Sydney's frantic voice brought me back to the present, and I lay on my back, open-mouthed, gasping for breath. "Hey! Come back to me! You're dream-ing; you're only dreaming. Shake it off, Matt!"

I lay alongside her, catching my breath. "Sorry," I managed to gasp out.

"Go back to sleep. Just calm down and go back to sleep."

Easier said than done, but eventually I dropped off into a dream-less sleep.

Next morning, I woke to sweat-soaked sheets and an empty bed. The smell of coffee brought me to the kitchen, where Sydney sat with a bowl of cereal in front of her. "You scared the crap out of me last night."

"Good morning to you too. I did warn you about my recurring PTSD."

I grabbed a cup of coffee and sat down at the kitchen table op-posite her.

"Jesus," she said as she stared at me. "You look absolutely ter-rible."

"And thank you for that."

"I know, I know. I decided to sleep in the guest room once you settled down. You did whimper a little, by the way, once you were asleep. Let me tell you, what happened last night was the rudest awakening I've ever experienced."

"Again, sorry. You know, it hasn't happened once since you moved in. I thought you might've helped me kick it at last."

"You think maybe being reunited with your Marine buddy might've triggered it? Brought back the memories?"

"Could be. I don't know."

"I'd hate to think this is going to become a regular thing with you."

Sydney returned her attention to the cereal, and I got up to fix some eggs. She was on her second bowl when I sat down again with my breakfast. Normally, I might've slipped my hand into her robe before sitting back down, but this morning my heart wasn't in it.

"I'm wondering how the Burkes can afford next door," Sydney said between bites. "I mean, they didn't buy their house for a dollar like you did. They've got to be carrying a hefty mortgage. And then there's the property taxes on top of that. I mean, my town house's taxes are outrageous; I can't imagine what theirs are. And yours, for that matter; but at least you don't have a mortgage."

"Amos's family lived in base housing, if I recall, which helped them save some pennies," I said. "And Lily taught French on whatever base they were assigned to. She has a graduate degree, which helps her salary-wise, and Amos has his retirement pay. I think they're good."

Sydney took her empty bowl to the sink and returned to the table. She sat down, and her face told me something was bothering her. She looked at me with hooded eyes. "Mind if I ask you a question?"

"Since when would I mind? What's up?"

"Between us, now. Strictly confidential; I mean it. It's your friend Amos." She affected a tone that bordered between coyness and discomfort. "I'm just wondering, and again this is strictly on the QT. Is it true what people say about black men? Like, once you have black you don't go back?"

Shit. I knew it had been too much to hope for. You can't live with a father who's a bigot your entire childhood without having some of his prejudice rub off on you. I tried to keep my voice neutral as I said, "Meaning?"

"Come on, honeybunch. You must've seen him in the shower. I mean, all you guys shared the same shower room, right?"

"Oh. You mean that."

"Yes, that. I mean, I've got no experience there, which is obvious, but I kind of wondered what Lily sees in him, no offense intended. Okay, I'll say it. Is he, like, hung like a horse?"

There it was. I was hurt by, embarrassed by, and ashamed of Sydney. To cover my feelings, I sought release in barracks-type humor.

"Is he ever," I said sardonically. "We used to call him the human tripod. Uh huh; that's right. He needed his trousers specially made; one leg wider than the other. And he had to tuck his foreskin into his sock. Back in the States, after work he'd pole vault home to Lily." I asked myself: did I mock her southern accent a little there?

"All right, all right, I get it. Sorry I asked. Jeez; no need to make a federal case out of it."

After a brief and uncomfortable silence, Sydney smiled and stood up. "More coffee, honeybunch?"

Reserve duty occupied one weekend a month and two weeks during the summer, and in seven days it would be time for me to take my temporary leave of civilian life. I suggested that Sydney might want to stay in the house while I was gone, and Lily, ever gracious, said she'd be happy to set another place at dinner for the time I was away. Sydney said thanks, but her secretarial position at school limited her vacation time to four weeks, two of which we'd already consumed.

"I live closer to the school," she explained to Lily, "so I'll go back to my job for two weeks, and then when Matt comes back, I'll take my remaining two weeks off. But thanks, really, and when our hero returns, we can have a welcome home party. I make a wicked jambalaya, Cajun style."

I told the Burkes that the pool was theirs whenever they wanted to use it. We'd already had a couple of pool parties with them since we came back from the shore. Amos would do his ribs on my grill, Lily would prepare a huge salad, and Cheri—Cheri was a regular water rat. Her exuberance made me remember myself from back in the day.

Sydney's earlier question about Amos was the only blot on what she called our summer of love, and neither of us brought it up again. I had to privately remind myself that she was, after all, a product of her home environment and that her question was born out of her own naïveté.

The school year began with me on a high. I had my first year under my belt, and I approached September with a hundred percent more confidence than I had on the opening day of school the year before.

Cheri entered seventh grade and made friends immediately. She was an eager student, which made her a favorite with her teachers as well. It was no one's business that we were neighbors, so we kept that information to ourselves. And despite Sydney's apprehensions, Cheri honored her commitment to secrecy about our relationship. In fact, she seemed to enjoy being in on a high-level conspiracy. If we happened to pass each other in the hall, she would sometimes give me a sideways look and wink.

The problem with the highest of highs, as I would soon learn, is that they're often followed by the lowest of lows.

As Veterans Day approached, our principal, Mrs. Martin, asked me if I'd do a presentation in the auditorium on the meaning and importance of the holiday. I'd never mentioned to students or staff that I'd served; it was easier not having to field questions that I didn't want to answer. The board and administration were the only ones who knew. And Sydney, of course. I didn't mention my upcoming command performance to her, because she would surely object, fear-ing it would trigger further nightmares. And more and more often I'd wake up in the morning to sweat-soaked linens and an otherwise empty bed.

"I'll arrange for a substitute for your classes," Mrs. Martin said, "and call an afternoon assembly for all sixth, seventh, and eighth graders. I expect you'll wear your uniform, right? Of course, you will," she teased. "Nothing like a man in uniform to set a girl's heart aflutter. Even an old bat like me."

It wasn't something I'd have volunteered for, but Mrs. Martin was an excellent principal; I couldn't say no. Furthermore, I was only in my second year, and a teacher had to be on the job for three years and a day before earning tenure. Before that time, he could be fired for any reason—like refusing the principal's request—or even no reason at all. If I did try to beg off, that would mean I'd have to advise the administration of my PTSD. And that might cause uneasiness among them relative to student safety.

On the afternoon in question, Mrs. Martin took the lectern on the auditorium stage as I waited in the wings, alone and antsy. "Veterans Day," she began after checking the microphone and greeting the students, "is designed to honor the men and women who have fought—and died—in order to secure all the freedoms you and I enjoy. As our guest speaker will tell you, from the American Revolution up to the wars in the Middle East, our freedom, your freedom, has been paid for in blood—and yes, also in tears, from the families of those who paid the ultimate price.

"Our speaker is a decorated Marine Corps veteran who served in the war and received a medal called the Purple Heart for wounds he suffered in combat. Boys and girls, faculty and staff, please welcome Sergeant Matthias Hayes, United States Marine Corps Reserve."

I walked out in full dress blues, eyes on Mrs. Martin, my white gloves clutched in my left hand and white barracks cap clasped under my left arm. Amid the stunned applause, I detected murmurs, most of them from my eighth graders in the front rows. Mrs. Martin shook my hand, smiled, and walked off the stage, leaving me alone in a cavernous room that was absolutely silent. I placed my gloves and cap on the lectern in front of me, with the polished brass eagle, globe, and anchor emblem on the cap facing the audience.

"Good afternoon," I said, sweeping my gaze over the auditorium. "In the days when I was sitting where you are now, I thought of my teachers as, well, just teachers. For all I knew or cared, after we left school for the day, they just pulled out a cot from their closets and slept in their classrooms." The kids chuckled with me. "We knew absolutely nothing about their personal lives, and frankly we weren't all that interested. Ring a bell with any of you?" Heads and smiles acknowledged. "I teach American history, as my eighth graders know, but what they don't know, what none of you knows, is that eleven years ago, I played a very small role in a very large part of American history."

I told them about my decision to enlist after high school, to do my part to thank America for all it had given me; brought them through recruit training, where the drill instructors' job was to transform undisciplined civilians into combat ready Marines; and stressed again that every living American citizen owes a debt of gratitude to those men and women who stood, and stand today, willing to sacrifice their very lives for millions of people they would never even know, including every person in this auditorium.

"The next time you meet a veteran," I concluded, "you might want to thank him or her for their service. And I think I can speak for them, in saying it was our honor and our privilege to serve; and... you're welcome."

I took a step back from the lectern as applause filled the auditorium. Some shouted, "Thank you!" and I smiled and nodded back.

Mrs. Martin returned to shake my hand. She faced the audience and gestured toward me, and the applause and cheers grew louder. I began to breathe easy. Then she checked her watch and said, "I'm sure many of you have questions for Sergeant Hayes, and we do have some time before the bell for the next class."

No! I thought. *No! Please, no questions!* Because I knew what the first question would be. And sure enough, it was.

"Did you ever kill anybody?" asked one of the boys, and I could see hundreds of students and staff leaning forward, hanging on his question, waiting for my response.

I closed my eyes and drew a breath as the worst of my nightmares suddenly flashed back, the ones that would wake me up sweating in the middle of the night. When I reopened my eyes, mind and body were once again trapped in the sandbox. I wasn't a teacher now; I was a combat Marine, and I relived those hellish moments, words tumbling from my mouth unchecked.

"It was hot, unbearably hot—well over a hundred degrees, and that was in whatever shade we could find. We swam in our own sweat and carried enough gear to equal half our body weight. Everything around us was yellow—the sand; the sun; the jagged walls we took shelter behind. Wind drove dust and sand into our noses, our ears, our mouths, and our eyes. And directly in front of us, people were firing automatic weapons at us. From somewhere down the line, I heard a scream as one of our men was hit. In his dying breath, he called for his mother.

"I was a squad leader, in charge of keeping my twelve Marines alive and functioning. The enemy had us pinned down behind these broken walls, maybe three feet high tops—the ruined walls of what had once been a family's home.

20

"The closest gunfire came from the bed of a pickup truck. Two men operated a machine gun, mounted on a tripod, while the driver sat in the cab. They fed the gun with bullets attached to a long ammunition belt. One man would fire at us while the other fed the ammo into the side of the gun. There happened to be a lull in the shooting, and I peeked around the corner of the wall. The enemy fighters had run through one ammo belt and were getting ready to load a new one. It would be a matter of seconds before they could begin firing again.

"Acting purely on instinct, I pulled a grenade from my vest and ran across the field, totally exposed, heading for the truck. The men saw me and fumbled as they tried to load the ammo belt. When I was close enough, I pulled the pin and threw the grenade. It landed between them in the truck bed.

"Again, if I'd been thinking, I'd have made a zigzag run back to cover; instead, I crouched there for just a second to witness the explosion. I won't forget what I saw then, and I won't describe it for you now. But what I did not notice was that another truck had pulled up, with another pair of fighters loading another machine gun. I ran for cover as they began firing. The first round tore a chunk out of my thigh and chipped my pelvic bone. The force spun me around, and then my body caught more rounds. A lot more. The enemy was using armor piercing ammunition, so my plated vest couldn't protect me. The impact from the bullets spun me around a few more times before my wounded hip gave out and I fell. The sand around me began turning red."

The bell rang for the last class of the day. No one moved.

The sound jarred me back to the here and now. All eyes were still glued on me. Committed to finish, I took a deep breath and continued.

"As I lay there, another Marine rushed out from behind the wall and ran toward me, dodging bullets in a helter-skelter pattern. The others in the platoon gave him cover by firing at the men in the second truck. My rescuer got hit in one leg, but he kept coming anyway. He reached me and somehow, using only his one good leg, managed to drag me back to relative safety. If he hadn't done that, I would have bled out and died in a foreign land. That Marine lived too and was later awarded the Bronze Star for conspicuous valor in combat. He happened to be my platoon sergeant, and today he is my hero as well as my best friend; in every way but by birth, he is my brother. I need to mention this because that hero's daughter sits among you today."

Heads swiveled and voices murmured. They became silent when I said, "It's not my intention to embarrass her, but if she doesn't mind, I'd ask her to stand and ask you to let her take your applause home to share with her father, to thank him for his own bravery and his own sacrifice."

Slowly, from halfway back in the auditorium, a self-conscious Cheri Burke stood.

The room erupted, all eyes on Cheri. She looked at me and mouthed a thank you.

When the applause died and Cheri returned to her seat, Mrs. Martin turned to me and extended her hand. Then she dropped all decorum and hugged me, to more applause.

When she released me, I glanced around the room and saw, standing in the rear of the auditorium, her expression blank but her blue eyes blazing, Sydney Brand.

Cheri and I went home that day with a stack of letters from the students, written during the last period of the day—thank-you notes addressed to me and also to her father. She walked over to my house after dinner to thank me as I was sitting at the dining room table grading papers. I was wearing chinos and a tee shirt, my uniform returned to its garment bag in the bedroom closet. I welcomed her and asked her to sit down. "Pop never told me anything about what happened, except that you were both wounded in combat. He just now told me to thank you for telling me what he couldn't tell me himself. I don't think even Mom knew the full story. Although she does now, because I told them both soon as I got home."

"Your father's a humble man. I'm sure he said he was just doing his job."

She smiled. "That's exactly what he said."

At that moment the front door opened with enough force to make it slam against the wall. Then we heard an unmistakable voice, shouting in a southern accent: "What. The. Fuck! Where are you, you son of a bitch?"

"Bathroom, now!" I whispered, and Cheri disappeared down the hall just before Sydney Brand stormed into the dining room and slammed her front door key onto the table with enough force to scar the wood.

"What's going on with you?" I said, standing up and trying not to shout back.

"What the fuck's going on? Suppose you tell me! We're together for over a year, you never let me see you in your uniform, and you've had me put up with your stupid fucking dreams. But does that count for anything? Obviously not, because instead of sharing your story with me, you stand there all decked out in your precious uniform and blurt it out to three hundred snot-nosed, shitty-assed kids—most of them perfect fucking strangers!"

"Sydney," I protested, leaning toward her, "wait a minute. What happened after my planned presentation was unscripted and unrehearsed. The boy's question triggered the memories, and you know what? You know what? When I was done, I felt a huge weight lifted from me. It was a catharsis. Sydney, if anything you should be happy for me." I took a breath. "And as for your foul mouth, that's totally inappropriate."

"You still should've told me first. I asked you, and you said no, forget it, you don't want to talk about it. Okay, I can get that. But did you say that to the kids today? No. You. Did. Not. What the hell is wrong with you? What am I to you? Someone to get your rocks off with? Some whore you can just kick to the curb?"

"Stop. Stop now."

She wasn't finished. "And what's with you and that skinny little pickaninny bitch next door?"

"You've just stepped over a line, Sydney."

"Oh, does that word offend you? So sorry. Then how about mulatto? Or high yellow, like what my daddy calls 'em? That work better for you?"

"I told you to stop. I won't tell you again."

"Ooh, so scared now. You ever think about the way you two behave at your pool parties?"

"You mean with her mother and father always there? Come on. Cheri and I tease each other all the time. It's called rapport."

"Oh, she's teasing you, all right. Teasing your cock."

"That's *enough*. You can't be jealous of a thirteen-year-old girl."

Sydney snorted and headed for the stairs. I murmured something obscene and hoped that Cheri hadn't heard me. No sound came from the hall bathroom; no coffee-and-cream-colored head peeked out the door as thumps sounded from the bedroom above.

About fifteen minutes later, Sydney came back, the suitcase she'd kept in the closet making a thump on each stair tread. She rolled it to the front door and stomped back into the dining room. She stood there, hands on hips, glaring at me.

Forcing myself to look at her, I suspected why arguments with her ex had turned physical. Because right now, I wanted to...

No. Nothing I could say would satisfy her; and frankly, there was nothing I cared to say. She'd crossed the line when she slandered Cheri. I returned my attention to the students' papers.

"Yeah, you keep ignoring me, shithead," she shouted. "I've got two words for you, and they're not Merry Christmas." With that, Sydney stormed out of my life, leaving the front door ajar as she made her way to her car and peeled out of the driveway.

"Shut... the front door," I mumbled mockingly. Then I heard Cheri's footfalls running down the hall. I stood and she ran sobbing into my arms. I hugged her for a long time.

"She had no right to say that about you," I finally said as her tears soaked the front of my shirt.

"I can deal with that," she sobbed, her voice halting. "I'm crying for you."

"For me."

"She said horrible things. She hurt you."

"Cheri, please don't be sad."

"I am sad." She took a deep breath and let it out. "But in a way I'm happy too, because now you know what she's really like." She sniffled. "I couldn't tell you before."

"Excuse me?"

Cheri took a step back and wiped her eyes. We returned to the table and sat across from each other. "When you were away on reserve duty last summer, she came by your house. From my bedroom I saw her scoping out our place from one of your second story windows."

"Why was she doing that?"

"You know that Mom does the week's grocery shopping every Wednesday at one o'clock, right?"

I nodded. "It's a ritual with her, yes."

"Well, when Mom drove away, Ms. Brand—no, she's Screech from now on—she walked over to our house and rang the bell. Pop answered, and she came in, and they talked."

"I didn't know about that."

"You weren't supposed to. I listened from upstairs. I couldn't pick up everything they said; she wasn't screeching then. It was like she was asking Dad to tell her something. I thought it might be about you, but I didn't like her tone, you know what I mean? It bothered me."

"You heard nothing specific, then?"

"No, but Pop got really mad and told her she had to leave, and they'd best forget this ever happened. After she was gone, I asked him what it was about, and he just shook his head and told me not to say a word about her being here. Especially not to you."

"I think I know what she was doing."

Cheri sucked in a breath. "Sure. She wanted to go to bed with him."

"What?"

"Mr. Hayes, come on, why else would she want to get my father alone? I didn't grow up in a bubble. I know that some white women want to have sex with black men. They want to compare them to what they're used to." She smirked. "It's a Mandingo thing, happens sometimes down South." She looked down, as if avoiding my eyes. "Least, that's what I hear."

"You are wise beyond your years, Cheri Burke. Your dad once told me you're thirteen going on twenty-five. And now, you and I have a secret of our own, don't we?"

"Can I at least tell my folks you broke up?" I said yes.

She looked up with the conspiratorial smile I'd seen so often, especially as we'd pass in the halls at school. "God, I *hate* that damn woman."

Next morning, I walked into the office to sign in and Sydney, feigning indifference, announced that Mrs. Martin wanted to see me in her office. The door was open. I greeted the principal with an apology for my behavior yesterday.

"Don't apologize, Matt. You held those kids spellbound, and when you opened up about your experience—I think you surprised yourself as much as the rest of us—well, we got a real-life look at war from a man who'd actually lived it. Those letters you and Cheri Burke got at the end of the day were all spontaneously generated; no teacher solicited them. More than one told me that as soon as the kids got back to class, they took out their notebooks and began to write."

"Thank you."

"I think it's best that I not ask you to do a Veterans Day presentation again, though. Agreed?"

I nodded. "Agreed. Again, thank you."

"A few of your students came in early and asked to go to your room. I gave them permission. Get going before they tear it apart."

I left the office without a look or a word to Ms. Brand.

When I walked into my room, four of my homeroom students, two boys and two girls, had just finished posting a computer-generated banner across the whiteboard. *Semper fi, Sgt. Hayes*, it read, with the words bookended by the Marine Corps emblem.

Cheri told me after dismissal that day that her classmates had greeted her with cheers too, and her homeroom teacher gave her a note of appreciation addressed to her father as well as one for me.

Back home, Amos came by and said a little bird told him Sydney was out of the picture. With that established, he invited me over for dinner and what he called a confab.

The confab concluded with our agreeing that should anything happen to Amos and Lily, I would become their estate's executor and assume guardianship of Cheri. Likewise, should anything happen to me, Amos would serve as my executor. After Cheri went to bed, Lily told me they thought their daughter might have a crush on me. I assured them that would pass when the boys her own age began to notice her. Amos grumbled and said that's what he was afraid of. Meanwhile, he would call an attorney in the morning and arrange for a meeting to draw up the documents. With a handshake from Amos and a kiss from Lily, I left for home floating on air.

A few weeks later, as I passed Cheri in the hall, she gave me no sign of recognition, but I was quick to see her eyes were bloodshot. After I returned home, there came a timid knock on my front door.

Her eyes were still red. I brought her inside and sat her at the dining room table. I offered her water, but she refused, twisting her hands together, almost afraid to look at me. Once her breathing returned to normal, I asked what was wrong.

"Mona." She said the name as if that explained everything. I had no idea who Mona was or what she'd done.

Cheri seemed to realize it and said, "She's my friend. But she's telling lies about me behind my back."

"Why is that?"

"I dunno. Maybe she's jealous? She likes Kevin, but he hangs out with me at lunch."

"I see. You're saying she's telling lies about you for revenge." I paused to formulate my response. "Answer me this, Cheri. Does a friend tell the truth about you, or does a friend tell lies about you?"

She sniffed. "Duh. A friend tells the truth."

"Uh huh. You've just told me Mona lies about you, so by your own definition she's not your friend at all. Which means you haven't really lost a friend, am I right? You've just realized that someone you thought was a friend really isn't. That's what's upsetting you, yes?"

She thought about it a moment and nodded. I said, "So why aren't you happy that now you know the truth?"

She choked back a sob. "But it hurts!"

"Well, that's your fault, isn't it?"

She snapped back in her chair. "What?"

"Cheri. You know you can't trust her anymore. Should the words of a liar mean anything to you?"

Another sniffle. "I guess not."

"Then if her words mean nothing, why do you give her the power to hurt you? I mean, you have the power, not she. If you give the power to Mona when you don't have to, that's on you, not her. It's kind of like... you know."

Cheri thought a moment. "You mean like Screech?"

I laughed. "Like Screech."

She frowned. "So that's why you weren't all upset when she broke up with you?"

"Don't get me wrong. I was hurt; I was hurt a lot—at first. But that night, after what she said—and the way she said it—especially what she said about you, I lost all respect for her. Instantly. Yes, I'd grown up with this hopeless dream about this idealized, perfect woman, and then when that dream came true, I was hooked. But then, in one fell swoop, she shattered the dream. I'd been wrong all that time. I decided I needed to take my own advice and not give her the power to hurt me. Because I know now what she is—and that's nothing. So, in your situation, you can refuse to give Mona the power to hurt you. Just blow her off. Maybe say Thank you for sharing, and then walk away. It's all up to you, girl."

Cheri wiped her eyes and smiled. "So why aren't you sitting in the guidance counselor's office instead of standing in front of a class-room?"

Having been a veritable twig in seventh grade, Cheri blossomed physically in eighth. It was like Mother Nature had apologized for not letting her develop sooner, and as a consolation she threw in some extra-curvy curves. I found out who Kevin was, and Mona, as they were all in my homeroom that year. Cheri's attitude was polite but dismissive around Mona and flirty around Kevin, which made Mona steam. Cheri had the power, and she was using it.

Returning from Christmas break—she'd spent the vacation ski-ing with her parents in Park City, Utah—Cheri surprised us all by walking into homeroom with her long black hair in dreadlocks. I pre-tended to be frightened and warned the class to beware "The Walking Dread." She in turn responded with a zombie act I christened the Burke lurk. The kids got a charge out of it.

Needless to say, Cheri wasn't about to let me get the upper hand. Once the class had settled, I greeted them with my usual good morning. That's when Cheri decided to zap me back. She put on her sassy face and said, "It *was* a good morning, Mr. Hayes." She paused a beat. "Case you didn't hear me, I said it *was* a good morning, Mr. Hayes." Everyone laughed, including me. I loved that kid.

A few weeks later, I overheard Mona accuse Cheri of being the teacher's pet. Cheri smiled and said, "That's because he can't afford a dog." Score another point for Cheri.

Later that day, Cheri visited me at home for a soda and a chat. She confided in me that she'd put the dreads in her hair because she was confused about her racial identity. Was she white, or was she black? "Mom told me I might want to talk to you about it."

Mom was either shuffling her off to me or was being very clever. I believed the latter, and later Lily told me I was right.

I looked Cheri in the eye and told her she was neither and both. "You're a perfect blend, Cheri. You have your father's deep dark eyes and a lighter version of his dark skin, plus you have your mother's soft hair and classic facial features. Your looks are a gift, girl; don't question them, and don't reject them." She took my advice, shed the dreads, and from then on wore her black hair long, loose, and casu-ally wavy.

Career Day in the spring was always a big eighth-grade event, and one of the presenters that year was a former professional model who now ran her own academy. She took one look at Cheri and after her talk told her privately that she was born to model. She stayed after school to elaborate with her and me about the possibilities for Cheri's future. Later, she met with her parents and me at their house.

"Keep modeling throughout high school," she told her, "and you'll never have to worry about student debt in college." That pleased her parents immensely, although they didn't say so in front of Cheri.

Also that spring, Sydney Brand requested a transfer to the elementary school, a switch that would allow that school's secretary to move to the middle school. Mrs. Wilhelm was thrilled that she would get the chance to keep up with "her babies" and observe them as they progressed through middle school. An additional benefit for me was that I didn't have to ignore a dirty look every morning when I signed in.

Finally, later in the spring, the board of education traditionally met to discuss the status of non-tenured teachers—who would be retained, who would be let go. My second and third years had been so successful that I assumed I'd be a shoo-in for tenure. My personnel file already contained numerous letters from parents commending me.

After school a week before the board meeting, Mrs. Wilhelm said Mrs. Morris wanted to see me in her office. I walked in and saw her with Dr. Hoffmeister, our superintendent. He asked me to close the door and sit down at the table opposite them. Neither was smiling.

Dr. Hoffmeister was a small man, with a round face and curly brown hair that made more than one staff member compare him to a hobbit in a three-piece suit. Very popular among the board members, he used his PR skills to charm the community as well. The teachers were wary, however; they suspected another face might lurk behind the cherubic one he presented.

He turned to Mrs. Morris, expecting her to initiate the meeting. She said, "Matt, I hate having to tell you this, but someone has charged you with unbecoming conduct with one of your students."

I was stunned. My entire body went numb, starting from my ankles and working all the way up. If I'd been standing, my legs would have given way. For a moment I sat there looking like a simpleton. Finally, I managed to stammer, "What? Who? When?"

"You forgot the where and how," Dr. Hoffmeister said with a smirk. Mrs. Morris turned her face to his, her frown saying not funny. My own thoughts returned to Parris Island, where my drill instructor advised us, if we didn't respect the officer, we must respect his office. I chose not to respond.

The superintendent continued, "Mr. Hayes, nothing so far has been placed in writing, and as of now this is strictly confidential, just among the three of us. I'd prefer it didn't become public."

"I honestly don't know what you're talking about. Who's the student? Who's charging me? Do I get my Sixth Amendment right to confront my accuser, or are teachers exempt?"

He scowled. "Remember, you haven't been formally charged. If you are, then you'll be allowed—"

"Dr. Hoffmeister," Mrs. Morris said, "Matt deserves to know all the particulars. Please."

He nodded grudgingly. "All right. In light of your principal's support and your military service, which I appreciate, I'll allow Mrs. Morris to give you the particulars. But as hers is an extraordinary request, I'm going to have to leave the room. Best that I know nothing of your conversation. We will, however, need your decision before the board meeting in two days."

"My decision?"

"Excuse me," he said and left, making sure to tell Mrs. Wilhelm to have a lovely day on his way out.

"Plausible deniability," Mrs. Morris said, shaking her head. "All right, Matt, from the beginning. You'll recall your Veterans Day presentation, of course. Sydney Brand told me that as your former high school classmate, which I wasn't aware of, she was really proud of you and drove to your house to tell you how impressed she was. She knew you lived alone, but she had the feeling someone else was in the house. She said you were quick to dismiss her, which she thought was odd. The next day, a female student dropped something off in the office, and before leaving she looked Sydney in the eye and repeated what she had told you that night, almost word for word. Then she snickered and walked out of the office."

"That's what Sydney said? Did she identify the student?"

Mrs. Morris shook her head. "I asked her not to. But she told me that if the board recommends you for tenure, she will go public and warn parents about allowing their girls in your class."

"My God. Sydney actually said she'd do that? Mrs. Morris, full disclosure, I'll tell you that up until last year, Sydney and I were living together on weekends and during the summers. We broke up after Veterans Day, and it was pretty rancorous, but I thought she was over it by now. I'd never have expected she'd stoop to this."

It was Mrs. Martin's turn to be stunned. "You and Sydney? Matt, you're one surprise after another. Your former relationship may be moot or not; it depends upon your answer to my next question, which I wish I didn't have to ask. Was there a female student in your home when Sydney arrived?"

I sighed. "Yes. My next-door neighbor. But there was nothing improper about her visit. Her parents and I have been close friends for years."

"Were her parents in the house when Sydney arrived?"

"No."

Mrs. Morris shook her head. "You know, Matt, perception is everything. If word of Sydney's suspicion gets out, your career will be over, and you'll be blacklisted in every board of ed office in the state."

I hung my head. "This isn't fair. Sydney knows better; she knows nothing inappropriate was going on."

"No, it's not fair, and for the record I believe you. But Matt, you can't afford the charges being made public, and as I just reminded you, perception is everything. Parents in the town won't trust you anymore."

"What happens next?"

"Dr. Hoffmeister is offering you two choices. One, submit a letter of resignation he can present to the board; or two, deny all impropriety, in which case the board will consider the public relations fallout, deny you tenure, and fire you."

"There's really no choice at all in the matter, is there?"

"The best I can do is this. If you do write the resignation, I will hand you the most glowing recommendation anyone has ever seen, and you can present it to your next prospective employer."

I shook my head and stared at my lap as Mrs. Morris waited for my answer. Finally, I looked up and said, "I'll resign, effective at the end of the day."

She let out the breath she'd been holding. "Let me suggest you address your letter to the board president, with copies to the other members, Dr. Hoffmeister, and me. Tell them you've enjoyed working here, but you feel it's time to pursue other avenues. Thank them for the opportunity to teach in an outstanding school system, yada yada yada."

Mrs. Morris stood and offered me her hand. "I'm so sorry," she said. "I'll get a permanent sub for the rest of the year. When the kids ask, and they will ask, I'll tell them you've decided to leave for personal reasons and that it has nothing to do with them. I'll say you're sorry to leave them, and that you genuinely care and wish them well."

"Couldn't ask for more, I guess."

"Oh, and I'd advise you not to pay a visit to the elementary school, if you get my meaning. Stay away from her." I shook her hand and said goodbye.

I drove home trembling, walked into the hall bathroom, closed the door, and screamed. Again and again, I screamed, impotent at Sydney's betrayal, of her threat to destroy not only my reputation but Cheri's as well. If the bitch were to go public, Cheri would be hurt far beyond my ability to grasp. And Amos and Lily, what would become of them? Lily's teaching career could be cut short as well as mine; her contract was up for renewal as well.

I walked out of the bathroom, went to the dining room table, and opened my laptop. Before I could begin composing my letter, the bell rang. It was Cheri, all bright and bubbly, there to tell me that she and Mona had mended their fences and were friends again. Kevin was totally out of the picture for both of them.

She saw my computer open and asked what I was doing. Writing a letter, I told her. Then she sat at the table across from me. "So not only are we BFFs again, but with our old friend Screech gone to the other school, we don't have to see her squirrely face anymore. I like Mrs. Wilhelm, by the way."

"Cheri," I said, "one question. Did you say anything to Ms. Brand a while ago that might've made her mad?"

She flashed me her million-dollar smile. "Oh, it was so cool. One of the other teachers asked me to take something to the office. I handed the envelope to Ms. Brand, and then I said, 'This is from Mrs. Ross, courtesy of your favorite high yellow mulatto pickaninny.' God, she practically jumped out of her skin! Good one, huh?"

I looked down at the table. "Oh, Cheri," I said.

"What? Wasn't it cool? I got her."

I sighed. "You got her."

Cheri frowned. "Something wrong? I thought that would make your day."

"No, I just have this letter to write, and I need to get it out tomorrow."

"Say no more, Mr. Hayes. I'm out of here. See you in homeroom tomorrow."

"No, you won't," I mumbled after she'd left.

Lily received her contract approval for next year, but she was shocked at the board meeting when the president read my letter. Afterward, she and Amos rushed to my house and demanded to know what the hell was going on. Lily said Cheri was heartbroken and wanted to come with them, but they told her this was grown-up business.

"I'm not supposed to say anything, so you must promise me what I tell you will never, I mean never, leave this room. Not even to Cheri. Especially not to Cheri." They agreed, and I detailed the whole sordid story.

Amos shook his head. "You're saying that if Cheri hadn't smart-mouthed Sydney Brand you'd still have a job?"

"Don't blame Cheri, Amos. She's a kid. She didn't think it through. But this is why you can't say anything to her. It'd kill her. Promise."

"Hmph."

Lily was weeping silently. "*Merde,*" she muttered. "I am so sorry. Maybe we shouldn't have let her come over so much. But we're family; why should we be concerned? We still aren't concerned, by the way, so you know."

"Thanks, Lily. It's all about the image of a young girl alone with her teacher in his house," I said. "I should've been more aware of it. But you're right, we're family, and we operate on that premise. However, if we let the harpies get hold of it, the court of public opinion will ruin us all, including your career, Lily. Better I take the fall."

"What'll you do?" asked Amos, still grumbling. "If it was me, I'd rip that bitch a new asshole."

I chuckled ruefully. "If what Cheri thought Sydney talked to you about that day is accurate, I imagine Sydney would have welcomed it."

His eyes grew wide. "She told you that?"

"Remember, she'd just heard Sydney call her a high yellow, a mulatto, and a pickaninny, all practically in the same breath. She couldn't let that slide."

"Well, something's got to be done about this."

I shook my head. "The resignation's official. Now I have to start looking for another job. Maybe get a real estate license or something."

"No!" he said, more forcibly than I'd heard in a long time. "You're a natural born teacher, and she's not going to get away with this."

I thought what Amos said was enraged bluster; I'd forgotten what a tenacious, take-charge guy he was.

For the next couple of weeks, I did maintenance chores around the house and got the pool ready for warmer weather. Cheri came by often, but on her father's advice—that is, his warning—she didn't pursue questions about why I'd left school. She'd tell me about what was going on in class, the sub was okay, but she wasn't me, the kids missed me, some sorry and others resentful.

I decided to take a weekend and remove the indoor-outdoor carpeting from the laundry room, replacing it with self-stick tile. Cheri asked to help, her parents approved, and we stripped the carpeting, nailed sixteenth-inch plywood over the subfloor, and laid out the tile. We worked together like a well-oiled machine, and when we were done, she invited her parents over to see the results.

Lily oohed and aahed, and Amos told Cheri she could grow up to be a carpenter; but Cheri reminded them of what the former model had said on Career Day—that if she modeled through high school, she'd have enough money saved to pay for college. Amos rescinded his job advice.

Amos's phone rang, he excused himself to take the call, and when he returned, he said he had to leave, but he'd be back before dinner.

"That's good," said Lily, "because I'd remind you, you're cooking tonight. And you'd better not make it SOS."

"Nothing wrong with Marine Corps SOS," he grumbled as he walked out the door.

I asked what business Amos had that could draw him away on the spur of the moment like that, and Lily said she didn't know; he'd been pretty guarded of late about his recent mysterious calls and meetings.

Cheri teased and said her father was checking in with his girl-friend, and Lily laughed and said that'll be the day. This was the kind of family I'd longed for, at one time blindly, with Sydney. Being denied that, I took comfort that I was part of another family I deeply loved.

"All right, people, listen up," barked Amos a few days later. I was in his living room along with Lily, Cheri, and a stranger he'd brought with him. When we were settled, Amos said, "This is Mr. Richard Dunbar, and he's a private investigator. Say hello, people." We all said hello. "Mr. Dunbar has some news for us that I think you'll want to hear."

Dunbar was a tall man, mid-forties, and fit. He was dressed in a hound's-tooth sport jacket over a knit tie. His trousers were pressed and his shoes were shined. In other words, not the movies' version of a gumshoed private eye.

"Mr. Hayes," he began, "Mr. Burke sought my services in regard to the libelous charges that caused you to resign from your position."

My jaw dropped for the second time this month. "Amos?"

"Shut your pie hole and listen."

"Mr. Burke asked me to investigate a woman named Sydney Brand, someone you all know and obviously do not love. My first visit was to the local courthouse to see if there were any legal matters pending; litigation and the like. It's not often I strike pay dirt on my first attempt, but there it was."

"Litigation?" said Cheri. It was a new word to her. Amos scowled at her, and she zipped her lip.

"Ms. Brand, it seems, sought a divorce from her husband a few years ago based upon spousal abuse. I assume she told you that?" I nodded. "Well, it seems her case was fraudulent, and she'd been planning it for months before reporting to the police station with a black eye and bruises. Did she ever mention a friend of hers, a make-up artist?"

"Leslie Benson," I said.

"Ms. Benson is quite skilled at simulating cuts and bruises with make-up. They look real as can be, in photographs at least."

"You're kidding."

Dunbar chuckled. "Over a weekend, Ms. Benson doctored up Ms. Brand with what looked like evidence of serious abuse. Ms. Brand took selfies of each different job, making sure she was wearing a different set of clothes each time. She took the photos against various backgrounds inside the house, as if she were beaten in different locations, shot them some time after her husband had left the room. Very convincing."

"But when she reported it to the police," I said, the damage was real, right? I mean, they would've known it was false as soon as they examined her."

"You're right. For the coup de grâce, she had Ms. Benson really beat her up. It hurt something terrible, but she knew the reward would be worth it. And in case you're wondering what Ms. Benson was getting out of it, Ms. Brand promised her a third of her monthly alimony payments in return for her services. All she had to do was keep her mouth shut."

Lily said, "The woman is devious; I suspected it from the beginning. The way she looked at Amos; it made me queasy."

"We know that now," I said. "But—"

The detective put up a cautioning hand. "There's more. What makes this more interesting is that a month ago Ms. Benson discovered a lump in her breast. She's an hourly employee at a gift shop during the day and has no health insurance. She asked Ms. Brand to help her with her upcoming medical costs, perhaps increase her share to half. Ms. Brand said that wasn't part of their deal, and she said no."

"I so hate that woman," mumbled Cheri.

"And now for the fun part," Dunbar said. "Since Ms. Benson could find no financial support from Ms. Brand, she visited the home of her former husband, the alleged wife abuser who'd always claimed innocence—but at the time figured no price was too high to be rid of the shrew he'd married. Ms. Benson confessed to her part in the plot and showed him prints she'd duplicated of her artistry, to add to her make-up portfolio. She'd hoped to break into film work—special effects make-up."

He looked around the room, smiling at the smug look on Amos's face.

"The ex reacted as one would expect. After all, his former wife had ruined his reputation, and once he was single again, he was off limits to any and all available women who might otherwise be interested. They wanted nothing to do with a wife beater. As for the alimony he'd been compelled to shell out every month—he could easily afford it; he's a multimillionaire real estate developer these days—he wanted it back, with interest. He filed papers in civil court."

"Fascinating," I said. "But what about Leslie?"

"He has agreed to pay her medical expenses in return for her courtroom testimony."

Cheri cheered; Amos gave her a look, and she zipped her lip again.

I said, "But Sydney can't possibly afford to give back all that he's paid her over the years."

"No, but that's not our problem, is it? I did, however, approach Ms. Brand a few days ago with what I discovered, which naturally she'd been hoping to keep out of public view. No one, including her parents and her colleagues at work, are aware of the upcoming litigation. She's hired a lawyer to help her make it go away. Using her ex's money, by the way, which I find amusing. What I did was suggest that in return for my silence she write a full confession to the board of education, saying all of the charges she'd brought against Mr. Hayes were false, and she was just trying to exact revenge following an acrimonious break-up."

"Wow. What did she say?"

"She's already written the letter and hand-delivered it to the board secretary. I've made a copy for you. Bottom line, the board held a meeting in emergency session and decided to award you tenure in the district. You can return to work on Monday if you want, with their apologies."

We all cheered then, and I gave Amos a bear hug that was almost as strong as his.

"I'm paying Mr. Dunbar's expenses," I said to Amos, and he barked me down. "This is our treat. After all, it was our daughter got you into this mess in the first place."

Which meant he had told her.

Cheri's face flamed. "I'm so sorry," she said, and her eyes filled with mist. "Me and my big mouth." I hugged her and told her it was all right, but in the future, she should consider the fact that all actions, including speech, have consequences. She sniffled against my shirt and promised she'd learned her lesson.

Amos said, "I spoke with the principal, who was very nice, and she told me to get your written commitment to return to class Monday so she could release the sub. I told her you would be there, no ifs, ands, or buts."

When Cheri finished eighth grade, I opened the pool to her friends, and Lily, Amos, and I hosted her graduation party poolside. I was still getting slaps on the back from some of the boys, and everyone said they'd miss my classes when they went to high school. Some of the girls said they'd really, really, *really* miss me.

When everyone had gone home, leaving the Burkes and me to lie on towels and gaze at the moon, we spoke about what we meant to each other. And when they got up to leave, Cheri threw her arms around me and said, "I love you, Mr. Hayes."

"Love you back, Cheri. And now that you've graduated, I'm not Mr. Hayes to you anymore; my name's Matt."

Over the next four years, the Burkes and I enjoyed many a shared vacation and holiday. Cheri modeled throughout high school, and she decided that she liked the field enough to pursue a business degree in college, with the idea of eventually opening her own agency.

She went off to the University of North Carolina's Charlotte Belk College of Business, and I realized it was finally time to reactivate my available bachelor status. I'd been celibate since the Sydney Brand fiasco—once burned and all that—and at thirty-four I was still a young man in my prime.

A few unattached women on staff had shown passing interest, but for obvious reasons I wasn't comfortable with any school-based relationship. It was by chance that I found female companionship during my reserve obligations. By this time, I had advanced in grade and was serving as company first sergeant, reporting directly to the company commander, Captain Carole Hills, USMCR.

Recently freed from an ugly divorce, Carole saw me strictly as a friend with benefits. She made it clear from the start that there would be no strings attached to our one-weekend-a-month and two-week summertime liaisons. I welcomed her stipulation.

After our initial coupling, we managed to disentangle our sweaty bodies as we lay, spent, on her bed in the CO's quarters. Carole turned to me and said, "I have waited so long for a really good roll in the hay." I mumbled something appreciative, and she said, "Yup. Still waiting."

Then she laughed and kissed me. "Kidding! You gave me exactly what I needed."

"Likewise. Would you like an encore?"

"No more tonight, cupcake," she said with a smile. "Reveille comes early, remember?"

"That's Sergeant Cupcake to you. Ma'am."

One night I happened to see a catalog on Carole's nightstand. It advertised bras and foundations for curvy women, which Carole definitely was. When she saw me do a double take, she asked what it was about. "That model on the cover. She grew up next door to me. Her parents are my best friends."

"Gorgeous woman," she said. "Are you close?"

"We were, when she was a kid. But I've barely seen her in years. She's in college now. I knew she was working as a model, but I'd never seen her likeness in print."

"Uh huh. Because you probably don't get lingerie catalogs mailed to your house. You don't, do you?"

"Hey. You should see how I look in my push-up bra."

"Shut up and kiss me."

After another really good roll in the hay, Carole said, "I loved it when you called me chéri."

Cheri? No! What was I thinking?

I fought to keep my breath steady. It must've been seeing Cheri's photo on the catalog cover. And speaking of cover: "*Oui, madame,* a term of endearment in ze French fashion."

"Ooh-la-la," she said.

Even though we were compatible sexually, Carole and I were never intimate emotionally, and while it worked for us, I admit to missing that deeper connection. We officially called our affair off when she showed up one weekend sporting an engagement ring. "Second time's the keeper," she said. "But thanks, Matt. It's been a great ride."

Cheri graduated cum laude with her business degree. She'd wisely continued modeling throughout her college years, and now she returned to New York, where she signed with a well-known agency. Before long, she was not only modeling but also helping with administrative work. She was busy but still managed to find time to spend weekends with her parents. And me.

Most kids tend to forget their teachers after they move on and their universe expands. Cheri, however, proved the exception. When she came home, the four of us were family again.

On one of her later visits, Cheri asked how my parents were doing, and I reported them hale and hearty, still swimming every day.

"How about school?"

"The good news is, the superintendent, Dr. Hoffmeister, left for greener pastures—as in, a larger district with more green in his paycheck. The better news is, his replacement is Dr. Camille Caron."

"Camille Caron. Sounds French."

"She is. She picked up her earlier degrees in France before earning her doctorate here. When she and your mom are together, they speak French all the time. They've become good friends."

She remembered my near downfall years earlier. "So, I never asked before. Whatever happened to Screech?"

"Well, as you know, with her letter exonerating me of all wrongdoing she also added that she'd resign effective the last day of the school year. The board told her she didn't have to wait that long." Cheri grinned. "That much you already know. Her ex-husband's civil suit took a while to resolve; you were in college when things finally got hammered out. Thanks to Leslie Benson's testimony, Sydney ended up losing everything she'd conned her husband out of. He had grounds to sue Leslie as an accomplice, but a deal was a deal; he arranged for her cancer treatments. Sydney, meanwhile, declared bankruptcy and crawled back to her parents' house. They moved away soon after. Where they might be now, I don't know; nor do I care."

"How is this Leslie woman doing today? Just curious." I shook my head. "Oh. Too bad. Sorry."

"Here's something you might find interesting. Leslie testified that she and Sydney had once been more than friends. She'd loved her and would do anything she asked, which included abetting fraud. She also testified that during that time their relationship had been more than platonic."

"Whoa. You mean Screech worked both sides of the salad bar?"

I chuckled. "That's one way of putting it."

"Wow. The things you don't know."

"You said it."

"And speaking of things you don't know, I've got a confession of my own to make."

"Really. Do tell."

"Okay. See, I was seriously dating this guy in college named Mike. And one night in the heat of the moment, so to speak, I called him Matt." She peered at me from beneath half-lidded eyes.

"Busted?"

She laughed. "So busted."

"All right, since we're confessing, while you were away I dated a woman named Carole and mistakenly called her Cheri. I'd just seen your cover photo on a lingerie catalog, so you were obviously on my mind."

"Uh oh. Guess we're even. So how did she react? Kick you out of bed?"

"No. She thought I was speaking French; you know, being romantic. I didn't see the need to correct her impression."

"Nice save. And you know vat zey say about ze French, right? Zey fight wiz their feet and—"

"I know the rest," I stammered and felt the blood rise to my cheeks.

"What's the matter?" she said, playing the flirt. "Cat got your tongue?"

"Um..."

She laughed softly. "You are soooo cute when you're flustered."

Cheri stood, stretched, and ran her fingers through her long black hair. "Time for my beauty sleep. Got to go to work tomorrow and look gorgeous for the camera."

After I went inside and turned on the shower, I realized that both her parents could have—in fact, probably already would have—answered her questions about what was going on in school, what had happened with Sydney and Leslie. So why had she been making small talk with me about it before confessing her heat-of-the-moment faux pas?

Sometimes I could be really thick.

That winter, horror struck.

Amos and Lily had arranged for their annual ski vacation out West during Christmas break. According to the National Transportation Safety Board's report, their commuter plane had entered sudden blizzard conditions; it iced over too quickly for the on-board de-icing equipment to handle; and the plane went down into a mountain. There were no survivors.

Cheri had had work commitments that prevented her from joining them on their vacation—one of those quirks of fate some say is coincidence and others say is ordained. We both took bereavement leave, and for a long time we huddled together, embraced, and wept. There were days we could barely function.

I fought to keep a stiff upper lip as I offered the eulogy at her parents' memorial service; and struggled too when Cheri joined me as I probated their will. After the estate was settled, she decided to sublet her apartment, move into her family's home—now hers alone—and commute to New York. She assured me that without my love and support she'd be lost, that she needed me close to her now more than ever.

My nightmares kicked in again; not as frequently as before, but strong enough to wake me up in a cold sweat. All over again, I relived Amos's battlefield rescue of my sorry ass. The dream segued to Amos and Lily, hopelessly trapped in a stricken airplane, whose lives I had been powerless to protect.

I figured that sooner or later I might have to contact the VA for an appointment with a counselor.

As summer approached, Cheri told me that her parents' house was too big for her alone, and it seemed the right time to move on from the memories that anchored her there. I suggested that since her sublet New York apartment was no longer available, she put the house on the market and move into mine while she waited for a sale. She mentioned that she'd been hesitant about asking me to share my home. "Although you have to admit, Matt, your décor is pretty severe; it could use a woman's softer touch."

Together we staged her house for the realtor's showings, and when the For Sale sign went up Cheri moved in with me, insisting she share expenses and take the guest room for herself. "It's your house; I know you're gallant and all that, but you're not giving me the master."

Once settled in, Cheri began to add some feminine touches to the décor, which I had to admit was an improvement, but it made me wonder privately how long she intended to stay. The real estate market had gone flat, and that was fine by me. How would I feel, I wondered often, if she sold her house and moved out of mine?

In July, two months into our platonic living routine, the nightmare came again. I snapped awake with a start and began to shake and cry out—no words, just shouts and grunts and moans. Seconds later, the hall light went on, and Cheri, clad in white satin pajamas, appeared in my doorway. She rushed to my bedside, pulled down the sheet, and placed the palm of her hand against my tee shirt. "Matt. You're soaking wet, and you're trembling," she said. I nodded, breathing hard. "It's back, isn't it, what happened over there? When Dad saved you?" I nodded again, still trying to catch my breath. "He used to have those dreams too; Mom was always right there to comfort him."

Cheri climbed into bed beside me. "And I'll be here for you," she said. "Don't try to argue; I'll win. Now go back to sleep. You need someone with you, and I'm not going to leave you alone." As I drifted off, I thought I heard her whisper something that sounded like, "Not ever." But by then, I could've been dreaming already.

I woke up again with a scream, and I heard Cheri's soft voice. "Shh, shh, it's okay, I'm here. Shh." She smoothed my hair and stroked the side of my face, and I remember clasping her hand with my own, holding it to my lips, and kissing it as if I were a suitor and she were a lady of the court. I fell asleep again with the warmth of her calm, steady breathing wafting against my ear.

The next morning, I awoke to an empty bed. Leaning forward alongside it, sweeping my face with her soft, sweet-smelling hair, was Cheri. "Wake up, Marine," she said as she straightened up. "You've had quite a night. You need to shower and shave now, and after breakfast we'll change the bed linens."

"Change them?" I muttered, still half asleep.

"They're soaked in sweat. I've already taken my shower, and by the time you're done I'll have breakfast ready. Cheri's famous blueberry pancakes."

I swung my legs over the side of the bed, and by the time I looked up Cheri had left the room. Shaking my head to clear the cobwebs, I remembered her presence as she lay next to me. Nothing erotic, but maybe something even more intimate. I made for the bathroom and a steamy shower.

With a close shave, clean body, and wearing shorts, a tee, and flip-flops, I let the smell of bacon draw me into the kitchen, where Cheri stood at the stove, her back to me. Her glossy black hair cascaded well below the collar of her pale cream polo. She wore mid-thigh navy shorts and flip-flops.

She heard me pad into the room and turned around. "Last pancake, ready for the warming oven," she said as she appraised my appearance. "You clean up nice, Matt. Smell like a soap bubble, too." She added, "I have news. As they say on TV, this just in. The head of my agency called this morning and mentioned that she'd like to set up a satellite office on this side of the river. If she did, I'd get the chance to run it."

"Really? Great news."

"Want some better news? The site she's looking at is only about ten miles from here."

"Even better."

Over breakfast I became aware of a certain awkward question hanging between us. As we drank our second cup of coffee, Cheri said, "Would you like me to sleep with you again tonight? I promise not to try to ravish you." She flashed that sassy grin. "Unless you want me to, that is."

I stared at her for seconds that seemed like minutes.

Cheri raised her eyebrows. "Well?"

"You've got me trembling inside."

"Yeah, I can tell. Talk to me."

"I don't know if I can."

"Talk already. I'm listening."

"Cheri, I keep reminding myself you're one of my former students."

She shook her head. "*Former* being the operative word. I haven't been your student for years and years, so please don't play the ick card on me. I'm a card-carrying adult now."

"I don't want to risk turning you away."

She sighed softly and looked me in the eye. "Okay, Matt, I'll start. At home once during college, I confessed to Mom that strange as it might seem, I still harbored feelings for you. It was a schoolgirl crush at first, I'll admit, but over the years, with our holidays and vacations spent together, our barbecues and gatherings at your pool, I have to tell you those feelings grew, and there was no stopping them. You were the gold standard; no one else measured up, at least for me. Yes, I was fearful to acknowledge it. But Mom told me that if after all this time I was still in love with you, I should accept no substitutes. Bottom line, I do happen to love you, Matthias Hayes, and if you love me the way I think you do, all I can say is I believe Mom and Pop would have gotten a real kick out of referring to you as their son-in-law."

I paused to let her words sink in. "But the fact that I'm, what, fifteen years older doesn't bother you?"

"It never bothered me. And I hope it doesn't bother you, because I'm dead serious."

Relief washed over me. "I do love you, Cheri Burke. But I was afraid..."

She stood and gave me a come-hither smile that spoke volumes. "Some fearless Marine you are. Now that we've established our feelings, why is there still a table standing between us?"

We made love in the guest room, where she'd slept, and afterward we had two sets of linens to change.

We decided to set our wedding inside the house, and we invited some of Cheri's friends from the modeling agency and some of mine from the school staff. We told them to dress casually and bring their swimsuits for later.

When the reception was over and the guests had left, Cheri and I walked into the bedroom and embraced. I said, "I love you, Mrs. Hayes," and she giggled and said, "I love you back... Mr. Burke."

"Still sassy," I said, laughing.

"Still classy," she countered. "Wait; I have a wedding present for you."

"Didn't we agree not to exchange gifts?"

Cheri ignored me and told me to sit on the bed. She reached into a nightstand drawer and presented me with a polished walnut box with an enameled Marine Corps emblem affixed to the top. "I was saving this for you," she said as she sat alongside me.

Inside were the badges, medals, and ribbons won by or awarded to her father—his marksmanship badges, battle ribbons, and on top of them all, his Bronze Star. I held it before my eyes and choked down a sob as my bride embraced me. "He'd have wanted you to have this," she said, tears forming in her own eyes.

I returned the medal to the box and placed it on the nightstand. "Long ago, Sydney Brand told me that if your father got a medal, I should've gotten one too. She said it wasn't fair."

"You have to bring Screech into the conversation? On our wedding night?"

I held Cheri's face in my hands and kissed her. "Guess what," I said as my eyes drank in every contour of her dusky, lovely, exotic face. "She got her wish." Cheri blinked. "But not in the way she intended. I have my own bronze star now. What greater award could I ever receive than you?"

Cheri wrapped her arms around me and kissed me, hard.

"I think we should go to bed now," I murmured.

"Ooh-la-la," she cooed.

Two Two Tango

One

When my flying club announced it was putting its fifteen-year-old Piper Cherokee Six on the market, I jumped at the chance to buy it. I'd used it as a training platform for my instrument rating, and because I was the club's trustee for the plane, I knew the single-engine airplane intimately. Except for an aging paint job and worn upholstery, Piper's venerable six-seater was in cherry condition.

Mike Fox, the club's president, joined me on the ramp at Florida's Naples Municipal Airport and handed me the keys and the airplane's logbooks; at the lawyer's office earlier that day we'd closed the deal, leaving me with a spanking new mortgage and a whole new slate of responsibilities.

Mike owned Foxtrot Construction. He was a bear of a man in his forties with a gravely voice and a pipe stem constantly between his teeth. If you wanted to find him on the job site, all you had to do was follow the odor of cherry blend tobacco. Mike's homes sold for well above what a guy in my pay grade could afford; my girlfriend Juliet and I were very happy renting a cozy one-bedroom condo a dozen miles from the airport.

I'd joined the flying club as a student pilot, and Charlene Baker, a.k.a. Charlie—a regional airline pilot, fellow club member, and flight instructor—had been my mentor for both my private pilot's license and instrument rating. She and her psychologist husband Oscar lived in a town home in the same complex, and she and I frequently carpooled to the airport for my lessons and for the monthly club meetings. The four of us became friends, and today we, along with Mike and his wife Sierra, were going to celebrate my purchase of the Six by flying up the coast for what pilots call the hundred-dollar hamburger.

Oscar drove the women to the airport, and after a round of congratulatory handshakes and hugs, they loaded themselves into the plane. "Where are we bound for today?" Mike asked as I fired up the engine. Charlie, who would be flying right seat, mentioned one of our favorite small restaurants in Sarasota.

"You mean the one near the Salvador Dali Museum," he said.

"Uh oh," said Sierra from the back row alongside Julie. "Don't you dare do it, Mike."

But her husband wouldn't be denied. He began to croak, "Hello, Dali, well hello, Dali."

Charlie turned to face him where he sat alongside Oscar in the center row and said, "One more sour note out of you, Mike, and you'll be making your first skydive over the Gulf. Trust me."

Oscar said, "That'd make the payload a lot lighter, save fuel besides," and Mike protested that his seatmate, being of the male persuasion, was supposed to be on his side.

We landed at Bradenton International, squeezed into an Uber minivan, and headed for the Dry Dock Waterfront Grill. We made for a motley group as we walked inside. Oscar was a buttoned-down shrink even when he wasn't working or teaching, and hadn't changed from the suit and tie he'd worn this morning for his appointments. Mike wore shorts and a polo that might have been blue once, and I wore chinos and a short-sleeved sport shirt that Julie had bought for me, because I'm not a shopper. Besides, she loved to dress me. Conversely, I loved to undress her.

As for the women, I'd have to say we all married above our stations—except for the fact that Julie and I weren't married. I can't say which of them was the more attractive, but they were definitely the objects of other men's surreptitious—some not-so-surreptitious— glances. If I were to compare the ladies to fine wines, Julie—my five-foot-two, blue-eyed blond firecracker—was the sparkle in champagne; Charlie—a tall, long-haired brunette with pale hazel eyes and a face and figure mortal women would kill for—was the brightest Beaujolais; and Sierra—maybe a decade older and more handsome than beautiful—was the tried-and-true Pinot Noir. Those were the wines they ordered, and with which they toasted me on my airplane. Oscar drank Manhattans and Mike downed a pint or two of stout. Following the "eight hours from bottle to throttle" rule, I limited myself to sparkling water.

Dinner conversation that night, as usual, began with the praise of our significant others. Oscar said thanks to Charlie's airline job, they flew free and spent many a weekend in Nassau. I praised my good fortune to have found a position with the same company Julie worked for. Only Mike seemed to hit a sour note when he said he kept Sierra in the lap of luxury, meaning his wife didn't have to work.

"I do lead a charmed life," she admitted dryly. "And did Mike tell you we have a maid to make the bed and do the dusting, vacuuming, and overall cleaning, and another to do the laundry and ironing, plus a chef to buy the freshest foods at the farm market every day and prepare delicious meals for Mike's dinner? Did he tell you that?"

Knowing her answer, Oscar said, "Do tell."

"Oh yes," she answered and pointed a thumb toward herself. "Right here."

Charlie and Julie gave Sierra high fives while Oscar glanced from Sierra's ironic expression to Mike's jovial grunt as his eyes rolled back. I could almost hear the gears turning in the shrink's head.

Among the appetizers was a plate of what the menu listed as crab balls, tiny orbs of seasoned crabmeat. Mike took a look and said, "I didn't even know crabs had balls."

Charlie affected a faux haughty look along with a British accent. "Surely, Michael," she said, "even you must have heard of the Vienna Crab Choir."

"Ouch," I said, cupping my lap while the others laughed.

When Julie and I arrived home, Julie fixed us with a nightcap and put on some soft music. We sat back on our loveseat and sipped the drinks. I closed my eyes and said, "Big day."

Julie agreed. "How lucky we are," she toasted as we clinked glasses. "Good friends, good times, good fortune."

Good fortune indeed. After my discharge years earlier as a Navy corpsman serving at the Marine base in Quantico, I found work as an EMT at the Walter Reed Military Medical Center in Bethesda, Maryland. After a few years of suffering the bitter Washington winters, where the tiniest snowfall tied up traffic and made passage of emergency vehicles almost impossible, I high tailed it to sunny South Florida, where in Naples I stumbled upon a company called X-ray Medical Supplies, Inc.

When I walked into the building, I was greeted by a vivacious blue-eyed blonde who introduced herself as Juliet, the bookkeeper-cum-secretary-cum-receptionist. I told her my name and the reason for my visit, she placed a call, and said the boss would be with me shortly. I noticed she had a habit of curling a few strands of hair around one finger as she made conversation.

Julie asked my background, thanked me for my service, asked if I'd seen combat—no, I was lucky—and commiserated with me on the harsh D.C. winters. "I'm an ex-pat myself," she said. "Vermont. You want cold? You want snow?"

"But at least the roads got plowed, right?"

"True, but I don't ski or ice-skate or do any of the other winter activities everyone else seems to love. I got frostbite once, and that was it for me. No more. Hello, Florida."

Her phone rang, and she directed me to the boss's door.

When I came out an hour later, I found myself the new Southern Florida sales and service representative for the company. My job would entail visiting hospitals, outpatient centers, and surgical supply facilities on both Gulf and Atlantic coasts, promoting the company's latest hardware. I had a thick loose-leaf notebook under my arm, with instructions to familiarize myself with it ASAP.

Before leaving the building, I asked Juliet if she knew a good local restaurant, and when she gave me a name, I asked her to go with me. Three months later we were renting a condo together, and life was good.

When I had to cross to the Atlantic Coast cities, the only way to get there was to drive across the straight-line Interstate known as Alligator Alley. I always had to plan for an extra hour's travel time, because if there were an accident somewhere along the way, the road became a parking lot.

I remembered flying in Medevac helicopters in the Navy and happened to idly mention to Julie that if I were a pilot with my own plane, I could fly across the state, not worry about traffic, and schedule more daily appointments up and down the coast. She said, "Why not see if your GI Bill will pay for flying lessons?"

That was all I needed to hear. After work one day, I moseyed on over to the Naples Municipal Airport and asked about flight training. "Cheapest way to learn is to join a flying club," I was told. "And we just happen to have one on the field."

Two

The Southwest Florida Flying Club boasted four single-engine aircraft and had a charter that limited membership to one hundred pilots. It almost never took on student pilots, but there were several vacancies when I applied, and dues were dues, no matter where they came from.

Mike Fox welcomed me into the fold and told me the club had a few certificated flight instructors available for lessons. Privately, he took me aside and told me to look up Charlie Baker. "She's beautiful, with a body that won't quit... not that I'd know personally," he corrected himself, with a look that seemed to tell me he wished he did.

I met Charlie at my first official club meeting, and it was not difficult picking her out from among the roomful of mostly men. Mike was right. She had a face that looked like she'd modeled for a Barbie doll, and her figure could've come from the same shop. She was wearing a short-sleeved white shirt with captain's epaulets, and when Mike introduced us, she apologized for her work uniform. "I just came back from a flight and didn't have time to change if I wanted to make the meeting on time."

Charlie was happy to take me on as a student, especially when I informed her a commercial license was my final goal. I told her my reasons, and she said that was a terrific idea. "You'll start with nothing and end up as a pilot for hire. I appreciate your ambition."

46

After the meeting ended, Charlie took me outside the clubhouse to introduce me to the planes. "The one here with the retractable landing gear is a Mooney Executive. It's a speed demon, and guys use it mostly for extended trips."

She walked me to the other end of the line. "The high-wing plane is a Cessna Skyhawk. It's a very stable platform, and it's what we'll use for your training." Next to it was a low-wing plane she identified as a Piper Archer. "The basic difference, if I can draw an analogy, is that the Cessna flies like a sedan and the Piper flies like a sports car."

Finally, she brought me alongside the Cherokee Six. To me, it looked like someone had attached an Archer to a taffy-pulling machine and stretched the nose another six feet or so. The inverted U-shaped split windshield and the elongated nose reminded me of a cartoon hound dog. The side windows looked like they came from the same parts bin as the Archer, and the wings reminded me of old-fashioned Hershey bars. "Kind of ugly," I said.

"She won't win any beauty contests," Charlie replied. "But the Six is wide, it's comfortable, and because there's a luggage compartment between the engine and the cabin, it's not nearly as noisy as the other planes. I'll check you out in it after you master the Archer."

"Which is after I master the Skyhawk."

"Correct. Now, let's see if we can coordinate our schedules."

For our first lesson the next Saturday, Charlie led me through the pre-flight inspection of the Skyhawk and told me that this would be the first and last time she'd do it with me; from the second lesson on, I'd have to do it while she observed from a distance.

After inspecting everything on the outside of the plane and checking the fuel level in the wings, it was time to continue to the inside.

"Above your side window is a shoulder harness that's separate from the seat belt. You have to link them manually. Some people consider it a bother to fasten, Mike for one, despite my nagging him about it. You will be using it, yes?"

"Absolutely."

"Atta boy. Okay, now for the startup..."

Charlie explained the flight controls, and once airborne, she gave me the controls and grinned good-naturedly as I made like a porpoise. "You'll get used to the sensitivity of the controls," she said. "Everybody does that on their first flight. Pretty soon, you'll be finessing the wheel with two fingers of your left hand."

An hour later Charlie landed, we secured the Cessna, and I wrote a check for the bill at the clubhouse desk. When Charlie told me her instructor's fee, I suggested that she was undercutting herself, and she assured me I got no favors from her. "Club discount," she explained. "For non-club members, it's double. But if you're feeling guilty, you can buy me a coffee."

One Saturday morning a month was devoted to an airplane wash party, with club members, often joined by family, showing up to wash down the birds. Afterward, the volunteers headed to a pizzeria and ate heartily on the club's dime.

As the club's newbie, I was eager to join the dozen or so members who showed up, and Julie joined me. Charlie came too, with Oscar in tow. She gave me an approving look and told me it's good for student pilots to contribute to their plane's welfare. Mike Fox was there too, and he gave Julie a second look, which he probably thought I didn't notice.

Mike said, "Oscar. You actually get your hands dirty?"

Oscar looked down at his sudsy bucket and said, "I thought I was here for a manicure."

Charlie and Julie hit it off right away, which pleased me, considering that the beautiful lady pilot would be sitting side by side with me in a small airplane for the next who knew how many hours; or even, how many years.

Mike had a shadow that day, a busty young redhead with braces on her teeth he introduced to Julie and me as Dee.

Julie said, "Dee. Short for Deborah? Deirdre, maybe? Delilah? Just curious."

She almost looked embarrassed. "Delta," she said. "Weird, huh? Papa named me after his favorite song."

Mike began to sing, "Delta Dawn ..."

Dee held up her hand. "Please, please don't sing; I left my earplugs at home."

"Hey, gang, don't let the braces fool you," Mike said. "She may look like a teenager, but she's not. Her dad was one of our original members; introduced me to Sierra as a matter of fact. He used to bring Dee with him when she was a little girl; kind of like our club mascot growing up."

"Where's your dad today?" asked Julie.

"In a wheelchair, unfortunately," Dee replied. "Alzheimer's."

"Oh, I'm sorry," said Julie. Seeking to change the subject, she said, "Are you a pilot too?"

"No. I'm just here for the company. Like the club mascot, as Mike says."

Julie looked around and said, "Mike, isn't your wife coming? We've never met her."

He shook his head, a wreath of cherry blend smoke forming a broken halo around his head. "She tells me she doesn't need to spend another day cleaning. Instead, she goes out and spends my money." He smiled and shrugged. "Women."

Dee giggled. "Watch it, mister. There's three women here who just might hose you down along with the planes."

"Hear, hear," Charlie said.

We finished the Cessna, and Charlie, Oscar, Julie and I went to work on the Six.

"Pardon me for saying so," said Julie, "but this is not a pretty airplane. It's kind of homely, if you ask me."

Charlie agreed. "It's like the man said when someone told him his wife was ugly. He says, 'She may be ugly, but she sure can cook!' That's the Six. She's a wonderful airplane. Some Saturday or Sunday, I'll fly us somewhere for lunch in it. Good for Vic here to get experience with an unfamiliar aircraft."

As we soaped down the plane, I couldn't help but notice that Dee, now working with Mike on the Archer, seemed to give him as much attention as she did the plane.

Charlie seemed to pick up on what I was thinking. "We know Sierra Fox," she said. "Nice lady; you'll like her when you finally meet her. She's a little older, like Mike; still darned attractive, if you ask me."

"Bird in a gilded cage," added Oscar. "We've gone to dinner with them a few times. And personally speaking, if I were Mike and had Sierra waiting for me at home, I wouldn't be spending my time basking in the hero worship of a redheaded Lolita."

"You're not doing so bad yourself, Oscar," said Julie, and Charlie thanked her.

"Just saying," Oscar said. "Professionally speaking, you understand."

Charlie flicked some water on him, he chuckled, and then we all continued soaping the Six.

Three

We made arrangements for the following Saturday for the four of us to fly out for lunch. Charlie had Oscar and Julie sit in the second row and told me to take the right seat. "This'll let you see what I'm doing and give you a feeling for the Six," she said.

We flew up the coast to Tampa and had lunch at a restaurant that overlooked the water. Over the meal, Julie brought up the subject of Mike's relationship with Dee. Charlie said, "With her mom dead and her father with Alzheimer's, Mike's become like a surrogate father to her."

Oscar raised his eyebrows. "I don't know if that's a totally accurate description of their relationship."

"Really? What makes you say that?" asked Julie.

"Let's just say part of my job entails reading people's body language. Theirs, and I hope I'm wrong, suggests that familiarity has grown into something deeper."

"How old is the girl?" I asked. "Mike was right; she does look like a teenager."

"Early twenties, I believe," Charlie said.

Julie said, "I can imagine what kind of life the girl has. Caring for an Alzheimer's patient is a total commitment. She probably lives for Mike's visits."

"I think we should leave it at that," Charlie said, having noticed Oscar's raised eyebrow. "What we should do is get together with Sierra and Mike so you can meet her, maybe get us together for dinner. Oscar grills a mean steak."

The rest of the meal was accompanied by good-natured banter, and when we returned to the airport Charlie told me to take the left seat. "Did you bring your logbook with you?" she asked. I told her Julie had it in her purse. She smiled and said, "Be prepared, right? I'll talk you through engine startup and I'll handle tower communications. And once we're at altitude I'll deal with the radio, so all you have to concentrate on is flying. You'll see it's different from the Skyhawk, but the principles are the same."

I couldn't believe my good fortune—Charlie and I had logged just a few training hours in the Skyhawk by that time. She told me that since we were splitting the rental cost of the plane already, she wouldn't add her instructor's fee, which humbled me more.

"Come on, Sky King," said Julie from the middle row. "Let's see what you can do."

Sitting at the end of the run-up area, I heard the tower tell us we were cleared for takeoff and eased the Six onto the active runway. "Give us one notch of flaps, feed throttle, and remember to give us right rudder to correct for prop torque," Charlie said. Her fingers were barely touching the wheel on her side, and I figured she also had her feet poised above the rudder pedals. At liftoff speed, she told me to ease back just a little on the wheel, and we were airborne again. "I didn't touch the controls," she said. "You did that all by yourself."

"I think I love you," I said as Julie cuffed my head from behind.

As we approached Naples Municipal, Charlie said, "Here's something you should keep in mind. The Cessna has a very efficient glide ratio, which means if the engine quits, you'll have some time to pick an emergency landing site. Pipers all glide like a piano."

"Really?"

"You'll need to keep some power into the flare. You've done okay so far. I haven't taken the controls yet. I'll continue to have my hands and feet ready, and if during the approach you need me to take over, you'll say, 'The plane is yours.' Got it?"

I said yes and flew the traffic pattern just as Charlie had trained me to do in the Cessna. She was right about the Piper's sink rate, and I kept some power on during final approach until we crossed the runway threshold. "Slowly pull back just a little on the wheel," Charlie said, "and ease the throttle to idle." The long, hound-dog nose came up just enough to obscure the far end of the runway, and we heard a squeak as the main wheels touched down. From the back, Julie cheered, and Charlie said, "You did that on your own too, you know. Natural-born pilot here," she announced, and my head swelled.

"I like this plane," I said. "She may be ugly, but she sure can cook."

"Just for the record," I said to Julie after we got home, "you're not going to be jealous of me spending hour upon hour, sharing a small plane with another beautiful woman, am I right?"

Julie laughed. "Long as you said *another* beautiful woman, we're fine. Hey, I like Charlie. No opinion on Oscar yet. I kind of feel I have to watch myself that I don't say or do something, and he decides to analyze and pigeonhole me."

"You mean the way he analyzed Dee and Mike's body language?"

"Exactly. And I wonder how he'll feel about his wife and you spending so much time together."

"Oscar spends a lot of his time with both students and patients, some of whom I'd suspect are women, and some of whom are probably attractive. Point being, I'd think neither of their professions poses a threat to their relationship. It seems pretty solid."

Julie began to unbutton her blouse as she walked toward the bedroom. "Speaking of relations..." she said.

Four

Two weeks later Julie and I finally met Sierra Fox. She was a short-statured woman, barely five feet tall, with short sandy hair that showed a trace of gray. As we socialized over drinks on Charlie and Oscar's patio, we quickly realized she was diminutive only in height; intellectually, she was more than a match for her loquacious husband. After we'd eaten, relaxing with after-dinner drinks, Julie asked each couple the details of how they'd met, and Oscar said that as the newcomers, we had to go first. Julie and I told our story together, with one person finishing a sentence or two and the other taking the tale from there.

When it was his turn, Oscar said, "I was a nervous flier once upon a time, and the puddle jumpers really scared me."

"By puddle jumpers," Charlie said, "he means the regional jets."

Oscar acknowledged her and told us he had been on his way to a conference in Nassau. His seatmate was this beautiful brunette with gorgeous light hazel eyes.

"He means me," Charlie said with a wink.

"I didn't know that she was a pilot for the airline, of course. She was taking a comp flight to spend a couple of days in the Bahamas. We hit some turbulence and I jumped, but Charlie calmed me down by telling me I'd already survived the most dangerous part of flying—namely, the drive to the airport. By the time we landed she'd agreed to have dinner with me. That's how it all began. Your turn, Sierra. We've heard it, but our newbies haven't. Meanwhile, Charlie and I can go inside and get the dessert ready."

"I don't know how much my infinitely lesser half told you already," Sierra began as Mike twisted his mouth and rolled his eyes, "but I used to be the office manager for Alpha Window and Door Company. I'd just come off a relationship that ended badly, and my boss, whom everyone called Papa, knew I was hurting. Well, one day he collared me to go with him to an airplane wash party at his flying club, and he 'happened' to run into this high-end builder who bought his windows and doors from him. And the rest, as they say..."

Mike said, "Then his wife died, leaving Dee without a mother."

Sierra picked up the story. "His wife burned through at least two packs a day, and as you might guess it was lung cancer that took her."

Mike said, "Dee was in high school then, and she and her mom had been more like sisters. Sierra and I started taking her to lunch on Saturdays, and her dad would join us when he could take an afternoon off."

"Then," Sierra said, "he developed Alzheimer's, just as Dee was getting ready to go to college. She gave up her plans in order to care for him, and that's what she's been doing for the past couple of years. Mike still visits on Saturdays, but I had to stop when Papa called me by his wife's name and started yelling at me for being unfaithful—with Mike."

"Wow," said Julie. "That must've been tough."

"So tough I quit my job as soon as I could train a replacement."

Julie said, "On the days Dee goes to the club, can she leave her dad alone?"

"He has a home health aide now," Mike said, "a Cuban woman, who comes in three days a week. I'm there on Saturdays, and when we wash the planes, I pay for her to come in. She's happy for the overtime."

"Not to sound insensitive," I said, "but I guess now it's just a waiting game. What will Dee do once she doesn't have the responsibility of caring for her dad anymore?"

Mike said, "Well, the business is privately owned, and Dee has power of attorney, which means her major duty these days is signing the checks the bookkeeper gives her. She says one day she still hopes to start college."

"Maybe she'll be one of my students one day," said Oscar as he and Charlie returned with the dessert.

"There you go."

"And maybe I'll get my husband back on Saturdays," added Sierra.

"Permit me to philosophize," I said after we'd eaten dessert and gone inside for coffee.

"Lay it on us, Socrates," joked Oscar.

"I remember from basic training when we were told you don't make friends in the Navy; you just make military acquaintances. Why? Because your best buddy today can be transferred out tomorrow and you'll never see him again."

"I'd never thought of that," said Julie as she placed a hand over mine.

"It was true. And it was true when I was an EMT in Washington; our crews were tight professionally but not socially. So, as I sit here among five amazing people, I think it's finally time to safely say that for the first time in my adult life I've found real friends."

Two years later, I had earned both my private license and instrument rating and was well on the way to earning my commercial license, when the board of directors decided the Six wasn't being flown enough to justify the expense of maintenance and insurance. The planes' trustees were automatically members of the board, so I was part of the club's unanimous decision to part with her.

And that was when the Southwest Florida Flying Club's Piper Cherokee Six, model PA32-300, registry number N4122T, radio call Two Two Tango, became mine.

I soon finished my commercial training, thanks again to Charlie. I showed my boss at X-ray Medical my new license, which legally allowed me to fly for hire. X-ray Medical covered my hourly flight expenses, which made up for the non-productive clock hours that I formerly spent driving at speeds one third of the Cherokees on the best day.

Life was good. Julie's salary paid for the rent and groceries, and mine paid the mortgage and maintenance expenses on the Six. She and I always marveled at our good fortune, hoping that the blissful bubble we found ourselves in would never burst.

But one day it did.

Five

Weather-wise, Monday promised to be a beautiful day, and I left early, kissing Julie goodbye as she was just waking up. I drove to the airport and preflighted the Six, which I'd loaded up the day before with samples of our latest medical equipment. Today, I'd be flying to meet clients in Fort Lauderdale, West Palm Beach, and Vero Beach. If I'd been driving, it would have taken two days, which would have added lodging to my expenses. With 22T, it would be a long day, but I'd still arrive back in Naples by sunset and home for dinner.

The day went as planned, and I signed the Vero Beach firm to a hefty long-term contract. After I got the signatures, I returned to the plane and called the boss with the news. When he didn't answer, I checked my watch and realized it was past quitting time, so I left a voice mail saying I would report in tomorrow with some very good news. Then I enjoyed a lovely evening flight back to Naples.

I stopped on the drive home from the airport to buy a bottle of champagne—cheap champagne, but still champagne—to celebrate my sales with Julie. When I walked in the door, I saw her sitting on the sofa with Charlie and Oscar flanking her, and their expressions were the opposite of celebratory. Julie, in fact, had tear tracks down her cheeks.

"What's up?" I asked, all cheer gone from my voice.

Charlie and Oscar nodded at Julie. She took a breath, and her eyes misted over again. "I went to work this morning, but the door was locked. I'm usually the first one there, so I have a key. The first thing I noticed when I went inside was that my books were open. I never leave the ledger out in plain sight; it's locked in a safe over-night. Then I walked into the inner office and found it stripped of everything—even down to the boss's Buccaneers helmet and his Marlins ball cap."

Julie took another deep breath, and Charlie put her hand over hers. I still stood dumbly by the door with a bottle of cheap champagne in my hand and feeling my entire body go numb.

"I went online to check the company's balance, and it was zero. Zero! Then I called the bank, and they told me the funds had been sent to a numbered account in the Cayman Islands." She looked at me forlornly. "Vic, we don't have jobs anymore! We're broke!" More tears spilled from her eyes, and I put the bottle on the table to wrap my arms around her as she stood up.

As Julie continued sobbing, Charlie said, "When Julie found out, she called the police. Then she called me, and we called Mike and Sierra. We've been here with Julie all day. Vic, we're so sorry."

I thanked them both weakly as my mind watched dollar signs fly out the window. "We have some money saved up," I said, "but that won't last, what with rent on the condo and a loan on the plane. That son of a bitch."

"What do we do?" Julie asked, and I was at a loss to answer.

The doorbell rang, and Mike barged in, pipe clenched in his teeth, clouds of smoke riding above his head. "Sorry. Couldn't get away earlier." He wrapped Julie in a bear hug and took my hand inside both of his beefy paws.

"All right, look," he said. "I've been doing some thinking on the way over, and maybe I can help dig you out." I was about to protest when he said, "This isn't charity, Vic, so don't play the too proud to accept help card. I fight with the bank every month, because I've been keeping the company books for years, and frankly I suck at it. The bank always wins; always. But I don't know anyone I can trust enough to see my financial records. Except now I do. Julie, I can use a bookkeeper. Again, it's not charity; I really need someone I trust to keep my books straight."

Julie sobbed and said, "Are you sure, Mike?"

He grinned. "Depends. How much was the asshole paying you?" She told him. "Well, I think I can do a little better than that; not much, but a little."

I sighed. At least the basic necessities were covered.

"Wish I could help you too, Vic, but there's no way the club can buy back your plane. You're using it more now than it ever got used before, if that's any consolation. Which I know isn't, but still."

"Thanks, Mike. You've done plenty. I'll probably have to sell the plane, maybe take a loss. Let's face it—as of now, Tango isn't a plane; she's an albatross."

Charlie said, "Just thinking out loud here. If you hired yourself for sightseeing flights—no, you'd have even more expenses and the work's unsteady in the best of times. No, forget I said it. Grasping at straws here."

But Julie didn't forget it. She wouldn't start with Mike until the following Monday, and while I contacted my former client list to tell them the bad news, she burned up the Internet doing research. Soon the printer was churning out paper.

"All right," she said after a lunch I barely tasted. "This could be a long shot, and it might bring the wrath of the holier-than-thou group upon us, but desperate times, desperate measures."

"What are you talking about?"

She shoved the papers she'd printed under my nose. "Can you believe businesses like this actually exist?" she said. "They're in vacation destinations all over the country."

I shook my head; no, I couldn't believe it. "Do you think? Would it bother you if I tried something like that?"

"Babe, like I said, desperate times. It's not like you're running drugs or anything illegal. Our goal is to keep the plane in the family, right? And the middle row of seats does come out; you told me they can be removed for cargo. One site even mentioned a Six that carries skydivers."

"But this isn't the kind of diving you're talking about," I said as I went through the other papers.

"Listen: you incorporate as a business, take out the middle row, and, well, you can figure out the rest."

I was torn. This wasn't the way I'd envisioned using my airplane. But I didn't see any other viable option. I incorporated as Two Two Tango, LLC. Then I removed the middle row of seats, filled the area between the front and rear seats with an air mattress and pad, pillows, linens, tissues, and sanitary hand wipes. Feeling as nervous as if I were about to dive off a hundred-foot tower into a wet sponge, I placed a tiny ad in the tourist magazines hotels pass out that describe all the things to do in that area.

The bold print read, "It takes Two Two Tango." The text continued, "Couples: Join the Mile High Club. Discretion Assured" and was followed by a dedicated cell number. The latest edition came out two weeks later, and I held my breath until two weeks and one day later, when the phone rang.

My first customers were a young couple honeymooning on Captiva Island. They introduced themselves as Jack and Jill—and answered my "sure you are" look by displaying their driver's licenses. They dressed as if they were clones of each other— leather sandals, white shorts, high-end powder blue polo shirts. Their suntans even looked identical. They were both slim and obviously fit; probably met on a tennis court back home in the Hamptons.

I introduced them to the Six and gave them my introductory spiel as I opened the double passenger/cargo door on the port side of the fuselage. "For takeoff and landing, you'll strap yourselves into the seats against the aft bulkhead. After we reach cruising altitude, I'll flash you a thumbs-up signal from the cockpit, and you can unbuckle."

Jack gave me his credit card, and I swiped it through my tablet. It cleared, and we were ready to go.

"We'll cruise at sixty-five-hundred feet, which puts us more than a thousand feet above a mile. The ride over land might be a little bumpy, but it's usually still over the Gulf." Jack asked why a thousand feet higher. "Under visual flight rules, planes heading west fly at even thousands plus five hundred feet; going east, it's odd thousands plus five hundred."

"Thousand-foot separation," Jack said. "Makes sense. So, what's next?"

"Looking inside, you can see that between your seats and mine is an air mattress, covered by a mattress pad and a sheet. You have two pillows as well, but you might not be using them for sleeping." Big grins. "Once you've achieved mile high status, you can use the tissues and sanitizers on the starboard—that's the right—side of the bulkhead. There's a button mounted next to them. Once you're ready to return, strap yourselves into your seats and press the button. That'll flash a little light on my instrument panel, and I'll know we're good to head back to the airport."

Jack said, "You'll be eyes front all the time, right?"

"Absolutely. What happens between the front and rear seats is your business; getting you to altitude is mine. My eyes will be scanning for traffic anyway, and headphones will cover my ears so I can listen for radio transmissions. For all intents and purposes, you'll enjoy complete privacy back here."

Jack looked at his bride. "Ready, hon?"

"Roger, dodger," she replied.

Once over the Gulf, I gave the thumbs-up. I could feel the plane's center of gravity shift as Jack and Jill unbuckled and moved forward onto the mattress. The headphones couldn't completely block out their moans and groans, and when those sounds became a shout accompanied by a squeal, I knew they'd consummated their experience. Ten minutes or so later, the green light flashed on the panel, and I descended for our return to the airport.

Back on the ground, and before saying goodbye, I presented each of them with a tiny enamel pin, suitable for a man's lapel or a woman's collar. It pictured the Six, and below it the numbers 5280. They couldn't have been prouder.

And I couldn't have been more pleased.

After they drove away, I checked voice mail and downloaded three messages from people seeking membership in the mile high club. When I got home, Julie kissed me and coyly asked, "How's business?"

I couldn't resist. "It seems to be taking off."

Six

Mike, Sierra, Julie, and I were seated on Charlie and Oscar's patio shortly after my maiden mile-high flight. Needless to say, the topic of conversation was my new business.

Mike thought it was a great idea, saying it filled a vacuum. Actually, he said it filled a hole, but when Sierra scowled at him, he said, "Just saying, honey. No offense. In fact," he added, "maybe Vic could take you and me up sometime, add a little spice to our lives. Complimentary, of course."

"Fat chance of that," she said, and it was clear she wasn't referring to the complimentary part.

Charlie was only half teasing when she cautioned me about the vice squad coming down on my neck. I asked her if she seriously thought what I was doing was immoral, unethical, or even a little bit illegal. She echoed Julie's "desperate times" mantra. Then she looked at Oscar and said, "Don't you get ideas either, mister." He shrugged.

Julie said if the business became profitable, I should get a Web site, and Oscar cautioned, "Not the best idea." She asked why, and he said, "As one whose patients sometimes suffer psychological harm from online trolls, social media can be ruinous to one's health. Once malcontents latch on to you, they can make your life a living hell. Therefore, if the business will pay the bills, I'd just keep advertising in the local throwaways." Oscar turned his attention to me. "You do have a separate cell for calls, I assume." I nodded. "If I were in your shoes, when enough money rolls in I'd rent hangar space, because your plane could become a target, like from the folks who throw red paint on women wearing fur coats."

Julie said, "Oh. That would be a problem, wouldn't it?"

"And—now I don't know how much it would cost, but again when the money comes in, I'd invest in a new paint job and new upholstery. Make the plane look new again."

Julie said, still a bit uncertain, "So you're saying a Web site wouldn't be practical. But my research was done online, and the other operations all have a web presence."

"Think about this," Oscar said. "You're local; the web is by definition worldwide. You don't need that kind of coverage. And for heaven's sake, stay away from Facebook, Twitter, and all the other sites. Again, speaking as a shrink, I can tell you that horrible postings have led people to commit suicide."

"I've read about some of them," Charlie said. "You don't have to be a celebrity to get a following, and with followings come troublemakers who have no reservations about assassinating your character while they remain safely anonymous." She added, "Freeloaders, breathing air others could put to better use."

"First Amendment," said Sierra. "That's what they hide behind. 'Course, they've no idea what the First Amendment actually says, and the Constitution itself has no meaning for them, mainly because schools don't teach it anymore. Not sure they ever did," she added, remembering her own education. "In college, the motto with the professors seemed to be 'Blame America first.' I said screw that, and instead of signing for a second term answered a want ad from Alpha Window and Door Company, and eventually wound up with... Mike."

"You make it sound like a curse, doll," Mike said.

Before Sierra could add another dry retort, I asked about her former boss's health.

"It's beyond terrible," said Mike. "And poor Dee is worn to a frazzle caring for him. He doesn't even recognize her now. I don't know how she does it."

"You help," Sierra said, her tone non-committal.

"Yeah. Sometimes if I can get off a construction site early enough during the week, I'll come over and visit with her and her dad."

"Don't tell me he recognizes you but not his own daughter," said Charlie.

"Nope. Once he thought I was the sheriff come to lock him up. I'm telling you, I don't expect him to last much longer."

"Does Dee still aspire to college?" asked Oscar.

"Far as I know."

Charlie changed the subject and said, "So Julie, what's it like working for Mike?"

Julie rolled her eyes and grinned. "The work's fine, but the boss is a jerk." We all laughed, and she said, "Seriously, his books were a mess. You needed a detective license to figure them out."

"She's definitely worth what I pay her," Mike said.

Two weeks later, Dee's father died. Mike led her through casket selection, funeral arrangements, and the obituary notice. Dee bravely delivered her father's eulogy at the funeral home, as her family had no religious affiliation. Her voice quavered, and tears spilled out of her eyes as she spoke, but she managed to continue without dissolving into tears.

Many of the old timers at the flying club attended to pay their respects. Oddly, I thought, not one of his employees or business associates showed up.

Mike sat next to me, and as Dee spoke, he whispered, "She looks good up there without the braces on her teeth, doesn't she?"

"Not appropriate, Mike," I whispered back through clenched jaws.

Only the six of us accompanied Dee to the cemetery.

Afterward, we all went to Mike and Sierra's home, where Sierra had arranged for a small, catered reception in honor of her former boss. Dee was touched to see Charlie, Oscar, Julie, and me there, as in the past she'd only seen us at the airplane wash and wax parties. "It's like you're the only family I have left. Like I'm your little sister or something."

We all agreed that her description was fine by us.

After the caterers left, we adjourned from the living room to the den and sat on leather-upholstered settees as Mike and Sierra shared with Dee and the rest of us memories of her father—anecdotes here, snippets of conversation there, mention of working for him and flying with him—and she herself contributed memories of both her parents.

"I hated the fact that Mom smoked so much," she recalled. "And some of her last words to me were she hoped her smoking wouldn't affect my health later in life. Part of me wanted to say, 'You think?' But I just told her I loved her, that she was the best mom. And the next day she was gone."

I saw tears in Julie's eyes, and Charlie looked like she was on the verge of tears too.

"Dad... I wish you'd had the chance to know him when he *was* my dad," Dee said to the four of us. "You'd have loved him."

Oscar asked if she'd made plans for her future.

Dee nodded and said she'd thought about attending the local junior college and going on from there for her four-year degree. He asked her if she had a major in mind, and she told him that based upon her life experiences over the past few years she'd consider grief counseling. "It takes one to know one," she said, her eyes downcast.

Oscar handed her his card. "Dee, I teach Introduction to Psychology at the college two nights a week. I'd be happy to welcome you as a student. Also," he added, "I'm also available if you'd like to see me professionally."

"You mean, like a patient?"

He nodded. "Sometimes it helps to talk with a third party, someone who can be objective and maybe offer advice."

"Thanks, Dr. Baker," she said as she studied Oscar's card. "I just might do that. This would be confidential, right?" she asked with a snap-quick glance at Mike that I'd guess only Oscar and I picked up on.

"Doctor-patient confidentiality is protected like lawyer-client and priest-confessor confidentiality, so yes."

"He never brings home stories about his patients," Charlie assured her. "Or his students, for that matter. I only know he's a real psychologist because I've been to his office. Loose lips sink ships, they say, and if Oscar were to betray a confidentiality his career would definitely be sunk."

"Thank you," Dee said. "Um, can I ask how much you charge?"

"First consultation's on the house, Dee. If you'd like to come back afterward, we can discuss my fees. Fair enough?"

"Can I hug you?"

"As a friend, yes; as a patient, no. But you're not a patient yet. That said, hug away."

On the drive home, Julie remarked that it was Mike who'd made all the arrangements for the funeral, the burial, and the reception. "But she didn't hug him once, did she? She hugged Oscar, and she hugged Sierra, but she didn't hug Mike."

Seven

Months passed. Dee enrolled in junior college, and if she became a student or patient of Oscar's there was no way he would ever tell us. Julie continued working the books for Mike, frequently casting good-natured jibes at him when we were socializing—which he seemed to love. Mike decided he didn't want the responsibility of presiding over the flying club any longer, so Charlie volunteered to take his place, and at the next meeting she was elected unanimously. She nominated me for vice president, and no one objected then, either. Frankly, no other members even wanted the jobs, so we were a shoo-in by default.

A couple of the club members teased me, telling me I was the luckiest guy on the planet. "You get to live with one beautiful woman, helm the club with another beautiful woman, and get to fly other beautiful women to the mile high club. You sure you don't have a hidden video system in your plane?"

I sometimes thought about that *beautiful women* reference. It's true that both Julie and Charlie were strikingly beautiful, but we'd all been together so long by now that their good looks were irrelevant. Not that I took them for granted, but that our relationships had gone deeper than the surface. Julie was my friend and lover, and Charlie was my friend and partner. We could share joy as the club's ranks filled to capacity, with many of the new members women, along with a sprinkling of minorities both male and female. And we could bitch to each other when we got the insurance and maintenance bills and realized we had to up the monthly dues.

Unlike our supportive—if envious—members, not everyone saw my latest career in a positive light. I began getting crank calls on the business phone. Callers claimed I was operating a flying cathouse and contributing to the delinquency of minors, even—ironically—adding sex trafficking to their list of complaints. At first, I tried being polite, assuring the callers that I checked the IDs of all my clients, and that they were all consenting adults. It didn't work; they just spewed more invective at me. I grew to simply thanking them for their concerns and hanging up. And grateful for Oscar and Charlie's earlier advice about staying away from social media.

One couple made an appointment for a mile high flight, but when they arrived, I saw they were middle-aged sourpusses, dressed more for a funeral than a romp at 6500 feet. "You!" they cried pointing fingers at me and the plane. "You're the whoremaster, and this is your flying whorehouse!"

I remained calm and asked them to leave. They harrumphed and said I hadn't seen the last of them. The next morning, I found the word *pimp* spray-painted in black on both sides of the fuselage.

I filed a complaint with the police, but the callers had used fictitious names and a burner phone when they made the appointment; in other words, they were well versed in how to remain anonymous. My only recourse was to scrub the paint from the plane and make arrangements for a hangar.

By this time, I had enough money in the account to pay hangar fees, and the one I rented had a motorized roll-up door, a lavatory, an additional 220 electrical outlet, and a dorm-sized refrigerator and freezer along with shelves galore. Julie and I spent one Sunday adding a washing machine and dryer, and exchanged the shelves for cabinets, thanks to Mike, who'd taken them from a kitchen-remodeling job. Thus, we had linen closets as well as storage for oil, filters, tools, and cleaning and waxing materials. Next to the shelving and cabinets we put in a bottled water dispenser. A shop vac stood in one corner. Finally, we gave the walls a coat of sky-blue paint. I put no sign on the outside to identify the business.

That said, the morality police didn't give up their attacks, and one group played lawyer roulette seeking to file suit against me for any number of violations they thought might stick. To a man, the attorneys told them no lawyer other than a shyster would touch their claim. It would lead nowhere, but the shyster would still bill them for fees.

One of the lawyers they'd contacted happened to be mine. He explained that precedent for my business had already been set in various venues nationwide and even supplied them with a list of Internet links. Legally, the couples who hired me were, for all intents and purposes, booking a sightseeing flight—and what consenting adults did in the privacy of the plane was no one's business but theirs. He told me, "We call it the 'What happens in Vegas' defense."

Eventually, the cranks got tired of harassing me and moved on to the next topic that offended them.

And the mile high calls continued to roll in.

After each flight, I'd throw the linens in the wash, replace the mattress pad, remake the bed, and set the plane up for the next couple. By now I needed to make an appointment schedule, as on a single day I might have four or five couples reserving a flight. I reflected driving home one day that thanks to a crooked boss, I was now a successful entrepreneur. I'd made lemonade from lemons, and this lemonade tasted sweet indeed.

Upon arriving back at the condo one day, Julie hit me with the news that Mike and Sierra had separated. "He told you himself?" I asked.

"No, actually it was Sierra. She dropped into the office while Mike was on the job site. She didn't say why they were separating, but just felt I should know. I asked if she had a place to go. She said yes; she'd stay in the house. Mike, however, refused to leave. Bottom line, they still live in the same house but sleep in separate bedrooms."

"Wow. Awkward much?"

"Also, she refuses to be his maid any longer. She cleans her room, her bathroom, and the kitchen. She does only her own laundry and cleans only her own dishes. And she buys food only for herself. Mike eats in restaurants." Julie added, "She's hired a lawyer to begin divorce proceedings. One of her stipulations is she wants ownership of the house."

"Big house for one person."

"If Mike wants to buy it back, she'll make him pay above market value."

"Did Mike say anything to you at all?"

"No; he didn't mention it, so I didn't ask. Sierra only told me so we wouldn't invite them anywhere together."

Charlie and Oscar came for dinner that night, and Julie told them the news. Charlie was shocked, but Oscar remained stone-faced, once or twice fidgeting in his chair. And when Charlie asked Oscar what he thought about it, he shrugged and said, "It happens." If he were privy to any of what had been going on between them, he wouldn't have told us anyway.

"Well, I have some bad news of my own, Mr. Vice President," Charlie said to me. "It seems one of our club members landed the Mooney gear up. The prop is ruined, the engine needs attention, and the belly suffered some major damage."

That wasn't bad news; it was horrible news. "Did he do it locally?"

"We should be so lucky. No, he was flying to Albuquerque to see the balloon festival. He called me with the news, all apologetic, and explained that in his excitement he simply forgot to lower the wheels."

Julie shook her head. "So glad our Six has fixed landing gear."

"Happens to the best of us," Charlie said philosophically. "There's an old maxim that says when you fly a retractable gear airplane, it's not a question of *if* you'll land wheels up but *when.*"

"Albuquerque's a towered field," I assumed. "Couldn't the tower tell him he was gear up?"

Charlie nodded. "Maybe they didn't notice. The airport had to close the active runway and have a truck drag the plane to the repair shop on the field. The estimate isn't going to be pretty."

"What are our options? I know the member will see a fat fine in his future."

"And the club will see a hefty insurance renewal fee. Unless..."

"Unless?"

"We leave the Mooney in ABQ and offer to sell it as is. It's a great plane, and whoever restores it will get a lot more years out of it. I'm only guessing here, understand. We'll have to do some research on how to deal with the situation. If we write off the Mooney, the insurance cost goes down, but a lot of folks in the club love it, so there's that."

"We could replace it with another Mooney?"

"I'm thinking that's the way to go. But it's too soon to make decisions, and the final one will have to be made by vote at the next meeting. Which means we're going to have to brief the membership on costs and options."

"Going to be a long evening, isn't it?"

"That it will."

The membership decided to survey the Mooney. In Navy terms, that means we exchange one for another. The errant and embarrassed member resigned, after paying the hefty insurance deductible plus a fine to the club, and the plane's trustee moved on to securing a replacement.

As to the Mike and Sierra separation, no one at the club knew, and Julie told me he still hadn't mentioned it to her. "It has to be awkward being separated but still both living in that big house," she said.

"Never mind that," I said. "He's lost his maid, his cleaning lady, and his cook."

"That's right," said Julie. "Like the song says, you don't know what you've got 'til it's gone."

Eight

Early one morning, Charlie and I were poring over papers regarding the club's insurance policy, not at home but in the clubhouse. During a break to clear our heads of the minutia, Charlie mentioned that Mike had called her at home to inform her of his separation. He'd told Julie the day before, so now everything was out in the open.

"He didn't give me a reason for their split, and I didn't ask. Just told him I was sorry; that we were sorry."

"That's pretty much what Julie said when he told her—no explanation. She told me she hugged him and wished him well. And she did not mention that Sierra had told her about it first." I also told Charlie about Mike and Sierra's modified living arrangement, which was something Mike also didn't mention.

"He's probably too embarrassed to admit it," she said. "I would be."

We finished what we could, relative to the plane and broke for early lunch at the local burger joint. I looked at my watch and told Charlie I'd have to get back to the airport, as a couple had reserved an afternoon flight.

"This probably sounds perverse," Charlie said, "but do you think they'd mind if I rode right seat?"

"I think that might be a great idea—having another pilot aboard, a woman at that, might be calming to an insecure wife or girlfriend."

When the couple arrived, I introduced Charlie as an airline pilot who would join me up front.

"Like a co-pilot?" asked the girl.

"More like redundant pilots," offered her boyfriend.

"When you're flying an airplane, redundancy is good," I said.

Charlie couldn't help herself. "You can say that again."

The two clients chimed in with, "When you're flying an airplane, redundancy is good!"

When we returned from a somewhat bumpy ride in the normally smooth air over the Gulf, the couple gleefully accepted their 5280 pins and promised to refer Two Two Tango to their friends. They walked to the parking lot arm in arm, leaning into each other with a nudge here, a playful hip bump there.

Charlie and I prepared the plane inside the hangar for the next passengers, and then I pulled up two metal-framed, canvas-covered chairs I'd recently added. I got a bag of tortilla chips from one of the cabinets, grabbed some dip from the fridge, and filled two plastic cups with chilled water.

"Well," I said as we relaxed, "do you think I'm a dirty old man, doing what I do?"

She crunched on a chip and shook her head. "I'll tell you the truth, Vic. At first, I wasn't all that thrilled. I pretended to be for your sake, because times were tough, and I knew how much you loved the Six and would do anything to keep her. For the record, while some people may happen to think you're a sleaze of the lowest order... I happen to *know* you're a sleaze of the lowest order." She laughed at my reaction and poked my shoulder. "Gotcha! Listen, Vic, you've discovered a need and found a way to address it. You're discreet, and you've got a fresh-faced little boy look about you that the clients immediately trust."

"I have a fresh-faced little boy look?"

"Yeah. It's kind of attractive."

I wasn't sure where to steer the conversation next, so I copped out and asked Charlie if sometimes she'd like to switch seats and become pilot in command.

"Depending on my work schedule, I'd love it. You're a great pilot, Vic, thanks to me." Before I could make a remark about her modesty or lack of it, she laughed and went on, "Seriously, I'm not only proud of my former student, but I'm also even prouder to have him as my closest friend."

I half expected her to say, "Except for Oscar." She didn't, and I had the sudden urge to lean over and kiss her—chastely, mind you, friend to friend. But I didn't. And as if to underscore that my impulse was ill advised, Charlie popped another tortilla chip into her mouth.

"Almost out of dip... dip," she said.

We all showed up for the next wash, and Mike was as jovial as ever. None of us made mention of his separation, but we did mention that Dee hadn't been at the last two monthly parties.

"Yeah, she's pulling Saturdays at her dad's business these days. Finally getting the hang of it. Plus, she's going to school at night."

Mike turned to Oscar. "She happen to be in one of your classes, professor?" he asked. "She never mentioned it one way or the other."

Oscar gave him a slight smile and said, "If she didn't mention it to you, then she must feel it's none of your concern."

"Ouch. That hurts. I'm talking school, not whether she's your patient."

"No offense intended, Mike."

Charlie reminded him, "There's nobody more tight-lipped than my husband."

"Well, I guess that's a plus in your business, Oscar. And more power to you. You're probably a great shrink."

"I am. I'm the sultan of shrink."

Charlie laughed and said, "Have you ever seen Oscar shrink? Watch this." And she tossed a soapy sponge at her husband.

To say we were shocked would have been an understatement. But then Oscar dipped the sponge in his bucket and threw it back at his wife.

The washing of the planes stopped as hooting club members made a circle around Charlie and Oscar as they soaked each other through like kids playing at an opened fire hydrant. Someone said he was putting money on Charlie, and someone else said he'd wager fifty on Oscar.

When the drenched combatants had had enough, they bumped their foreheads together and continued laughing. Charlie faced the raucous group and affected her high-class accent. "A little respect here, please. After all, I am your esteemed president." That brought more hoots.

"You folks will have to go to the pizzeria without us," Oscar said. It went without saying; both of them were soaked to the skin. I'd never seen Oscar shed his professional persona before, and it was refreshing.

Driving back to the condo after lunch, Julie mentioned that something Mike had said earlier didn't ring exactly true.

"What do you mean?"

"Well, I order building supplies for Mike, and when I call for an order of windows and doors, I usually get Dee on the phone. The last couple of times someone else answered. I asked for Dee, and she told me Dee wasn't in the office that day."

"So?"

"She hasn't been in the office any day since, as far as I can tell. I called this morning to see if she'd be at the wash party, and I got the same answer. I don't know. Sounds pretty cryptic to me."

Something else seemed cryptic, not to me but to Charlie. We were in the clubhouse the next day setting up chairs for the monthly meeting, when she asked me what I thought of her and Oscar's shenanigans at the wash party.

I told her I thought it was hilarious.

"So did I, at first."

"It never got nasty."

"No. It was good-natured fun, right?" I nodded. "Vic, Oscar doesn't do good-natured fun. Have you ever seen him have good-natured fun? It was like he was trying too hard."

"Did you talk with him about it?"

"He said it was about time he loosened up around my friends, wasn't it?"

"And?"

"And I dropped the subject."

After the meeting, I drove home to find Julie engrossed in one of those cable shows about home building. She told me Mike wanted her to familiarize herself with the trade. I asked why—she was a bookkeeper, not a saleswoman.

She raised her eyebrows. "Who knows? Maybe there's more in the offing for me he hasn't told me about. I'm just doing my homework here. Do you happen to know what a mortise and tenant joint is?"

"I think you mean mortise and tenon, Jules. And yes, I do."

"Oh." She shrugged. "Tenon, right. Live and learn."

"Tell me, what did you think about Oscar's behavior at the wash party?"

"Funny as hell. I never knew he had it in him."

"Yeah. That was what I was thinking too."

Nine

Southwest Florida's weather often includes daily showers and occasional thunderstorms, a hazard to general aviation pilots. It was a couple of weeks later, when severe thunder bumpers over the Gulf moved toward the mainland, that I had to call my afternoon clients to tell them not today.

"Tomorrow looks good, though, and I have the same slot open, if you'd like to try again."

"No way we can go today, then?" said the man.

"I can't risk the precious cargo in the back of the plane."

He laughed. "You're the precious cargo. If we go down, so do you."

I chuckled. "Yeah, there is that."

He said, "Tomorrow will be fine. Make sure it's worth the wait."

"That'll be up to you," I said, and we both laughed before ending the call.

The sky was already getting dark when I secured the hangar for the day, and as I got into my car the clouds opened up. Lightning flashed, thunder crashed, and the rain was so heavy I had to pull over to the shoulder—along with other motorists—because the windshield was nearly opaque. I could barely make out the emergency flashers on the car in front of me.

I finally pulled into the condo's parking lot and saw Julie's car. Mike had probably seen the storm coming and given his crew the rest of the afternoon off. I pulled my ball cap low and dashed from the car to the front door, where I stood under the portico to shake the water off me. Finally, I put my key in the lock, opened the door, and called, "Honey, I'm home."

Julie was nowhere to be seen. My ears picked up the sound of the shower. I thought it might be cute if I got undressed and surprised her by slipping in with her. Then my nose picked up a familiar and chilling scent—that of cherry blend pipe tobacco.

The shower shut off, and a few minutes later the door opened, and Julie stepped out in a robe, saw me, and shrieked.

Behind her stood Mike Fox, a towel wrapped around his waist, his mouth hanging open, and his eyes big as swim goggles.

They both started talking at the same time, one over the other. Finally, Julie stepped toward me as Mike ducked into the bedroom, where his clothes probably lay scattered over the floor.

"Vic, I'm so sorry," Julie said. "It just... you know, happened."

"I guess I do know—now. How many times has it just... happened?" My temper was hot, but my voice was cold.

"It's not what you think," she said, tears ready to pop from her eyes.

"I think it is, don't you?"

Mike came out of the bedroom, dressed in work shorts and boots. He pulled a dirty polo over his head and yanked it down over his gut.

"Vic, I'm sorry, man, I really am. We were going to tell you."

"I think you just did."

"Can we sit down and talk about it?" he said, trying to sound conciliatory. I didn't want to do conciliatory.

"I have an idea; let's do something else instead. First, Julie. You will immediately pack everything you own and toss it in your car."

"I can't do all that now—there's too much, and besides, it's pouring outside!"

"Let me put it this way. Anything you don't remove today will be on the sidewalk tomorrow. You betrayed me, Julie. I never would've expected that, ever. You have no idea how much you've hurt me."

"We can start over, Vic."

"What you can start is packing." Then I turned to Mike, who'd picked up his pipe, put it into a pocket of his cargo shorts, and looked at me with a mixture of embarrassment and fear on his face.

"Vic, buddy, she's right; it just happened, you know? We've been working together, we became friends, and then... it just happened. I mean, you work with Charlie all the time at the club and everything. Haven't things ever gotten... you know what I mean... between you?"

"For the record, no." I turned to look at Julie, still standing there in her towel. "Julie, why are you still standing there?"

Julie wailed and ran into the bedroom. I heard drawers and closet doors being opened and shut.

"Mike, here's what I suggest you do. First, you might want to find someplace for Julie to stay, because she's not coming back here. Second, you will write a letter resigning from the flying club. You can give any reason you want; I don't care. But once it's done, you will place it in an envelope along with your clubhouse key and mail it to the club's post office box. Charlie will read it aloud at the next club meeting and accept your resignation with regret." Mike cast his eyes to the floor and nodded weakly. "Because if I see your face at the clubhouse, even once, I will expose you to the membership. Do you think I won't?"

"No. I'll do what you say."

"I didn't see your truck when I pulled in."

"It's around the back."

"Uh huh. Convenient. Well, I'd suggest you bring it around to the front, and throw what Julie can't fit into her car into your truck bed."

"It'll get soaked back there. Besides, the bed's dirty."

"How ironic. Tell me, Mike, do I look like I give a shit?"

"Okay, Vic. Whatever you say."

"Know this, Mike. I'm speaking to you calmly and matter-of-factly. But for your own good, you stay away from me, because right now I'm boiling inside, and if I see you again, I just might boil over."

Mike looked down and saw the tension in my clenched fists, which I was fighting to keep at my side.

"I'm leaving," he said and hurried out the door. Moments later I heard his truck back up to the condo door. He rushed inside without looking at me and flew into the bedroom.

They returned with suitcases and plastic trash bags filled with her things. "Nothing in the bathroom?" I said. She shook her head. "Leave the house key on the table; you won't be using it again."

Tears flowed down Julie's face. I stood to the side, giving them a clear path to the door.

When it closed behind them, I checked the bedroom and bathroom and satisfied myself that nothing of Julie's remained. Then I opened the front door, made sure her car and Mike's truck had left, and turned on the ceiling fan. I left the door open, hoping to get the smell of cherry blend out of my house. I listened to the rain hammer against the metal-roofed portico. The deluge continued unabated.

Ten

Later that evening, I threw out a lifeline and Charlie and Oscar came over. They were soaking wet when they arrived, their umbrella having been inverted by a gust of wind. Oscar said he hoped my news was worth their drenching, and Charlie said she should squeegee herself down before walking into the living room. I led them inside and suggested we sit at the dinette table, asked if they'd like something to drink.

"We've had our fill of liquid refreshment," Oscar said. "What's up? Why did you drag us from our dry and comfy home so close to bedtime?"

I returned his half-smile and led them to the kitchen. When we sat down, the empty fourth chair alerted Oscar. "Uh oh," he said.

"Where's Julie?" asked Charlie, frowning. "Come on, Vic, out with it."

I told them. Oscar sat back, alert to every word. Charlie placed her hands over mine and leaned toward me, her tone suffused with empathy. "I'm so sorry, Vic. I know it must sound trite, but I don't know what else to say. God, I'm sorry."

Oscar asked how I was dealing with the situation. I told him I didn't really know how. "How do you love and hate someone at the same time?"

He suggested that after a while reason would overpower emotion.

"Maybe that drink is in order now," Charlie said.

I broke out wine for Charlie and beers for Oscar and me. We sat in silence for a few minutes, pretending to concentrate on the booze.

"Should we tell Sierra about Mike and Julie?" I said.

"That," Oscar replied, "is what we call a conundrum."

"Why?"

"Vic's right. She deserves to know," said Charlie.

"Telling her about Julie, whom she trusted as a friend, might cause her some real hurt. As for Mike, I suspect not so much."

"I wonder where Julie's going to spend the night," Charlie said idly. "Mike can't take her to his house, can he? Sierra's still there."

Oscar said he had a theory. We turned our attention to him.

"Julie, I assume, will continue as Mike's bookkeeper?"

"Makes sense," I said. "He'd want to keep her close now more than ever."

"You mean because he loves her?" asked Charlie.

Oscar gave a smile that someone who didn't know better would characterize as condescending. "I believe for a more practical reason," he said. "Right now, Julie has the upper hand when it comes to Mike and Sierra settling their divorce. See, if Sierra knew her husband was romancing Julie, she could add adultery to her reasons for asking for a divorce. And adultery would increase her chances for a larger settlement than, say, simple incompatibility. Julie would probably be aware of that."

"All right, but should we or shouldn't we tell Sierra? You guys are dancing around my question."

Oscar continued without answering. "Mike's developments have model homes, beautifully staged with furniture, artwork, and whatever; in other words, they present as functioning houses."

"Sure. Oh; oh," I said.

"Yes. Mike can easily put Julie up in one of the models. She can do her bookkeeping there, and after working hours the house is hers. She just has to set her alarm early enough to get the house ready for prospective visitors the next morning."

Charlie said, "Being there when they show up, she can act as a sales rep. You don't need a realtor's license for that. Every house these days has a home office in it, so as far as visitors are concerned, her books and computer would just seem like part of the staging."

I said, "Which makes total sense. I don't know how he does it. Mike's the kind of guy who could fall into a septic tank and still come out smelling like a rose."

"Or cherry blend," said Charlie, suppressing a sneer.

Oscar said, "You may think of yourself as a victim now, but I believe you should think of the first time you were a victim; namely, when your former boss left you high and dry. You transformed yourself from victim to victor, no pun intended. You can do the same now. By the way, I'm not suggesting you rebound romantically with some, oh, I don't know, casual acquaintance, perhaps someone you might meet at a bar."

"No, Vic; no way," Charlie said emphatically.

"I don't see that happening," I assured her. "But I don't think that's what Oscar's talking about, is it?"

"No. I'm suggesting you turn your attention to something positive, like, oh, expanding your business. Maybe get access to another plane if the demand warrants. You can always lease one, I'd assume."

"Too ambitious for now. And the only other pilot I know I can trust already has a job, flying big iron—all right, big aluminum—out of RSW."

Charlie's home base at the Regional Southwest Airport in Fort Myers was an easy drive from Naples. Her flight schedule was erratic at best, as she occasionally had to fill in for another pilot who'd called out sick.

"Just an idle thought," Oscar said. "Then again, you could build your public relations image by making the plane available for transporting patients with specific medical issues to specialized hospitals. As a former Navy corpsman, you'd be more than a pilot to them; you'd be an EMT as well."

"You're brilliant, Oscar, you know that?"

Charlie's face brightened. "Listen, I'm flying to Nassau tomorrow, but I'll be back in time for dinner. Why don't the three of us go out to a really nice restaurant, our treat?"

The rain had cleared by the time they said goodnight. Oscar shook my hand, and Charlie gave me a strong hug and a long kiss on the cheek. "Tomorrow, seven o'clock," she said softly into my ear. "Our treat."

I might have held on to her a little longer than appropriate.

But she didn't pull away.

Eleven

Sierra called a couple of weeks later and invited herself to dinner. She told Oscar to brine a turkey, because Thanksgiving was just around the corner, and she had some news we might all be thankful to hear. "Just don't make any of those disgusting candied yams," she ordered Charlie, in case she'd planned to make them. Which suited Charlie fine; we were all of one opinion when it came to candied yams.

We ate dinner inside and spoke about all things but Mike and Julie. Sierra saw Julie wasn't there, but she didn't ask, and we didn't volunteer to tell. She seemed happy to keep us in suspense about her news as she downed glass after glass of Sauvignon Blanc. Charlie cleared the table afterward and suggested we wait to let the dinner settle before dessert and coffee. Sierra said this would be a perfect time for... after-dinner drinks. "Do you have any limoncello?" she asked.

Charlie took the bottle out of the freezer and poured the liqueur into tiny glasses. As we sipped, Sierra downed hers and asked for another. We began to wonder if she intended to drive home tonight.

"Okay, folks, I've kept you in suspense long enough. Are you ready for my news?"

"It better be good," Charlie said. "You know you've been keeping us on tenterhooks ever since your phone call.

"I know; apologies for that. You know how as kids we couldn't wait to open our Christmas presents? We'd see them under the tree, wondering what was inside those boxes?"

"I think we can identify with that," Oscar said.

"Well, for our parents, our anticipation was part of the fun. For them. They loved seeing us squirm before they allowed us to open them."

"And we're squirming," I said, laughing. "Okay, Sierra, we get the message. Give."

She put down her glass, sat back in her chair, and looked around the table with a self-satisfied smugness.

"Okay, kids, here we go. First, you remember that Dee took over the window and door business after her dad died. She wasn't motivated, but Mike—you remember Mike, I assume—convinced her to at least try. She did. Problem was, she suffered the stigma of being the boss's daughter, totally unqualified to run a company. In fact, she was happy to let the manager run the business while she manned the phones, took orders, and made sure they got bundled and delivered. Challenging at first, boring later. And the manager's attitude toward her was less than encouraging, if you know what I mean."

"I can guess," Charlie said.

Sierra tilted her glass toward Charlie, and she poured another.

"Well, Dee asked me if I could consider coming on as manager. From my marriage to Mike—you remember Mike, I assume—I know a lot more than most people realize about the building trade. I said yes. As soon as I reported to work the first day, Dee gave the manager his marching orders. And the rest of the crew was quick to accept my authority. Better yet, they gave me respect. And that transferred to Dee, who'd finally made a command decision."

We congratulated her and asked how she liked the work. She said she loves it, but they've severed relations with Mike's company. "You remember Mike, right? Well, he's not the only builder out there, you know. But wait; there's more. And this time it's personal."

"Tell us," Charlie said as she leaned across the table.

"Okay, and this is between us, you understand. We all know Mike was porking Julie—sorry to be blunt, Vic; I figured it out early on after she left you—and he probably still is, for all I know or even care. But it seems Julie's not the Lone Ranger. My son of a bitch soon to be ex-husband was also banging young Dee. Seems his weekend visits had less to do with visiting her dad and more to do with seducing her."

"Whoa," Charlie said. "She's half his age."

"Seems their affair started sometime after her mom died. But here's where he more than stepped over a line—the bastard got her pregnant. And the reason she stopped showing up at the airplane wash parties was because Mike ordered her to get an abortion. He said no way was he going to support a child, and why wasn't she on the pill in the first place?"

"Which means getting pregnant was her fault," said Charlie. "I am so disappointed. I mean it was bad enough he betrayed Vic with Julie, but this... this is unforgivable."

"Dee didn't want the abortion, but Mike convinced her, as only Mike can. He said she needed to be free to pursue college and a career. It was tearing her up inside. But she finally had it done, and then she went into a deep depression. She told me if it weren't for Dr. Baker here, she'd probably have killed herself."

Charlie's and my eyes turned to Oscar, who glared at Sierra.

"Oh, shit. I shouldn't have said that, should I? I'm so sorry, Oscar; I know she told me in confidence. I shouldn't have let the cat out of the bag."

"We won't discuss it," Oscar said firmly. "But I think I should drive you home, Sierra."

She looked at her empty glass and said, "You're right; I've really overdone it tonight, haven't I? In more ways than one."

After they left, Charlie and I cleared the table and began cleaning the kitchen. At first, we didn't speak. Finally, she said, "I feel so horrible for Dee. And what a burden that must've been on Oscar. To counsel a bereaved and traumatized girl we've all known, a girl whose dad's funeral we all attended—and not be able to share any of it with me or either of us. I feel so sorry for Dee, for Oscar, for both of them." She turned to me. "I'm hurting. Hug me."

Twelve

Hard as it was to adjust to Thanksgiving without autumn's nip in the air, it was harder still to see people putting up Christmas decorations in eighty-degree heat. My winters in D.C. may have been brutal, but at least they were cold. However, I appreciated the fact that having Santa fly over in a hot air balloon or drop in by parachute was something I could get used to. And you could hang a wreath on your door and then spray it with artificial snow. Voila.

With the holiday season soon upon us, the hotels were jammed. What did this mean for me? Not much. The visitors by and large were families who'd been to Orlando enough times to become jaded and now only wanted to swim and relax in Florida's Gulf waters, where the waves were small and the dolphin made frequent appearances—real dolphin, not Disney animatronics.

Another group that came down in numbers were senior citizens, snowbirds escaping the Northeast cold. Needless to say, these folks weren't interested in hiring my services either. My best months were May through October, newlywed season, when adventurous honeymooners eager for bragging rights to their friends—but definitely not to their parents—swamped me for rides. I'd schedule each flight for three hours, but most were over by two, which gave me time to change the linens and get the plane ready for the next thrill seekers. If my day began at seven, I could schedule three, sometimes four flights before securing 22T for the night.

Now, with the winter doldrums, business-wise, setting in, I volunteered for Angel Flights and even puppy runs, taking rescue dogs to homes across the country. If Charlie were free, she'd join me and charm the kiddies and puppies while I flew them to our destination. On the return flights, she always flew left seat. On one return, Charlie told me I should get further training for my flight instructor's certificate, which she would be happy to shepherd me through. "Your instructor's fee won't make or break you, but you'll be getting new pilots into the air, and that's gratifying in itself."

The current college term would end in mid-December, which gave Oscar a month to recharge his teaching batteries. At the same time, Charlie began to see that clothes were starting to disappear from his closet. "Time to upgrade to a decent wardrobe?" she teased him, while offering to take his old duds to Goodwill; but he told her it would be more meaningful to him if he dropped them off himself. After the Christmas season, he said he'd snap up some post-holiday sales.

He never mentioned Dee's name since Sierra blabbed, and we had the good sense not to intrude. But Dee's name did come up during a casual dinner at Oscar and Charlie's, again from Sierra.

"I'm staying sober tonight," she announced as she sipped a glass of wine with the appetizers. "Besides, I have news. And don't worry, Oscar, I'm not going to reveal any privileged information." He stared at her stone-faced.

Sierra's face beamed. "You are now looking at the new owner of Alpha Window and Door Company."

"What?" We cried as one.

"Yup. It seems Dee has found a beau who wants to take her away to some island in the Caribbean, as in permanently. Don't know who and where, because unlike me she doesn't blab. She tells me he knows her history, including the abortion, and tells her he loves her and will always treat her like a princess. Which sounds pretty hokey to me, but she really seems to love him."

"Wow," said Charlie. She winked at Oscar. "I should be so lucky."

"As if you're not."

Sierra continued, "So Dee and I made arrangements for me to buy the business, with her holding the mortgage. She's put her parents' home on the market, and I'll be working with her realtor to get the best price. Anything we get over her bottom line will be applied to my payments for the business. Hey. Maybe I will get drunk after all," she said, laughing as she held her empty glass for Oscar to refill.

We congratulated her on the news, and Charlie asked when Dee's Don Juan was planning to take her away. Sierra said they planned to leave as soon as the paperwork is done.

Over dinner, Charlie reminded me that my flight review was coming up. FAA regulations require each pilot to submit to a periodic review with a licensed instructor. The airline gave Charlie her review, and she gave me mine. I told her I didn't have anything planned for tomorrow, and she said she didn't either, because Oscar was wrapping up the term and would be busy with grades, so that was that.

Sierra got drunk again, and Oscar drove her home.

I drove Charlie to the airport next day and parked on the ramp as she quizzed me on assorted Federal Air Regulations. Only after I'd answered them satisfactorily did we leave the air-conditioned car and head to the hangar. When I opened the overhead door, we were hit by a wall of heat. Yes, it was December; yes again, it was Florida. "You should get a commercial air conditioning unit in here," Charlie said. "Really. Temperatures like this don't do the plane any good, especially the electronics. You know that." I agreed and said once the money started rolling back in regularly, I'd invest in one.

Meanwhile, Charlie watched while I preflighted 22T, noting my proficiency on her mental checklist. Then we pulled the plane out, closed the hangar door, and headed for the Everglades, flying east this time.

As we approached the Glades, a voice cut in on the common traffic advisory frequency. "Hey, you all, wuzzup?"

Charlie and I stared at each other, and when the call repeated, again, and yet again, we realized that some fool had gotten his hands on a portable transceiver and was playing games. This was a huge violation, bigger than the average jamoke could ever imagine. By commandeering the airwaves, he placed all local air traffic in jeopardy, from tiny Cessna 152s to heavy twins.

I picked up the microphone. "Person cluttering the common traffic frequency. You are in violation of Federal law. You must stop your transmissions immediately."

"What chew gon' do, asswipe?" came the reply. I replaced the mic, took a deep breath, and looked at Charlie.

"I know," she said. "And he's right; what can we do? We don't even know where he is."

Then another call broke through. "Mayday, mayday, Cessna 2724 Quebec, engine failure over Everglades; will try to land on Alligator Alley."

Charlie and I started. As one, we shouted, "That's a club plane!"

Thirteen

"My God, we've got to find him," said Charlie. "If he can't make the road he's going down in the Glades."

"At least we're at the west end of the highway. We head east and we've got to spot him."

We flew on, eyes outside both sides of the plane, because the panicked club member didn't announce whether he was north or south of the road. Finally, we saw a jackknifed tractor-trailer across the highway blocking westbound traffic, and just in front of it we saw the high white wing of the Skyhawk, nearly buried in the grasses.

"He must've come in low and panicked the truck driver," I said.

Charlie keyed her microphone and radioed that we'd found the plane and gave our GPS coordinates.

"Tell them Piper Two Two Tango is going to land and render aid."

Charlie cast a puzzled look at me, then looked down to see traffic at a standstill behind the trailer, and radioed my message. The road in front of the truck was now empty.

"Do you think I'm doing the right thing?" I asked. "I'm asking you as an instructor."

"Have you ever made an off-airport landing before?"

"No. Have you?"

"No."

"Well?"

"You're the pilot in command," Charlie said. Her tone was non-committal, in accordance with protocol. I nodded and began my approach.

I turned to put us well behind the truck to give us room to descend to the west. I touched down a hundred yards ahead of it, and once our rollout slowed to taxi speed, I pivoted us around and taxied back to the truck. The driver was outside, waving his arms and pointing toward the tail of the Cessna and the tear in the boundary fence.

I shut down the engine, and before the prop stopped, Charlie had grabbed the plane's first aid kit and opened the door. I followed her out the door, and together we raced toward our downed club plane.

"You smell anything?" Charlie asked as we came up to the plane, its tail high and its nose buried in muck.

"I can't smell any gas fumes. Damn it to hell; the guy ran out of fuel."

"No excuses," she said as she reached the pilot's side door and looked through the window. "And the fool isn't even wearing his shoulder harness."

The pilot was slumped forward, his head jammed against the instrument panel, his face covered in a sheet of blood. He wasn't moving.

The impact of the crash had buckled the aluminum skin, and it took both of us to open the sprung door. Charlie backed away to give me room, silently acknowledging my proficiency as an EMT.

I reached into the plane and gently tipped the pilot into an upright posture. He was breathing, at least. And then I smelled it. Not gas; the unmistakable smell of cherry blend tobacco.

"Holy shit!" I shouted and looked back at Charlie. "It's Mike!"

"What? What? That son of a bitch!" Fury flamed in Charlie's eyes.

Mike screamed when I eased him out of the plane, and I saw the raw and jagged end of bone poking through his thigh, just below the hem of his shorts.

"Compound fracture of the femur," I said as we laid him on the swamp grass. I reached into the plane and took out the metal tow bar to use as a splint. I held it against his leg, and Charlie used multiple thicknesses of gauze to tie it in place. Then she used a gauze pad to wipe the blood from his face. She wasn't gentle.

Mike Fox looked up and saw who was treating him. "Aw, fuck," he said.

Without a word to him, I checked his vitals. Other than the leg and a severe gash in his forehead, which had already soaked through the pads I'd taped on, he seemed all right. "You'll live, asshole," were my first words to him. "Better for you if you didn't."

"You freaking stole the club plane," Charlie seethed, standing over him with fists clenched. "Before you turned your clubhouse key in, you made a duplicate, didn't you? You've committed grand larceny, you bloody idiot. And don't think we won't prosecute you to the max." She took a deep breath, her eyes spitting fire. "Your life as you know it is over."

He groaned. "Charlie, listen. I just wanted to take a ride is all. I was gonna leave cash on the counter when I got back, so no harm, no foul."

"But you didn't check the fuel level during preflight, did you?" she said.

"Uh, well, no I didn't. Kinda in a hurry to get out before someone saw me, you know? Shoulda been full anyway, though. No excuse for low fuel, right?" His tone had grown whiny, which infuriated me even more.

"But there is," I said. "It was going into the shop tomorrow for its annual inspection, and we left a note telling the last person to fly not to bother filling the tanks."

Charlie stood up straight and looked down at Mike's pained face. "You're going to jail, shithead. And you're going to lose everything— your house, your business... and Julie too. Because she's sure as hell not going to wait around for you to get out of prison, is she?"

"She... already left me. Went back to Vermont."

Suddenly I started to laugh. I couldn't help it. Despite everything, I laughed and couldn't stop. A few seconds later, Charlie joined me, both of us perversely savoring Mike's past, current, and future suffering.

Charlie's ears perked up. "Vic, we've got to stop and get serious. I just heard a siren. Company's coming."

When the emergency crew arrived on scene, I described Mike's condition, and they got a backboard ready to haul him out. The EMT re-dressed his scalp wound and asked how he felt.

Through tears, Mike said, "They were laughing at me."

"He's delirious," Charlie said somberly, and the tech nodded.

"You might want to get out of here yourself," he said. "Pumas have been spotted in this area. They smell blood, they'll come running."

As the emergency truck drove away, Charlie and I returned to the trusty Six. "You're shaking," she said. "Want me to fly back home? You've passed your review, by the way."

I told her that was a good idea but noted a vehicle out on our side of the median, a van with a dish on top and a local TV station logo on the side. "We're trapped."

"I'll take care of it."

Eventually, the news bunny got what she needed from Charlie as I performed a hasty preflight check. "Good to go," I said. "Your turn to make an off-airport takeoff."

She gave me a sudden peck on the cheek and hopped into the plane. "This'll be fun," she said as she started the engine.

"It's not going to be fun later," I said, thinking of the inevitable police statements, insurance paperwork, and media interviews. "Not to mention towing the plane out of the swamp and back to the airport. And telling the membership what happened."

"I think by the next meeting they'll already know everything. Let's fly, partner."

Airborne again, a crackly voice came over the common frequency. "Yo, you all, wuzzup?"

I shook my head, disgusted. "I'd like to put my size ten up his ass."

Charlie radioed the FAA to report him. She said if they had other planes in the air, they might be able to triangulate his position. "Who knows? Mike might have a cellmate soon."

Fourteen

A news van was already in the parking lot as Charlie taxied us to the hangar. "News travels at the speed of light these days," I remarked sourly as I pressed the remote to open the hangar door.

Charlie pivoted the plane so we could back it into the hangar, and as she shut down the engine a cameraman and an on-scene reporter, a man this time, approached the plane. "Here we go," she said. "I wonder if you'll still be hailed as a hometown hero if they connect you to your full-time pursuit." I said ouch. "Not to worry," she said, chuckling. "We'll tell them of your volunteer work with Angel Flight and the other missions. They'll have you walking on water by tomorrow."

"And the next day, they'll move on to something else. Unless..."

"Unless?"

"Unless the morality police make the link to the mile high flights."

"Hopefully, they've gone on to other pursuits, like preserving the snail darter or the spotted owl."

"Cynical, are we?" I chided.

"Time to face the music, partner."

We climbed out and noticed a second and third van, each emblazoned with the logos of the local national broadcast affiliates. The first reporter on scene approached us, but Charlie held up a hand and said, "Let us back the plane into the hangar, please? You can have first dibs at us, promise."

"How do you do that?" he called. "Does it have a reverse gear?"

"Wouldn't that be a godsend?" she called back.

He waited and the cameraman began shooting as I took the metal tow bar from the baggage compartment. I attached the forked tong to the steerable nose wheel, then grabbed the T-handle at the other end. Charlie and I muscled the plane into the hangar, she pushing on a wing's leading edge, me pushing on the tow bar and steering her into place. Once inside, I climbed into the cockpit and applied the hand brake.

Charlie primped her hair, smiled, and called coquettishly to the reporter standing outside, "Ready for my close-up, Mr. DeMille."

We answered his questions about landing the plane on the highway, freeing the pilot, and triaging him. The reporter asked how I was qualified to do the triage, and I related my stint as a Navy corpsman and my time as a med tech in Washington. We didn't mention the pilot's identity.

Next, he focused on Charlie, who told them she'd been my instructor. "You... were his... instructor?" he asked, expecting the opposite answer. She smiled and told him she also flew for an airline, and that set him back another pace.

"Vic's not my student anymore," she explained and told him I was a commercial pilot myself.

He noticed her wedding ring. "Are you two married?"

As Charlie blushed, I said, "She is; I'm not."

He opened his mouth as if to ask another question, thought better of it, and thanked us for the interview.

Once the reporter was done, he yielded to the next one, who in turn yielded to the third. We told them the same story, and each one asked if we were married. Charlie answered that we were long-time friends and current officers in the Southwest Florida Flying Club. The third reporter, a woman, asked for details about the club, and after the camera stopped rolling told Charlie she was a single mom, and now that her kids were grown and out of the house, she was contemplating getting a pilot's license. "It's been a dream of mine."

Charlie wrote her number on the back of the reporter's card and invited her to the next meeting. She shook Charlie's hand and said she'd be there.

"That went well," Charlie said, grinning. "At least no one asked if you were the flying whoremaster."

"We have more company," I said, pointing to two uniformed officers waiting outside. We invited them into the hangar and thanked them for waiting until the reporters were done. They told her they'd been listening and already had a feel for the narrative, but would we mind going with them to the station to make official statements?

"Happy to," I said. "What we didn't mention to the reporters was that the plane was stolen for a joyride." That piqued their interest significantly, and they said they were very eager to hear the rest of the story—at the air-conditioned station.

When we arrived home, Oscar was standing outside the townhouse door waiting for us. "You're all over the local news," he said. "Is it true that the pilot you rescued is Mike? He's being treated in Miami as we speak."

Charlie gave him the details as we sat on their patio with drinks.

"His girlfriend's gone back home, his ex-wife runs a business that won't do business with his, and he faces a fine and prison time for aircraft theft. I'd call that a trifecta."

I raised my beer. "To trifectas." We drank as my phone rang. It was Sierra.

"That true what I'm seeing on the news?" she said without preamble.

"I'm sorry, Sierra. We should've called you as soon as we got back to the airport. But there were the reporters to deal with, and then the police wanted statements, and—hell, no excuses. We just forgot."

"Understood. Hey, you know what? Sorry about the plane and all, but as for what's coming for Mike, I'm as happy as a pig in shit."

I laughed, apologized again, and we said goodbye.

Charlie said, "I feel terrible. I should've called. Not good to get bad news from the TV."

"I think she considers it more good news than bad."

Charlie said, "You know what really sucks, Oscar? Mike must've anticipated doing something like this all along. He made sure the clubhouse was empty, unlocked the door with his duplicate key, and picked up the key to the Skyhawk. Took off without even checking the fuel, and he didn't secure his shoulder harness. Which makes him the consummate asshole. Bottom line, all of this is Mike's fault, but who has to suffer for it?"

"Besides Mike?" said Oscar.

"Don't tell me he's suffering," said Charlie. "We're the ones, Vic and me. We've already submitted statements to the police; the FAA will be calling posthaste for another statement; and in addition, we'll have to submit documentation to them, and to the insurance company. The NTSB will be on scene to determine probable cause for the crash—obviously a no-brainer. Then we have to get the plane towed out of the Everglades and brought back to the airport. Once it's back, we have to have the shop determine if repair is more feasible than resale. If it's cheaper to let it go, like with the Mooney, the trustee will have to look into securing another Skyhawk. That'll require a vote from the membership. And—"

"Whoa," said Oscar. "Slow down. You're in motor mouth mode. Take a breath. Things will work out. Over time, things will get better."

"Right," she said. "Because right now they can't get much worse."

Fifteen

The Friday before Christmas week, Charlie was scheduled to fly to Kingston Airport north of Manhattan, where she'd stay overnight before making a run to Atlantic City International, which would entail another layover. On Sunday she would return to Fort Myers, arriving at around two in the afternoon.

I mentioned to Oscar, half-kiddingly, that while Charlie was away the timing was right for a boys' night out, but he told me he had scheduled group sessions Friday and Saturday nights; perhaps another time. "You work nights too?" I asked.

He shrugged. "Why I get the big bucks."

At six o'clock Sunday evening, getting ready to prepare dinner, I heard my doorbell, accompanied immediately by a banging on my door. Charlie rushed inside, kicked the door shut behind her, and ran into my arms, sobbing. Finally, she backed off and looked at me, agony writ large on her face. She was still dressed in her flight uniform, and her mascara made black tracks down her face.

"Charlie, what's wrong?"

"Get me a drink. No, just hold me. No, I need a drink. No, I need you to hold me first. Then I need a drink."

I held her, our bodies swaying from side to side as she wept. Finally, she looked up at me and said she'd be okay with that drink now. "Make it strong," she said.

We moved into the kitchen, and as she plopped down at the dinette table, I mixed her a gin and tonic with twice the gin. She gulped it down without tasting it—until her eyes opened wide at the kick. "Another?" she said.

"How about you tell me what's going on first? I've never seen you like this."

Charlie took one, two, three deep breaths, and said, "You remember when I mentioned things could only get better, because they couldn't get much worse? I lied." She looked at the empty glass. "The ice cubes look lonely in there."

"Later. Explanation first."

"I'm sure you never noticed this, because he put up a good front. But for the past couple of months, Oscar's been... I don't know, maybe distant would be the best way to describe it. Maybe bordering on cold, now that I think of it. But I figured he was just busy with preparing for the end of the term, grading exam papers, and figuring out final grades, you know? He did tell me his patient load was growing, and he was feeling a little overwhelmed. At least, that's what he told me. Here."

She reached into the pocket of her uniform blouse and handed me a creased letter. It had been composed on a computer and printed, with Oscar's scrawled signature at the bottom, first name only. Charlie began talking before I got a chance to read it. "I got home after the flight, took off my blazer, and hung it in the walk-in closet. Figured I'd take it to the dry cleaner's tomorrow. Oscar's side of the closet was empty. I thought at first, he was taking his wardrobe makeover to the extreme. But that didn't seem quite right, so I checked the dresser drawers. His clothes were gone too. All of them, down to underwear and socks. And his bathroom gear was gone too."

"Holy... no, that's not right."

She sobbed. "I went into the kitchen and found this—he couldn't even hand-write it, the bastard; it's so impersonal—anyway, the letter. It was on top of a large official-looking envelope in the center of the table. I haven't even looked inside the envelope yet. Probably some legal crap, I don't know. This letter was all I could deal with. And even now, after reading it a dozen times, I still can't deal with it. Go ahead, read it."

I saw water stains on the paper—Charlie's tears. In the letter, Oscar admitted he'd been counseling Dee since Mike had forced her into an abortion. She was so deep in depression he feared she was becoming suicidal. He counseled her almost every day, and their relationship deepened beyond doctor-patient. He knew his actions violated every professional code of ethics, but he couldn't help himself. He was truly in love for perhaps the first time in his life.

"For the first time in his life!" Charlie wailed.

It had been he who'd suggested Dee put her house on the market and sell her father's company to Sierra. He wrote a letter of resignation to the college, and now the two of them, Oscar and Dee, were starting a new life, relocating to some unnamed Caribbean island.

The letter concluded with Oscar telling Charlie he felt guilty at taking the coward's way out and not confronting her directly. He said he'd been conflicted because he couldn't betray doctor-patient confidentiality, so he couldn't tell Charlie what he was going through. The overlap between his professional and personal lives tormented him for a long time. He concluded by wishing her a happy life.

I put the letter on the table and fixed both of us a gin and tonic, this time not spiked so heavily as Charlie's first. She sipped it and reached across the table. I took her hands and held them tight. On impulse, I brought one of her hands to my lips and gave it a supportive kiss. She gave me a half smile through her tears.

"So now Oscar's in love for the first time. What does that say about me? Was our marriage a lie? Was I just a convenient bedmate? Maybe a status symbol to show off to his snooty peers? 'Yes, my wife is also a professional; she's an airline pilot, you know.' He was the passive one in our relationship; I don't know if you ever picked up on that. I'd make the plans and he'd go along. I never felt he was all that interested, all that involved. But I figured well, that's Oscar. I knew his temperament before I married him, and I figured that's okay. We're like yin and yang, you know?" She held her head in her hands, reminding me of myself when Julie left. "Sorry to dump this on you, Vic" she said weakly.

"I want you to dump it on me, Charlie. I've always been here for you, and I always will be."

Charlie sniffed and tried to smile. "Vic, there's no dearer friend than you. I so love you for that."

"I love you too," I said. But I wondered if I meant it in quite the same way she did.

Sixteen

I'd told Charlie to come by for breakfast next day, and when I opened the door, I saw her eyes were bloodshot. She said good morning—which her tone told me was anything but a good morning—and when I closed the door, she turned to face me and practically fell into my arms.

"You give the best hugs, Vic," she said a full minute later when she eased out of my embrace. She sniffed and said, "What smells good?"

"It's just coffee."

"Coffee, please."

I followed her into the kitchen, where she reached into a cupboard and pulled out two mugs. She filled them with coffee, added sugar and cream to both, and brought them to the table as if she were the host, not I.

"You've been crying," I said lamely.

"All night."

"I'm sorry."

"Don't be. Now I know how you felt when Julie left you; or when you kicked her out. I wish I'd been there more for you at the time."

"I healed; you will too."

She sipped her coffee. "If you say so. Now, what's for breakfast?"

"I'm thinking of bacon and waffles, and maybe a fried egg on the side."

"That sounds delicious. How can I help?"

The condo had a large kitchen, which allowed us to work side by side. Charlie fried bacon while I prepared the batter. As I made the waffles, she heated syrup in the microwave and got butter from the fridge. "We make a good team," I said, and she said we do, don't we?

We put the bacon and waffles into a warming oven as I prepared the eggs. With the heat low, I cracked them into a frying pan and placed a glass lid on top, so the tops would cook without having to flip them over easy.

"Sunny side up," I announced as I added one to her plate.

"Like me, huh?" she said.

"Like you; or like you will be. Dig in."

Charlie savored every bit of her meal, and when we were done, she took the dishes to the sink.

"I'll get them later," I said. "Sit down and I'll pour you more coffee."

"I'm supposed to be a strong, modern woman," she said as she returned to the table. "Tell me, Vic, how did you feel when you found Julie and Mike together?"

"I was furious at first, like you. And after she left, I felt as if one of my limbs had been severed." I took a breath. "Then the grief set in."

"But you survived."

"And you will too. Listen, Oscar's affair is no more your fault than Julie's affair was mine. When I realized that, the wound began to heal."

"Thanks."

"You said his letter was on top of a flat envelope?"

"I opened it last night before I went to bed. I was really afraid to, figuring it contained something horrible. But it was verification that he'd taken his name off our joint bank accounts. That was the first paper. The next was a lawyer's statement that Oscar was willing to agree to a no-fault divorce and would not contest me for any assets. It directed me to call the lawyer's office to begin proceedings."

"He'd represent you both? He can't, right?"

"Right; his lawyer would give me the name of a colleague. But the letter said the divorce would be open and shut, quicker than a Vegas wedding."

"He really did cut all ties, didn't he?"

"Well, not exactly. I went online to check our accounts. Seems before he had his name taken off, he withdrew half of everything in our checking and savings accounts. Which I can't fault him for. At least he couldn't touch my IRA or pension."

"We should call Sierra. Let her know what's happened, who Dee's mystery boyfriend was."

She nodded. "You make the call, all right?"

"I'll put it on speaker."

Sierra's first words after I gave her the news were, "What a scumbag. How's Charlie doing?"

"I'm okay," Charlie said from across the table, her voice quivering. "Vic's just made breakfast for me."

"Comfort food," Sierra said. "I mean that literally." She paused for a beat. "Listen, amigos. Christmas is in two days. How about I fix us dinner with all the trimmings? Just the three of us. You game?"

I looked at Charlie, who nodded. "You're on, lady. What can we bring?"

"Bring your cute little bodies, that's all. No, wait; bring booze. Whatever you like; I'm not fussy. As you know."

"How about a walk on the beach?" I suggested.

"Walk off the breakfast? Good idea. Let me go change into shorts, and I'll be right back."

When Charlie returned, she was wearing abbreviated denim shorts that highlighted her gorgeous legs and a cream-colored sleeveless top, modestly cut at the neckline. Sandals were on her feet. I wore dark khaki shorts and a light tan polo, which she said looked good on me. I told her everything looked good on her, and she gave me a playful cuff. "Come on, Romeo; you're just trying to make me feel good," she said.

We took off our sandals as we stepped onto the broad white beach. Pale-skinned tourists sat on beach chairs or lay on blankets, while children played nearby. We walked to the barely rippling water and let it wash over our feet as we strolled north, with no destination in mind.

Behind us, we heard a high-pitched shriek. We spun around, expecting to see someone in trouble; instead, we saw a little girl of about six or seven years old, jumping up and down in glee as a pod of dolphin rolled by not fifteen feet from shore.

We watched the dolphins as they swam north and then continued our stroll. My sandals were hanging from my left hand and Charlie's from her right. She tentatively closed her fingers around mine. We exchanged smiles and continued hand in hand.

Back at my car, Charlie said, "Let's stop at the market, and I'll buy a couple of steaks. You cooked breakfast for me; I'm going to cook dinner for you."

She grilled the filets to a turn and accompanied them with baked potatoes slathered in sour cream and fresh string beans. We ate outside, and after dinner, with wine making us mellow, we retired to side-by-side patio chairs and looked up at the stars. The humidity was uncommonly low, and the sky was clear enough to make the stars seem close enough to touch.

We held hands again.

"Thank you for today," Charlie sighed. "There's no one better than you to ease a girl's broken heart."

"I'd be happier to be able to heal it."

"Mmm. You know, I'd kiss you now, but I wouldn't want you to think I'm rebounding from losing Oscar."

"Oscar who?" I said, and she chuckled. But she didn't kiss me.

"May I make a suggestion?" I said.

"Of course. Please."

"Remember when we first flew to Tampa in the Six for dinner?"

"Seems like forever ago, but yes."

"Tomorrow's Christmas Eve. Let's do it again."

"Just the two of us? There's plenty of room for Sierra, too."

"Just us, if that's all right with you."

"I was kind of hoping you'd say that."

Seventeen

The next day early, my phone rang. Charlie.

"You're making breakfast again, right?"

"Come on over."

She arrived wearing dress slacks and a flowered top, carrying a sweater.

"What's up?" I said.

"I'll do breakfast. You put on some nice duds. I'm belaying the Tampa trip and taking you to Charleston."

"Huh? What for?"

"Some delicious Low Country cuisine." To my frown, she said, "Four hours up, four hours back. We leave at ten, arrive at two, rent a car, have a leisurely late lunch, be back at the plane by four, home by eight."

"Wow. That's taking the hundred-dollar hamburger to a whole new level."

"I suggest I fly left seat going north; you fly left going home. Now scoot. Breakfast will be ready by the time you are."

Charlie's calculations, airline pilot that she was, were on the money. By three o'clock we were at The Ordinary on Charleston's peninsula—which proved to be extraordinary. Charlie ordered mustard crusted amberjack, and I tried the pumpkin swordfish saltimbocca. Sounds weird, but it was delicious.

At no time did the subjects of Oscar, Julie, Mike, or the Skyhawk accident come up. She told me about her first hire as an ATP—air transport pilot.

"Starting salary was equivalent to a McDonald's trainee," she said, smiling, "but I did get to fly."

I asked her what her passengers would say if they knew how little she was paid, how that would translate to proficiency. She said that fortunately, no one asked.

"I made a lot of Nassau runs from Miami in turboprops before graduating to the bigger jets, better routes, and bigger salary. When the airline assigned me to a permanent base at Fort Myers, I began looking for someplace to put down roots."

"Like a town house in Naples."

"Yes. And once I got situated, I realized I missed flying the little planes and joined the flying club."

"They were happy to get another instructor as a member, I'd guess."

"They were happy, I was happy, and look at us now."

We arrived back in Naples, filled up the plane, and backed it into the hangar. When we got home, Charlie spoke the words no one likes to hear.

She stood by her door and said, "Vic, we need to talk."

My stomach dropped. If she noticed, she gave no hint.

We sat on her living room sofa, with the center cushion serving as a metaphoric bundling board. I was growing more nervous by the minute.

"Wait. Let me get some wine. We couldn't drink at the restaurant, so we can make up for it now."

I wasn't sure I wanted to wait. All manner of horrid thoughts fought for attention. Finally, she returned with two goblets and a bottle of Malbec. We filled them and each took a swallow. Charlie looked at me over the rim of her glass. "About that talk," she said.

I nodded.

"I'm wondering if you're the reason Oscar decided to leave me."

I almost blubbered out my wine. "What?"

"Seriously. You and I have known each other for, what, four years now? Maybe a little longer?" I nodded. "And we've grown close, wouldn't you say?" Another nod. "Well, I never mentioned this to you, but there have been times that Oscar mentioned he thought you and I might be getting a little *too* close."

"He was jealous?"

"I told him that was ridiculous, because let's face it, you and I were never really alone together, except in an airplane, and we had other things to occupy our time. After Julie left after you'd set up your mile high enterprise, that's when he really began to grow suspicious."

"Oh. No, I didn't know any of that. He was always pleasant—a little aloof at times, but pleasant. I figured he was just preoccupied with work."

"Preoccupied with Dee. I'm wondering if it's my fault for not showing him as much attention as I might have."

"I... can't relate to that, Charlie. There's no one more... attentive, empathetic... than you."

"Yet here I am, unburdening my soul to you."

"Who else would you trust with your soul?"

She sat back on the sofa and put her wine glass down. "Vic. Was Oscar right? Were we getting too close?"

I swallowed. "We could never be *too* close."

There, I'd said it.

"If I were to kiss you now, Vic, what would you think? Would you think I was getting revenge on Oscar for leaving me? I'm so confused right now."

"In that case, I have a suggestion for you."

"Yes?"

"Kiss me and find out."

The center cushion wasn't a bundling board anymore.

After our first kiss, tentative on Charlie's part at first and then, sensing my desire, stronger and more passionate, I said softly, "I do love you, Charlie."

"Thank God," she said.

We kissed some more, and Charlie said, "When I got Oscar's letter, and you held me and comforted me, I called you a friend, because I was kind of afraid to say what I was really beginning to feel. To realize."

"Truth to tell, when you called me a friend, it kind of broke my heart."

"I will never break your heart, Vic."

Eighteen

The gentle rhythm of Charlie's breathing woke me up. She lay on her side, her head resting on my outstretched arm, her arm resting across my chest. I brought her hand to my mouth and kissed it. She stirred.

"Good morning," I murmured.

"Mmmm."

"Merry Christmas."

"Mmmm."

"Want to get up?"

"Mmmm. Tomorrow."

Charlie snuggled up to me, draped a leg over my hips, and kissed my cheek down to my ear. Her eyes were still closed, but her lips were turned up in a contented smile. I kissed her lips lightly, and her smile grew.

I ran my fingers through her long dark hair, hair she pinned up when in uniform but was now loose and long and fine. She sighed and cracked open her pale hazel eyes.

"Thanks for my Christmas present," she whispered.

"I didn't get you a present."

"Yes, you did." She rolled on top of me and kissed me after pulling the sheet back. "Now I'm about to open it." It was another thirty minutes before we rose from the bed.

All my bathroom gear—shave cream, razor, and toothbrush—was down in my condo, so I excused myself to freshen up, but not before Charlie suggested, "When you're done, why don't you bring them up here? When does your lease expire, by the way?"

I fixed us a light breakfast, because we knew Sierra would be stuffing us like turkeys at dinner.

"Well, it's about time," she greeted us later as we stood at her door holding hands. "Come on in, and Merry Christmas. What did you bring us to drink?"

Oscar had a stash of fine liquors, which he only broke out to impress his colleagues when he and Charlie entertained. We brought over bottles of scotch, rye, bourbon, and gin and told Sierra to take her pick of any or all. And that we planned to leave them there when we left. She said that's why she loves us.

"What am I smelling?" Charlie asked. "It's not turkey, is it?"

"It's goose. A German tradition on Christmas. Or at least in my family."

"It smells delicious," Charlie said. "My mouth is watering already."

Sierra led us to the living room of the spacious house that for years she'd shared with Mike. She fixed us drinks and placed a platter of appetizers on the coffee table. "Tell me, you moon-eyed calves," she said. "When did... this... finally happen?"

"Yesterday," Charlie said, her face beaming. I guess mine was too, because Sierra called our attention to it.

"I'm happy for you. Vic, I got the impression from the start that Julie was trouble, though I really didn't have reason to; just intuition, I guess."

"Which proved correct," I said. "Hope she's enjoying her Vermont winter."

"And Charlie, there was something about Oscar that rubbed me the wrong way too. Like he was analyzing everything we said. I knew it was his profession, but we weren't his patients, and I felt like he was intruding that way."

"He tended to do that," Charlie admitted. "I used to admire his insights. Notice, past tense."

"As for my beloved ex, he called yesterday from the hospital. Told me he was doing all right, like I give a shit. Had the gall to ask if I'd look in on the business while he was gone."

"Wow," I said. "That's chutzpah."

Sierra laughed. "What he doesn't know, and what I didn't tell him? As soon as what he'd done made the news, his officers voted him out of his corporation as president and CEO."

"Were they afraid the company would be targeted in legal proceedings?" asked Charlie.

"I guess. I mean, what with his legal fees, fines, and penalties, in addition to his liabilities to the club over the loss of the plane, they were afraid all his assets were endangered. As I'm sure they are. Again, who gives a shit. They ousted him, with no golden parachute."

"Can they do that?" Charlie asked. "He founded the company."

"You mean like Steve Jobs founded Apple, but later the board fired him anyway?"

"What happens to him now? Do you know?" I asked.

"Frankly, my dear," she rasped, affecting a Southern accent, "Ah don't give a damn." She added, grinning, "Shouldn't have seduced his innocent little Scarlett O'Hara in the first place. And knocked her up. And made her get an abortion against her will."

"And that's not to mention Julie," I said.

She scoffed. "Julie was nothing compared to poor Dee."

"Who's now living in a tropical paradise with my soon-to-be ex-husband."

We nibbled on appetizers and sipped our drinks for a moment. Then Sierra asked, "You want me to tell you about Mike's business?"

"Please," Charlie said. "You started to, and I interrupted you."

"Not to worry, doll face. And I mean that as a compliment, by the way."

"Compliment taken," she said.

"And seconded," I added. Charlie leaned over and gave me a quick kiss.

"The other guys on the board thought Mike was a real shit for cheating on me; they told me they liked me better than him, can you believe it? Anyway, they wondered if I'd consider coming back."

"Whoa," I said.

"It gets better. They've approached me to ask about the possibility of Foxtrot Construction merging with Alpha Window and Door. I told them I'd think about it."

"And?" asked Charlie.

"What do you think?"

We drank to Sierra's new venture, and as we did a bell sounded. "Our goose is cooked," she said.

We sat down to a table whose cream-colored cloth was festooned with red and green trim, and a bowl filled with Christmas ornaments as a centerpiece. Sierra said, "Tradition says the man carves the goose, but you probably haven't done it before, Vic, right?" I acknowledged her. "Which means I'll carve. Goose is fatty, you know, which makes the meat moist. And the breast meat is dark. You won't find it dry like a turkey's."

When she finished carving, I said, "For a bird that big, there doesn't seem to be a whole lot of meat. There's plenty for us, but I don't think you'll have much left over."

"That's the beauty of it," Sierra said. "I hate leftovers. Here, have some Spätzle and red cabbage. Another German tradition."

For dessert, Sierra brought out what she called *Bienenstich*, which translates as bee sting cake. Two layers of yeast cake sandwiched a creamy filling, and the top was coated with a honey-and-almond topping.

"I'm in heaven," Charlie said after her first taste.

"Love at first bite," I added. "This is incredible."

"It's really complicated to make, so I only serve it when I have special guests."

Afterward, filled to the gills and mellowed out, we sat back sipping Jägermeister and reflected on a perfect day. Something came to mind, and I chortled.

"What's funny?" asked Charlie.

"Back in the Navy, I was a corpsman stationed with a Marine unit. The Marines called their enlisted men's club the slop chute. Behind the bar, up high where everyone could see it, was posted a sign."

"Well?" demanded Sierra.

"It read, 'Tuesday night is poultry night. Every lady gets a free goose.'"

Charlie winked at Sierra and said, "Don't you love it when he talks dirty?"

Epilogue

"An email! He sent me a freaking email!" Charlie ranted. "What's the matter? Don't they have phone service on St. Thomas? I'm not worth a freaking phone call?" She was laughing through her outrage.

Almost a year had passed since Oscar had left. During that time, I air-conditioned the hangar and treated 22T to a paint job, which made her look new again. Business from May through the first half of October had been brisk, and we had enough money in the plane's account to eventually replace the original instruments with a digital glass panel. Charlie, when she wasn't on call, flew the Six almost as often as I, either alongside me or alone, if I happened to be otherwise occupied with club duties.

We'd been re-elected to our offices unanimously, following being hailed as heroes for our actions during and after Mike Fox's off-airport landing—and for our efficiency in processing all the tedious administrative work that followed. The Skyhawk was inspected and restored to airworthiness by our skilled on-field shop, all expenses paid, "courtesy" of Mike—who lost everything due to fines, penalties, aircraft towing and repairs, and lawyer fees. When he learned to his surprise that Sierra had no intention of welcoming him back to Foxtrot Construction, newly merged with Alpha Window and Door, he had no option afterward but to declare bankruptcy.

In October, a hurricane ravaged the Keys, making roads impassible. In the aftermath, Charlie and I organized a number of club convoys to fly emergency supplies to Summerland Key Cove, the last private airport before Key West. The club's action was featured in newspapers from the Keys all the way to Tallahassee.

The lease on my condo had expired the previous March, and I didn't renew, as by that time Charlie and I were sharing her town house. Now it was mid-November, and we were getting the clubhouse ready for our first annual Thanksgiving dinner for families in need. Club members volunteered to enhance their experience by setting up tables outside and staging a spot landing contest for their enjoyment. Tower personnel volunteered to close the airport to other traffic for the afternoon's festivities.

We'd just returned home when Charlie picked up the email that had her flying into a rage, accompanied by a simultaneous fit of laughter.

"He wants me to take him back!" she said, and of course I knew who *he* was. "Can you imagine? He says he made a mistake; that Dee is a lovely person, but they're completely unsuited for each other, and he still loves me and misses me. He calls his fling with Dee a midlife crisis—which is ridiculous, unless by *midlife* it means you're planning to die at seventy-four. Which I wouldn't wish on anyone, even him."

She handed me a copy she'd printed out.

"I feel sorry for Dee," I said. "Poor kid's been through a lot in her life, and now this."

Charlie acknowledged that and wondered if there might be something we could do for her. We called Sierra and asked if Dee would be welcomed back to the company, and she said she already had it covered. Dee had been emailing her on occasion, and her latest indicated that there was trouble in paradise. Sierra emailed her, saying the company would pay for her airfare back to the States if she was willing to return.

"Her flight lands in Miami three days from now," Sierra reported that evening. "She'll be flying unaccompanied. And I told her she can stay with me for as long as she likes. House is too big for one anyway. And we'll both volunteer to help at the club's Thanksgiving fiesta."

We told her she was the best, and we meant it.

"I can fly us into Miami to pick her up," said Charlie, which was a relief. She was used to flying into the busiest airports; I tried to avoid them.

We disconnected and stared at each other over the kitchen table. The printout of Oscar's letter lay between us. I looked down and asked what she was going to do with it.

"Let's fire up the grill and have a cremation," she said. "We can grill some burgers over the ashes."

The Second Time Around

The chime on my smart watch sounded, signaling it was time to wake Casey from her pre-celebratory nap. I stretched, clicked Save on my document, closed the laptop, and walked down the hall toward the guest bedroom.

My sister-in-law slept on her back, with one arm at her side and the other across her belly. Her honey blond hair fanned out across the pillow, and her lips were turned up in a half smile. She was clad in a cotton tee over abbreviated denim shorts that made her legs seem to stretch on forever.

Casey had been eighteen when she served as Bek's maid of honor at our wedding. Now, she was living temporarily with us—well, with me now, full disclosure—while pursuing her Ph.D. in psychology. Last week she'd defended her dissertation, and tonight, Friday, two of her girlfriends were taking her out to celebrate.

"Casey, it's time," I said. When she didn't respond, I nudged her shoulder and said, "Come on, sleepyhead. It's five o'clock. Your friends will be waiting for you."

She stretched her arms and legs with a satisfying "Mmmmm," and cracked open her sky-blue eyes. "If I'm late, I can always tell them it's because you seduced me and ravished my poor helpless body."

"Like that's going to happen. Come on, brat, get up."

Casey pivoted, cast her legs over the side, and placed her palms on the edge of the bed. Looking up at me, she said, smirking, "Well, if you're determined to leave my virtue intact, I might as well get up and get dressed." She extended her hand, and I helped her to her feet—not that she needed help. She gestured toward the vanity table that stood in a small alcove, much like the one in the master bedroom. "See you after the metamorphosis."

I chuckled as I returned to the dining room, where my laptop awaited my renewed attention. For a reason I couldn't define, that happened to be my favorite place to write. My formal office was the fourth bedroom—chock-a-block with reference books, a slew of trade magazines, and a few reams of printer paper, along with a desktop computer and multi-function laser printer. Bek had insisted upon installing a trophy case there in which to display my novels. Compared to the magnitude of her own successes, Bek's penchant for showcasing my modest body of work sometimes reminded me of the mother who lauds her five-year-old's finger-paintings as mini-Picassos and tapes them to the refrigerator.

Rebekkah Brozek, my wife of ten years, was the granddaughter of an émigré from Poland who came to America penniless, as had so many others of his generation. He was a cloth merchant by trade, made a living in the city, and raised his only son in the business. His son expanded the business into ready-to-wear women's clothing, and named the company Bek, his nickname for the older of his two daughters. She in turn went to fashion school and became an entrepreneur, designing and selling her own eponymous line of casual wear, formal gowns, and intimate apparel.

I was an aspiring writer when we met on a double date. What happened that night would be obvious to anyone familiar with rom coms, but this was real life. At least my date and hers got along well enough to live together for a while. Bek and I, however, respected her parents' old-world tradition and got married before sharing a bed.

Two weeks after the wedding, her parents died in an automobile accident—hit head-on by a drunk driver—on their way to the airport to pick us up as we returned from our honeymoon. And suddenly, Bek and Casey were orphans.

Casey—born Katherine Celine and nicknamed KC by her schoolmates—had already been accepted at a prestigious university on the West Coast. She almost didn't go, wanting to stay with what remained of her family, but Bek insisted she follow her dream. They would keep in touch through social media, and they could get together during school breaks.

After seven years away, Casey had earned two degrees and begun her doctoral studies in psychology. When she learned she could continue her program back East, she decided to return. "Southern California is so boring," she'd said. "Sunny and warm all the time. I miss the seasons." Then she admitted the other reason—she was terminating a relationship and needed to get away. Far away.

Bek and I insisted Casey move in with us. "Don't refuse the offer, sis," Bek had said. "Save your inheritance money to buy a house after you get those three new letters after your name. You never know where you'll end up working."

Casey came back East, got a teaching job nights at the university's extension campus—a twenty-minute drive from home—and insisted on depositing the bulk of her adjunct's salary in Bek's and my checking account to pay for room and board. Meanwhile, she continued her doctoral studies, which meant she was usually either at school or busy working on her dissertation. I'd offered her the use of my office, and after a few days of perching on her bed with a laptop resting on her knees, she saw the wisdom of my suggestion. The office became Casey's, and mine continued to be the dining room.

By the time Casey moved in, Bek and I had been living a platonic life for about two years, despite still sharing the same bed. She had finally admitted intimate relations had become unpleasant, if not downright off-putting. She assured me she still loved me, but sadly not in *that* way. Bek became more roommate than wife, while Casey ironically became the forbidden fruit in our private little Eden.

Casey had been with us for a year when Bek and I admitted our situation to her—she'd already suspected by then—and decided to separate officially. Bek relocated to the city, bought a high-end condo, and moved in along with her executive assistant, a former model named Gigi. Which left me alone with a beautiful woman five years my junior, in a four-bedroom ranch house on a wooded lot in a northern New Jersey suburb—with a heated swimming pool out back, in which Bek and I had regularly skinny-dipped early in our marriage, our privacy assured by a tall stockade fence.

As the song goes, those were the days.

These days I spent mornings and afternoons and sometimes evenings working on my latest novel. One day a week I'd devote to a stem-to-stern housecleaning, and if Casey were available, she'd join in. We shared a breakfast ritual every morning, taking turns cooking, and when the weather was warm enough, we would occasionally sit by the pool on the rare nights she wasn't on campus, and over a bottle of wine we'd philosophize about everything and nothing.

She asked me one evening why, since I was officially separated, I didn't put myself out there on the dating scene. "You could really benefit with some good female companionship, you know?"

"I already have good female companionship."

She scoffed. "Thanks for that. But you know what I mean."

"Okay. Understand, and this is just me, but until the divorce papers come through, I still see myself legally married. I'd be uncomfortable seeing someone else until it's final."

At the time we separated, Bek had been so busy with her fashion empire that filing for divorce had not been on her agenda. I had no agenda of my own except to continue writing, so the delay didn't matter all that much to me either. But I finally called and suggested perhaps it was time, and she apologized and promised to get the proceedings started immediately.

"Wow," Casey said. "Well, I have to respect your position, I guess." She took a deep breath of the night air. "Seems a shame, though. You're a real catch, Jay. Or will be someday."

Casey and I continued our sister-brother act, living under the same roof and sleeping in separate rooms. Today we'd finished the housecleaning early, so she decided to shower and take a brief nap before heading out with her girlfriends to party.

I was back at the keyboard, typing furiously, when Casey walked into the dining room and did a little pirouette as I looked up. "All ready to paint the town. How do I look?" she said.

"Like an angel fallen to Earth."

"Fallen angel, you're saying?"

"No, just visiting with permission, to make mortal women feel inadequate. You look gorgeous, Casey."

She did indeed. She wore her long hair loose, with gentle waves framing her face. Her make-up was subtle—the merest trace of shadow above her eyes, a touch of color on her cheeks, pale lipstick that matched her fingernails and, with a glance at her sandaled feet, her toenails as well. Her blouse was a long-sleeved deep blue satin that complemented her eyes, and she wore it untucked over a modestly cut white skirt whose hem barely reached her knees. In one hand she held a small, beaded clutch.

"Do I look like I'm ready for the runway at one of Bek's shows?"

"Hardly. Bek's models are flat chested enough to pass for boys. You, my dear, don't meet that standard."

She looked down, then back at me. "Maybe I should button up a little, you think?"

"Depending on how many wolves you want baying at you, you might want to close up one or two."

She sat opposite me, placed her forearms on the table, and leaned forward, ignoring for a moment my fashion advice. I tried to keep my eyes focused on her face, and not—as I've already established—as a lesser man, whose attention would've drifted southward.

"Won't you be late for your date?" I asked.

She shrugged. *Eyes up,* I cautioned myself. "You know, I still wish you were going out with the girls and me instead of being chained to your computer."

"Thanks again, but as the only male member of your clique, I'd be an outlier for sure. And your friends' conversations might be stilted, with a representative of the male persuasion listening in."

"Actually, I think they'd love to meet the famous author I share a house with."

"Famous author? If your friends are anything like you, they'll be reading Freud, Maslow, Piaget, those guys. Not some hack writer who puts out a new bodice ripper every six months or so."

She reached across the table and placed her hand over mine, her expression serious. "Jay, I want you to stop demeaning yourself. Seriously, if you have a major flaw, it's that. First, you don't write bodice rippers. You write serious romantic fiction that really connects with your female readers. Like me, for instance. And my friends, who are always asking me about you. Your books are our escape from all the clinical reading we have to do."

"Your friends? Really?"

She patted my hand before withdrawing hers. "Does that mean you'll come? You still have time to put on some glad rags and join us."

"I can't tonight, I'm afraid. I'm at a turning point in the narrative and I've got to get it written while it's still fresh in my mind. But thanks for the invitation—and the sound advice. Another time, promise."

"Okay, then, you've got a rain check. Meanwhile, to reinforce your fragile ego, I want to tell you why we enjoy your books so much, not that you asked."

I slid the laptop aside, focusing on Casey's eyes. "Have you wondered why I've never asked?" She admitted she had. "I was at some soiree a few years ago with your sister—this was while you were finishing up your master's work in SoCal—and she introduced me to one of her highfalutin' friends, a very well-placed socialite, as 'my husband, the author.' 'Oh, I just love your books,' the snob said, but when I asked her what she liked about them, she hemmed and hawed and finally excused herself to mingle with the other guests. Bek was mortified, although she tried to hide it, and I knew never to ask that question again. I also begged off future events like that, and Bek didn't argue."

"Obviously, this elitist hadn't read your books. Well, we have, and I'm happy to tell you why we love them. It all boils down to one word—*respect*."

"Respect," I repeated, thinking it best not to spell it now.

"Your love scenes—especially your erotic scenes—are incredibly sensitive." She paused when she saw me frown. "Here's what I mean. You seem to worship your female characters; metaphorically, you put them on a pedestal. And when you refer to their physical attributes, you never use pejorative terms."

"Good word, *pejorative*."

"I'm serious."

"Thank you for noticing that. Seriously."

"I swear, Jay, you write like a woman." My face fell. "No, I mean that as a compliment. Your appeal is to women. I'm telling you, sensitive and loving as you are, what woman wouldn't be thrilled to have a real gentleman like you for a husband—or at least a live-in lover?" She screwed up her mouth. "I think my sister's nuts, frankly, for leaving you."

"Do you think if I got a sex change, she'd come back?"

She laughed, a full-throated laugh, and walked around to my side of the table. She bent down and kissed me on the cheek. "Let's not go there."

She walked away, leaving me to continue with my writing. But I'd lied—there was no turning point; at least, not yet. What there was, was a wall.

A swim in cold water sometimes cleared my mind. This time, it didn't.

Afterward, I called out for Chinese and ate moo goo gai pan while watching a baseball game on TV.

I never watched sports on TV.

The next day, Saturday, I looked in on Casey. She was sound asleep, her clothes draped over the valet stand, and from the look of her bare shoulders above the sheet I figured she hadn't bothered putting something on to sleep in.

I decided to let her sleep and padded to the kitchen in my robe—I'd slept naked since Bek and I got married and didn't bother with pajamas after she left—put the coffee on, and broke out the waffle maker. As it was heating, I put sausage in a frying pan and some rashers of bacon on a microwave tray. Just as I finished preparing the batter, I felt a tap on my shoulder.

"What smells so good?"

"Ah, Rip Van Winkle is up. Morning, sleepyhead." Casey was wearing a white terry robe that Bek had ordered years ago from a luxury hotel's website. It was a match for mine, and there were a few more in the bedroom closet, for pool guests.

"How could the sleepyhead possibly stay in bed with all those delicious aromas drifting into her room?"

"Look, how about you get the syrup and butter from the fridge while I make myself presentable."

"Oh, that's right. Bek warned me you sleep in the altogether, you naughty boy. Be prepared, right, Mr. Boy Scout?"

"Just get out the syrup and butter, and then you can set the table, if you don't mind."

Casey snapped a saucy salute. "You got it, boss."

"Very funny. Hot today already. I'm thinking of a swim after breakfast. How about you?"

"Sounds like a plan."

I came back in swim trunks and a tee and sat at the dinette table opposite Casey. "Good timing," she said as she placed a hot waffle on my plate. "Help yourself to some bacon and sausage. You can fix your own coffee."

Casey finished making the other waffle and joined me. She closed her eyes and sniffed. "This smells soooo good," she said. "How did you know I was in the mood for waffles?"

"Male intuition."

"Riiiight."

I asked Casey how her evening went, and she said fine, but her friends missed meeting me—again. "They're getting the impression you're a recluse."

As we ate, I noticed that the sash around Casey's waist had loosened when she brought breakfast to the table, and the robe had parted slightly to reveal the beginning of cleavage. "You see more than that in my bathing suit, you know," she said with a giggle. "But I'll close up anyway. Don't want to make you blush, Jay. You really do blush easily."

She was right. It's a curse I've suffered with all my life. Some girls, when we were growing up, thought it made me adorable; but my high school buddies would take every opportunity to bring color to my cheeks whenever we were hanging out with girls. I didn't know if it was their bawdy jokes or my reaction in their presence that made the girls giggle. I took their teasing good-naturedly, and one girl eventually got me into her bedroom when her parents were away for a weekend and *really* made me blush. Thank goodness she was discreet and didn't blab about it in school. After we graduated, she and I went our separate ways, but it was lovely while it lasted. And it taught me the rewards of being a gentleman when it came to making love.

"I'll clean the kitchen while you put on your suit," I said when we'd eaten. "Meet you by the pool."

Casey was wearing her string bikini when she walked out to the deck. By that, I mean the bikini was barely—and I do mean barely—a string. She didn't appear self-conscious about her body at all. Maybe it was a California thing. Or maybe simply because she saw me as a brother. No tension there.

No, no tension there at all.

Casey lay on one of our four chaises, face down, and asked me to rub sunscreen on her neck, back, and shoulders. She knew I'd turn the rubdown into a ritual that went from her neck to the soles of her feet, with me being careful not to devote any untoward attention to her shapely behind.

"That's heaven," Casey said as I finished. "Thanks, Jay. I can do the rest."

I gave her the bottle and jumped into the pool before I embarrassed myself. *Note to self: wear a jockstrap from now on.* When Casey followed me in, her first comment was, "Damn, the water's cold."

"I forgot to turn the heater on last night; sorry."

"I'll bet you're sorry," she said as she watched the effect it had on her top.

I felt the heat rise in my cheeks and said, "Honest mistake." She smirked and said she'd forgive me—this time.

We swam some laps, took a few dives off the springboard, and finally lolled on our backs under the late spring sun, beach towels between our bodies and the chaises.

Later, we decided to go for lunch in a storefront deli we'd found nearby. I wore deck shoes, shorts, and a knit polo. Casey emerged in a summer-weight pale denim sundress. It was sleeveless and fastened from the waist up with a nylon zipper. She wore the same cork-soled sandals she'd had on last night.

I drove to the deli, and Casey ordered her usual—their Reuben sandwiches, she said, were to die for. I ordered a large crock of onion soup topped with crusty Italian bread, with a slab of mozzarella on top of that, the whole shebang put under the broiler until the cheese melted and got all stretchy.

"Onion soup," remarked Casey wryly to our regular server, a young woman with a tattooed sleeve from shoulder to wrist and whose name was Melissa. "The mouthwash for lovers." They both laughed, and laughed harder when I accused Casey of sauerkraut breath. When we'd finished and signaled for the check, Melissa brought us a familiar-looking trade paperback along with the bill.

"I just finished your latest book," she said. "Would you mind?" She placed it on the table and handed me a pen.

"Seems you have a fan," said Casey as I autographed the book.

"Great title, by the way, *Bedside Manor.* I loved it." Having learned my lesson years before, I didn't ask for a review. Melissa gave it to me anyway. "I'm on my break now. Mind if I tell you what I like most?"

Casey gestured to an empty space alongside her in the booth. "Please."

And lo and behold, Melissa proceeded to review the entire plot, virtually page by page. "I have all your books, but I like this one the best. I'd love to see it made into a movie." She slid out of the booth and said to Casey, "Let me tell you, if you weren't his girlfriend, I'd be all over him like flies on honey."

I blushed furiously as Casey smiled but didn't correct her about the girlfriend remark. "He does that a lot," she said, pointing to my reddened cheeks. "You'd think he's ashamed to be seen with me." Once again, the two of them shared a laugh.

Leaving Melissa an even more generous tip than usual, I drove us home. "So, what did you make of your new groupie?" Casey asked, flashing an impish grin. "Flies to honey, she said. Better watch out. She could be a stalker."

"As if. My critics would probably say *honey* was the wrong word, considering what flies also gravitate toward."

Casey slapped me on the thigh. "I'm telling you, stop with the self deprecation. All right, you're not a Hemingway or a Faulkner or a Salinger. You've found a niche that works for you, and you've obviously found an audience that appreciates you. Enjoy it!"

I thanked her and promised yet again to take her advice.

"Moving on, what did you think of her ink?"

"Not fond of it, to tell the truth. For me, a woman's body is a work of art in itself. You don't make the nudes of the old masters any more beautiful by painting panthers or daggers on their arms, or a heart with *Mother* on their chests."

"I don't have any tats, you know."

"I'd have noticed if you did."

"And no piercings either."

"Except for the ears."

"Except for the ears, but just one in each lobe." She leaned back in her seat and grinned at me. "Do you want to know why I've never gotten a tattoo?"

"I await your answer with bated breath."

"You don't put decals of where you spent your vacation all over the windows of a Rolls-Royce."

We'd no sooner arrived home than a courier came to the door. He presented me with a thick brown envelope and had me sign. Casey remarked, "That looks official."

"My lawyer's return address. Must be important to pay a courier for Saturday delivery. Let's have a look." We went to the living room and sat on the sofa.

Casey leaned toward me as I opened the envelope. "Mind if I look over your shoulder?" I said that would be fine and she leaned closer. I could feel her breath in my ear as I tore open the envelope. My lawyer's cover letter was on top, and Casey and I read it together. I let out the breath I'd been holding and realized that she'd been holding her breath as well.

"It's official," I whispered. "Bek and I are divorced." The formal declarations were still inside the envelope, and I was about to pull them out when Casey stopped me.

She took the envelope from my hand and laid it on the coffee table in front of the sofa. I looked at her, puzzled. "Now that you're divorced, would you like to kiss me?" she said. "Because I would like to kiss you."

"Don't you—" I couldn't complete the question, because Casey's mouth covered mine. When she broke the kiss, I said, "What—"

"Isn't it obvious? Now. Shut. Up." She held my head between her hands and drew her mouth to mine again. This time, she used her tongue, and I nearly flinched. Bek had never allowed me to use my tongue.

And there it was. Casey had been pretending all this time, the same as I.

She smiled. "You have onion breath."

"You have sauerkraut breath."

"I love onions."

"I love sauerkraut."

We kissed some more, and then Casey straddled my legs. She leaned back, gripping my knees for support. "Do you need a written invitation?" she asked, looking down at her zipper.

She'd been right—I did worship my women characters. And now I was worshiping one who'd come beautifully to life.

We never made it to the bedroom.

"I love you, Casey," I said when we finally relaxed on the sofa. I spoke the words directly into her mouth, and she kissed me again. Then I pulled my head away.

Casey knelt upright, looked at me, and said, "Something wrong, Jay?"

"I didn't wear protection. I don't even *have* protection. Casey, if you were to get pregnant—"

She placed two fingertips over my lips. "I'm on the pill. I've been anticipating this moment ever since you told me you and Bek were separating." She surveyed our bodies, still linked, although precariously. "We're soaked in sweat, you and I. But it's a good sweat." I had to agree. "Maybe we should grab a shower, and then we can relax with some wine, and later we can order take-out. Does that work for you?"

After showering, we put on our terrycloth robes. I called out for pizza, and soon after I hung up Casey's phone rang. She stood close enough to me to hold the phone in one hand while the other snaked into my robe.

"Sorry, Viv, I meant to tell you I couldn't make it tonight. No, I knew nothing was definite, but I should've called you anyway. Something"—she winked and squeezed—"came up. I'll call you later, okay?"

When I greeted the pizza delivery boy, he looked at my robe and said, "Early night, huh? Must've been a busy day."

"You have no idea."

As we sat at the dinette table sharing the pizza and drinking wine, I said, "So this Viv is one of your friends?"

"Yep. Viv and Miyuki are the ones who took me out to celebrate my Ph.D. They're both on staff, and Viv is up for tenure next year. Miyuki's an adjunct. She's in the position I was in two years ago, master's working on her doctorate."

"And these are the ladies with no taste in literature you said would love to meet me?"

"The same. And you're being self-deprecating again. Do you understand the implication that it transfers to me? That the woman who loves you isn't worthy of respect either? That's psychobabble, by the way."

I blinked. "Oh. I see your point. But you know I would never— okay, for the record you may call me Mr. Shakespeare."

She laughed. "That's more like it, Mr. Shakespeare."

"And as we are intimate now, my lady, you may consider yourself free to call me Will." She chuckled and leaned across the table to kiss me. "I have an idea. Instead of taking me out to meet your friends, why don't you invite them here for a pool party, like tomorrow? It's Sunday; they won't be working."

Casey's face lit up. "Yes! Oh, and this time you'll put the heater on beforehand, right?"

I laughed. "I'll make sure it's set tonight."

"And tomorrow morning we can hit the stores early for salads, burgers, whatever, and have everything ready by early afternoon. Say, have them come around three? Swim, dinner from the grill, more swimming, some late-night philosophizing. Then they go home and we go to bed. Does that sound doable?"

"I like it. Especially the last part."

Casey smiled. "You never asked what my friends look like."

"What would it matter? I only have eyes for you."

Let me amend that. My heart belonged to Casey, but my eyes did in fact enjoy the sight of Viv and Miyuki. Two more delicious examples of eye candy I'd never seen this side of the silver screen. Casey gave them a tour of the house, and when they walked into my office, Viv said, "So this is where the magic happens."

Casey corrected her. "No, the magic happened yesterday, when Jay's divorce became final."

"Whoa," said Miyuki. "That means he's not your brother-in-law anymore?"

"With all that implies?" said Viv, arching her eyebrows.

"You... know?" I asked, frowning.

It was Casey's turn to blush. "Sorry, Jay, but I had to share with someone, and while you were officially married it certainly couldn't have been you."

Viv said, "This girl was so hot for you. And the fact that she couldn't do anything about it, well, you can imagine. The way she fidgeted sometimes, she could've been the object of a psych study all by herself."

"But now, no barriers, right?" asked Miyuki.

Casey gave them a smile and a wink, and they cheered and congratulated us both.

They certainly made for a diversified group, ethnicity wise. Casey was American as apple pie; take the most glamorous movie stars, combine their best features, and you've got Casey. Miyuki was the product of an American father and a Japanese wife; her face carried the delicate beauty of her mother.

As for Viv, there was no way I could pin a specific ethnicity on her. Her skin was the color of caramel, her hair was black, long, and wavy, and her almond-shaped eyes—similar to Miyuki's but not as pronounced—were a brilliant green. I wondered if she wore colored contact lenses.

So here we all were, in my office, the ladies looking at my titles, pointing to them and reviewing plots and love scenes. Unlike Bek's snooty friends, they actually had read my work. They told me they loved my writing, especially the more erotic bits. Viv winked and said they actually made her hot. Miyuki added, "And wet, too," and they both giggled. "My husband loves your books," she said, "and he's never even read one of them. Baby number two's already on the way, in fact, thanks to you."

We looked at her belly; her bare midriff was flat. "Ten weeks," she said. "First one didn't show until twenty."

"And that's why Friday night you just drank tonic water," said Viv. "Well, congratulations, you oversexed tart."

After the congratulations ended, Casey directed her friends to the guest bedroom to change into their bathing suits. She'd already moved her stuff into mine, where we'd slept naked last night, after once again—to borrow an image from the esteemed Mr. Shakespeare—making the beast with two backs. If we hadn't had a more urgent agenda this morning—the laying in of supplies for later—we could've happily spent the morning in bed. As it was, we gave each other a lick and a promise for later.

When the women—all of whom taught classes at the college— walked through the sliding glass doors to the pool, I wondered why none of my teachers ever looked like that. Viv, the only Ph.D. currently among them, was decidedly curvy, with what in earlier times would be called an hourglass figure. Of course, that was when people knew what an hourglass was. It could even be described as a Coke bottle figure, but when was the last time you saw Coke in its original six-ounce bottles?

Miyuki, on the other hand, was slender and had the lithe body of a ballet dancer. Like Viv, she had shapely, well-toned legs but stood barely five feet tall, whereas Viv was half a head taller than Casey's five foot six—which meant that in heels she'd stand eye level with me. Viv's most striking features had nothing to do with what she'd stuffed into her bikini, either; it was those mesmerizing eyes. "No, I don't wear contacts," she said when she caught me staring. "Only thing I can think of to explain them is my ancestors must've slept around. A lot."

Casey caught me appraising her. "Like what you see?" she teased.

I mumbled so the others wouldn't hear, "Both of them combined couldn't make one of you." That wasn't *exactly* true, but it earned me points for later.

Casey said, "Miyuki's husband's babysitting number one son today, but Viv's still available, she's an incorrigible flirt, and very much on the prowl."

"I heard that!" Viv said to laughter. "And by the way, mister romance writer, if Blondie over there ever decides to dump you, I'll teach you what a real woman can do." She laughed again as she opened her eyes wide. "Oh, look, girls, I did it! I got him to blush. Casey, you were right!"

I turned an accusative stare at Casey. "All right. What else have you told them?"

She winked and they all laughed, enjoying their little joke at my expense. But to tell the truth, I realized I enjoyed it too.

We all swam for a while, and when we'd dried off, I started the gas grill. "Burgers, franks, and chicken, ladies. Take your pick."

Viv sidled up to me and purred, "About that chicken. Tell me, Jay, you like the dark meat?"

Casey called from a chaise, "You stop that."

"I just like to see him blush. It's refreshing in a man."

Without thinking, I blurted out, "I prefer the breast," and immediately wished I'd bitten my tongue.

Viv had a comeback, of course. "Farm raised, all natural... as you can see."

"You weren't raised on a farm," Casey retorted.

"No, but the second part is true." She giggled and jiggled. "Why, Casey, I'd swear your boyfriend has a bad case of sunburn. Funny, though, it's only in his face."

Miyuki joined in with, "Jay, feel free to tell her to *butt* out." Which caused more glee from the ladies.

Viv turned herself around and looked over her shoulder at me as she displayed her shapely brown behind. All sweetness and light, she said, "Did Miyuki just mention my butt?"

"Casey told me you could be *cheeky*," I came back, hoping it would control the blush. It didn't work.

"Here we go again," Viv said. "Look at that color rise. Like an elevator heading for the top floor. You, my friend, are a marked man." Then she cast an eye at the pool and said, "Do those hot dogs come with... *buns?*"

The rest of the day and evening went just as Casey and I had hoped. I gave them all robes to ward off the early evening chill, and we arranged the poolside chaises like four flower petals, so we could face each other and make conversation easier. The outdoor lamps cast a warm glow, and it was still too early in the season for bugs; in other words, the perfect night for a friendly symposium. Casey's girlfriends proved witty, intelligent, and insightful.

I mention insightful especially, because as they were getting ready to make their goodnights, Miyuki called out, "Epiphany!"

The other women turned to her, questions writ on their faces.

"You two academic elites have obviously forgotten the lessons of Psych 101."

"What are you talking about?" asked Viv.

Miyuki leaned toward me. "Jay, tell me. When did you begin writing romance novels?"

"I'd say about two years before Casey came to live with us. Why?"

As one, the women cried, "Sublimation!"

Casey said, "I, uh, did happen to mention that you and Bek were living platonically."

"Great. No secrets here."

"And..." Miyuki spoke for the three of them, "you channeled your frustration into another outlet, namely your writing. Hence, sublimation."

"You created fantasy women to take the place of your ex." Viv smiled. "And one or two of those sexy women in your books happened to be of the darker skinned variety, didn't they? Hmm?" She gave me a lascivious grin, and Casey shook her head and laughed.

"Too bad that I got him first, you shameless slut."

I reached over for Casey's hand. "And for the record, Casey is my ideal fantasy woman."

"Just so you know," Casey affirmed, and her friends said, *Aw, rats,* and snapped their fingers.

Miyuki asked if this meant I wouldn't be sublimating my energies into more romance novels, now that my needs were being met. I told her I happened to be working on one now, and I didn't think Casey's influence would affect me one way or the other. "How long 'til publication?" she asked, and I told her it was nearly finished, so maybe early next year. Miyuki patted her stomach. "If baby number three comes about because of it, I'm naming it Jay."

"What if it's a girl?" asked Viv.

"Then Jaye with an *e.*"

They made their goodnights with hugs and kisses—on the cheek—and promised to get together again soon. Miyuki said, "Since you love women; and you write for women; you might as well hang out with women. Join us any time. Who knows? We might inspire you. Maybe you can consider writing a beautiful Asian woman into your next book?"

"I just might. In case you'd be eager for baby number four."

Once their cars pulled out of the driveway, Casey turned to me and said, "What do you think of my friends?"

I smiled and said, "In three words, piquant pulchritude prevailed."

"Come on, you didn't just make that up."

"No, I thought of it when the three of you were cavorting in the pool while I was getting the food ready. And speaking of, the perishables are put away. Do you want us to clean up the rest, or should we wait for tomorrow?"

"They'll still be there tomorrow, right?"

"Question answered. Now I've got another question,"

"Shoot."

"Viv."

Casey arched an eyebrow. "What about her?"

"I'm curious about her heritage. She probably thinks of herself as, what's the phrase, a woman of color, but her loose hair doesn't fit the stereotype, and her eyes are almond shaped and green."

Casey laughed. "Let me tell you, Viv thinks of herself as Viv. Period. Zero racial identity, and wants no part of it. She says labeling is libeling. She hates the word *race* and says it's only used these days for political reasons; you know, to pit one... tribe, if you will... against another; or multiple others. Divide and conquer, that's the politicians' game. She used to enjoy a rum and Coke, but when Coke went woke and moved out of Atlanta, she flipped. Hasn't picked up a Coca-Cola product since."

"How amazingly refreshing."

"I have to admit, with her diverse heritage she does make a very pretty package."

"Not as pretty as you, though."

"Enough with the flattery; you're going to get what you want without it."

"All right, then. Tell me about Miyuki."

"Miyuki was brought up by a tiger mom—strong and resourceful. The girl helped finance her undergrad studies by selling locks of her own hair to a chemistry major who was testing formulations for hair dyes. After she earned her bachelor's degree, she married him."

"I really like your girlfriends."

"Sure; the way they massaged your ego in your trophy room? What's not to like?"

"You know what I mean. I was comfortable with them right from the start."

"Be careful with Viv, though. She's a dyed-in-the-wool flirt, but she's loyal, so don't you get any ideas about sneaking in a quickie when I'm not around. She'll shut you down, fast and hard."

"Then make sure you're always around."

"Oh, I'll be around. Let's go to bed." She took my hand and led me through the sliding glass doorway and past the living room, where my divorce decree still sat on the coffee table. "That'll be there tomorrow, too," she said as she led me to my bedroom.

Our bedroom now.

Next morning, I awoke to the brush of a bare breast against my face. "Who's the sleepyhead now?" Casey teased. Before she could pull back, my arms flew behind her and pulled her tight. She giggled and squirmed out of my embrace. "Breakfast is on," she said, standing up and closing her robe.

After we'd eaten and cleaned the kitchen, we went to the living room, where the divorce papers lay on the coffee table. Casey had never asked about the terms other than ascertaining from me that the procedure went amicably—which is unheard of in most divorces, according to our lawyers, no matter how good the couple's intentions.

Our lawyers had been wrong. Maybe we'd set a precedent.

It goes without saying that Bek had been the breadwinner in our family; despite my modest success as a romance writer, my current royalties didn't give me the financial wherewithal to continue what had once been our shared lifestyle. So, after agreeing that Bek's condo in the city would be hers and the house would be mine—it was already mortgage free—my ex would automatically send a stipend to my account every month. More generous she could not have been, and yes, we still had a bond of friendship that our divergent sexual orientation couldn't deny. It's safe to say we still loved each other unconditionally.

"She's a great gal, my sis," said Casey just as her phone rang. "Hey, Bek, we were just talking about you. Yes, all good. When's graduation? Two weeks, why? Oh, damn. No. No, I understand, I do. You can see the video when you get back from Paris. Great. Yes, he's here." She handed me the phone.

"Hi, dear," Bek said, asked how I was doing with my latest novel, and wished me luck. "Someday you'll hit it big time, I know, and I'll be beaming right along with you if not alongside you." I told her if and when that happened, I'd return every penny of her accumulated stipends, and she said absolutely not.

"And speaking of money," Bek continued, "look at all the legal fees we saved simply by being sensible. Listen, I just told Casey that my fall fashion show is in Paris beginning in ten days, so I have to miss her graduation. Which galls me, but I really don't have a choice."

I told her that naturally I'd be there representing Casey's family, and she had a couple of girlfriends to cheer her on as well when she walked across the stage.

As we signed off, Casey said, "You two are just the best. How lucky can one girl be to have a sister like her and a lover like you?"

"You didn't mention that we're sharing the same bed now," I said.

She shook her head. "Time enough for that later. Listen, why don't I clean up last night's dirty dishes outside and let you get back to your writing. Oh, and would you mind if I gave the girls an open invitation to come by for a swim any time?"

"My pleasure." I kissed her and said, "I'm happy to take you up on your offer. I've almost reached the end of the manuscript."

"Think I can read it before you send it off?"

"Ordinarily, I'd rather not. But in your case—and there's a reason—the answer is yes."

"Well, that's pretty cryptic," she said, pecking me on the lips. "You get busy now, and I'll do the same."

Viv came for a swim two days later. She told us that Miyuki and her husband had left their son with his grandparents while they took a week at a B and B in Cape May. "But she'll be back in time for your graduation," she assured Casey.

"Jay's told me I can read his manuscript before he sends it off; it'll be the first time he's done that."

Viv gave me a buss on the cheek, and as she did, she said in her most sultry voice, "Maybe someday you'll let me see what's in that laptop of yours, too. Know what I'm saying?"

"Mine, all mine!" cried Casey, and they laughed when Viv repeated her elevator going up jibe.

"Vixens. Vixens, I say."

I excused myself from the ladies outside so I could work in my office, my real office, with the door shut. An hour or so later Casey knocked with a tray of deli sandwiches. "Your new groupie Melissa delivered them personally. I think she really does have a thing for you."

"No, thank you. To Melissa, not the sandwiches."

"Although she is quite the cutie, you must admit."

"For a high school senior, sure."

"Bite your tongue. She told me she just finished her second year of junior college." I shrugged and said my mistake, to which Casey said, "Maybe she's the infatuated coed who wants you to be the father of her child."

"Yeah, right. And for the record, please note that no infatuated coed has ever made an appearance in any of my novels." I helped myself from the tray and made an exaggerated gesture. "Now begone, wench."

Casey curtseyed. "Yes, master."

While Miyuki was away, Casey and Viv and I became a threesome. We swam every day and went out to dinner every night. It did wonders for my self-esteem to be seen with two gorgeous women, one on each arm. When the restaurant offered a table or booth, we'd choose the latter so I could sit facing them. That way I could bask in their beauty while enjoying the envious stares of many a male diner.

Viv managed to get my blush up seriously one evening when we entered a fancy restaurant and she said to the hostess, "Man Sandwich, table for three." The hostess noticed the scarlet flush and tried to hold back her giggle. It didn't work any better than my attempt to stop my face from flaming. When she led us to our table, the ladies flanked me, each locking an arm in mine. I had a flashback of how the guys in school used to make me blush in front of the girls as a joke on me.

"Look who's laughing now," I said under my breath.

"What's funny?" Viv asked when we were seated, and I told her. She placed her hand on mine and said, "Wouldn't it be poetic justice if some of those same boys were in this room right now? Casey and I could give them a show, you know, cuddle up to you, make them think we were a ménage à trois."

"Every man's dream," said Casey. "Right, Jay?"

"Now you're doing it too?" I asked, shaking my head.

Graduation day promised to be a scorcher, and the ceremonies were scheduled to take place outside. I was sitting on a folding chair close to the speakers' platform, saving a seat on either side of me. As the family and friends of the graduates gathered, Miyuki and Viv sidled in alongside me. Miyuki wore a white blouse and navy skirt, Viv a flowered sundress with a V neckline that plunged perilously deep.

"How was Cape May?" I asked, and Miyuki closed her eyes and smiled, said it was wonderful. I looked at Viv, who looked incredibly lovely with her striking green eyes and long black hair pulled forward across her shoulders.

In an exaggerated whisper, Viv said, "Stop looking down my front, mister."

"I'm not looking down your front," I protested.

"Well, why not?"

She placed her hand over mine during the ceremony, releasing it only to applaud. At one point, I turned my palm up, and her fingers interlaced with mine.

Miyuki noticed. "Careful there," she advised me. "You know Viv."

Viv replied, "He knows I'm safe. Not necessarily by choice, but I'm true to my friends." She gave my hand a squeeze and directed her attention to the stage as the presenter announced, "Katherine Celina Brozek, Doctor of Philosophy, Psychology." The audience applauded politely, but we gave her a standing ovation. Casey had made us promise not to shout or cheer, so we kept our dignity intact, and our mouths shut but clapped as loudly as we could.

We held a small reception afterwards at the house, encouraging the guests to bring their swimsuits, and thanks to the behind-the-scenes efforts of Miyuki and Viv it was a huge success. Faculty and spouses attended, Casey's advisor telling me she did a brilliant defense of her dissertation. Many of the staff took advantage of the pool, and it was late in the evening when the affair officially broke up. Viv and Miyuki insisted on cleaning up without help from the newest doctor in the house, and so Casey and I retired to the sofa to recap the day.

"I wish we could call Bek right now," she said, "but it's what, six hours later in Paris? Maybe I'll call tomorrow."

"Why don't you let her call first, when she has some free time between shows?"

"You're right."

"I have something for you. No, not a gift, because you ordered me not to do that." I handed her my laptop.

She gasped. "It's done?"

"Awaiting your approval."

"*My* approval?"

Our comely cleanup crew said they were done and would now leave us to continue the graduation celebration in private, wink wink.

I asked Casey if she were ready for bed, and she said maybe later, because she wanted to read at least the first chapter before turning in.

When I woke up next morning, I was still alone. Upon finishing my bathroom routine, I walked into the dining room, where Casey sat at the laptop. She didn't hear me padding barefoot behind her but saw my reflection in the glass. On the screen I saw the last page. She'd stayed up all night reading.

Casey stood, her face inches from mine. "It's our story," she breathed. "Jon and Angie are Jay and Casey—you and me. That's why you let me read it."

"What do you think? Be candid now."

"I love it, just love it. And you know what I love best? The ending." She hugged and kissed me, her breath stale but no worse than sauerkraut. She pressed her body, still clad in the shorts and top she wore at the pool yesterday, against my robe and just held me tight. Finally, she murmured, "Now that you don't have a need to sublimate your emotions into your writing, how will you continue producing romance lit?"

"Maybe you'll inspire me."

"Maybe I can start now."

"You're tired. You haven't slept all night."

"I can sleep later. Feel like a celebratory quickie?"

Like swimming in the ocean, a person's life rides a series of waves, some gentle, some brutal. The tallest waves are always followed by the deepest troughs. And once you're past the crest, it's a long way back down.

It was three o'clock that same afternoon, while we were enjoying a late lunch, when Casey's phone rang. She frowned at the number on the screen and excused herself to answer it. When she came back and sat down across the table from me, her eyes were red.

"Oh, Jay," she said. "I don't know how to begin." She took a deep breath and leaned toward me. "My ex, he—no, back to the beginning. When you and Bek asked me to move in with you, I mentioned that I needed to break off a relationship in California. You probably thought it was a brief affair; it wasn't. I was engaged—to another grad student, Josh. He was a great guy, and his parents—his parents treated me like I was their own daughter. I mean, they truly loved me, and I loved them back. But Josh, well, he grew clingy, and that morphed into possessiveness. I couldn't do anything without him just being there, hovering. Sometimes I used to visit the bathroom, even when I didn't have to go, just for some privacy. Does that make sense?"

"Okay. Now what?"

"When I broke off the engagement, Josh's parents understood the reason and said they still considered me a member of their family. That's how wonderful they were—they are. And Josh's mom just called to tell me he's in the hospital, in a coma. He'd been surfing—that was his hobby, and he was good at it—when a novice caught a wave the wrong way, the board flipped him, and caught Josh from behind the head. It knocked him out, and if it weren't for another surfer who pulled him out of the water, he would've drowned."

"So sorry, Casey, really."

"His mom just asked if I might come back to California to stay with them for a while. They think that if I sit with Josh in the hospital and talk to him, the sound of my voice may help bring him back."

I sat straight in my chair. "Whew. That's a lot to digest. You've got the summer off anyway, so yes, off you go."

"Do you mind?"

"Mind? Of course, I mind. But he needs you. His parents need you. I can survive without you for a while. Besides, now that you mention it, I'm wondering if I'm starting to get a little clingy myself; maybe you could use a break from me."

"I love your style of clinging." She leaned across the table and kissed me, sniffing and wiping her eyes with a napkin. "I'll call back and tell them I'll be there as soon as I can. Tell Bek goodbye for me and I hope she enjoys the graduation video. And can you call Viv and Miyuki too? I'm not up for a lengthy conversation just now."

"Understood. Call me when you get there."

"I will, promise."

She didn't. Not until two days later, all apologetic, saying everything was happening so fast that she'd forgotten to call. "Jay, if you could see him lying there, with all those tubes in him and those monitors beeping, it would break your heart."

I told her I understood.

Then she said, "I have a feeling I'll be here a while longer than I'd thought. Can you ship me my clothes? Do you mind, Jay? I won't need the winter ones, obviously. Love you."

I packed up her summer clothes in boxes from the post office. Then I got two more boxes and filled them with Casey's spring and fall wardrobe. Those I didn't send out; but I began to get a nagging feeling I eventually would.

And for another reason I couldn't immediately grasp, I decided to wait to send my latest manuscript, the one that fictionalized my love for Casey, to my agent.

Before shipping Casey's clothes to California, I sent the graduation video to Bek and then called Miyuki and Viv.

"She left without telling us?" Viv said, annoyance evident in her voice.

"That's exactly what Miyuki said. To be fair, Casey suddenly had a lot thrown on her plate," I explained. "Packing her suitcase, booking her flight; she was preoccupied, to say the least."

"I don't know, Jay. Doesn't sound like the Casey we know."

Naturally, I didn't tell Viv that Casey was so preoccupied that we didn't even make love the night before she left. If her mind was elsewhere, I reasoned, there would be no reason drag it back for sex.

At my invitation, the next day Miyuki and Viv stopped by with wine, and we sat by the pool. There was none of Viv's flirtatiousness on exhibit, and Miyuki too seemed subdued. I told them I hoped they wouldn't forget their open invitation to use the pool or just to visit. They were welcome with or without Casey. Happily for me, they continued to come by, and many an afternoon we'd swim, grill our dinner, and sit around philosophizing into the wee hours.

Viv never once put on her flirty act.

June bled into July, with no word from Casey in the seven weeks she'd been gone. I'd thought about calling her myself, but I didn't want to intrude on her time with her former fiancé and his parents. She would touch base when she was ready.

Bek called near the end of the month to tell me, belatedly, that she'd enjoyed the graduation video and to ask if I'd heard anything from Casey. I told her no, not since two days after she'd left. There was a pause, followed by, "Damn."

"Bek? What's wrong?"

"She did it again."

"What are you talking about?"

"Casey called me with her news last night. Me, not you, not the guy she should've called first."

"News? What news?"

"Okay. Take a seat, because you might need to. It seems Casey's ex-fiancé died ten days after she arrived. The parents were naturally heartbroken, and she did all she could to comfort them. Which makes sense, because she was like a daughter to them. Well, the doctors and administration were so impressed by her counseling they asked for her CV—which she just happened to have with her. And they offered her a job in their psych rehab unit."

I'd been standing, but now I sat. "She took it?"

"She said this was the direction she wanted her career to go; so, yes. But wait, because it gets better. And I mean that ironically."

"Explain."

"Her dead former fiancé had a cousin from upstate. She met him when he visited his comatose cousin in the hospital. Long story short, he's an MD who just relocated his practice to be near her. From what she said—I'll spare you the details—I'd say it's serious or getting that way fast."

"Wow. That was quick."

"I assume you had no inkling about this, am I right?" She paused. "I can't see you nod, you know." I said yes. "Thought so. I got the feeling she was hoping I'd be the one to tell you. All her life, she's shied away from confrontation with people she cares about. You didn't know this, but when she was a teenager, I had to tell a boyfriend she was breaking up with him—because she didn't want to face him herself. I told her then I'd only be doing this once. Well, yah. Looks like I did it again. And I am so ashamed of my sister, Jay. You deserve better. Oh, and she asked me if you'd ship the rest of her clothes out whenever you can. Whoop-de-do."

After we said goodbye, I called Miyuki and left a message. Viv was home, and she said she'd be right over, with a bottle of wine to drown our sorrows.

We sat on neighboring chaises, with a glass-topped table between us, where we sat our wine bottle.

"You and Casey never considered a bi-coastal relationship?" I said no. "You know, a writer can write from anywhere. You could've moved out there to be with her."

"I know. But it wasn't my place to suggest it, Viv."

She nodded and drank some wine, looking across the pool toward the stockade fence, her eyes seemingly unfocused. "I have something I'd like to run by you, and you can tell me to shut up if you want."

"Viv, I'd never tell you to shut up."

"Wait until you hear what I have to say. You were living with Casey for two years, right? And during that time, you each saw the other as forbidden fruit. Day after day, week after week, month after month, that temptation simmered in both of you. And by the time you were free to admit your feelings, well, maybe the fantasy couldn't stand up to the reality."

"Too hot not to cool down, as the song says?"

"Exactly. Does that make sense to you?"

I looked across the table at her and nodded. "Will you be my personal shrink?"

"You can't afford me, bub."

The next day, after shipping what was left of Casey's clothes to California, I decided to visit the deli that she and I had thought of as ours. Melissa took my order for onion soup and asked where my girlfriend was. I told her we weren't together anymore.

"Oh, I'm so sorry," she said as she leaned over and placed a hand on my shoulder. "How are you doing?"

"I'm coping. She's been gone a while now, and I've pretty much adjusted."

"Well, good on you."

When I finished my lunch, Melissa returned to the table—not with my check, but with a solicitous smile. "On me," she said. I insisted on paying; she insisted I not; and in the end she won.

I chastised myself as I got back into my car. "You idiot. What Pandora's box have you just opened?"

She rang my bell at seven that night, as I'd both anticipated and feared. Melissa had once delivered take-out from the deli, so she knew where I lived. And now she was at my door again. "May I come in?" she said.

Melissa wore low-rider jeans below a bare midriff that featured a tiny diamond stud in her navel, along with a red knit tube top that hugged her breasts and terminated just below them.

I offered her something to drink, thinking maybe a soda, and she asked for a glass of wine. I poured two glasses of Riesling, and we sat at the kitchen table.

We sipped our wine, and because I needed something to say, I asked about her tattooed sleeve. She extended her arm across the table for my inspection. Flowers of many varieties and colors were inked from wrist to shoulder. "Do you like it?"

"The artwork is impressive," I responded as tactfully as I could.

"My parents hate it."

"Long as you like it, Melissa, that's what counts."

She put her wine glass, now empty, on the table, took a breath as if to build up her courage. "Okay, so much for small talk. You remember what I told you when you signed my book? That if you weren't attached to *her,* I'd be all over you like flies on honey? Well, you're not attached to her anymore, are you?"

I nodded, my expression doubtless not the one she wanted to see. "Melissa, I'm not sure I'm ready for—"

"I'm not looking for a long-term affair," she said, as if to reassure me. Had she known me, she'd have realized that was exactly the worst thing she could've said. "Melissa, another time, another place, I'd be yours to command," I lied. "But it's too soon. I hope you understand."

"You told me you were coping."

"I wasn't being truthful. I'm sorry."

She looked hurt at first, then stood and yanked her top down to flaunt her breasts. "You're sure?" she said. "Men would die to get their hands on these."

Nipple rings.

Ugh.

"You're very attractive. Can we leave it at that? Please?" I stood up, signaling our conversation was over.

Melissa gave me an ironic look. "Can't blame a girl for trying." She pulled up her top and scowled as she walked away.

A minute later the bell rang. Thinking she'd decided to try again, I opened the door a crack to find Viv standing there. "Who was that?" she asked as I ushered her inside.

"Her? She's a server at the deli Casey and I like. Make that used to like. I won't be going back. Why?"

"Because she told me she hoped I had better luck with you than she did. What did she mean? That hussy try to put the make on you?"

"I suppose." I shrugged. "All right, I mean, yes."

"Let me guess. You had lunch, she saw you were alone, and she figured you were fair game?"

"She asked where my girlfriend was, and I told her we were no longer together. Also, a while back I signed a copy of *Bedside Manor* for her; she's a fan. Or at least she was."

"Well, Casey was right—you've got your first groupie."

Before I could respond, the bell rang again. It was Miyuki, carrying a bag of groceries. "What's going on?" I asked.

"We've decided to cook you dinner," she said. "You've cooked enough for us, so it's reciprocity time."

As they turned toward the kitchen, my phone rang. Caller ID said it was from my agent.

"Honey, have I got a surprise for you," she said, her voice raspy from a lifetime of smoking. "You sitting down?"

"That's the second time someone's asked me that. What's up? I know you're waiting for my next manuscript, but I've got a bit of a snag."

"Forget the snag, sweetie. You're getting a contract for *Bedside Manor*."

"Hello? Hasn't it already been published?"

She laughed. "Jay, this is for a mini-series on cable. We're talking big buckaroos here, kid."

"All right, I'm sitting down. Talk to me."

"It's an option for now, right? But they've already found a producer who can't wait to begin filming."

"That... is the best news I've had all day. All week. All month. Wow."

"Am I the best agent in the world, honey?"

"None better."

"I've reviewed the contract, and it looks good. I'll courier it over to you tomorrow. Now go and celebrate."

"I know just the people to celebrate it with."

Before I broke the news to my lovely kitchen staff, I called Bek. After her bubbly congratulations, I reminded her of my intent to return every dollar of her monthly stipends once money started coming in. She told me she wouldn't take a dime of it; a deal was a deal.

My ex-wife was still my best friend.

And two other women weren't far behind. As we sat down, they told me I looked like the cat that had swallowed the canary, so I told them the news. Hugs and kisses all around—chaste ones, of course, on the cheek.

Miyuki, whose baby bump was finally beginning to show, was first to leave. Viv stayed behind and made coffee. As we talked, I decided to make her an offer.

"After the graduation party, you remember I let Casey review my unedited manuscript before sending it off. That's something I never do, because—because it takes an editor to make my writing look good. No, don't say it; every writer needs an editor. Anyway, I'd like to offer you the same option, and you may interpret that as you wish."

She gave me a half smile. "Where is it?"

I went into my office and bought back my computer. As I handed it to her, I said, "Just think—now you'll be finding out what's in my laptop, just like you said you wanted."

"Oh, so now you're trying to make *me* blush, white boy? Doesn't show on me, you know. Score one for the Cappuccino Kid." She opened the laptop and saw Page One cued up on the screen. "I'll take this home, and I promise not to let anyone else know I have it. Not even Miyuki."

"Casey read it overnight," I reminded her.

"Guess that means I have to, too."

"No; I mean, take your time."

"I plan to. Goodnight, mister romance writer."

I went to bed hoping Viv would like the manuscript.

The next morning, my phone rang. It was Viv.

"I'm a grump today, Jay. I did a Casey and read the manuscript at one sitting. Now I can barely keep my eyes open."

"Oh. Is that good news or bad?"

"Let me put it to you this way. Right now, I'm going to go to bed. But I'll be around tonight, say around eight, if that's okay. I'll give you your laptop back, and we can talk about it then."

"How about if you come at seven and I'll make you dinner?"

"Oh, we're alternating chef duties now, are we? Okay, I'll see you at seven. But for now, it's good morning; or good night. Whatever."

Viv arrived with my laptop in one hand and a bottle of red in the other. She wore blue shorts and a white cotton sleeveless blouse, and her hair was pulled back in a ponytail. I ushered her poolside, where I had a grill going and salads prepared on the picnic table. She took off her moccasins and sat on the edge of the pool with her feet in the water and watched me grill two filets alongside two ears of corn still in their husks.

Summer was winding down, but the night was still uncomfortably warm. With Casey's clothes gone, there was no indication that she had ever lived here, and her name didn't come up once in our conversation. It was as if neither of us wanted to bring up her name. There was also no mention of my manuscript, which made me a little uncomfortable. I decided to let her bring it up. To continue the conversation, I did ask Viv if her full name was Vivian, and she curled a lip.

"Close, but no cigar. I really prefer just Viv, okay? Short for vivacious. You know, like me?"

"Also short for vivisectionist."

"Bite your tongue. Or I'll bite it for you."

"Promises, promises."

"Ooh, so now who's the flirt?"

After we ate, we went inside for dessert. I brought out a bowl of trifle I'd made from a recipe Bek had brought back from a trip to England. Viv dived into it and asked for more. "I don't think we should do this every night," she quipped. "But every other night would be fine."

We cleared the dishes, set up the dishwasher, and returned to the dining room.

Viv excused herself to use the bathroom and afterward remembered she'd left her moccasins outside, where dew could collect on them. She retrieved them, plopped down on the dining room chair opposite me, and asked if I were ready to hear what she thought about the manuscript.

I took a breath and leaned back, said yes.

"You know I love you, Jay, right?" She caught my startled expression. "Your writing, kemo sabe, your writing. Don't get all rebound-y on me. I happen to love your trifle, too."

"Not rebounding, Viv. Seriously. You just took me by surprise."

"Well, since we're friends and you want an honest critique, I have to tell you right off the bat that I didn't like it."

I made as if to say something... defensive? But kept my mouth shut as I nodded for her to go on.

"First off, I thought it was a little too smarmy."

"Smarmy."

"Yes, smarmy. But that's incidental. Obviously, it's the story of you and Casey, but come on, Jay, where's the conflict? The plot goes in a straight line from point A to point B and ends happily ever after. I knew after the first ten pages where the story was going to go. This is not like you; or not like your writing, anyway."

"Um, okay. Should I trash it and go on to something else?"

Viv placed her palms on the table and leaned forward. "No, Jay, no. But if I were you, writing as you that is, I'd make some serious changes. We start off with the author and his wife financially independent upon each other. His income is from steady royalties, and hers is, say, from a high-level corporate job. They've been married a while, and the bloom has faded from the rose. Then little sis moves in, and the guy finds himself seriously attracted to her. But of course, he has to keep his feelings hidden; he's a faithful husband." She paused to let it sink in.

"Okay," I said. "What's next?"

"Okay, the wife has a brief affair and hubby finds out. He kicks her out of the house and files for divorce. The wife contests the divorce. It gets ugly. As for little sis, she doesn't know which side to take. She loves her sister, but she's also been harboring a secret crush on her brother-in-law. Now we have real conflict." She paused and stared at me. "Jay?"

I stared back, mulling over what she'd said. She was right. My stare turned into the smile of discovery. "You're right, Viv; absolutely right. I love you." Catching her look, I grinned and said, "Your insight, I mean. After all, I love trifle too."

She laughed. "You think what I said makes it better?"

"Better? Makes it brilliant. You're not only a brilliant shrink, but you're also a brilliant writer."

Viv sighed and sat back in her chair, relieved. "I held off telling you what I thought, because I didn't want to take the chance of hearing you get all defensive." She beamed across the table. "But you came through with flying colors. Now tell me, are you really over Casey?"

"Believe it or not, Viv, I am. Your impromptu counseling session made me see through the haze. When Casey bolted, I said I understood, but her leaving hurt. When she didn't call for two days, I suspected there was trouble in paradise. Then, when Bek called to tell me Casey'd broken up with me, but didn't have the strength of character to do it herself, I knew my feelings were based on fantasy. Too hot not to cool down, as you said. Or did I say that? Doesn't matter, you were right. Casey's ancient history. She has no more appeal to me anymore than Coca-Cola has for you."

"She told you about that, right? Of course, she did. God, I hate this woke culture."

"For the record, I couldn't agree more." I took a tentative breath. "And I've never felt closer to you than I do now. You can interpret that any way you want."

Viv trained those hypnotic eyes on me for a moment before standing up, her expression unreadable.

"I screwed up just then, right?" I said.

She walked out the door without a word, leaving me to stew. "Don't feel sorry for yourself," I said to the empty room. "You were being honest. And you weren't rebounding; sayonara, Casey, and frankly, good riddance. I just hope I didn't drive Viv—"

The front door opened. Viv walked in without a word, carrying a large pocketbook, and headed down the hall to the bathroom. I turned my chair around and waited, for heaven knew what.

A few minutes later, the bathroom door opened, and I saw, walking down the hall toward me, a caramel-colored vision wearing the same low-cut sundress she'd worn to Casey's graduation. I stood up to face her, and saw she'd let her ponytail down. Her hair was a sable cascade, and her face was subtly made up. Viv placed her palms against my chest, and I smelled the barest trace of perfume.

I stood speechless, which was the right thing to do, because it was Viv who spoke first. "You remember my accusing you of trying to look down my dress back then?" I nodded dumbly. "You were pretending not to, right?" Another nod. She tilted her face up to mine and we kissed, both a little tentatively, before she took a step back and slid the straps from her shoulders. She reached behind her back and unzipped the dress. It fell to the floor, and Viv stood before me, fully nude. I took in a breath, mesmerized.

"Wanted to make it worth the wait," she said, and then she pressed her perfect body against mine and kissed me again.

In the ocean, the deepest troughs are always followed by a second wave. And for the swimmer, sometimes that wave is more towering than the first.

Next morning, I awoke first and nuzzled my nose against the nape of Viv's neck. She stirred, turned toward me, and kissed me. Her breath smelled of mint, and it dawned on me that she'd actually gotten up earlier and washed her mouth out before returning to bed—to wait for me to wake up. My breath was probably bad, but she didn't even curl up her nose.

We made love again, and Viv told me she was going to take me to her favorite place for lunch. "It's a ways away, but it's worth the drive."

I thought of her flowery sundress, still puddled on the dining room floor. I asked if she were going to wear that.

"You're not serious. That dress was for a special occasion; two special occasions, now that I think of it. No one will ever see me in it again; well, unless you want to see me in it before you take it off." At that moment I was ready to take her up on it. "After breakfast, I'll drive you to my condo, throw the dress and yesterday's shorts and blouse into the washer, and put on some fresh duds. Nothing fancy. Shorts and a polo, like you wore yesterday, would be fine."

Viv's condo was a one-bedroom affair, furnishings courtesy of IKEA. "You know I'm up for tenure this year, right?" she said as she took her clothes to the washing machine. "If I make it, then I'll be able to splurge on new furniture."

I held my impulsive tongue.

Later, Viv drove us to the next town over, to a place called Dobkin's, which she told me was owned by one of her former students and her husband. It stood at one end of a strip mall, and most of the cars in the lot were parked near the eatery.

"Hey, Doc, long time no see," the owner said as we approached the hostess station. They exchanged friendly kisses, and then she asked, "And who might this good-looking fella be?"

Viv smirked. "Just my latest conquest. You know, of the many."

Damn, she did it again.

"And he blushes, too? Wow. What a find."

"Pick of the litter," Viv said. "Mollie, this is my dear friend Jay." We shook hands and Viv said, "How's the baby doing these days? Still driving you and Mel nuts?"

"If you only knew. And I suppose you're getting ready for the new school term?"

"Uh huh. I'm up for tenure, so wish me luck."

"Absolutely. If anyone deserves a lifetime position, it's you." Mollie turned to me. "Best teacher I ever had. And a lot of people will back me up on that."

Now I wished a blush did show on Viv.

Mollie led us to a table and said, "Margaret will be taking care of you today."

When she went back to her station, Viv whispered, "Thank goodness she didn't try to show us pictures of her baby. Sorry to sound so cynical, but can you think of anything more boring than baby pictures?"

Margaret, a heavy-set older woman, brought us two tall glasses of iced tea as we studied the menu. When she returned to the table, Viv ordered a cheeseburger, onion rings, and a side salad with poppy seed dressing. As she spoke, she ran a foot up my lower leg. I said, "I'll have what she's having."

Margaret laughed heartily. "That's my favorite movie," she said. "You two just made my day."

"Esmeralda," I said as Viv drove me home.

"Esmer-who?"

"Esmeralda. Named means emeralds. Like your eyes."

"Okay, but I really prefer Viv."

"No, no, no. It's you but it's not you. Esmeralda's going to be in the book."

"How?"

"I haven't figured that out yet. But the hero's sister-in-law will leave him for someone else, and Esmeralda, who's always been on the scene, say as a friend, comforts him."

"That sounds familiar."

"Or maybe she's his lawyer, who gets his ex to settle. Or his therapist; writers can be notoriously insecure, you know."

"All kinds of possibilities. Tell me, what's this Esmeralda like?"

We'd reached my place and Viv shut off the car. She turned her face to me and waited for my answer.

"She's tall, of mixed ethnicity, and smart as a whip. She has long dark hair, large green eyes, a face that cries for a Rembrandt to paint it, and a figure that belongs on a pedestal. Venus de Milo, with arms. In other words..."

"In other words..."

"Esmeralda would've picked up on that immediately."

"Come here, you idiot," she said as she drew my lips to hers. "Now get inside and start writing."

With a week to go before her classes resumed, Viv became reflective. "Jay, you and I are professional people in our own right, with our own career commitments. We have our responsibilities—mine to my students, yours to your readers. I'll need time alone to prepare for my classes, and you'll need time alone to continue your writing. As for where you and I are headed, unlike my dear friend Miyuki, I don't want marriage, and I don't want children. That said, I wouldn't mind having a lover all to myself." She paused. "Um... listening."

I thought for a moment before responding.

"Marriage doesn't come with a warranty, does it? Once I thought Bek and I would last forever. Then I thought Casey and I might do the same. But I can tell you this, my Esmeralda. For now, and for as long as I can envision, you will be my love as well as my muse. You are honest, you are direct, and you don't mince words." I didn't need to add *gorgeous* to my description. "In the revised manuscript, Esmeralda plays *the* pivotal role in the narrative. She is exactly what my broken-hearted protagonist needs. And then, if you have no objections, it will be *our* story."

Viv stayed with me that night, and the next day she said she'd leave me to my writing while she prepared for the new term. Before leaving, she asked if I had come up with a title for the book yet. I looked into her blazing green eyes and said I was thinking of *Second Time Around*.

"As in, love is even lovelier?"

The months between September and May flew by. I finished the manuscript and sent it to my agent, who loved it. Then Bek called with the news that as *Bedside Manor* was filming in a right to work state, where union rules didn't apply, she was hired to be costume designer.

I didn't ask, but she told me anyway that Casey was married, and she and her doctor husband seemed very happy. I said good for her, seriously. I recalled how Viv had characterized our relationship—the consummation couldn't live up to the anticipation.

Miyuki had her baby, a girl she named Vivica. She asked Viv and me to be godparents, so now we had a godchild between us. We took lots of photos.

Speaking of Viv, a.k.a. Vivica, she earned her tenure and brought in tons of grant money to the university through her research into the role sex drive plays in ambition and achievement in asexual professional pursuits.

In other good news, my agent called to tell me *Second Time Around* was being rushed into print. The publisher loved the character of Esmeralda. And I told her I'd been invited to the set of *Bedside Manor* as a consultant. The only downside was I'd have to leave Viv for a month or so. But I promised to call every day, and I did. Viv assured me that she'd keep the bed warm for me. And she did.

The launch party for *Bedside Manor* brought Viv and me together with a number of luminaries, but none looked more luminous than she. She wore a V-necked floor length gown, slit up the leg, red with an emerald-studded necklace to complement her eyes, to say nothing of her fictional alter ego. Instead of wearing her hair up that night, as most of the fashionistas did, she wore it elegantly long with gentle curls that framed her face. I introduced her to Bek, and they hit it off immediately.

"I learned something tonight," Viv said in the hotel later as we prepared for bed. "From your ex-wife."

"Oh? From Bek?"

"Do you have another ex-wife I don't know about?"

"I'll never tell."

"We'll leave that discussion for another time. What Bek told me was that every month nearly a year now, when you began making steady money from your book sales and movie rights, an anonymous gift has been made to her foundation's charity."

"Do tell."

"Oddly enough, it matches the amount she sends to you as part of your divorce settlement. And stranger still, it arrives in the charity's account the day after it's posted to yours."

"That's quite a coincidence."

"I thought so."

"Well, good for Bek. Did she tell you her foundation's a children's charity?"

"She did."

"And do you hate me for not telling you?"

"I love you for not telling me."

We were living together full time now, deeper in love by the day, but strict in giving each other time for our professional pursuits. Viv inherited my office, and I continued to pound away at the dining room table.

And no week went by without visiting our goddaughter and taking photo after photo. Miyuki was sporting another baby bump, and she said it was due to *Second Time Around*. "Another one thanks to you, Jay."

Her husband rolled his eyes. "At least when we're in bed, she doesn't call me by your name. And if she ever does, you better watch out."

We became a foursome, spending evenings together and sometimes weekends. Cape May proved a favorite destination. Their kids called us Aunt Viv and Uncle Jay.

It had been a while since Viv and I had returned to Dobkin's for a comfort food lunch. Mollie was as effusive as ever, congratulating Viv on her tenure and me on the television series.

After we'd finished our dessert, Mollie took a break and came to the table for a visit. Viv asked for the latest on her baby. And before long, we were all sharing baby pictures on our phones.

Last Dance
Prologue

Their teachers and closest classmates referred to them as Team Triple Threat, or T3. Frank Populski, Popeye to any and all, was the darling of the English teachers and drama coach. Donald Greene was the history nerd and captain of the swim team. And Staci Rousseau was the math whiz and cheerleader captain. Together, the three made up one well-rounded, nay, near perfect student.

Staci and Donald had gone steady since eighth grade. She was a blue-eyed blonde with Cupid's bow lips and sky-blue eyes and stood five feet two, ten inches shorter than her beau. Donald, lean and lithe thanks to his daily swimming regimen at the Y, made some of Staci's girlfriends look upon her with unabashed envy.

Frank stood nearly as tall as Donald. Although reasonably athletic, he never participated in team sports; rather, his interests focused on creative writing and drama. In his sophomore year he played a sailor in the school's production of *South Pacific*. The next year, he played Will Parker in *Oklahoma!* And in senior year, he played the title role in *Pippin*. The role of his love interest in the last two plays was played by Staci, who'd scored acclaim earlier as Nellie Forbush in *South Pacific* and Ado Annie in *Oklahoma!* Her Catherine in *Pippin* was her crowning achievement in high school.

To the delight of his senior English teacher, Frank declared his love for all things Shakespeare. And he wowed his classmates when during a reading of *Macbeth*, he recited the bitter "Tomorrow, and tomorrow, and tomorrow" soliloquy from memory, completely losing himself in the role.

Summers found the three inseparables spending days on the beach and nights on the boardwalk at Seaside Heights. And upon graduating from Toms River High School South, they all enrolled in Ocean County College to earn their AA degrees before transferring their credits to a four-year school.

Two years later, with their Associate degrees in hand, they spent what would be their last summer together at the Jersey Shore. In late August 2001 they reluctantly parted company for different colleges.

Then came September 11. And the day after the terror attacks, Donald Greene bid farewell to Monmouth University and enlisted in the Marines. A tearful Staci took time off from Ryder to spend their remaining days together until he was due to leave for boot camp. The night before, Donald asked her to marry him. Staci said yes, a thousand times yes. Then they repaired to the local Holiday Inn, where they made fervent and desperate love until dawn.

Frank was at Northwestern when the buildings came down. Having assumed a double major in English and Drama, he was loath to leave his studies, unsure if he'd be welcomed back should he take on a four-year enlistment. When Donald phoned with the news of his imminent departure for Parris Island, Frank expressed guilt at not having signed up himself, but Donald assured him there was no reason for regret and explained that taking up arms for his country was something he just had to do for himself.

Private Greene stood at attention on the painted yellow footprints with seventy-five fellow recruits, some trembling as their three drill instructors screamed abuse inches from their faces. The first week was filled with one group humiliation after another, and after lights out at 2130, Donald could occasionally hear soft sobs from other bunks. Later he would think of it as the What am I doing here? syndrome.

Donald's senior drill instructor, noting his first name, called him Private Duck, which Donald privately admitted was better than Private Quacker. Over the three-month training period, as the former civilians morphed into Marines, all three drill instructors recognized his leadership skills, and the senior DI called him aside prior to graduation and informed him he needed to go to OCS. It wasn't a request. Therefore, instead of going on ten days' boot leave, he boarded a bus for Quantico and Officer Candidate School.

Second Lieutenant Greene graduated near the top of his class and shipped out to Iraq, where at age twenty-one he assumed leadership of a thirty-six-man infantry platoon, some of whose members were older than he. He and his unit distinguished themselves in combat, and although some received grievous wounds, all survived, many claiming they owed their lives to the actions of their platoon commander.

As an officer, Donald had a six-year obligation to the Corps. Following his tour overseas, he was assigned to embassy school and then joined the American Embassy in London, England. Along with two other lieutenants, he supervised the enlisted embassy staff and rotated duties as Officer of the Day. Once during his off-duty hours, he attended a performance of Shakespeare's *Comedy of Errors* at the New Globe—he laughed until he cried—and realized how much Popeye would've enjoyed it. In the lobby afterward, he met an elementary school teacher named Julia, who, upon learning he was a history buff, invited him to her classroom to speak to her children on the Colonial Revolution. After his talk, Julia declared him a gifted teacher—

and also hinted that a romantic relationship might be in the offing. He demurred, citing his engagement to a woman back in the States, leading Julia to commend his fidelity.

When his commitment was up, First Lieutenant Greene was on track for captain, but he opted instead to muster out. He had a degree in American history to complete, with aspirations for a master's and then a doctorate. As a staunch Jersey Shore native, his goal was to teach in his local alma mater, Ocean County College. But the overriding reason was waiting for him at home in Toms River.

Staci Rousseau had completed her master's degree by now and was applying her formidable math skills as an accountant. Frank had also returned to the nest, sporting a master's degree in English and Drama and was already established on the faculty of OCC.

They were the T3 all over again.

Staci and Donald married in a civil ceremony attended by their parents, with Frank standing as best man. They'd booked a local hotel for their first night as man and wife and drove in his compact Honda the short distance north from town, stopping at the traffic light on busy Route 37. As they waited for the light to change, Donald told Staci to ask him what the second thing was that he'd do when they checked into their room. When she did, he told her it would be to shut the door.

She laughed and leaned over to give him a passionate kiss. A horn behind them alerted them that the light had turned green. Donald bolted into the intersection—and heard Staci scream as a speeding car crashed into her side of the Civic, crumpling it like an accordion. Her head whiplashed against the shattered window, then caromed back to strike Donald. Gouts of blood and brain matter gushed from her head, spattering him and turning her gold hair red. Her beautiful face was now a Halloween horror mask, all shredded skin and blood, embedded with shattered shards of glass.

Donald felt his right leg shatter at the impact, but the shock blinded him to the pain. Then his world went dark.

Chapter One
Eleven Years Later

"Good evening, all, and welcome to American History 101. We will meet on Tuesday and Thursday evenings for the next fifteen weeks, from six to eight, with a ten-minute break at seven so you can congregate outside and pollute your lungs." Gentle laughs greeted his remark. "Is there anyone who's in the wrong room?" He scanned the seventeen adults in the classroom. "Good. To my undergrads I'm Dr. Greene, but as we're all adults here, I'll answer to Donald. I've printed my college email address on the board behind me, should you need to contact me between classes. But before we begin, I need to take attendance; that's right, just like when you were kiddies in grade school." More smiles from the class as he picked up the roster. The names were not arranged alphabetically but in the dates the students enrolled.

"Robert Goulding." A hand went up. "Maria Palladino." Another hand. Next, "Christopher Giglio."

"Pronounced it right the first time, Doc; I'm impressed. You speak Italian?"

"Only when I'm angry. And my vocabulary is limited."

Donald continued to read the names, placing them with faces. "Calvin Jackson." A surly-looking young black man in his late twenties, wearing a purple tee silk-screened with "No justice, no peace," raised his hand and said, "Yo."

Donald continued. "Perry White?" An older black man raised his hand. "Great Caesar's ghost!" Donald exclaimed, feigning frustration.

"I get that a lot," Perry replied, laughing. When he looked around at mostly confused faces, he added, "Metropolis? *Daily Planet?* Editor? Come on, folks, you're not that much younger than me."

Donald went on to the next name. "Hannah Soong." She looked to be in her early- to mid-thirties and presented the exotic appearance of a beautiful South Seas islander—long jet-black hair, skin the color of coffee and cream, dark oval eyes, straight nose over delicate lips. She was dressed in business attire; probably came to class directly from work. She raised her left hand, and Donald noticed the ring.

"Brian Snowden." A uniformed Toms River police officer raised his hand. He too might have come directly from work. He sat tall in his seat, eyes casting about as if alert for any trouble. Or perhaps trying to make an impression?

"Walter Ballew," he continued, and when he was finished, he placed the roster on his desk, and favoring his right leg, walked to the front of it and sat down on the edge.

"Thank you all for being here—and no, I don't say that to my undergrads; they have to be. You volunteered for this class; you're the ones paying for it, not your parents; and it's my goal to give you your money's worth. First, though, some housekeeping. When my daytime kids walk into my room, they place their phones in the cubbies you see on the wall and collect them when they leave. We're all grownups here, so I'll just ask you to turn your phones off while you're in class. Shut them down or silence them so the ringtones don't distract the rest of us." Hands reached into pockets and purses. The only person who didn't make a move was the policeman.

"As for your evaluations, my daytime students get quizzes and formal tests during the term. I don't assign them essays, because the topics are too easy to Google—and copy word for word—and then try to pass off as their own writing. Doris Kearns Goodwin and Stephen Ambrose these kids are not. You, however, bring not only your motivation to the class but also your life experiences. Therefore, this is the routine I'm suggesting—all right then, prescribing. Toward the end of Tuesday's class, I'll assign an essay in which you will recap the lesson and offer an opinion, editorial style, for Thursday. I'll return your essays the following Tuesday."

"How long do they have to be?" said Brian Snowden, his voice crisp as the military creases on his uniform shirt.

"I'm not looking for a thesis. Two pages, three max, Times New Roman, twelve point, double-spaced, justified left. You'll want to fold them in half the long way and write your name and date on the outside at the top. I'll write a comment or two below your name and write the grade inside."

"Will there be a final?" asked Walter Ballew.

Donald nodded. "That will be done in class the last night. I'll give you a list of topics on Tuesday, so you can make your choice, review your notes, and maybe even write a rough draft at home. That'll be up to you. Then on Thursday you'll type your final draft on your laptops or the classroom computers, using the whole two hours to complete it, upload it to the printer, and hand it to me on your way out. You won't be allowed to bring your notes or first draft; you'll have to write your essays from memory, to assure me of your command of the subject."

He asked if there were any questions. When no one raised a hand, he said, "Here's your first assignment. About those four-by-six-inch index cards you see on your desks: please print your name on top and take a few minutes to write a few notes about yourself and what you hope to gain from this class. And please don't say a passing grade."

Early Friday evening, with the first week's evening sessions completed, Donald sat at the horseshoe-shaped bar of the Office Lounge nursing a draught of Theakston's ale, which he'd developed a taste for during his embassy duty in London. As he checked his watch, Frank Populski walked through the double doors and made a beeline for the stool Donald had saved for him.

"I'll have one of those," he said as Mary greeted him from behind the bar. He looked at Donald. "Crowded tonight, Ducks. Think we can snag a booth, or did you think ahead and reserve one?"

"Oh, ye of little faith."

Popeye took a swig from the frosted glass and glanced over to the seating area, where he saw Cindy waving. "That's us," he said, and they brought their drinks to the booth, Donald trailing.

"The usual, guys?" asked Cindy. "Bacon cheeseburger for Don, liver and onions for Frank?"

They said yes, and Donald shook his head.

"What?" said Frank.

"I've said it before. Liver and onions: the mouthwash for lovers."

"I gave my harem the night off."

"You do know what passes through that liver."

"Didn't you tell me you ate kidney pie when you were in London?"

"Tried it once; that was enough. You know, it really does taste like piss."

Their dinners arrived, and as Frank waxed rhapsodic over his liver and onions, Donald relaxed with his burger and fries, with a side of slaw.

"Well," said Frank between bites, "at last it's September and the bennies have gone home to North Jersey and Staten Island. Now the beaches won't be crowded, and the water'll be warmer too."

"And we won't have to buy beach badges either," Donald groused. "Only in Jersey do you have to pay to go on a public beach in the summer."

"Hear, hear."

Donald finished the last of his cole slaw. "Well, Pops, how's the new crop of coeds shaping up? Found anyone to ask you to be the father of her child yet?"

"Hey, I only dated one student, remember? And she was a senior. It ended when she graduated and moved on."

"I'm glad you never told me who she was. Speaks well of you, Pops. End of compliment."

"Gossip sucks, Ducks. And I wouldn't have compromised her under any circumstances."

"So, the young lady must've been what, twenty at the time. And you are?"

"I *was* thirty-three then. Thirteen years' difference. Hey, Carlo Ponti was twenty years older than Sophia Loren, and they were still madly in love when he died."

Changing the subject, Donald asked if Frank, who not only taught English but served as the school's drama coach, had decided on the play he'd put on this year. Frank was renowned locally for the annual presentations, in part because of his attention to authenticity. He rented the players' outfits from a Broadway costume shop, duplicated the original stage sets, and hired a professional band to provide orchestration. He was a stern but loving taskmaster, and his efforts always paid off with packed auditoriums, rave reviews, and sometimes holdover performances. He tagged his productions as Broadway at Your Doorstep.

"Doing my favorite, Ducks."

"*Pippin?* Didn't you stage that like five years ago?"

"Yup. But this year I found a choreographer in New York who knows all the Bob Fosse moves and is willing to teach them to the kids. And the guy who's doing the Leading Player is a dead ringer for Ben Vereen. With all that talent available, how could I *not* reprise it?"

Donald nodded. "The story's universal and the music's unforgettable, I'll give you that."

"You'll never forget because you were there at every rehearsal when we did it in high school, making sure Staci didn't slip me tongue when we had to kiss."

"Up yours, Popeye."

"So, how's your night class looking this term? Anyone stand out?"

"I'm getting positive vibes from them. Really looking forward to the new term."

Cindy came unbidden with two more draughts. Frank commended her on her ability to read minds. She grinned as she told him that to read his mind, she'd have to find it first.

"All right, my class. There's a cop who I suspect thinks his excrement isn't odorous, to use the PG term. He strutted into class in full uniform both nights and probably found it hard to sit down with that broomstick up his ass. Then there's a twenty-something woman, broad as she is tall, Betty Boop hairstyle, make-up so thick it makes you wonder if the circus is in town. She might be a problem too. I've yet to see her do anything but scowl. The rest are pretty typical. Most are folks with families who've decided to go back to school."

"Uh huh. And?"

"And what?"

"Very nice. But I'm talking about foxes, Ducks."

"Naturally. What else would you be talking about?" Donald took a swallow of beer. "All right, there is one. She comes to class wearing either a business suit or dress. Very professional. Judging by her surname, I'd assume she's part Korean. Actually, she looks like a *wahine* from some Polynesian island. Very striking. And she sits in the T."

"Excuse me, what?"

"The T. If you let students sit where they want, the most motivated kids will sit in a T formation—across the first row and down the center."

"Really. I'll have to try that with my own classes, see what they do. They're arranged alphabetically now. Tell me, where does your *wahine* sit?"

"Third seat back in the center."

"She available?"

"She wears a wedding ring. And yes, I noticed right off."

"I'd remind you that you wear a wedding ring too."

"Yeah, but that's different."

Frank drained his glass. "Right. You seeing anyone?"

"Here we go again."

"Listen, you need a woman."

"I've been on dates," Donald said defensively.

"Come on, dates. You don't take off your wedding ring, and it tells them they're competing with a memory. That's a massive turnoff, as if you didn't know. I'd call you Teflon Don, but that title's already been taken."

"I'm sorry if I haven't found anyone who could measure up to Staci's standards."

"You think maybe you've embellished those standards a little? Or maybe a lot? You know I love you, Ducks, and I loved Staci too, but she's not an icon. I really think you're not being logical about this."

"We've been over this before, Pops. I'm not ready."

"Bummer. Sucks to be you, Ducks."

Chapter Two

Sunday morning, Donald drove to St. Paul's Lutheran in Beach-wood, an oval-shaped church whose roof was designed to look like an overturned fishing boat from the Sea of Galilee. Back in the day, he would sit in the same pew with Staci and both their parents. Today he sat alone. His own mother and father had retired and moved to a golf community in South Carolina. Staci's parents left New Jersey after the unrepentant drunk who killed her was found guilty of ve-hicular manslaughter and sentenced to prison; Donald never heard from them again.

Participating in the familiar liturgy allowed Donald a measure of comfort. He could almost hear Staci's clear voice as he joined in the hymns and participated in the responsive readings. But today no one sat on either side of him. Church attendance had ceased to exist during the pandemic lockdowns and later never returned in the numbers it had shown before. Donald attributed it to inertia. But he himself rarely missed a service.

After church, Donald treated himself to lunch at the Water Street Bar and Grill, a waterside restaurant in Toms River with views across the river to Beachwood. It was still warm enough for him to sit out-side and gaze eastward down the river toward Barnegat Bay and the narrow peninsula that stretched from Point Pleasant in the north to Island Beach State Park in the south. It was at Island Beach in years past that he and Staci would spend summer days swimming and sunbathing and trading dreams for their future together.

After lunch he returned to his modest townhome, sat at his desk, and opened his attaché case. He took out the index cards he'd had his evening students prepare and reviewed them again.

Most were garden variety responses: I want to learn about Amer-ica; I want to brush up on/extend my high school history; I'm return-ing to school now that my kids are grown; I hated history as a kid and want to make up for lost time.

Then there were the others:

Calvin Jackson. Black, dreads, obviously with a chip on his shoulder. "I want to know real history, not the bullshit stories they tell you in school."

Brian Snowden. White, cop, possibly with a superiority complex. "I want to compare what you teach with what I already know." Hmm.

Cassandra Bright. Clown girl. "It's a required course. I'm an undergraduate and I have to work days." *In a doughnut shop?* Donald wondered, then chided himself for being unprofessional.

Then there was Hannah Soong. "I'm here because a friend advised me to sign up for your class."

Now that was intriguing. He spent some idle moments wondering who that friend might be. He decided not to ask her, at least not in front of the class.

Three weeks later, Donald's class of seventeen had lessened by two. First to go was Cassandra Bright. "I'm not getting anything out of this," she declared for all to hear. "You're a shit teacher."

Keeping his expression neutral and trying not to sound patronizing, Donald said, "Ms. Bright, research shows that a failure to learn does not necessarily mean a failure to teach." She scoffed. "But if you'd like to transfer to another class, with a better teacher, I'd be happy to facilitate the move." She stood, huffed, and said she could do it herself as she stormed out of the room.

In the faculty room one morning a week later, Frank and Donald sat at a table getting caffeinated for the morning's classes. Frank said, "I've got some news for you about your dropout; you know, the one who looks like an overinflated beach ball."

"I know who you mean, Pops. There was only one."

"Seems she transferred to Ed McCrohan's class on Mondays and Wednesdays. A couple weeks in, she told him, in front of the class, that he sucked as a teacher. He was no better than Greene, and she was going to go to the dean and file a complaint about both of you."

"And did she?" Donald asked.

"She sure did. But Ed warned him she'd be coming, and when she plopped herself down in front of the dean, he was ready for her. After hearing her spout off, he took her transcripts from his desk drawer. This was her second term at the college. It seems she had Incomplete, D, or F grades in every other subject. The dean suggested the Ds were gifts."

"So, if she's not in either of our classes, Ed's and mine, where might she be now?"

"Who knows? Who cares? Enjoy your day, Ducks. I know I'm going to enjoy the shit out of mine."

The second dropout was involuntary. It was the police officer, Brian Snowden. Although admonished to leave his cell phone off during class, Donald could count on hearing it ping at least once every session. Brian would remove it from his pocket, say, "I've got to take this," and leave the room for a few minutes. The first time it happened, Donald called Brian aside after dismissal and reminded him of the classroom rule. "Yeah, I understand, but I have to take these calls."

"Do you have a wife about to go into labor or a sick relative who needs your attention? Because I can't think of any other reason for the distraction."

"I have a side job as a handyman. People call me and I have to get back to them. They could have an emergency."

"I'm sorry, but I can't see that as a valid excuse."

"All right. I'll tell them not to call during class time."

Either he didn't tell them, or his clients didn't care. Finally, again after class and in private, Donald said, "Brian, you've got to make a choice—either the phone or the class. Let me know which it is." Brian didn't respond; he turned and walked away.

The next meeting Brian showed up, in full uniform as usual, his expression defiant. "Just so you know, I'll be staying in class, but I do need to keep my phone on," he proclaimed for all to hear.

Eyes on Donald again as he sat on the edge of his desk. His game leg had been bothering him lately, and he didn't like sitting behind the desk, which in itself tended to form a subliminal barrier between him and his students.

"The next time your phone goes off, Mr. Snowden, I'm afraid you will have to leave."

"I paid for this course, Doc. You can't make me."

"I'd remind you that everyone else paid too, and your rudeness toward them is clearly unacceptable. Make your choice." He smiled subtly as if reminded of a private joke. "Don't you think it would be ironic if I had to summon a campus policeman to escort a municipal policeman out of my room?"

Brian's eyes became slits. He jutted out his chin, baring his lower teeth, and stood, projecting an imposing figure in his form-fitting shirt and leather utility belt. The fingers of his right hand began to twitch by his side. Donald noticed and stood tall to confront him.

"You wouldn't happen to have anger management issues, would you, Brian? I ask you this because you appear to be itching to uncase your weapon." Everyone stared at Brian, some with fear evident on their faces. "Now, I feel I should advise you, Brian, that I've been shot at before, many times in fact, and I never really took kindly to it."

The room fell silent. Some glanced briefly at Donald's right leg. Brian beetled his brow.

"I served in uniform too, Officer Snowden. It was a Marine Corps uniform, I served in a war zone, and my platoon was constantly under heavy enemy fire. All of which should suggest to you that I'm not easily intimidated." Donald kept his expression neutral as he stared Brian down.

The officer seethed and briefly lowered his eyes. Having broken contact, he looked up again. "I'm leaving. But know this. You're a marked man, Doc. You better hope I never get to pull you over at a traffic stop. Because if I do, your ass is grass, and I'm the lawnmower."

Donald affected a juvenile tone. "How about, your tail's a sail, and I'm a hurricane." Students looked from one to the other as if they were watching a tennis match. Donald gave him a wry grin. "Truly, Brian, have we devolved into schoolyard taunts? Has it come down to that, Officer Snowfla—I mean, Officer Snowden?"

The class burst into laughter as Brian slammed his textbook onto the floor and stormed out of the room.

Perry White spoke up. "He threatened you, Doc. You want, I'll testify on your behalf."

Hannah Soong looked at Donald with a nod and a smile that seemed to say, nicely done.

Chapter Three

"Gotta hand it to ya, Ducks," said Frank as they quaffed their first beer at the Office Friday night. "That T formation really works. After you told me about it, I told my freshmen they were free to choose their own seats. And what do you know? The go-getters fell right into the T."

"And so now you..."

"And now I engage the kids outside the T more than the ones inside it."

"Ah, my Polish grasshopper, you learn."

Cindy beckoned them to their booth. They brought their beers, greeted her, and began to place their orders. "I already put them in," she chirped. "You guys are totally predictable."

"Someday, Cindy, we'll surprise you."

"Oh, yeah. Like Don will order a side of mac salad instead of slaw."

Frank gave her a dismissive wave, as if he were a British lord. "Begone, wench."

Cindy smacked him on the shoulder and left to turn her attention to her other customers.

Frank said to Donald, "After the butterball left, anybody else jump ship?"

Donald told him the story of Brian Snowden.

"Shitbird with a gun," Frank concluded. "Worst kind."

"Amen, brother."

Their dinners arrived. "That was quick," said Frank.

"Told you," said Cindy with a wink.

Frank said, "Cindy, if you weren't already married, I'd be knocking at your door, begging to ask you out."

"Well, as a consolation prize you can have my two boys. They're in the terrible teens."

"Oh, my condolences. Consider my offer rescinded."

Cindy gave him a weary smile and left them to their meals.

Donald took a bite of his burger as Frank put knife and fork to his liver.

Midway through the meal, Frank said, "So Ducks, how's your *wahine* doing? She have the brains to match her good looks? Her off-limits good looks, I'd remind you."

Donald nibbled on a French fry before he answered. "Seriously, Pops, she's the best student I've ever had, bar none. In fact, maybe she's too good."

"Care to elaborate? Like she echoes your words of wisdom, for example?"

"Actually, she doesn't speak up at all; she just listens, takes notes on her laptop, and smiles at my jokes. I don't call on my adult students for comments. If they want to share, they're welcome, but I don't force the issue."

"Then what is it that has you going ga-ga over her?"

"Her writing. It's organized around a thesis, with supporting information, and bookended with an intro and conclusion that tie in with each other as well as the thesis. That, plus her reasoning is sound, her syntax is beautiful, and her command of language is impeccable. Totally professional."

"Wow. Now tell me what you really think."

Donald picked up his beer and tilted the glass toward Frank. "I'm not bullshitting you, buddy. And I'll tell you this, although I hate to admit it."

"I'm all ears."

"Obviously, I have never met the lady's husband; I have no intention of ever meeting her husband; and despite all that, I've grown to despise her husband."

They shared a laugh. Frank said, "You know, Ducks, I'm wondering if we're having a breakthrough moment here."

Donald shrugged. "Forbidden fruit, Pops, forbidden fruit."

"But if she were unmarried and available?"

"It's frustrating to deal in hypotheticals; you know that. How's your love life, by the way? Still pining over the one who got away?"

"When she graduated, we made our goodbyes in an adult and civilized manner."

"Tell me you didn't break up in an email."

"No, I sent a text. Come on, Ducks, that's not me and you know it. No, when she left for grown-up college," he said with a twist of his mouth, "I sent her off with a bang."

"You're a sick puppy, you know that?"

"I know, crude. We actually spent a lovely evening: dinner at Il Giardanello and later a lovelier night at the Best Western in Lakewood. Such sweet sorrow, as the Bard happened to mention somewhere."

Early in the term, when the topic focused on America's beginnings, Calvin Jackson mumbled that it officially began in 1619. Donald affected a bland expression and asked him what's in a name. He could say that America began in 1492 with Columbus, even though he never actually arrived on the continent; or five hundred years earlier with the Vikings. Or in prehistory, with the Asians who we think migrated across the land bridge to Alaska. If Calvin wanted to say America's history began with the importation of slaves, that was fine by him. It's all about perspective.

Calvin wasn't sure how to respond. Instead of refuting his contention, the teacher neutralized it.

Calvin's wardrobe that evening included a gray tee shirt with a black fist silkscreened on the front. Another time, he'd worn a white shirt featuring a portrait of George Floyd; he also had a black one with the word *Police* in white letters inside a red circle with a red slash through it. The next time he smiled in class would probably be the first.

But he attended every session and even took notes. His essays were competently written, but many made reference to what he perceived as racism. Regardless, he would probably pull a B for the course.

Midway through, Donald addressed the Civil War. "Your textbook tells you that northerners were able to avoid being drafted into the Union Army by paying other men to serve in their place. You might want to address the ethical implications of that in your next essay." Which was his way of saying you *will*. "Now, let's focus on how the rich Southerners managed to do something just like it. That's something you won't find in your textbook."

All eyes focused on Donald. Some students, including Hannah, leaned forward in their chairs.

"You've seen how the actors playing Confederate soldiers in the movies are dressed, right, Rebel gray right out of the wardrobe department? And how motivated they were to fight the Yankees? Let's put that myth to rest."

Faces grew expectant. "It's about the haves and the have nots. Understand, the wealth in the South was concentrated among rich plantation owners; most others, the have nots, if you will, were poor to middle-class farmers and merchants. A goodly number of them objected to secession; in fact, they wanted no part of the war. Regardless, they were conscripted forcibly from their homes and farms and forced to serve the Southern cause. These folks went off to war not in fancy uniforms but with only the clothes on their backs. They had to leave their wives alone to manage their farms and homesteads. And those draftees, for the most part, never owned slaves, never wanted to own slaves, and thought slavery was an abomination in the sight of God. In other words, they didn't have a dog in the fight."

"But they fought for slavery anyway," countered Calvin in a damning tone.

"Well, Calvin, it was a choice between serving and being shot or hanged; and more than a few deserters were. The other non-volunteers had to slog through mosquito-infested Southern swamps, where alligators lurked, and cottonmouths draped over tree limbs or slithered out of the putrid water. They wore through their boot soles and still had to march, on bloody feet, to the next battle. They couldn't bathe, and their clothes ended up stuck to their bodies. Everyone had lice. They were so starved for food, sometimes they slaughtered their pack mules. And the first aid tent was basically an amputation station. Is it any wonder that men deserted in droves?" Heads nodded. "To make matters worse, back on the farms, men claiming to represent the Confederacy would casually make off with the corn and cotton and livestock from whatever homesteads they happened upon, which left the wives running them destitute. They justified what they were doing by telling the poor women it was for the war effort. You try plowing a field without a horse or a mule. Try making clothes without cotton. Try making bread without cornmeal."

Perry White raised his hand. "So how did the rich Southerners get out of serving?"

Here it comes, thought Donald, thinking of Calvin. "That's what I'm leading up to, Perry. Have you or anyone else heard of the Twenty Negro Act?"

Calvin's eyes narrowed. "That's racist," he growled. "You can't say Negro."

"Sticks and stones, Calvin. Slaves at the time were in fact referred to as Negroes, which as you know is the Spanish word for black. It might not be PC by today's standards, but it was accepted then, and it was never intended as a slur. Neither was another socially accepted word at the time that also began with an *N*."

Calvin shook his head.

Donald continued, "To your question, Perry. Those rich, slave-owning plantation owners didn't want to suffer the unpleasantness and inconvenience of going to war, so a delegation went to the legislature to complain that they couldn't *possibly* leave their plantations to their frail womenfolk to manage. Why, they needed a master on hand to supervise and discipline the slaves. And they certainly didn't want their innocent wives and virginal daughters to fall victim to those black savages' animal urges. To placate these plantation owners—after all, these were the men who paid the most taxes and had the real political clout—the legislature passed the Twenty Negro Act, which decreed that any landowner who had twenty slaves or more was exempt from serving the Confederate cause in battle."

"Which means it was left to the non-slave owners to serve," said Perry.

"Yes. The Southern insurrection was basically a rich man's war that the poor man had to fight." He looked at his watch. "Ready for your break? See you in ten." The room emptied and Donald was alone.

For some reason during the break, he couldn't take his mind off Hannah Soong. He looked down at his desktop and realized he was toying with his plain gold wedding ring. He'd never done that before.

When the class returned, Calvin shot his hand up. "We been talking outside, and what you said kinda reminds me of how in Vietnam the black man fought the white man's war."

Donald was not averse to digression. "Excellent point, Calvin. Well, with one exception. White men were drafted too and had to fight alongside their black brothers. I say *brothers* not in the way you might think, but in the way that the man sharing your foxhole is your brother in arms, and the amount of melanin he carries in his skin has nothing to do with it. As a footnote, during Vietnam too there were men of means who fled to Canada as a way to avoid the war. So, I'll give you that."

"But black men were still slaves to a country that didn't care about us."

"Calvin, I hate to break it to you, I really do, but the African tribesmen who were sold to the white slavers were already enslaved, by *other* African tribesmen. They were captured from neighboring tribes and sold like property. Call it the original black on black crime."

"But still, the white men in America slaved us, and they should be held accountable for it."

"You're talking reparations, I assume." Calvin nodded. "Why?"

"Because they owe it to us."

Donald saw Hannah Soong forcibly repressing a smile.

"All right, to your point. If you want reparations for slavery, then I want reparations for the six hundred and twenty *thousand* Union soldiers who died fighting against slavery. I'd call that fair, wouldn't you? In fact, I'd call it a wash."

Heads were turning again, from Donald to Calvin and back.

"This'll blow you away, Calvin, and if you can prove me wrong, more power to you. We all agree that slavery was a shameful, horrible institution. But for Calvin Jackson, today, it's the best thing that could've happened to you."

"Whoa!" someone said under his breath. Calvin's face registered shock. He scowled and slapped his palms flat on his desk, as if he were going to stand and fight.

"Calvin, if your ancestors had never left Africa, never come to America, where would you yourself be right now, and what would you be doing?"

Perry White turned to Calvin. "I'll tell you what you'd be doing. You'd be living in a hut, and carrying a spear, and drinking cows' blood mixed with milk. You'd have a wife who washed clothes against stones in the river, hoping she wouldn't get snapped up by a crocodile. Grow up, son. Our ancestors had no hope, but you and I do. This is the land of opportunity for all of us, my man."

"Huh. I still say America's a racist country."

Donald played his hole card. "Calvin, if I were to tell you that I'm married to a black woman, would you call me a racist?"

"What?"

"And if I told you she's a high-powered civil rights attorney who earns more in a month than I do all year, would that make me an even worse racist for taking advantage of one of your black sisters?"

Calvin simmered for a minute. "How do I know you're telling the truth?"

Donald chuckled. "If you're waiting for a dinner invitation, it's not coming."

The others laughed; all tension was broken. And then Hannah Soong surprised Donald by raising her hand. "I'd like to say something to Calvin, Doctor Greene."

"Of course. Please. Go ahead."

She turned in her chair to face him where he sat on the fringe of the T formation. "Calvin, my father is a black man, and my mother is half white and half Korean. How would you color me, racially speaking? Would you say I was black, white, and yellow?"

He looked at her dumbly. Finally, "Yeah, I guess. I don't know."

"I wouldn't. Not to be jingoistic, but feel free to color me red, white, and blue." Calvin scoffed. "Listen, my friend," Hannah continued, authority in her beautifully modulated voice. "You've been suckered into playing identity politics, which means you're what politicians call a useful idiot." Calvin opened his mouth. "No—no, don't interrupt; here's what I mean. In countries all over the world, it's the government that rules the people. But only in America is it the people who, in theory at least, rule the government. Can you understand that?

Calvin lowered his eyes but didn't respond.

"Now, you and I both know there are elites in government who don't want to be held accountable by everyday Americans like you and me. So, what do they do? They follow their age-old playbook—identify, isolate, intimidate, and incite." All eyes were on Hannah now, ears attuned to her voice. "Playing the race card? That's step one, identifying us by race, or religion, or sexual orientation. Then they isolate us into tribes. Racially speaking, think about the Congressional Black Caucus, Black Entertainment Television, magazines like *Ebony*. Some colleges now have black-only dorms. That's pure segregation, and it's what civil rights activists, both black and white, have fought against for years. If our society is divided into warring tribes, that gives politicians the opportunity to step in and take control. Make you depend upon government to"—she made air quotes—"set things right. And if you need an illustration of how that works, just look at Nazi Germany—from the yellow stars, to the ghettos, to *Kristallnacht*, and to Auschwitz."

As the others in the class sat in awe of their heretofore silent classmate, Hannah directed her attention to Donald. "Sorry, Doctor Greene, if I derailed your train of thought."

"You absolutely did not, Ms. Soong. You steered the engine. Thank you." He looked around the room. "What say we call it a night, folks? You can go home and think about what Hannah said, and while you're at it take a close look at our national motto: Out of many, one. One *united* people, not divided. And when you see politicians trying to tribalize us, remember they're doing it to make us useful idiots, serving their cause, not ours. Good night, all. For next time, please read the next chapter, on Reconstruction."

As the class left, talking excitedly among themselves, Donald asked Hannah to wait. "Thank you for what you said tonight. It means more to the class to hear it from one of their own than from the teacher."

She smiled pleasantly. "Happy to do my part, Dr. Greene. See you next time."

The door closed behind her and Donald sat alone in the room, gathering his thoughts. Staci Rousseau, his petite French sparkler, had been his high school love. Cheerleader captain, 4.0 GPA, voted most popular in the yearbook, and totally devoted to Donald. As was he to her. But they were eighteen then. Years later, his military obligation fulfilled, it was like they were still eighteen, locked in some kind of time warp. They still looked at each other with moon eyes; they still possessed that overpowering youthful optimism; and they still believed that their love would last forever.

Until it didn't.

But if she had lived, could Donald today honestly assert their love would have endured? Might they have grown apart as they matured and their professional paths diverged? When he came home, Staci was an accountant, a career that held as little interest for him as teaching held for her. Would their relationship have eventually devolved from yin and yang to oil and water?

Donald forced himself to ask the hard questions. Had Staci become an icon, as Frank had suggested? Was it finally time to give up the ghost of romance past? Finally, would Staci have approved his forsaking others for the sake of her memory?

How ironic that after all these years, the one woman for whom he could feel a genuine bond was already married.

Chapter Four

In early December the term ended. Donald collected two sets of papers from each student—the final exam and the teacher evaluation form, the latter to be delivered, unread by him, to the department head's office. The evaluations were to be anonymous; the students placed the separate papers in a pair of boxes by the door on their way out. Calvin gave a grudging nod to the teacher, and Perry White shook Donald's hand and thanked him.

Hannah Soong was last to turn in her paper, and Donald told her what a joy it had been to have her in class. She smiled and said, "May I tell you a secret?"

"All right."

"I signed up to audit your class. That's why I was more of an observer than a participant. At least until Calvin went into his rant. I figured if you challenged him as the classroom authority figure, he'd turn you off; ergo, I butted in."

"Again, thank you. But now I'm curious. I know that as an auditor you didn't have to turn in any essays. But you did anyway, and frankly, I found them brilliant."

"Writing them served two purposes," she acknowledged. "One, it sharpened my skills, and two, it was rewarding to share my opinions with someone I respect and who would be objective."

"I remember on your note card you wrote that you were advised to enroll in my class. Can you tell me now who advised you?"

"One of your former students, Emily O'Neil. She's my paralegal and raves about you. You know, I never liked history in school: basically, it seemed like just a collection of dates and wars. In law school, I realized there was a void in my knowledge, and finally, at Emily's urging, I decided it was time to fill in the gap."

"I remember Emily. She played Lola in the college production of *Damn Yankees*. She brought the house down when she sang 'Whatever Lola wants.' Wait. You said she's your *paralegal?*"

"Yes. I started out as a civil rights attorney, like your wife. Junior member of a Manhattan firm. I eventually left to open my own office in Point Pleasant, and I poached Emily to come with me. She's originally from Beachwood, so she was happy to get the chance to live at home again. Now we enjoy regular hours, no major stresses, and our weekends are free to enjoy. Plus, no tedious litigation to slog through." Hannah smiled contentedly, then added, "Another downside of the former job was the predatory attitudes of some of the senior partners. You probably remember how beautiful Emily is, with her red hair, green eyes, and her dancer's body."

"I assume you garnered your share of unwanted attention too."

Hannah nodded. "I overheard someone say that they privately referred to me as the ice queen and Emily as my frigid princess. Rumor eventually began that we were gay anyway, the classic sour grapes defense. It made for an uncomfortable work environment.

"Soon after we'd established our practice back home, I happened to mention to Emily my regret at not having paid attention during my history classes, and she told me about you—what a great teacher you are, how you make history come alive. I never knew a teacher like that, and she said I should sign up for your course in night school. I figured what the heck, my nights are free anyway. Well, I'm happy to assure you that Emily's assessment was spot on. I learned some history I didn't know before, but I also learned a lot about you, from your remarks on my essays." Her face assumed a pensive expression. "Please understand, I wouldn't want to give your wife cause for alarm, but would you mind if I asked you to join me for a coffee sometime?"

Donald smiled. "Hannah, I'm not married."

She stepped back, and her winter coat nearly slipped from the crook of her arm. "But you told Calvin you are, married to a black woman in fact. A civil rights attorney. One who makes more money in a month than you do in a year."

"Ah, grasshopper. You remembered what I said, but you didn't pick up on the nuance. I asked Calvin *what if* I told him I was married to a black woman."

Hannah's exotic eyes grew wider, and a grin blossomed. "You sly devil, you." He smiled and shrugged. "Well, now I don't feel so uncomfortable about asking you to share a coffee with me."

"What about your husband? What would he say?"

She held up her left hand so he could see the ring. "Beautiful, isn't it? It used to be my grandmother's. I'm not married either."

"Oh. In that case, let me grab my coat. I'll drive."

Donald escorted Hannah to the parking lot and pointed out his car.

"What *is* that thing?" she asked as she scanned the long and wide white sedan with its slab-sided body, squared-off fenders, and rear window that angled toward the car instead of sloping away toward the trunk.

"That, Ms. Soong, is a 1965 Mercury Montclair four-door sedan."

"It's huge. Wait. Did you say 1965?"

"I did. My grandfather bought it new and passed it on to my father, who passed it along to me as a gift when I got my doctorate and he and Mom were ready to live the golfing life in South Carolina." He opened the passenger door and Hannah slid onto the blue leather bench seat. "No seat belts at the time. The harnesses are new."

Hannah buckled in and Donald closed the door with a solid thunk. Then he got in on the driver's side and assumed his place behind the wheel. They were surrounded by silence.

"What do you think?"

"I think it's a tank." She looked around the interior. "No, more like a cruise ship. It's gorgeous. What's with the backwards rear window?"

"It slides down behind the back seat. Designed for ventilation."

"But wouldn't it pull in the exhaust fumes when you're driving?"

"Maybe. The design didn't last. But there's no danger of that happening here." She asked why. "Electric."

"What! They didn't have electric cars in 1965."

"Actually, there were electric cars in the early twentieth century. But they didn't go far. Double meaning there."

"I get it, but what's the story with electric?"

"When my dad told me he was giving me the car, we ferried it to a shop in Lancaster, Pennsylvania, where they remove internal combustion engines and powertrains and replace them with electric motors driven by a huge battery that's fitted under the floor. I had an electrician run a high-voltage line into my garage so I can charge it overnight."

Hannah laughed. "Which means Doctor Greene is a greenie."

"After the conversion, we took the Merc to a body shop that specializes in older cars and had the body stripped, dings and rust taken out, and repainted to look new. Finally, we had the seats reupholstered. For all intents and purposes, we're driving in a classic car made brand new."

"Does your chariot have a name?"

Donald smiled. "My friend Popeye calls it Moby Duck."

"Clever. But Popeye? That's his name?"

"It's the name we called him in school growing up. His name's Frank Populski, and he teaches English and drama at the college. Emily would remember him."

"Small world."

Donald pressed a button next to the steering column. The headlights came on, the dashboard instruments glowed a soothing blue, and they glided silently out of the campus parking lot.

Diagonally across the highway from the Office Lounge stands the Crystal Diner, open twenty-four hours. Donald and Hannah sat in a booth away from the front door and ordered coffee. Hannah said if he didn't mind, she wanted to order breakfast. "I leave my office at five to get to class by six and don't get the chance to eat dinner."

"I think it's a great idea. Breakfast any time is always in order. I normally just grab a sandwich between day and night classes."

They gave the server their orders—pancakes, two eggs over easy, and the Jersey Shore staple, Taylor pork roll—and then stared at each other across the table.

"You said in class your mother is half Korean, so your surname is hers, yes?" She nodded. "But Hannah doesn't sound particularly ethnic."

"Ah, grasshopper, as someone we both know is fond of saying. My Korean name is *Hana*." She spelled it. "It's on my birth certificate and translates as favored one. But to avoid confusion, we Anglicized the spelling."

"I'd have thought you'd have your father's surname."

"My mother divorced my father and took her maiden name back. I followed suit. Years later, when I told my mother how unhappy I was in Manhattan, she urged me to come home. She's a real estate agent, also in Point Pleasant. And before you ask, yes, she does refer her clients to me for their closings."

Donald smiled. "It's not nepotism if it produces the desired results. Is your father anywhere in the picture?"

Hannah screwed up her face. "He's in prison."

"That's not what I expected to hear."

"Not something I normally volunteer. But you asked, and I'm not going to hedge."

"Okay. We can change the subject."

"No, that's okay. My mother and father were high school sweethearts; don't ask me what she saw in him. After graduation, he found a job and they got married. He worked for a developer who builds retirement villages. More like Stalag compounds, really, but again not mine to judge. He painted the interiors of the houses. All day every day, he'd spray diluted eggshell white paint on Sheetrock walls and ceilings. Basically, it was a factory job—and numbing, as you can guess. Mom, meanwhile, went to real estate school and before long was making more money than he was. A lot more. That threatened his perception of his manhood, and he began to drink, and when he was drunk, he got abusive; verbally first, then physically. Mom served him with papers when I turned twenty. At the time, I'd just finished my AA at good old OCC and was on my way to a four-year college."

"Your dad's in jail for what he did to your mother?"

"No. That's another story—which if you don't mind, I'd prefer not to share right now."

"Then I won't ask again."

"Appreciate it. Oh, and speaking of appreciating..."

Their meals arrived and they turned their attention to their breakfast platters.

Over another cup of coffee after their empty platters were removed, Donald said, "That wedding ring had me fooled."

"Yes, I wear it to remember my grandmother."

"Also, to discourage the wolf pack, I'd imagine. It sure worked on me."

She smiled and briefly lowered her eyes. "I never married. Too busy earning my J.D., and after that I was accepted to the Manhattan firm. Too busy to form a serious social life. How about you?"

"I was married once."

"Divorced?"

"Widowed. A long time ago."

Hannah reached across the table and touched his hand. "I'm so sorry. I won't ask for particulars."

"Thank you."

She withdrew her hand, suddenly self-conscious. "Your turn to tell me about yourself, Doctor Greene. It's okay to call you Donald, right?"

"Promise not to spread it around, but Popeye calls me Ducks."

She chuckled. "I'm sure Mr. Disney would be proud. Does your friend Popeye like spinach?"

"Hates it."

"Ducks, huh?"

"Should've kept my mouth shut."

"Your secret's safe with me."

Donald told her about his passion for history, his joining the Marines after 9/11, his tour as platoon leader in Iraq and at the embassy in London—and skipped the part about Staci, instead going right from his discharge to enrolling in college. "By the way, I didn't get the limp in the war. I was in an automobile accident after I got home."

Hannah let out a breath she hadn't realized she'd been holding. "I didn't want to pry. You never mentioned anything about it in class."

He shook his head and smiled. "I don't mind. It's part of what makes me me, as some obscure philosopher might've said. Justifiably obscure, I'd imagine."

"Where do you call home these days?"

"Bey Lea Brook condominiums. They're town houses, right across Bay Avenue from the golf course."

"Do you play golf? You mentioned your parents do."

"No."

"Neither do I. One box checked."

He gave her a look. "We're checking boxes now, are we?"

"Mm-hmm."

"In that case, where do you live?"

"Also, a town home. Do you know the condos that line the Manasquan Inlet in Point Pleasant Beach?"

"Between the public parking lot and the jetty, yes. Never been inside one." *Okay; was that too broad a hint?*

If it was, Hannah ignored it. "My unit is on the eastern end. Looking out from my second-floor balcony I have an unobstructed view of the ocean. Sometimes, if I get up early enough, I can watch the sunrise from the south-facing bedroom." She made a check mark in the air with her finger. "My mom scored the place for me."

"You went to Point High, I guess."

She nodded. "Honors courses, but the only sport I took was swim team. I was a water rat."

"I was on the Toms River South swim team."

"Really. What was your event?"

"Two hundred free. Yours?"

"Hundred-meter butterfly. Was your friend Popeye on the team with you?"

"Popeye tried out for the breaststroke. But first time he tried it, he got his face slapped."

They laughed together. Hannah said, "Do you still swim?"

"I use the college pool whenever I can. Usually on Saturdays." He gave her a half smile. "I can bring a guest if I want, by the way."

"Sounds enticing; I'll think about it. How about your Sundays?"

"I go to church in the morning."

"What denomination?"

"Lutheran. You?"

"Episcopal. Close enough. Another box checked."

Donald cleared his throat and put his napkin on the placemat. "By the way, thanks for not asking to smoke in the car."

"You're welcome. But that's probably because I don't smoke. Never did, never will."

"You went out with the others during break; I thought—"

"The class clustered in two groups outside, smokers and non. Perry and I were in the non-smoking group. He's a very nice person, which I suspect you already know. How about you?"

"Just like you. Never did, never will."

"Another box," they said in unison.

Donald shook his head and smiled. "Should I suspect you had this little kaffeeklatsch planned?"

"Not as calculating as it seems. Remember, I believed you were married. In fact, I thought I might want to meet your wife, compare notes and all that, maybe become friends." She shook her head. "All right. No, that's not the main reason."

"Oh?"

Hannah lowered her eyes briefly. "I wanted to get to know you personally. And I'm ashamed to say, despite my best efforts not to, that I resented your wife. But believe me, I'd never try to insert myself between you."

"And I'm ashamed to say I resented your husband." He raised an eyebrow. "Um... we're flirting now, aren't we?"

She gave him a puckish smile. "Obviously, Doctor Greene, I can't speak for you."

Chapter Five

Driving Hannah back to the college parking lot, Donald asked if he might take her to dinner the next day.

"Well, that depends, doesn't it?" she said coyly. "What did you have in mind?"

"I was thinking Burger King. But if you'd prefer McDonald's..."

"Oh, Burger King would be great. Will they give me a paper crown to wear?"

"I'll make sure they have one on hand."

She turned her face toward him, and he could see her smile in the soft blue glow of the dashboard lights. "Would you like me to meet you at the Burger King?"

"No. I'll be a gentleman and pick you up at your home."

"Gentleman works for me. You remember where I live, yes?"

"Point Pleasant Beach, Manasquan Inlet, last condo on the right, with an unobstructed view of the ocean."

"Excellent. What time may I expect you?"

"I'm thinking seven."

"Seven also works for me. And I'll be sure to dress appropriately for Burger King. I'm thinking pigtails and a jumper; is that all right?"

"Great. The customers will think I'm robbing the cradle."

They arrived in the parking lot, where Hannah's Highlander waited alone. Donald parked next to it and left his car to open Hannah's door for her. She slid in gracefully and smiled up at him. "See you tomorrow," she said as she closed the door and started the engine.

Donald shivered in the cold as he watched Hannah drive away. Then he got back into the Merc and began to drive home. Suddenly he braked hard, and the big sedan nose-dived to a stop.

"Rats," he said. "Tomorrow's Friday, Office Lounge, Popeye." He pulled his phone out and turned it on. As it booted up, Donald said to himself, "I've got to let him know I can't make it." The dashboard clock read nearly midnight. Class had let out at eight; had he and Hannah been talking that long? Whatever, it was too late to call. He decided to send a text.

The screen came to life, and he heard the ping that signaled voice mail. The number was Frank's.

"Hey, Ducks. Afraid I won't be making our regular Friday night session. I made a date for tomorrow night and totally forgot about the Office. Sorry to stand you up; try to survive without me. Popeye out."

Hannah's condo stood close to where the inlet ended and the jetty extension began. Her door sported a wreath of holly, with red berries and bright red ribbon celebrating the joy of the season. He rang her bell at precisely seven o'clock. And at one minute past, Hannah appeared, clad in a black winter coat with a red knitted scarf around her neck. She was beautifully made up and wore her long black hair loose. No pigtails.

"Hello," she said brightly. "I'd invite you in, but I'm really in a hurry to get to Burger King. Do you mind?"

"Not at all. Your chariot awaits, my lady."

He drove south along Highway 35, the road that goes straight down the barrier peninsula. There was virtually no traffic on this cold pre-winter night. Occasionally they would pass a house festooned with lights, and Hannah called the owners year-rounders. "The whole strip is a ghost town in winter—as you know already, having grown up at the Shore."

"I do. But keep talking; I like the sound of your voice."

"You do know how to make a girl feel special, don't you?"

"Only when she happens to be."

Hannah leaned across the seat and whispered conspiratorially, "We're flirting again."

"Hold that thought."

They made a right at the ramp where Route 35 meets 37 and crossed tiny Pelican Island before reaching the Mathis Bridge that spans Barnegat Bay. A few miles later, he turned right onto Route 166, at the intersection where the Office Lounge and the Crystal Diner sit diagonally across from each other. Some minutes more, Donald pulled into the Il Giardanello parking lot.

"This doesn't look like a Burger King," Hannah said, sounding pouty.

"Yeah, sorry about that. The place was booked for a private party. Looks like we'll have to make do here."

She sighed. "If we must, we must. But I still want my paper crown."

Inside the restaurant, when Donald took Hannah's coat and scarf, eyes turned. In heels, she stood nearly as tall as he, and her exotic, finely chiseled face drew appreciative stares—in some cases, gawks. She wore a knee-length dress the color of rich burgundy whose cut bespoke modesty while being snug enough to leave a hint of the toned body beneath. Her lipstick and trace of eye shadow complemented her dress. Donald, in his three-piece charcoal suit, almost felt underdressed next to her.

The waiter took their wine order as they studied the menu. When he returned, Hannah ordered the chef's special Rigatoni Amatriciana and Donald chose veal saltimbocca. Then they settled back and sipped their wine. Hannah scanned the room, noticing the Christmas decorations with approval. "This is lovely," she said. "It's not Burger King, but it'll do." The waiter appeared with a tray of breads and overheard. "Private joke," she said, and he replied that he thought he got it.

"Where do we begin?" Hannah asked. "And I'm not talking about the food."

"We can pick up where we left off last night," Donald replied as he tore off a chunk of focaccia and handed it to her. Hannah dipped it into a small dish of olive oil infused with spices. When she placed it in her mouth, Donald noticed a small spot of oil glistening on her lips before she dabbed them with a napkin.

"Donald—I've decided Ducks won't do; that's between you and your friend—I've known you just for fifteen weeks, and then only for two hours twice each week, but in the spirit of full disclosure, I have to admit it's like we've known each other much longer. I hope you understand what I'm saying."

"I do. As for me, I got to know you through your essays. And when you schooled Calvin about race, I wanted to hug you."

"You can make up for that later."

"Promise?"

"Donald, when you taught the class, it seemed that you were speaking directly to me. That's nonsense, of course, but that's what I felt—a real connection. You made me think and rethink my own philosophy, and that made it personal. I hope the others in the class realize the gift they had in you."

"As far as I'm concerned, your being in the class was a gift to me." Hannah lowered her dark eyes and showed the ghost of a smile. "Your essay assignments were what drew me in. You'll remember my comment on your last one before the final."

"Yes. 'Next term you can teach the course.' You really touched me with that." She chuckled. "I don't know about you, but to me it was almost like we were online dating for three months."

"But with boundaries," Donald said, nodding toward her grandmother's ring.

"Boundaries we both grudgingly accepted. Until we realized they didn't exist."

Hannah shed her coyness and became suddenly quiet on the drive back to Point Pleasant—so quiet Donald asked if something was troubling her. She said no, just thinking. He didn't ask what she was thinking; he, meanwhile, harbored thoughts of his own.

They arrived, and Donald walked Hannah to her door. "May I see you again?" he asked.

Hannah remained silent for a moment, her arms huddled against the cold. She seemed to be struggling inwardly as she shivered in the cold air—or could it be something else? Finally, she said, "Donald, would you like to watch the sun rise over the ocean with me... tomorrow?"

They went inside, removed their coats, and hung them in the hall closet. Hannah led him into her living room and turned to face him. She placed her palms against his chest and leaned in for a kiss. It was barely more than a peck.

"You're shaking," Donald said as he touched her cheek. "Is something wrong? Maybe I should go?"

"No, don't go. Please. Bear with me; more than anything I want you to stay. But I don't want you to think I'm being too bold, too... is *unladylike* the word I'm looking for?"

"For me, that would be unthinkable," he said.

She offered a timid smile. "Can we try again?"

They kissed, and this time her lips were soft and welcoming. "Is that better?" she asked, and he kissed her again, gently, sweetly, no insinuation of tongue. She was still on edge, he realized. And he himself was apprehensive too.

She led him to her bedroom on the second floor.

Hannah's king-sized bed stood against an interior wall and faced a sliding glass door to a balcony outside. If the curtain were open, Hannah's first sight upon waking would be the Manasquan Inlet with the Brielle beaches beyond.

Hannah's face paradoxically registered both unease and longing, and Donald cupped her cheeks between his hands and kissed her. "You're trembling like a leaf," he murmured. This was not the flirty woman of yesterday evening and earlier tonight. "Are you sure you want to do this?"

"More than you know," she whispered and kissed him again.

Donald took a step backward and regarded Hannah, beautiful as any model, self-confident in public, suddenly timid in private.

As Hannah watched, Donald slowly removed his wedding ring and set it on her nightstand.

"Can we go slowly?" she asked as he faced her again.

"Hannah, I want this to last all night," he whispered.

Their lovemaking was gentle and unhurried, their bodies forming a leisure rhythm, and eventually they climaxed together, with a sharp intake of breath followed by a gasp from both. Donald remained supported on his elbows as he lowered his face and covered Hannah's with kisses. A tear ran down her cheek, and he kissed that too, tasting its salt.

Finally, Hannah whispered, "You were wonderful."

"I was afraid I might've hurt you. You seemed scared."

"Sometimes, you know, people cry when they're happy."

They formed the classic spoon position as they snuggled under the covers. Donald timed his breathing to match Hannah's and wrapped an arm around her waist. In moments, she took his hand in hers and slid it up to her breast. She sighed, mumbled something he didn't quite hear, and drifted into sleep.

They slept through the sunrise.

Daylight seeped through gaps in the curtains covering the sliding glass doors to Hannah's balcony. She stirred, turned, and looked at Donald, who lay on his side, awake, staring at her.

"It wasn't a dream," she said softly.

"My thoughts exactly."

"Don't move." Hannah slid out from between the covers and walked naked to her ensuite bathroom as Donald admired the fluidity of her form. Moments later, he heard the shower running.

When Hannah opened the door again, she stood there, still nude, regarding him.

"Venus on the half shell," Donald said as he sat up. "Polynesian version."

She frowned and cocked her head.

"The Botticelli Venus, emerging from the sea. You know the painting."

"Yes. But Polynesian?" She climbed into bed and knelt alongside him.

"When I first saw you, I didn't know about your mix of ethnicities. My first impression was that of a Pacific Island Princess. And now that princess has just stepped out of an artist's masterpiece and joined me in her bed."

"Make love to me again?"

"It would be my pleasure."

Afterward, Donald took a shower and gargled mouthwash. When he came out of the bathroom the bed was empty and made. He put on his briefs and trousers, then slipped into his undershirt, leaving the rest of his clothes where they lay. He smelled bacon and coffee as he walked downstairs. Hannah was standing at her stove, her back to him, wearing a white terry robe that barely covered her bottom.

Donald let out the breath he'd been holding and padded up behind her. He nuzzled her neck and slipped a hand inside her robe. Hannah tilted her head back and kissed him. "Don't make me burn the eggs," she said. "Please pour us some coffee and take a seat."

With breakfast done and the table cleared, they brought mugs of coffee into the living room. A decorated artificial tree stood before a sliding glass door that, like the one directly above in her bedroom, opened to a view of the inlet. Hannah turned the tiny white lights on and sat alongside Donald on the sofa. They sipped their coffee, and when they were done placed the mugs on end tables.

"There is something I need to tell you," she said.

Donald took a breath.

Had she read his mind? "No, Donald, not *that* something." She took a throw pillow from one end of the couch, placed it on his lap, and laid her head on it as she stretched out, looking up at him. Her hair spread across the pillow like an ebony halo. Donald stroked her hair with the fingers of one hand. The other rested on the terry cloth robe that threatened to part. He resisted slipping his hand inside, devoting his full attention to her misty black eyes as they stared into his.

"I'm being totally honest, Donald, and I know you'll understand." She took a breath and let it out. "I can't tell you that I love you—you know it's too soon—but I do love what you've done for me."

"I agree with the first part, but I'm afraid I don't understand the second."

"Your lovemaking... is gentle and sweet. There's no sense of urgency with you, no sense of domination. You seem to place my pleasure ahead of your own."

"That's because I'm being selfish, Hannah," he said. To her quizzical stare, he added, "Pleasing you is what pleases me most."

Hannah cast him a soft smile. "My dear Donald," she said. "What I need to tell you is that you have freed me from a trauma that has been crippling me for more than a decade."

Chapter Six

"I never told you about my father. In fact, I've never told anyone about my father—other than my mother."

Hannah sat up on the cushion, tucked her feet beneath her, and turned her body to face Donald.

"You only told me that your father's in jail."

"My father... this is killing me to admit it, so please bear with me, Donald. My father, you see, was... a rapist. He was, in fact, a serial rapist, a predator. And worst of all," she suppressed a shudder, "I was his prey."

Donald drew in a breath. He grasped her hands in his and brought them to his lips.

"I should be grateful he at least waited until I'd reached puberty."

"My God."

"The first time, I was thirteen, and Mom was out that evening showing a house she'd listed. I was doing my homework on the kitchen table. He came up behind me, moved my hair aside, and kissed me on the side of the neck. I thought okay, that was a little weird. Then he stroked the side of my face, as if he were petting a dog. I told him to stop; he was annoying me. Then he put his hands on my shoulders and told me I needed a neck and shoulder massage, get the knots out."

Hannah's eyes seemed to lose focus as she appeared to go from telling the story to reliving it.

"At first, it felt good; I had been under some stress. My mom was a tiger mom, and she demanded that I devote a hundred percent to my studies. So yes, the muscles in my neck and shoulders were stiff. He pressed his thumbs between my shoulder blades, and I told him that it felt good. Which it did."

Her hand gripped Donald's as she continued.

"He moved his paint-splattered hands from the back of my shoulders to the front. He said I was his beautiful baby girl and told me how much he loved me."

Donald said, "You were what, in seventh grade?"

Hannah nodded. "It was late spring, a warm day, and I was wearing shorts and a thin top. Before I knew what he was up to, his hands had slid into my top. I jumped up, and my head banged against his chin. But instead of pulling away, he pressed himself against the back of the chair and began squeezing my breasts until they hurt.

I tried to pull away, told him to stop, but he wouldn't, and I began to cry. This made him angry, and he ran one hand into my shorts. With the other hand, he gripped my face and pressed his thumb and fingers against my cheeks, making me pucker. He kissed me, and his breath smelled of cigarettes and beer. He shoved his tongue into my mouth. If I hadn't been so scared, I would've bitten it as hard as I could. He kicked away the chair and turned me around and told me to stand up and lean over the table. He forced me to brace myself on my hands and yanked my shorts and panties down. I heard the sound of a zipper, and then there was this horrible pain. He kept thrusting in and out, in and out, and I could feel blood run down the inside of my thighs."

With pain manifest on her face, Hannah continued, "He groaned as he came inside me. When he turned me around again, his face was like some vicious animal. He told me I'd better not tell my mother; if I did, he'd make me suffer. And then he'd make her suffer. Then he wrapped his big hands around my throat and squeezed until my eyes nearly bugged out. He let go and asked if I understood him. I whimpered yes."

Hannah paused, her eyes telling Donald she was back with him instead of bent over the kitchen table years ago.

"You said he didn't stop after the first time."

"It happened again and again. It was as if he was getting back at Mom too, because she was an excellent realtor and her commissions made his salary look like pocket change. That struck at his masculinity, and he couldn't stand it."

"You said he was abusive to your mother as well."

"But not sexually; that he reserved for his *beautiful baby girl.* And he began drinking heavily. When Mom finally left him, I left with her. I was almost fifteen, just out of eighth grade and ready for high school. She found a place for the two of us in Point Pleasant and filed for divorce. He wouldn't leave her alone; she got a restraining order against him, but he kept coming, stalking us. One night while we were asleep, he spray-painted *Bitch* in red letters on the side of her car. Needless to say, after the divorce Mom took her maiden name back, and I changed mine legally to hers."

"And you hadn't told her what he'd done to you?"

"I was too frightened. I was ashamed. I know, I know, I was never the one at fault; I mean, but having it out there that I gave in to being raped by my own father."

"Don't tell me she still doesn't know."

"I did finally tell my mother, but only after he was sent to prison. Understand, honor means everything to her, and if she had killed him after I told her—and I truly believe she would have—then she would have ended up in prison instead."

"And when you did tell her?"

"Her legs almost gave way, and I had to hold her up. Then she—do you know any Korean curse words?" He said no. "Well, she shouted them all, every single one. Over and over. I confessed that I had been too ashamed to tell her, and she held me tight and crooned to me like I was a baby again. We cried into the night. Next morning our eyes were bloodshot, and we spent the morning commiserating. Mom told me if she'd known, had even suspected, she would have slit my father's throat without thinking twice about it. She said no jury in the world would ever convict her. But of course, then my secret would have been a matter of public record. My mother's pain was as profound as my own. And the thought of having sex again? Frankly, it scared me. That's why I trembled in your arms, fighting my fear of intimacy but wanting you at the same time."

"I am so sorry, Hannah; I can't imagine."

"No, I don't think anyone can. But the only time, in all those years since, that I ever wanted a real relationship, was—no, is—with you. I'll admit I was frightened. Me, the independent, self-assured attorney, was afraid of opening herself up to a man." She grimaced. "Not the best choice of words there, right?"

"Hannah," he said and drew her lips to his. They were soft and yielding, and when he released her, he found more moisture to kiss away.

She noticed Donald glance at her gaily decorated artificial tree, and she reached up to draw his face back to hers. "No, Donald; just no."

"What do you mean?"

"You will not buy me a Christmas present; don't even think about it."

She'd read his mind. "I understand. It's too soon."

"Maybe next year, yes; but not this one."

"I like the sound of next year."

"As do I. But here's what you can do for me now."

"Whatever you want."

"What do you normally do for Christmas? Do you fly to South Carolina to visit your parents?"

"No, because they spend the holidays in Ixtapa. They love Mexico; I don't. I see them after the spring session ends, and they come to visit me before the fall term."

"Do you spend Christmas Day with your friend Popeye?"

"No, Popeye usually spends Christmas with his mother. She's in a round-the-clock nursing facility, Alzheimer's; his father's dead."

"So sad. Does she still recognize her son?"

"Not always. But she does love it when he brings her goodies."

"A bitter-sweet time for him, yes?"

"Yes, literally."

"He sounds like a good son."

"As for me, what I normally do is go to church that morning and treat myself to a dinner of roast chicken and stuffing." Hannah raised her eyebrows. "Don't look surprised; I can cook when I want to. And the leftovers last me for a couple of meals later in the week. Then I might watch a movie or read a book."

"I'm sorry, Donald, but aside from church, your day sounds pretty depressing."

He nodded. "I guess it does."

"Well, here's the favor I'd like to ask. Would you consider joining my mother and me for Christmas Eve services at our church?"

Donald blinked. "Hannah, I'd be—yes, of course."

She touched the side of his face. "I wouldn't ask you to give up going to your church on Christmas Day, so if you'd rather go home after the service, I'll understand."

He brought her hand to his lips and kissed her fingers. "I would love to stay here with you. There's only one reason I've continued attending that particular church, but for now at least I'd like to attend yours, with you and your mother."

"Are you going to tell me what that reason is, Donald?"

"That and more, that and more. You've shared your deepest secret with me. I'm ready to share mine with you."

Chapter Seven

They returned to the kitchen and Hannah made a fresh pot of coffee. When it was done, she set out small plates. Donald asked what they were for.

"For *yakgwa*," she said as she took a covered plastic bowl from her pantry. She placed on his plate a confection that looked like a little flower.

"Do I eat it, or do I frame it?" he asked. "It looks like a work of art."

Hannah smiled. "It's a honey and ginger cookie, deep fried, very chewy. Its name means sweet medicine."

"Did you make these yourself?"

"Don't make me feel guilty. My mother makes them for special occasions. Very time consuming."

Donald took a tentative bite and shook his head. "This is very nice."

"We sometimes eat them for dessert. Or with tea as a bedtime snack."

Donald took another bite and said, "I think I might want to marry your mother."

They laughed together, and then Hannah grew serious. "You said you have something you want to share with me, Donald. About your church."

"I do. I still attend only because that's where Staci and our parents worshiped together every Sunday."

Donald found it difficult to relate the details of the crash that took Staci's life.

"Next thing I knew, I was in the hospital in a lower body cast, and Staci was gone. My parents, and Frank of course, were with me every day. They tried their best to console me, but I was beyond consolation."

"Of course. And Staci's parents?"

"They buried her while I was still in the hospital. After the funeral, they put their home up for sale and left Toms River for parts unknown. We never saw the Rousseaus again, never heard from them."

"To lose a child. That's heartbreaking."

"When Frank and I were alone in my hospital room, I told him I wished it had been me who was killed; told him I wanted to die. But not before I killed the bastard who'd run the light and rammed us. Frank told me that the guy was, his words, shit-faced drunk at the accident scene and showed no remorse."

"Oh, Donald."

"I missed the trial, but I did see the guy's mug shot in the paper, and I'll never forget that face. I swore that if I ever saw him again, I'd kill him on the spot and let a jury decide if I was justified. Here's another thing that makes me want to scream sometimes. You know as well as I that a sentence for vehicular manslaughter, even with a DUI attached, runs only about five years. He'd be out of prison by now, but as it happens, when he ran into us, he was fleeing a murder scene. He'd invaded an elderly lady's home when he thought she was out. She wasn't. When she picked up the phone, evidently to call 911, he bludgeoned her with a table lamp. When he realized what he'd done, he downed half a bottle from her liquor cabinet before making off. He came to court with two manslaughter charges, one while committing a felony. That got him twenty years more."

Hannah stiffened briefly, and he asked if something were wrong.

"No; sorry. You told me how you remained faithful to Staci throughout your time in the Marines. Would that make me the second woman you've made love to in what, a decade or more?"

Donald nodded. "Popeye told me to stop obsessing over Staci. I was living with a ghost. Her memory was turning me into damaged goods, and there's no way she would've wanted that for me. I knew he was right, but casual dates, casual sex, they just weren't for me. I will tell you, Hannah, that last night was the first time I took off my ring. I intend to leave it off. And here we are. Here we are."

Hannah stood and walked around the table. She straddled his lap, let her robe fall open, and held his head to her breast. Neither spoke, but she could feel his warm breath against her skin. She held on to him for a long time.

Hannah had asked Donald to meet her mother and her at her town house at ten. The communion service, at St. Mary's by the Sea Episcopal Church in Point Pleasant, would begin at eleven and end at midnight. Then they could return to her condo for tea and more of her mother's homemade *yakgwa*. And on Christmas Day, she suggested, they might share the sunrise over the ocean.

Donald packed an overnight bag with a change of clothes and toiletries, which he would leave in his car until Hannah's mother had gone home. How much she knew about her daughter's relationship with him he didn't know, so he determined to practice discretion.

The New Jersey Shore seldom saw a white Christmas, and this year was no exception. The thermometer hovered in the mid-forties and the sky was gray following a powerful rainfall earlier that Christmas Eve. Donald dressed in his best suit and climbed into his car at nine. From the condo he drove east on Bay Avenue a half mile to Hooper, where he turned right to intersect Route 37 and then left, onto the direct link to the shore communities. Once over the bridge and on the strip, he planned to take the nearly deserted Route 35 north to Point.

Traffic was almost non-existent along 37. The car dealerships that lined the road were dark, as were all the other businesses he passed. Donald approached the traffic light at Fischer Boulevard, the last major light before the bridge that crossed the bay. The light was green, and there was no other cross traffic. When he was some thirty feet from the intersection, the green light turned amber. Donald's speed, just five miles over the limit, precluded hitting the brakes and perhaps inducing a skid on the wet pavement. The light was still amber when he crossed the intersection.

Before he reached the bridge, he saw flashing blue lights in his rear-view mirror. It was obviously an emergency vehicle, Donald thought, and he pulled over to the shoulder to allow it to pass. To his shock, the police car stopped behind him, lights ablaze.

This can't be happening, Donald thought. He reached into the glove box to take out his registration and insurance card, pulled his license from his wallet, and placed his hands on top of the steering wheel to wait for the officer's approach. In the rear-view mirror he saw the door open and the policeman approach. Seconds later he heard a tap on his window, and Donald lowered the glass.

"Well, what have we here?" crowed a familiar voice.

Donald turned his head and recognized him. Brian Snowden. The cop he'd kicked out of class in September.

"License, registration, insurance," Brian said curtly, and Donald silently handed them over. He took them back to his cruiser. Donald could see him work the computer under the dome light. Then he returned and tossed them through Donald's open window. They landed on the floor.

"Know why I stopped you, *Doctor* Greene?" he said, his face a sneer and his voice dripping scorn. Donald shook his head. "You ran a red light back there."

"Sorry, but that's not true. The light had just turned yellow, and I didn't have room to stop without entering the intersection."

"That's not what I saw. Now I need you to get out of the car."

Donald sighed and opened the door.

"I need you to walk a straight line for me."

"I haven't been drinking."

"Are you refusing to comply with a police officer's legal order?"

Donald stood on the white line that separated the highway from the shoulder. He took ten paces forward and ten back.

"You were walking erratically," Brian said.

"Excuse me?"

"You didn't walk straight; you wobbled."

"I've got a game leg, in case you haven't noticed. Plus, there was a puddle in front of me. I wasn't going to step in it."

"Oh, you stepped in it, Doc; you stepped in it big time."

"What are you going to do, Brian? Let's just get it over with; I'm on my way to Christmas Eve services."

"Oh, heading for church, is it? I question that. Way I see it, you're resisting an officer of the law in the performance of his duties."

"What!"

"You're going to leave your car on the shoulder, blinkers on. Then you're getting into mine. Back seat."

Donald couldn't hide behind propriety any longer. "You are such a *fucking idiot*, Brian Snowden! Just give me a ticket and I'll be on my way. And be assured, I'll fight it."

"Well, now I can add verbally assaulting an officer and resisting arrest to your charges. Don't make me draw down on you, Doc. You know, the way you hinted I wanted to do in class that time?"

Donald had no choice but to comply. He put his blinkers on, locked the car, and climbed into the back of the cruiser. Brian sat behind the wheel, cocking his head from side to side like a bantam rooster. "So, Doc, like one of those spooks in your class might say, when you fuck wid de whale's tail, you is apt to get slapped."

"Very clever. Racist, too. Young Calvin might want to have a word or two with you on that."

"Racist? Yeah, try to prove that when you get to court. I was polite and professional. You couldn't walk a straight line, you verbally assaulted an officer, and you resisted arrest. All that in addition to running a red light. Maybe I'll throw in reckless driving. Yeah. I'll write that I saw you weaving on the road, which made me suspect DUI. Uh... huh. Yeah, you're fucked, Doc. Merry fucking Christmas and have a shitty New Year. In fucking jail."

Donald was booked on Brian Snowden's charges. He told the desk officer he would post his own bond, but naturally, court was closed. Not only was it after hours on Saturday, and with tomorrow being Christmas, no way would Donald be able to post bond until Monday at the earliest. He was told to surrender his belongings, but before he did, he insisted upon his phone call.

In Point Pleasant, Hannah was growing worried. It was nearly time to leave for service, and Donald had yet to show up. Her mother admonished her to stop pacing and fidgeting. If he didn't come in the next ten minutes, they'd leave for church without him. If he did arrive late, he could join them at the church. Silently, she questioned her daughter's faith in a man who would break a commitment without so much as a phone call.

Hannah's phone rang.

When she disconnected, she turned to her mother with a look of disbelief. "Donald's in jail," she said.

Chapter Eight

Donald was arraigned on Monday, pled not guilty, posted bond, and got a trial date. Next, Hannah drove him to the impound lot, where he paid the ransom for his car. Then he followed her to her condo, where she prepared him lunch. He looked sheepish as he asked what her mother thought about her boyfriend's being a jailbird.

"I told her about how Brian retaliated for your kicking him out of class. She sympathized with you and hoped to meet you in pleasanter surroundings."

They finished lunch—cold poached salmon atop Caesar salad—and over tea Hannah asked Donald for all the details of what she liked to call the Christmas Eve Massacre. "Give me even the minutest details."

"Really?"

"Donald, when you appear before the judge opposite Brian Snowden, it's going to be his word against yours. And who do you think the judge will believe?"

"I figured that out already."

"And that's why I'm going to represent you."

Judge Albert Novins was sixtyish, with a full head of gray hair and steel blue eyes. He directed everyone to be seated and called the first case. Donald and Hannah crossed the bar and sat at one table while Brian Snowden, in uniform alongside his union-appointed attorney, sat at the other. The court reporter poised her fingers over the stenotype machine, ready to record the proceedings.

Hannah wore a navy pantsuit with a white blouse and red-and-white-patterned silk bow, and Donald wore his charcoal suit, without the vest. Brian wore a sharply creased uniform, his attorney a pin-striped dark blue suit. Hannah wondered what Donald would have looked like, by comparison, in his Marine Corps officer's dress blues. She was sure they would still fit him. He'd told her he couldn't wear the uniform on non-military business, but if she got the charges dropped, he'd give her a private showing later. She told him that now she was really motivated.

The judge glanced at the charge sheet before him, then looked down at Donald. "According to Officer Snowden's report, Mr. Greene, you were driving erratically and ran a red light, which gave him cause to assume you were driving while impaired. When he stopped you, he writes you couldn't walk a straight line. He confronted you with his suspicions, and you verbally assaulted him. He also says you resisted arrest. If his charges prove accurate, well, let me read you from the statutes. These are the maximum penalties, mind you."

Donald took a deep breath but kept his expression blank as the judge held up a paper.

"Resisting arrest, six months in jail and a thousand dollar fine; driving while impaired, thirty days in jail, five hundred dollars fine; reckless driving, sixty days in jail, two hundred dollars fine, and five points against your driver's license; running a red light, fifteen days in jail, two hundred dollars fine, and two more points; finally, assaulting an officer, eighteen months in prison and ten thousand dollars fine. If my math is correct, the maximum monetary penalties alone could exceed eleven thousand dollars. I'd say that's pretty serious. You've pled not guilty, so let's begin."

The four parties stood. "Stanley Wasielewski, representing Officer Brian Snowden, your honor."

"Hannah Soong, representing Dr. Donald Greene, your honor."

"Do either of you have opening statements?"

"Your honor, you've read the charges, and Officer Snowden stands by them."

"Very well. Ms. Soong?"

"Your honor, Dr. Greene is prepared to testify that Officer Snowden's charges are the result of a personal vendetta."

There was brief murmuring in the courtroom as Judge Novins raised his eyebrows and said, "Well. This could get interesting. Can you enlighten me, counselor?"

Hannah said, "In the interest of full disclosure, your honor, Dr. Greene teaches at Ocean County College, and I audited one of his evening classes last September. Officer Snowden was a fellow classmate during part of that term—until Dr. Greene expelled him."

"Hm. What do you teach, Dr. Greene?" the judge interrupted.

"American History, your honor."

The judge nodded and nodded for Hannah to continue. "At the first class meeting, Dr. Greene admonished the students to silence their cell phones during class. This is college policy. Officer Snowden refused, and after numerous class interruptions, Dr. Greene dismissed him from the class. Words were exchanged, and Officer Snowden threatened Dr. Greene as he walked out of the room. I have a witness from the class who can verify what I've just told you."

"Is he here? Have him stand up and introduce himself."

Hannah and Donald turned their heads, and he was shocked to see who it was smiling at him.

"Perry White, your honor."

"Perry White?" Judge Novins chuckled. "Great Caesar's ghost!"

Perry laughed. "Do you get that a lot, Mr. White?"

"Not much anymore, your honor. Nobody reads the Superman comics these days. But Dr. Greene said the same thing in class the first night."

"He did, did he? And what do you do for a living, Mr. White?"

"My wife and I run a souvenir shop on the boardwalk. Tee-shirts, caps, beach wear."

"What do you and your wife do off season, when most of the businesses are closed?"

"We have a condominium on Sanibel Island in Florida, your honor. We were going to begin our drive south when I got Ms. Soong's phone call."

"And you delayed your vacation to serve the interests of truth, justice, and the American way?"

Perry nodded and chuckled along with the judge.

"And you can testify that you heard Officer Snowden threaten the teacher on his way out of the room?"

"Yes, sir."

"Objection," said Wasielewski. "Dr. Greene's attorney never notified us she had a witness. And he hasn't been sworn in."

Hannah said, "As Mr. White mentioned, your honor, he told me during a classroom break last fall of his plans to head for Florida after the Christmas and New Year holidays. Frankly, I'd expected him to be long gone by now, New Jersey winters being what they are. I knew it was a long shot when I called, and I'm grateful that he was able to postpone his plans to support Dr. Greene."

"Objection overruled. It might not even be necessary to call Mr. White to the stand."

Perry nodded and took his seat.

"So, Ms. Soong, just so I get this straight, your position is that because Dr. Greene kicked Officer Snowden out of class, he took revenge by stalking him and later lying in wait to trap him? That's a very tall order."

"Yes, it is, your honor; but we believe we can prove it."

Brian Snowden took the stand and under his representative's coaching painted a picture of what happened on Christmas Eve. He spoke every word with conviction and authority. Then it was Hannah's turn to cross.

"You look very snappy in your uniform today, Officer Snowden," she began. He attempted a humble face and thanked her. "Now, I'm curious. You wore your uniform every night you were in class, is that correct?" He nodded. "Were you on duty those nights?"

He frowned. "No, of course not."

"Then can you tell the court why you came to class armed and in uniform?"

"Objection!"

"Overruled. Answer the question, officer."

"My shift ended, and I didn't have time to change."

Hannah asked, "What time did your shift end?" He said nothing. "Officer Snowden?"

"Five o'clock."

"Do you have a locker at the police station? Where you keep your civilian clothes?"

"I do."

"Objection. Where is this going?"

"Yes. Where is this going, Ms. Soong?" asked the judge.

"Your honor, Dr. Greene's class did not begin until six, and the college is only a couple of miles from police headquarters on Oak Avenue. Which means Officer Snowden had a full hour to change into civvies before reporting to class. But he didn't. I'd like to know why."

"Again, objection. What does what he was wearing have to do with anything?"

"I submit, your honor, that Officer Snowden wanted people to see him in his uniform. This might have been to assert authority. Or perhaps attract a female student or two." Wasielewski jumped to his feet. "Now before counsel objects again, I ask that the court disregard that speculation. I do, however, have another question for the officer that is relevant." She turned to Brian. "When Dr. Greene expelled you from class, did your fingers move toward your weapon? To me, it looked like they were twitching."

"That doesn't mean anything. I was angry, is all."

"And you followed that with the statement... let me be sure I remember correctly, because as you know I was there. Yes. You told Dr. Greene to watch his back, and then you said, 'Your ass is grass, and I'm the lawn mower.' Does that sound familiar?"

Brian sat and stewed. His face turned red.

"If anyone threatened anyone, your honor, I believe it was Officer Snowden."

The judge looked out at the spectators. "Mr. White. Is that how you remember the exchange?"

Perry stood. "Word for word, your honor."

"Thank you. Do you have any further questions, counsel?"

"No sir."

"Then we'll take ten, and when we come back, I'll hear Dr. Greene's side of the story."

When Judge Novins left the room, Donald leaned over the bar to address Perry White. "Perry, thanks so much."

"Hell, Doc, it's my pleasure."

"And you actually delayed your trip to testify for me?"

Hannah held up her hand. "A question best left unanswered. But thanks again, Perry."

The judge entered the room, called order, and focused his attention on Hannah. "Ms. Soong? Your turn."

"Thank you, your honor. I call Dr. Donald Greene."

Donald stood, was sworn in, and took the stand. He took a deep breath and let it out slowly. He looked at the spectators and noticed Frank among them, sitting in the back row. He must have taken a personal day from school to attend, thought Donald. He gave a nod, as if to say, Thanks, Pops, and Frank smiled back.

Hannah said, "Dr. Greene, I notice you carry a limp. Is that from an injury you suffered in combat?"

"No. It's from an automobile accident after my discharge."

"From the Marines?"

"That's correct."

"But you did see combat."

"I did. I was a platoon commander in Iraq."

Brian's counsel objected on grounds of relevance. The judge frowned a warning at Hannah.

"Your honor, Officer Snowden in his report testified that Dr. Greene had trouble walking a straight line. The line, he said, was the painted white stripe that separates the highway from the shoulder. We submit that a man walking with a limp could be mistaken for someone under the influence of alcohol."

"Overruled."

Brian Snowden scowled and thumped his fingers on the table. His attorney placed his own hand over Snowden's to make him stop.

"Dr. Greene, was there anything else that might have caused Officer Snowden to suspect you'd been drinking?"

Donald nodded. "I had to step to one side of the line to avoid a puddle. It had been raining that day."

"Tell the court about your difference of opinion from Officer Snowden's as to your alleged running of a red light."

He explained that the light turned amber when he was less than thirty feet from it; further, that there was no cross traffic waiting for the light. The road was wet, and applying the brakes, in his judgment, could have precipitated a skid. But even with sudden braking, he would have crossed the intersection before the light turned red.

"What did you do when the officer pulled you over?"

"I parked on the shoulder and placed my hands on the top of the steering wheel. When he asked for my license and registration, I handed both over along with my insurance card and he took them to his cruiser."

"Was everything in order?"

"Yes, it was."

"Then what happened?"

"He returned to the car, threw my credentials on the floor, and told me I had run the light; I told him I hadn't. Then he told me to exit the vehicle, walk a straight line..."

"Did he ask you to take a Breathalyzer test?"

"No."

Hannah frowned. "I would assume, if the officer thought you were DUI, he would ask you to take a Breathalyzer. All right; then what?"

"He grew argumentative. I suspected he was getting even for my expelling him from class."

"Objection. Calls for a conclusion."

"Sustained."

"Let me put it another way. What made you think he was getting even rather than simply performing his duties as an officer of the law?"

"He changed his voice to that of a Southern black man and said, I'm quoting now, 'Like one of the spooks in your class might say, when you fuck wid de whale's tail, you is apt to get slapped.'"

Murmurs rose, and the judge gaveled the room to order. He addressed Donald directly.

"Now, Dr. Greene, surely you don't expect the court to believe that Officer Snowden was stalking you, lying in wait to the detriment of his other duties. Do you?"

"No, your honor. I believe he happened to see my car and saw an opportunity."

"And how would he know your car from any other vehicle on the road?"

"Because it's the only 1965 Mercury registered in the state."

Hannah produced three photographs. She handed one to the judge and the other to opposing counsel. "This is Dr. Greene's car, your honor. Easily recognizable, and the fact that it's white would make it very visible on a dark night."

Judge Novins studied the photo. "She's a beauty. But," he added, "how would Officer Snowden know it was Dr. Greene's car when he stopped him?"

At that moment the door to the courtroom opened and a young woman with a shock of flaming red hair rushed in holding three sheets of paper. She glanced at Donald but quickly averted her eyes to fix them on Hannah.

It was Emily O'Neil, his former student and now Hannah's paralegal.

"Thank you, Emily," Hannah said. "You arrived in the nick of time." Emily handed the papers to Hannah and took a seat in the gallery. She sat alongside Frank, even though there were other seats available.

"What's this?" said Brian's attorney. "You can't present evidence without showing it to us first."

"As you can see, your honor," said Hannah innocently, "my associate just brought that evidence to me. I'd like to enter it." She handed a copy to the judge and another to Attorney Wasielewski. "It is a transcript from the Division of Motor Vehicles call log. It shows that Officer Snowden phoned the DMV shortly after he was expelled from class to ask for the plate number of the car that was registered to Donald Greene. He was also given the make and model of the vehicle. I submit that when he saw Dr. Greene's car on Christmas Eve it presented an opportunity he couldn't resist."

The judge studied the transcript, reading every word. He looked sharply at the prosecution table. "Do you have anything to contribute, Mr. Wasielewski? Officer Snowden?"

Brian's face was the color of rust. He had been holding a pencil above a legal pad. It snapped in his hand. His lawyer looked at him with disgust, shook his head, and said, "We have no comment, your honor."

"One more question, your honor, if I may." The judge nodded. "Dr. Greene, when you were arrested, did Officer Snowden Mirandize you?"

"He did not."

Judge Novins sat back in his chair, startled, as at the same time Brian Snowden began gnashing his teeth and the spectators in the gallery began talking among themselves.

He banged his gavel and called the court to order. When the gallery had settled, he turned his attention to the union's lawyer.

"Mr. Wasielewski, you've done your duty in representing Officer Snowden, who I believe might have been withholding relevant information from you. As for your client himself, I believe his behavior is a matter for IAD, don't you? Never mind answering; it's rhetorical. I'll contact Internal Affairs personally tomorrow. Dr. Greene, thank you for your service to the country. You may step down. Case dismissed."

He banged the gavel again.

Donald shook Hannah's hand formally; then they walked out of the room, trailed by Perry White, Emily O'Neil, and Frank Populski. Spectators on the aisle extended their hands as he passed for high fives. He never looked back at Brian Snowden.

Chapter Nine

On the courthouse steps, Hannah ordered them all to convene at her townhome, where her mother had prepared a victory party. Donald asked what if they'd lost, and Hannah told him then they'd have a pity party. Probably without him, as he'd be remanded into custody.

"Thanks for that," Donald said.

Perry White offered his apologies. "Sorry, folks, but our daughter will be going into labor any time now. It's her first. We—all right, mostly my wife, will help her out for the first few weeks. Then we'll head to Sanibel."

Donald frowned. "You're saying you weren't going to leave today?"

Hannah winked at him. "A question best unanswered."

Hannah gave Perry a hug and thanked him for his support. Donald hugged him as well and congratulated him on becoming a grandfather.

Frank meanwhile placed his hand behind Emily's back and guided her to his CR-V. "You two lead in Moby Duck, and Emily and I will trail you."

Hannah slid into Donald's Merc and strapped in. "Home, James," she directed.

"Am I imagining things, or are Frank and Emily in a relationship?" he asked as he merged into the Washington Street traffic bound for Route 37.

"Surprise," she said, with a pixie-like smile. "They can tell you all about it later."

Hannah instructed Donald to walk into the condo ahead of her. When he did, he was greeted by a miniature Hannah. That was his first impression. Her skin was lighter, her hair showed touches of gray, and she stood a full head shorter than her daughter. But in other respects, she was a preview of what Hannah would become. Donald thought her beautiful.

She took his hands in both of hers, smiled broadly, and said, "So you're the convict who's been dating my daughter. Come here!" And she hugged him, standing on tiptoes to kiss his cheeks. "You call me Daisy."

From behind him, he heard a familiar voice: "Daisy and Donald, straight out of the comics."

Hannah introduced Frank to her mother, who said it was nice to finally meet Emily's beau.

Emily's beau? thought Donald.

Daisy Soong told them to hang their coats in the closet and join her in the dining room, where she had a table set up for lunch.

Donald turned to Hannah, standing behind him, and kissed her. "I don't know what to say," was what he said. Then he looked askance at Frank. "Popeye, is there something you're not telling me?"

Emily returned from the hall closet and greeted Donald with a hug before wrapping her arm around Frank's waist. "Questions, Doc?" she said with a flirty smile. "Nice to see you again, by the way. I really loved your class."

"Thanks. For that, and for steering Hannah to me."

"Just call me Yenta." She looked at Frank and winked. "And before you figure it out, yes, I'm the naïve young student he seduced back when I was playing Lola in *Damn Yankees.*"

"Excuse me," interrupted Frank. "Who seduced whom?"

Emily affected an impish grin and said, "Whatever Lola wants, Lola gets."

"Get in here," came Daisy's voice from the dining room. "You can talk around the table."

After an abundant lunch prepared by Daisy, they pushed their chairs back from the table to make room for their bellies. Both bottles of champagne stood empty.

Emily said, "Doc, to answer your as yet unasked question, after Hannah and I left the big city to return to God's country, and after I convinced her to enroll in your class, I decided to look up my old drama coach and see if the flame still burned."

"And lo and behold, it does," Frank said, "brighter than ever."

"Hotter, too," she added.

"And I've convinced Emily to be my stage manager for *Pippin* in the spring production. Normally, I'd assign a student, but Emily has the experience, she loves the play as much as I do, and the kids will see her as a veteran trouper rather than one of their peers. In other words, they'll snap to when she gives an order."

Donald nodded and said, "Emily, I have another unasked question."

"Uh-oh; here it comes."

"Did you really come into the courtroom just in the nick of time with that call log? Those things just seem to happen in TV shows."

She and Hannah exchanged smiles. "You want to tell him, or should I? I'd suggest you."

"All right," Hannah said. "We had that information all along. I already had a text prepared on my phone. It read *Now*. When it was time for Emily to barge into the courtroom, I clicked Send. She was waiting outside the door and barged in. It was our modest attempt at creating a little drama."

He chuckled. "Okay. But I'm puzzled. If you already had the information, why didn't you hand it to the other attorney beforehand? He would've seen Snowden's duplicity and at the least advised him not to go to trial."

"But where's the drama in that? I wanted to humiliate Brian Snowden publicly for what he did to you."

"And he made you miss Christmas Eve service with us too," said Daisy. "Good riddance to him."

"Tell me, Daisy, is that your Americanized name, like Hannah is hers?" asked Donald.

"Yes. I was born *Deiji*, which translates from Korean as Daisy. My father was an Air Force colonel stationed in Osan. He liked to complain that he used to fly fighter planes, but now the Air Force in its wisdom—or lack of it—consigned him to flying a desk. My mother was his native interpreter. After a year's professional relationship, theirs became personal. They married and a year later I came along. A year after that, he was reassigned to McGuire Air Force Base here in New Jersey. He would introduce my mother to his friends as his Korean War bride. She would retaliate by calling him headlight eyes."

He chuckled. "But your mother kept her maiden name?"

"He insisted. And yes, he was ahead of his time. When I was a girl, my name was *Deiji* Soong-Porter. Later, when they enrolled me in school, I became Daisy Soong. Much more convenient."

"And the ring Hannah wears, that was your mother's?"

Daisy nodded. "Yes. And she'll wear it until some handsome young man replaces it with another."

"Mother," warned Hannah. Daisy only chuckled and opened a new bottle of champagne.

"What about her paternal grandparents?" asked Donald.

Daisy's smile vanished. "Pan Am 103, Lockerbie, Scotland."

"My God." Then, "Are your own parents still with us?" Daisy shook her head once, dismissing further inquiry.

Changing the subject, Frank said, "You know, Hannah, Ducks here once told me you reminded him of a *wahine* from the South Seas."

"He mentioned that, yes."

"You do know what a *wahine* is, right?"

"Of course. It's—"

"It's something you eat on a bu-*hun* with mu-*hustard.*"

Emily said, "Check, please," and they laughed.

Afterward, Frank said, "Ducks, let's let the ladies think we're sensitive, twenty-first-century men and do mess duty while they relax in the living room." Donald agreed, and they turned to, ignoring the faux objections of the ladies.

As they were loading the dishwasher, Frank said, "So, Ducks, is it serious? Has old Popeye finally convinced you to shed the doom and gloom persona? I hope so, because Hannah is one hot lady."

"It's not obvious? And how about you and Emily? I never even got a hint that she was the one."

"No one knew. We were utterly discreet."

"Again, to your credit; plural. So where is this going, do you think?"

"I think I've shed my wanderlust, Ducks. You may stick a fork in me, because I'm done."

Later, Frank and Emily left together arm in arm, and Daisy said goodnight soon after. She kissed Donald's cheek and held both his hands, her smile bright as the white lights on the Christmas tree that Hannah had left on for today.

"You be good to my daughter now," she said as she put on her coat and made for the door. Donald assured her he would, wondering if there might be a threat behind that sweet smile.

Hannah and Donald cuddled on the sofa, decompressing after the long day, her head resting on his shoulder.

"Thank you again," he murmured into her hair.

"I did it because I was being selfish, Donald, like you."

"Hmm?"

"Making you happy makes me happy."

"Touché."

"And I plan to do something else selfish, if you feel you're up for it."

"As Frank would say, *up* for it?"

"You get the picture."

"I know you represented me today pro bono. But may I now put you on permanent retainer?"

"Let's discuss that upstairs, shall we?"

"Um, right now? Because there's a garment bag in the car that happens to have my dress blues inside."

Hannah smiled broadly as she drew in a breath. "Yes, you promised, didn't you? And you know what women say: there's something sexy about a man in uniform."

Long as it's not Brian Snowden, Donald thought as he walked to his car.

Chapter Ten

The new teaching term began a week after the trial. Emily moved from her parents' home to Frank's, and after her workday ended on Tuesdays through Thursdays, she would join him in rehearsals. As he'd predicted, his cast and crew immediately looked up to her as a veteran performer. Etta Pourmel, whom he'd hired to teach them the distinctive Bob Fosse choreography, sparked an esprit-de-corps that would last them through the season and beyond.

During the week, Donald lived in his Bey Lea Brook townhome, where he devoted five days and nights to his classes at the college. Weekends he would spend with Hannah, and on Sundays he'd attend church with her and her mother.

In mid-February, the men decided that after due consideration, the time was finally right. They told their ladies, with tongues firmly in cheek, that on Saturday night they were going to take them to dinner at their exclusive, boys only, man cave—namely, the Office Lounge.

"I guess we've officially arrived," joked Emily, and Hannah pretended to swoon with glee.

The Lounge was busy as usual on Saturday, but when Cindy learned that her two favorite regulars had given up last night in favor of a booth for four tonight—four—she made sure it was ready for them when they walked in. She eyed the two women, the smashing redhead and the exotic brunette, and nodded her silent approval. Now, if the boys decided on proper dinners instead of Don's usual heart attack on a bun and Frank's halitosis-inducing liver and onions, she'd know things were serious. And, she concluded, it was about time.

"Greetings, ladies and gentlemen," Cindy said as she gestured grandly toward their waiting booth. "Your accommodations await."

"Hey," said Frank. "How come you're being so polite all of a sudden?"

Cindy dropped the pretense and lapsed into her casual banter. "Well, it's not for you guys, that's for sure. Welcome to the Office, ladies. My name's Cindy, I'll be your server, and seeing as who you're with, you have my condolences."

The women laughed and introduced themselves, extending their arms to shake hands. "I like you already," said Emily, and Frank cautioned her not to give Cindy a swelled head; it would ruin their years of hard work.

They settled in and ordered martinis to start. Cindy smirked and said, "That's a new one. You guys trying to impress your so-far-out-of-your-league dates?"

"You trying to talk yourself out of a tip tonight?" teased Frank.

Cindy looked suddenly remorseful. "Oh, gee, guys, never. Last tip you gave me, I went out next day and put a down payment on a Rolls."

"You're dead to me," Frank said as everyone laughed and Cindy walked to the bar to place their order.

"We love her," said Donald, and Frank told him not too loud, she might hear you.

Before long, Cindy returned with their drinks and said she'd be back in a few minutes to take their orders.

The four toasted their good fortune, clinked their glasses, and sipped their martinis. Hannah and Emily smiled their approval; Donald and Frank had to struggle to keep the first swallow down.

"Very dry," quipped Emily as she noticed the men's reactions.

"Isn't there supposed to be, what, vermouth in this?" asked Donald.

Hannah said, "The best martinis have the word *vermouth* whispered over the glass."

"Straight gin," Frank observed, sitting back in his seat and sliding his glass over to Emily. Donald did the same to Hannah.

"I think they're trying to get us drunk," said Hannah.

"Whatever could they have in mind?" replied Emily.

Donald said, "Um, ladies, maybe we should look at the menus for when Cindy comes back?"

They turned their attention to the bill of fare, and when they were ready to order Cindy appeared as if by magic—with two beers in her hand. She placed them in front of the men without comment. "Chef's special tonight is liver and onions," chortled Cindy. As Frank opened his mouth, she said, "Kidding. That's just Frank's standing order, ladies."

Emily cast a reproachful look in his direction. "He'd better not order it tonight."

The women ordered cedar-planked salmon, and the men blackened mako shark. "Really?" asked Emily. "Jaws?"

Donald said, "It's coated with Cajun-style blackening spices and fried in butter in a cast iron pan. When you first taste it, you'll think you're eating steak. Like from a cow."

"I'll believe it when I taste it," said Emily. "You will share, won't you, Frank?"

"It'll cost you."

"I'll bet."

"One of my clients a while ago," Hannah said, "would go to the docks at Point Pleasant and across the inlet to Brielle when the charter fishing boats came in. If he saw someone with a mako, he'd ask what they intended to do with it, explaining that sharks are trash fish and taste like ammonia. He'd offer to take the mako off their hands and grind it up for chum, and they'd be eager to get rid of it. Little did they know."

"But now they do know," said Donald. "Now mako brings a premium."

"Ah, the good old days," said Hannah. "Last time we saw each other he'd earned his captain's license and arranged to buy the *River Belle* sternwheeler in Point Pleasant. I handled the closing for him."

"That's the riverboat on the canal?" asked Frank. "I assume it's a reproduction, right?"

Hannah nodded. "A pair of diesel engines provides the power. The sternwheel's just for show."

Cindy placed their dinners before them with a flourish. "It does taste like steak," said Emily as she purloined a forkful from Frank's plate. "Promise me you'll never eat liver and onions again."

"I can neither confirm nor deny."

"Well, I can confirm that you'll sleep alone if you do."

"Busted."

The conversation turned toward the school's musical.

"I never heard of *Pippin,*" said Hannah. "I knew it was an old play, but beyond that…"

"You are in luck, my dear," said Frank. "Etta Pourmel brought a DVD of the play to introduce the kids to the Fosse choreography. The players are psyched, but of course they would be; they love the eroticism of the moves. I'll borrow the disc from her, so you can see it next weekend."

"I'd like that. Thank you, Frank."

Emily said, "You know, Hannah, now that you've got Donald going to church with you, I'm going to start dragging Frank to mass with me and my parents."

Frank grimaced. "What we do for love, with apologies to *A Chorus Line.*" He added, "Long story short, ages ago Mom had a fight with her priest over birth control. They had me, they knew they couldn't do better, and Dad got himself snipped."

"I love Frank's modesty, don't you? You know what couples who practice church-sanctioned birth control are called, right?" asked Emily rhetorically. "Parents."

"Then Mom and the priest got into it again because she never went to confession. Said she didn't need a middleman to talk to God. The priest, from the fire and brimstone school of theology, told her if she couldn't confess, she couldn't take communion in his church. And she flipped him the bird, figuratively that is, and never went back."

"That joker's long gone," said Emily. "Father Hafner's a good guy. And my folks really like Frank, even though he's practically a senior citizen."

"Hey."

She grinned. "But they see that we're kindred spirits, so they approve."

Donald said, "Do your parents know of your former relationship, when you were a student?"

"No. And if you tell them, I will cut. Out. Your. Tongue."

Hannah said, "Frank, what about your father?"

"Dad left the church when Mom did. When he died of lung cancer—he smoked two packs a day—Mom had him buried in a private ceremony, no clergy allowed."

Hannah added, "Donald tells me your mom suffers from Alzheimer's. I'm so sorry."

Frank nodded. "She's in Avalon Assisted Living in Bridgewater, which is more like a resort hotel than an institution. I see her every Sunday, bring her dessert. She's at the point where she sometimes thinks I'm Dad, tells me I shouldn't smoke so much; I could get cancer."

Emily frowned. "Frank, I want to come with you tomorrow."

"Why would you want to do that?"

"If I have to explain it to you..."

"Say no more. You've got a deal. You can make the dessert. I normally bring her pastries from La Scala."

"I like La Scala," said Cindy, who'd appeared like magic beside the booth. "If you're still too full for dessert, then I'll bring the check. Which one of you ladies wants it?"

Frank gave her an exaggerated scowl. "Like I said before, Cindy, you're dead to me."

Chapter Eleven

Donald arrived at Hannah's on Sunday holding the DVD of *Pippin*. "Frank warned me that the producers chopped it up in the editing room. Cut out verses from most of the songs, left out a major segment, and made Bob Fosse so mad that he sent a personal letter of apology to each of the cast members, saying the editing had been out of his control. But," he said, brandishing Frank's extra copy of the script, "we can read the full script and then watch the disc."

"That'll be a lovely way to spend a snowy winter's day. Oh, but first, some news."

"Speak to me."

"I was at a house closing yesterday, and guess who was sitting across the table from me, representing the sellers?"

"Surprise me."

"It was Stanley Wasielewski, the lawyer who represented Brian Snowden." Donald said huh. "He told me he appreciated my little trick at the trial—he saw when I signaled Emily—and thanked me for exposing his client. He said Brian never told him the back story, and so he believed the case was cut and dried. Stanley said he blames himself for not digging deeper before taking Brian on."

"No hard feelings, then. Good."

"There's more. Stanley told me that Internal Affairs recommended Brian be terminated, but the brass gave him a choice: be drummed out, or resign with his unblemished record—unblemished up to The Christmas Eve Massacre, at least—intact. These days, he's working as a guard at Trenton State Prison."

"Is that where your father is?"

Hannah nodded. She put on a sour expression to deflect further discussion, and Donald got the hint.

"So. Care to put on a fresh pot of coffee, and we can do a table read of the script?"

On that same Sunday, after early mass and brunch with Emily's parents, Frank drove her to Bridgewater to meet his mother. He'd been right about the cheeriness, she thought. There was no scent of alcohol or disinfectants, unlike what she'd expected. Nina White, a sixtyish RN who took special interest in Frank's mother, met them at the reception desk and escorted them to her room. "I have to caution you," she said to Frank, "Mom's been having some issues lately. Not violent, understand, but she sometimes experiences severe disorientation, and it makes her angry. I told her you were coming with her Sunday dessert, and she calmed down. When I left her, she was sitting in a chair watching TV."

Stella Populski appeared engrossed in a nature documentary—something about octopi being very intelligent creatures. "Hello again, Stella," Nina said. "Your son is here, and he brought a friend."

Frank put on a brave face and kissed his mother's cheek. It was the color of flour, and her eyes were filmed. She frowned, as if having trouble seeing.

"Who are you?" she said, her tone accusatory.

"I'm Frank, Mom, your son. And this is Emily, my girlfriend."

"So, you're cheating on me now? You can't wait until I'm in the ground before you pick up another woman?"

"Mom, I'm not Dad; I'm Frank. And Dad never cheated on you. He was as faithful as an old dog, and you know it."

Her angry frown transformed into puzzlement. "Oh. You're Frank."

"Yes. And this is Emily. She's the one who brought you dessert today."

Cautiously, Emily proffered the bag of cookies she'd been holding. "Hello, Mrs. Populski. It's so nice to meet you. And I hope you like the cookies. They're oatmeal chocolate chip with a sprinkling of walnuts. I made them this morning."

Stella took a cookie from the bag and cautiously nibbled it with teeth that were too perfect not to have been false. She nodded as Nina entered the room again with a cup of tea. She took the tea and sipped from the insulated paper cup. "It's good," she said and took another bite, a big one this time, as if satisfied that the cookie hadn't been poisoned.

"Would you brush my hair for me, Abigail?"

"It's Emily, and I'd love to, Mrs. Populski."

"And who are you again?"

"I'm Frank's girlfriend."

"You have red hair."

"And it's natural. It was lighter when I was born, my parents tell me." Emily picked up the hairbrush from the bedside table and began stroking Stella's hair.

"You're doing better today, Mom," Frank said as Emily gently brushed his mother's filament-thin white hair.

Stella turned her head violently to one side, startling Emily and knocking the brush from her hand. It fell to the floor with a clatter. "Who are you to call me Mom?" she challenged, her voice strained to the point of croaking. "You're not my son!"

Nina had stationed herself just outside the open door and softly walked in. "I think it might be time to go, Frank. When your mother gets agitated it isn't good for her."

Frank and Emily stood. She saw he was visibly shaken and squeezed his hand. "She's right; we should go," Emily said, and they walked to the doorway with Nina just behind them.

"Thank you, Nina, for all you're doing for Mom."

"It's not just a job for me," she said, and to Emily, "Thank you for coming. Stella might not appreciate it, but I do, and I know Frank does as well." Then she said goodbye and entered the room, where Frank's mother was wolfing down her second cookie.

Frank was trembling when he faced Emily, and his breath was halting and weak. She extended her arms and he fell into them, weeping openly.

Finally, he stood straight and she released him. "I'm sorry," he blurted. "I never did that before. It's just—"

"Shh," said Emily. "It's all right, Frank; it's all right."

"Thank you for being here," he said, drawing in a deep breath.

"I'll always be here for you, Frank," she said.

That was Sunday; Tuesday night, Stella Populski died in her sleep.

"How can I help?" asked Emily, who was sound asleep next to Frank when Nina called early Wednesday with the news. Before he could answer, she said, "Listen, as for the play, Etta can work with the dancers, and I can coach the principals on their lines and movements. You take all the time you need."

Frank put on a brave face and brought Emily's hand to his lips. "I love you, kid."

"I love you too. Listen, I'll call the college first thing to tell them you'll be taking bereavement leave. What are you entitled to, a week?" He nodded. "I'll call Donald too, and I'll tell Hannah at the office."

"It's not like I wasn't expecting this, but—I never expected it so soon."

Sitting on the edge of the bed, Emily wrapped her arms around Frank and murmured soothing words in his ear.

"When she first got Alzheimer's, Mom said she wanted to donate her body to research. She intended for scientists to study her brain for abnormalities that led to her disease." He took a breath. "So, no funeral. On the phone, Nina said I could come up this morning to say goodbye, but it had to be early. She said she'd stay up with Mom until I got there."

"I can go with you; Hannah would understand."

Frank shook his head. "You need to make those calls for me." He stood up and turned on the bedside lamp. "I'm getting dressed and leaving now. It's not fair for Nina to sit with Mom all night when I should be the one."

Early the next day, word spread throughout the college of Frank's loss. Staff members came to Donald for details, and he informed them of Stella Populski's wishes and that Frank, as a teacher, was terribly proud that his mother had volunteered to teach others after her death.

Wednesday afternoon, the players—having learned of their coach's bereavement—reported glumly to rehearsal. It took Etta Pourmel to set them right. "Listen," she said, "you're too young to remember *The Beverly Hillbillies* on TV; hell, I'm too young too. But I've seen reruns on cable. Point is, Irene Ryan, who played the grandmother in the show, also played Pippin's grandmother on stage. One day—before showtime, mind you—the cast was advised that Irene had died the night before. They were devastated; but still, they were professionals, and they played with Irene's standby in the role, fighting through their grief and performing as if nothing had happened. So, sad as you are for the coach, you know what he'd say to you if he were here? Suck it up, buttercup, the show must go on."

Privately to Emily as the dancers practiced their moves, Etta said, "Listen, while I appreciate the free hotel accommodations, it's time for me to head back to New York. The kids know their routines, and you know them as well as they do by now, so you can tweak them if they need it.

"I'll tell the kids after rehearsal tonight. Give Frank my condolences, and tell him that I've secured the costume rentals from Eaves-Brooks, so that's one more thing he doesn't have to worry about. It's two months 'til curtain, and I'll be back the last week for the final run-throughs. Plus, I've taken the liberty of hiring a friend who does professional make-up to school the dancers on how to apply their individual designs over the clown white base."

"What are you up to next?"

"I'm hearing the Paper Mill Playhouse is going to put up *Chicago* next fall, and they just might need a choreographer who knows the Bob Fosse style."

"Wow. Good luck with that. You know, I really don't know what Frank would've done without you."

"Hey, the college is paying me, remember? But between you and me, I love Fosse so much I'd do it for nothing."

"I won't tell a soul."

Chapter Twelve

Two weeks later, Emily hosted a small memorial service for Frank's mother in her parents' home, followed by a catered luncheon her mother had arranged. Frank offered a brief tribute, prefacing it with a line from *Pippin:* "When your best days are yester, the rest're twice as dear." He told of his mother's best days over the years, highlighting her love for his father; their support for his choice of career; her leaving her management position at Shop-Rite to care for his father when he got sick; her regrets that when she contracted Alzheimer's her memories of a life well lived would fade into darkness. "As you know, Mom donated her body to Alzheimer's research. I'm dedicating this year's play to her memory," he concluded. "I only wish she could've seen it with me." He looked lovingly at Emily. "With us."

Hannah had breakfast ready when Donald arrived at nine o'clock Saturday. Afterward, they wrapped themselves in their winter coats and walked the Point Pleasant boardwalk, stopping at every bench for him to sit and stretch his game leg.

"We don't have to do this, you know," said Hannah.

"I like to watch the waves curl and listen to them break in the surf. I like to look at the gulls, terns, and pipers. I like feeling the ocean breeze, and smelling the salt tang in the air. And I like the fact that this time of year, the boardwalk is all but deserted. It's like the universe is putting on a show for us and us alone. And beyond liking, I love being with you no matter where we are."

She snuggled against him and kissed his cheek before saying, "Your leg seems to be getting worse."

"I don't know. If it is, it's getting worse so slowly I don't notice it from day to day."

"Maybe it's my imagination." But she knew she wasn't imagining.

"As long as it doesn't slow me down in bed, I think I'll be okay."

Hannah smiled and kissed him again, this time on the lips. Then they stood and continued their walk.

"Blue sky, green water, sand sparkling like granulated sugar," Donald remarked. "What could be better?"

"Maybe you should apply for a job with the Chamber of Commerce."

"I'm happy right where I am, thank you."

The following Wednesday afternoon Hannah had a closing in her office, with a client of her mother's. Afterward, Emily having excused herself to attend rehearsal, Daisy said, "Now that we're alone, did you hear what happened this morning?"

"Something happened this morning?"

"The prison guard, Brian, the one who got Donald into all that trouble on Christmas Eve? He was killed."

"What? How?"

"No details yet besides that it was a prisoner who did it. Which had to be obvious."

"My God, Brian Snowden dead." Hannah looked suddenly contrite. "I had something to do with that, didn't I?"

"What are you talking about?"

"But I had no choice. I knew Donald was innocent and did what I could to defend him. And as a result, I got Brian fired."

"Brian Snowden wasn't the innocent party, dear. What happened before and after the trial was on him. You have nothing to feel guilty about."

They stared at each other, absorbed in thought. Finally, Daisy broke the silence. "Have you told Donald yet?"

"How could I? You just told me."

"I'm not talking about Brian Snowden."

"Oh."

"He has to know sometime. You owe him."

"Mom, I can't. Not yet. Donald is still fragile in some ways."

"Hah. Marine hero? I think not. I think you're the one who's fragile."

Hannah remained silent, her eyes on the paperwork before her. "The time's not right," she finally said.

"When will it be right?"

"I don't know, Mom, please."

"You and Donald are serious. There should be no secrets."

Hannah nodded. "You're right. But if I were to tell him now..."

"You're afraid."

"Of course, I'm afraid. I waited too long; yes, I admit it. But I can't afford to do anything now to threaten our relationship."

"And you're going to continue with this lie standing between you? Doesn't sound like love to me."

"It's not a lie, it's just—oh, darn it. Why do you always have to be right?"

"Then tell him. If he loves you, he'll understand."

"And if he doesn't?"

"Then you don't understand him as well as you think you do."

Hannah wiped a speck from her eye. "I'll tell him. But not now. I need time."

"It's your life. But I really like Donald. If you screw things up, daughter, it's on you."

Next morning before classes began, Donald and Frank sat in the faculty lounge preparing for the day with sixteen-ounce mugs of hot coffee. Donald put down his mug and told Frank he had news for him. Frank said he had news too, but Ducks first: age before beauty.

"I'm three hours older than you, Junior."

"Sucks to be old. Anyway, what's your news?"

"Remember Brian Snowden?"

"How could I forget? Great showdown in court; it belonged on TV."

"He's dead." Frank blinked. "I told you he left the local police force to be a prison guard, right?"

"Right."

"Well, some prisoner must've decided that prison would be a better place without him. He was DOA when his body arrived at the infirmary." He took another gulp of coffee. "Hannah called me last night with the news."

Frank considered for a moment. "Karma sucks, doesn't it? He should've kept his nose clean; no skin off yours."

Donald nodded. "Just came as a surprise."

"Are you sorry for him?"

"I didn't like him, but I don't like murder either. Changing the subject, what's your news?"

"We got a keyboardist for *Pippin*."

"Okay?"

"Ducks, you know the score for the play is heavy on piano. Anyway, last weekend Emily and I went to this upscale restaurant in Spring Lake, and the place provided entertainment in the form of a piano player. Now, this guy took requests all night, and he played them all without one sheet of music in front of him. Photographic memory? I don't know; encyclopedic at least. Plus, he has an obviously trained voice. During a break, we called him over and introduced ourselves. His name is Lou Parisi, he's a retired music teacher, and when we told him we were looking for a pianist for *Pippin,* he told us he loves the score and would love to do it. He also has friends in local bands he can draft for the orchestra. He's coming to rehearsal this afternoon to meet the cast and crew. He told me he knows Etta Pourmel too, from his daughter's dance school."

"You're golden."

"Come to rehearsal before your evening class starts; you can meet him."

Lou, Donald decided, was one of those people who upon meeting him for the first time, treats you like you've known each other forever. A tall, swarthy Italian somewhere in his sixties, with black hair and dark brown laughing eyes, he had the knack of immediately putting everyone at ease. And, to Frank's delight, he reveled in puns.

When Lou learned of Frank's love of Shakespeare, he asked, "What did Hamlet say when his cattle came down with mad cow disease?" To Frank's puzzled look, he said, "There's something rotten in the steak of Denmark."

Frank and Lou laughed; the others groaned.

"Did you know," he continued, "that Hamlet was a barbecue chef, famous for his ribs?"

Before he could give the punch line, Frank interrupted with, "Aye, there's the rub."

Lou laughed with him. "And you have to know that poor Hamlet sucked in algebra class, too. Remember when he said, '2b or not 2b, that is the question'?"

Finally, Emily brought them back to the play. "If you children don't mind, the cast is waiting for notes."

When Donald left for his evening class, Lou was accompanying the players on their numbers and coaching them on vocals as Frank and Emily beamed their satisfaction.

Chapter Thirteen

By the time the curtain rose on a Friday night in May, Hannah and Donald had viewed the DVD enough times to know the music and lyrics by heart. He marveled at Hannah's singing voice, which flowed from her like warm honey. "I can't read a note," he admitted to her one night. "My music education stopped at do, re, mi. Pitch, octaves, and sharps and flats are a foreign language. My only source of reference is the riddle about the tightrope walker's favorite notes."

"All right, I'll bite," said Hannah, smiling in the silence of the electric sedan as they drove to opening night. "What are a tightrope walker's favorite notes?"

"C sharp or B flat."

She groaned. "You've been talking to Lou, haven't you?"

"Oh, and by the way, he's invited Frank, Emily, and you and me to dinner at his house after Sunday's matinee. He lives in an old Victorian in Ocean Grove and loves to cook. What do you say?"

"What do you think I say?" She chuckled and Donald asked what was funny. "I hope Frank hasn't asked him to cook ducks; you know, in your honor."

"When did you become a wise ass?"

After the play's final "Ta-dah!" the audience rose as one, with applause reverberating like thunder. The Leading Player, a reviewer for *The Asbury Park Press* would write, was sweetly satanic, *Pippin* was charmingly naïve, and Charlemagne was properly bombastic. The Bob Fosse-inspired dancing was faithfully reproduced by professional choreographer Etta Pourmel, and the orchestra, featuring keyboard artist Lou Parisi, he deemed Broadway caliber.

Word spread, ticket sales soared, and demand required that the performances extend for another weekend. The dean dryly remarked to Frank that ticket sales might even cover expenses this year. Maybe.

Sunday dinner at Lou's was yet another festive occasion. A grand piano dominated his small living room, and after Donald praised Hannah's singing, he insisted she accompany him. She agreed, but only if Donald would join her in the play's "Love Song" duet. His voice, she knew, was at least passable, and Emily and Frank applauded when they were done, with Frank saying, "Ducks, I didn't know you had it in you."

Dinner began with Italian wedding soup, followed by antipasto and mounds of spaghetti with meatballs, hot and sweet Italian sausage, and homemade pomodoro sauce, the meal accompanied by a rich chianti. Dessert was mascarpone-stuffed cannoli. Later, they sat at the table, too stuffed to move, and Lou offered a selection of after-dinner liqueurs.

Conversation continued well into the evening until Lou's grandfather clock struck twelve and Frank said he had to get Cinderella home. They left with hugs and kisses all around and unspoken assurances that Lou had become part of their circle of close friends, or as Frank remarked, family by choice.

Donald was the designated driver for the evening—he abstained from the after-dinner drinks—and drove Emily and Frank to his home before returning Hannah to hers. When they arrived, she invited him in and asked him if he'd like to stay the night. She'd set the alarm for sunrise, and he'd still have time to get home and change for class.

They walked directly to her bedroom and slowly disrobed each other. Donald caressed Hannah's face as they stood before the bed and tilted her lips to his. "This has been a perfect day, hasn't it?" She nodded. "I do love you, Hannah," he whispered and kissed her tenderly.

"I love you too, Donald," she whispered against his lips. "So very, very much."

Donald fell asleep easily afterwards, his arm around her waist as they spooned. Hannah lay still, but her heart was racing. They had formally declared their love for each other, had consummated their love as if it were the first time, and now she found herself faced with a dilemma.

How would she tell him? And when? Where? Or, would she not tell him at all and hope he never found out?

By late May, the play had wrapped, the cast party produced tears at parting and promises to always remain friends, and Frank's tag line of Broadway at Your Doorstep became virtually carved in stone. The academic term ended, finals were reviewed and grades recorded, and even though Emily and Hannah still worked regular hours, Frank and Donald were free until their accelerated summer sessions in July.

Early June was when Donald regularly flew to Myrtle Beach to spend a week with his parents. This year, he invited Hannah to go with him.

"You've told them about me?" she asked over a dinner of cavatelli and broccoli at his Toms River townhome.

"I was keeping you close to the vest, frankly. But after Lou's dinner party, I knew it was time."

"Until then you weren't sure?" she said as she placed a cheesy floret into her mouth.

"I was sure long before that, frankly; I wasn't all that confident that you were. Remember, back in December, after our first night together, you told me it was too soon to tell me you loved me."

"And you agreed."

"I knew that you and I needed to get past the romance stage, to see if love would grow out of it. If I'd told them about you before—and I was bursting to, by the way—they'd have gotten their hopes up. They obviously knew how obsessed I'd been about, well, about Staci."

"You were saving your parents from possible disappointment in case we didn't work out."

"Profound disappointment, yes."

"You're a good son, Donald Greene. But," she said as she finished cleaning her bowl, "my calendar's full for the next few weeks. Tell me you haven't booked two tickets already."

He shook his head. "Just the one, last February. But I could try to book another."

Hannah laughed softly. "Donald Greene, you live in a fantasy world. These days, one doesn't just buy a ticket and hop on a plane. Before 9/11, maybe, but not today."

"I knew it was a long shot," he said as he picked up their bowls and brought them to the kitchen. "But hope springs eternal."

"You're so sweet. I am so lucky to have found you."

"And I'm so lucky that I met Emily back in the day," he called from the kitchen. "For dessert, we have tiramisu. Would you like it now or later?"

"Later, please, with decaf." She added, "I really would like to meet your parents. My mother loves you, and I'd like to think your folks would love me. When do you leave?"

"Next week. I'll be back the following Friday."

"Soon as you get in, call me. I'll have a welcome home dinner waiting for you."

The next afternoon, Hannah met with a young couple to set up a prenuptial agreement. Ann was a freelance bookkeeper for various small businesses in Ocean County, and Eric was a radio personality with the local FM station, WJRZ. At their initial meeting, Hannah remarked that she'd heard Eric on the air, and was impressed that he sounded not like an announcer but as a friend who was talking directly to her. She referred to it as a gift.

Eric said, "Want to know the secret? I post a photo of Ann on the glass behind the mic and pretend I'm talking to her."

Today, Emily joined them as they all went over the specifics. Ann and Eric were satisfied that every condition had been met, and they signed the documents happily. Emily notarized them and informed them that copies of the prenups would be on file here in the office. "But," she added, "Hannah and I sincerely hope that's where they stay."

The couple pecked each other on the lips, thanked them, and walked out hand in hand.

"Another happy customer; make that customers," said Hannah. "What?"

"Something's on your mind, boss. Let's sit down and discuss it."

"How do you know something's on my mind?"

"You haven't been your bright bubbly self for the last few days. What's going on? You know you can tell me anything."

They sat down and Hannah released a deep sigh. "You're right." She focused her gaze on Emily's deep green eyes. "I'm in trouble. I think."

Chapter Fourteen

Emily had been right, Hannah said to herself for the nth time as she picked up groceries for Donald's welcome home dinner. She would tell him tonight and pray he would understand. She placed two full bags in the back of her Highlander and drove home, her palms uncharacteristically moist as she took the wheel.

She parked the SUV, took out the groceries, and held the two plastic bags in one hand as she used the other to insert her key into the door. It swung open, she walked inside, and frowned angrily at the smell that hit her. "Who's been smoking in here?" she called out.

The door swung shut behind her, and she heard a man's voice, low, guttural, hatefully familiar even after all these years. "Hello, my beautiful little girl. Long time no see."

Hannah's legs liquified, and she dropped the bags onto the carpet. She would have fallen too, were it not for the pair of beefy hands that gripped her from behind beneath her armpits. She felt the stubble on his face as he pressed it to her cheek. His breath reeked of tobacco and whiskey. "No," she whimpered. "Not you."

"Yeah, me. You know, you and your momma never come to visit me once, all these years, did you? So now I'm come to visit you."

Marcus Washington, Hannah's father, pushed her into the dining room, where she saw her mother, bound to a chair with zip ties and duct tape over her mouth. Her eyes were wide, and her cheeks bore the trails of tears.

"I didn't know where you lived, so your momma graciously volunteered to take me. Ain't that right, Daisy?"

Daisy struggled against the plastic ties and made groaning sounds behind the tape.

Marcus forced Hannah onto another chair and told her to behave, "or you'll wind up trussed like your mother. Understood?"

Hannah trembled and fought to keep her bladder from emptying as she stared at the face of the creature who claimed to be her father but was in reality something loathsome, abhorrent, less than human. "You shouldn't be out yet," she managed to say. "Why did they let you out and not even tell us?"

Marcus grinned, his fleshy brown lips exposing nicotine-stained teeth. "Baby, I got out on parole."

"Impossible. We'd have been at the hearing."

"Yeah, well, don't ask me to explain how bureaucrats work. I did have a lovely lady there who did speak for me, explained to the panel I'd had a come-to-Jesus conversion in jail. Yeah, we were pen pals for years, and I told her I'd marry her when I got out. Dumb bitch believed me. When I walked out the gate a free man, I told her to fuck off, I didn't need her anymore."

"Bastard," whispered Hannah.

"Baby girl, you should be thanking me for defending your honor."

"What are you talking about, defending my honor?"

"See, there was this pig of a guard, thought he was hot shit, and I heard him tell another pig about this cunt lawyer who'd made him lose his job as a cop in Toms River, and that's why he was stuck in this shit job. He said he'd never forget that bitch Hannah Soong."

"Brian Snowden."

"Yep, Snowden, that was his name."

"You killed him?"

"Baby girl, no. Your daddy's too smart for that. No, I got someone else to do it for me."

Daisy Soong stopped struggling and let her head droop.

"How?" asked Hannah softly.

"There's this white dude, all jailhouse tattoos, worked out every day, mass of muscle, you know what I mean? And he has this foxy chick come visit him every week, his girlfriend. Or his ho, whatever. Anyways, I told him I overheard Snowden tell someone that he got the girl's name and address, and he was going to follow her home one day and bone her. Give her what she needed, understand? Course, it was all a lie."

"And he killed Brian for you."

"While I was leading a little prayer group in my cell, innocent as the day is long."

"You're a monster."

"But I'm smart. Smarter than I was in the old days, back before they locked me up."

"I need to go to the bathroom."

"Do you really, honey? Or are you just trying to find a way to get away? Because you're not."

"I'm about to leave a puddle on the carpet. I need to go, bad."

"Then I'll go with you, right behind. Hell, I seen everything you got anyway, so nothing new for me. Besides, I'll want you fresh as a daisy—no, not your mom Daisy—for when I make up for all those years I spent locked up. But I will want her to watch when I bend you over the dining room table."

"Don't," she whimpered. "Please, don't."

"Let's get you to the bathroom, my beautiful little girl, and then we'll discuss how this is going to go down."

Donald thanked his lucky stars once again that uncrowded Atlantic City Airport had direct roundtrip flights to Myrtle Beach. Newark was a nightmare and ranked among the unfriendliest of all airports. Plus, he didn't dare leave Moby Duck at the mercy of public parking in Newark.

Taking his carry-on from the overhead bin, he exited the plane and walked the short distance to the parking garage, where he tossed his bag into the trunk. He drove to the kiosk, where the middle-aged attendant gushed over the car as she ran his credit card for ninety-one dollars. From there it was a short drive to the Atlantic City Expressway and the Garden State Parkway. The drive to his doorstep took an hour, and every minute he felt nervous as a schoolboy on his first date.

He tossed his bag on the bed, opened it, and emptied the contents directly into the washing machine. All the contents but one, that is: a tiny square felt-covered box from Symbols Jewelers in Myrtle Beach. His mother had recommended the shop, citing some jewelry repairs she'd needed in the past.

It was now four o'clock, plenty of time to shower, dress, and drive to Point Pleasant by six, which was when he'd told Hannah to expect him before boarding the plane this morning.

He scrubbed his body clean, gave himself a baby-smooth shave, put on fresh chinos and a polo, and tossed his clean clothes into the dryer. Taking a deep breath, rehearsing once more what he would say to Hannah after dinner tonight, he returned to his car and drove the half hour to Point Pleasant Beach and Hannah's townhome. He parked next to her Highlander, took a deep breath, and walked to her front door. Oddly, it wasn't latched; the door rested against the jamb rather than being closed all the way.

One more nervous breath, and he pushed open the door. "Honey, I'm home!" he called in the manner of Ricky Ricardo in the old *I Love Lucy* shows. He detected an offensive odor and wrinkled his nose. "Honey, when did you start smoking? And why?" Then he saw the groceries scattered over the carpet.

From the dining room, he heard Hannah cry, "Donald, run! Get out and call 911! Now!"

But of course, he couldn't do that. As a Marine officer he always ran toward trouble, not away from it, and Hannah was clearly in trouble. He made his way the few steps to the dining room and stopped short as his eyes took in the shocking tableau.

Daisy Soong was strapped to a chair, her mouth covered in duct tape, her eyes wide and pleading.

Hannah was bent over the table, her skirt raised, her panties down around her ankles. Her arms were stretched across the table, her fingernails digging gouges in the wood.

And then there was the man: tall, black, heavy-set, his jeans lowered to his knees. He sensed a presence behind him and turned. His penis was large and turgid.

Donald's mouth hung open as his eyes found the man's face. His close-cropped hair was gray now, but the eyes, the broad flat nose, and the thick rubbery lips were unmistakable.

"You!" he cried and launched himself.

Chapter Fifteen

Marcus Washington stood dumbly for a split second. It was enough time for Donald to crash into him. Two bodies banged against the table as Hannah shrieked and hurled herself to the side. She fell to the floor as Donald and her father fought for an advantage. Donald leaned him back across the table drove his right knee hard into his antagonist's unprotected groin, making him shriek and double over, clutching himself.

But the blind lust for vengeance had fogged Donald's brain. It was his game leg that had made contact, the leg whose limp had grown more noticeable over time. Pain, sudden and piercing, shot through the leg up to his hip. He cried out and fell to the floor, where he lay on his side grasping his leg and writhing in silent agony. This gave Marcus the time he needed to recover, pull up his jeans, and stand over Donald, fists clenched and poised to rain hammer blows.

Hannah was momentarily forgotten as she scrambled sobbing to the kitchen on her hands and knees.

"The fuck are you?" Marcus shouted at his downed attacker.

Donald's eyes burned with hatred. His voice came out a croak. "You killed my wife, you piece of shit! You're a dead man!"

Marcus laughed. "Oh, so you're the guy was drivin', right? The happy bridegroom? And look at you now, lyin' on the floor, cryin' like a baby. Like you're in any fuckin' position to hurt me."

While his attention was on Donald, Hannah padded back from the kitchen with a ten-inch carving knife in her hand, blood lust in her eyes. She bent over to cut her mother's bonds and then stood, body tensed, and steeled herself to attack.

Marcus focused on Donald. "Leg hurt you, bright boy? How's *this* feel?" He delivered a powerful kick to the small of Donald's back. Something snapped like a dried twig, and he screamed again.

Marcus laughed in triumph. "So, I'm a dead man, huh? You can't even stand up, you honky cripple!"

He heard something behind him and turned toward Hannah, who stood trembling, the knife shaking in her hand. "What you gonna do with that, my beautiful little girl? You think you can take down your old man?"

Marcus chopped the side of his hand against Hannah's arm, and the knife flew from her grasp. Then he turned her around and forced her to her hands and knees, positioning her directly over Donald, now lying on his back and deathly still. "Glad your panties are still where I left 'em," he grunted as he lifted her skirt. "Now spread your legs, so your boyfriend can look up and see what a real man can do."

Hannah tried mightily to keep her legs together, but Marcus forced one of his between them, and then the other, driving them apart like a wedge. She screamed, from fear for herself and for the man she loved, pinioned beneath her and the brute who was about to sodomize her. Again. She heard the rustle of his jeans as he shrugged out of them.

Suddenly the air was split by an animal scream of sheer terror, and Hannah felt a rain of hot blood cascade against her back and down her legs. The next scream was cut off instantly as Daisy twisted the keen-edged blade inside her former husband's neck. She'd driven it in from the side, standing behind him. and the point of the blade glistened red as it emerged from the other side. She turned the blade toward the front of his neck, cutting through his throat and turning it into a second mouth.

Holding his head with one hand in a death grip, Daisy turned the knife again, the edge now facing his spine. She pulled him against her, finding strength she never knew she had, and pulled the blade back until it bit into bone. Marcus grew limp, and she dropped him onto the floor away from Hannah and Donald. "No more, you bastard," she said through gritted teeth. "No more!"

Hannah looked down at Donald's body, tears falling onto his face as she called his name again and again. His eyes looked blankly up; whether he was looking at her or the ceiling, she couldn't tell. She noticed the tiny box that had fallen from his pocket during the fight and knew immediately what it contained. She wept all the louder as she cradled his limp body to hers.

From behind her, Hannah heard her mother calling for police and an ambulance.

Donald finally managed to focus his attention on her. "Hannah," he murmured, panic in his voice, "I can't feel my legs."

Two teams of EMTs arrived at the scene at the same time as the police. One compared the scene to the carnage he'd witnessed while serving in the Mideast war zones. One man was down, immobile. A woman cradled him in her arms, covered in blood from her waist down. A smaller, older woman was also smeared with blood. Her hands were in fact drenched with it. One of her hands carried a cell phone and the other a ten-inch carving knife. Then there was the man lying on the crimson-stained carpet, head tilted back unnaturally from his opened throat as if his neck was on a hinge. The EMT's partner remarked that he looked like a Pez dispenser.

As the police radioed in to the station, one team of EMTs sat the older woman on a dining room chair—they noticed the zip ties and duct tape on the floor—and began their ministrations over her objections. "I'm fine. Just need to wash up." Then her eyes glazed as she went into shock, and the team slid her onto a backboard and carried her out the door.

The younger woman looked up as the older one was carried out. "Mom!" she called as the second team lifted her from the prostrate man, whose right leg was twisted at an unnatural angle. He seemed to be dazed, eyes blinking at the ceiling, mouthing words no one could hear.

They placed him on another backboard, and the woman handed one of them the tiny box with the jewelry store logo to take with him and add to his personal effects. She asked to go to the hospital with him, claiming he was her fiancé, but the police firmly but politely demanded she remain behind to give witness testimony. She was shaking as the EMTs took the man away, and when she heard the sirens from the two vehicles, she collapsed into the arms of one of the officers.

The police sat her in the same chair her mother had occupied. They offered her a glass of water, which she held in trembling fingers and couldn't bring to her mouth without spilling it down her blouse. The door opened, and two plainclothes officers entered, one a woman dressed in a pale gray pantsuit. She knelt before the younger woman, introduced herself as Detective Katina Hernandez, and asked the woman her name. With skilled words she comforted her and gently coaxed from her the story of what had occurred as her partner recorded her words.

She identified the dead man as her father, recently released from prison—and also as her childhood rapist, about to take up now where he'd left off, until the man she ID'd as her fiancé stumbled upon the scene and saved her. Tears tumbled from her eyes. The officers were similarly moved, exchanging glances that said the dead man got what he deserved. Hernandez's male partner mumbled, "Shoulda cut his balls off first."

Then the woman, through more tears, admitted that the injured man wasn't yet her fiancé—but she suspected that had the day turned out differently, he would be. Hernandez, ignoring the blood and what it would do to her pantsuit, hugged her tightly and whispered words of consolation.

She reached into her pocket as her cell phone vibrated. She answered it, listened, asked a few terse questions, thanked the caller, and disconnected.

"Your mother's been treated at Hackensack Meridian in Brick. She's fine and anxious to get back to you. They're going to keep her overnight to make sure she's okay. Also, they phoned her pastor, and he's on his way. As for your fi—the other injured party—he's being transported to the Spine Institute of Central New Jersey in Freehold. It's a half hour away; they tell me he just arrived."

"When will I be able to see him? Them?"

"I don't know any more details, but I'm sure your mother will be released tomorrow. For now, you understand that this is a crime scene, and you'll have to move out temporarily. When you return, your place will look good as new. Our cleaning crew is very detail oriented. Trust me on this."

"I may move out permanently," Hannah said. "I have a feeling I'm going to need a one-story home from now on." She wiped a tear. "At least I hope I will."

"Will you need a hotel room?" the detective asked. "I'd be happy to find you one."

The woman shook her head. "For now, I can move into my mother's place."

"I think that's an excellent idea. You can be there when she returns."

Chapter Sixteen

Frank was the first to arrive at the hospital. Immobile in his bed, Donald's first question was to ask how Hannah and Daisy were. "Are they hurt?"

"Not physically, Ducks, but emotionally? Sure as shit they're injured. Traumatized. Emily is with them now, doing what she can. Hannah says she needs to see you, but right now she's in no shape to do anything but hold onto her mom and cry."

"My parents know?"

"Their plane arrives tomorrow. I'm picking them up at ACY."

"How are they taking the news?"

"How do you think? Just after I called, they saw the story online, got all the gruesome details. The media are calling Daisy a hero. Big spread in *The Asbury Park Press* and *Newark Star-Ledger* today. I asked your folks not to call you; hope that's all right. On another note, did you know that Hannah's father raped her as a kid? Like continually?"

Donald nodded. "She told me early on. But she didn't tell me the rest of it."

"Oh. You're telling me you didn't know her father was the drunk who killed Staci?"

Donald's face darkened. "Not until I saw him. That's something we'll need to discuss."

"Hey, sucks to be both of you right now. I wouldn't go hard on her, Ducks; not now."

"She lied to me, Pops. Lied by omission. Why wouldn't she tell me that it was her father? What did she think I'd do, dump her? Visit the sins of the father on the daughter?"

"Uh, that's between the two of you. But between us chickens, I'd hate to see you lose her. You're a new man around her."

Donald grimaced. "I'm really a new man now. Her father's kick landed between my L-4 and L-5 vertebrae. The nerve's shot. The doc said they'd do some surgery to repair my spine, but it's dicey if I'll ever walk again."

"Shit, piss, and corruption."

"Yeah, about that. Imagine me, teaching from a wheelchair with a catheter bag hanging off one side and an ostomy bag off the other. Hi, kids. How do I smell today?"

Frank shuddered. "I don't want to imagine it, and I don't think you should either, at least until you know something definite."

"Can't wiggle my toes, Pops."

"Yet. Can't wiggle 'em yet. Let's postpone the pity party until we know something, okay?"

Donald sighed. "Look inside the drawer on the bedside table. There's a plastic bag with my personal stuff." Frank opened the door and pulled the bag out. "Open the little box."

Frank opened the bag and lifted the lid. "Wow. Serious. You were going to give it to her?"

"The day I came home from Myrtle. She was going to give me a welcome home dinner, and I was going to give her this over dessert. Then I walked in the door and heard her scream."

Frank shook his head.

They sat in silence for a moment. Then Frank said, "Lou Parisi called me as soon as he saw the bulletin on the news. He wants to come visit you, but he doesn't want to intrude on the family. Says he'll wait until later. But he does want you to know he's praying for you. He said he doesn't go to church much anymore, but he's going to go today so he can light a candle for you."

"Lou's a good guy."

"And the cast of *Pippin* send their best too, along with Etta. I expect you'll be getting a lot of cards and flowers."

"Yeah, I guess. The room'll smell like a funeral home."

"I can't tell you to suck it up, Ducks, but you know I hope everything turns out okay for you. For you both." He stood and grasped Donald's hand. "I'm going to go to Daisy's house now, see how she and Hannah are holding up. Emily's like a St. Bernard rescue dog around them. I love that girl."

"Make sure you tell her."

"Yeah. I tell her that a lot."

"And tell Hannah not to call. I'll let you know when I'm ready to see her."

"Don't be cruel, Ducks. She loves you."

The next day, Frank returned with Beth and Pete Greene in tow. Donald's mother smothered him with kisses and his father gripped his hand as he wiped his own eyes with the other.

"Still smoking that pipe, Dad? I can smell it on you."

"I keep telling him to quit. He doesn't inhale, obviously, but he could get mouth cancer anyway. Naturally, he doesn't listen to me; after all, I'm only a nurse."

Donald forced a smile. "Good to know some things never change. I noticed you didn't smoke when I was with you last week."

"I didn't need another lecture, frankly. You and your mother would call me out in stereo."

They grilled Donald about his condition, his hopes to be able to walk again, and he replied that as of now, everything was up in the air. Surgery was on the schedule for tomorrow; then they'd know better.

"Have you seen Hannah?" asked Beth. "We saw her photo in the paper. Beautiful girl. You're very lucky."

"I didn't give her the ring, Mom." She cocked her head and furrowed her brow, which she always did when she wanted an explanation. "Didn't get the chance."

"Does she know you have it? That you were going to give it to her?"

Donald shrugged. "I don't know. But if I'm going to be a paraplegic, maybe it's best she doesn't know."

"That's not fair, son," his father said, "and you know it."

"We did what we could," the surgeon reported the next day as Donald lay in the recovery room. "Now it's up to you. If the nerves reattach, you've got a good chance of at least partial recovery. But it'll take months of therapy, maybe a year, maybe more. We have an excellent program here, by the way. You won't have to go off site."

"So, I'll be wheelchair bound for, what?"

"I can't tell you how long. I don't want to discourage you, but I don't want to give you false hope either. If therapy works, you'll be able to use the bathroom with help. You might be able to get into a walker eventually. But I'm not going to sugar-coat this. You could be in a chair for the rest of your life." He paused to let that sink in. "But listen, you can still have a life. You just won't be skydiving or scuba diving anymore."

"Well, that's a break. Now I won't have to make an excuse when people ask me."

The doctor slapped him good-naturedly on the shoulder. "Keep your chin up. I'll check up on you later today and tomorrow. We'll be doing another MRI to assess the situation."

When Donald returned to his room after the MRI, he found Hannah waiting for him. She looked frail, like she hadn't eaten a thing since her abortive family reunion.

The orderly made sure he was okay and left them alone.

"Hi," she said softly.

"Hi yourself."

"How are you feeling?"

"I'm not feeling anything; at least, not below my hips." She winced. "Sorry; not funny."

Hannah approached his bed and took his hand. "I love you, Donald. Nothing has changed that."

"Move that chair over and sit down."

She did, returning her hand to his.

"Why didn't you tell me about your father? Did you even know?"

"Donald, I wish I could claim ignorance. But the day after you told me the story of how you lost your wife, I dug his court transcript out of my file cabinet. I hadn't looked at it since my father was sent away. When I read your name and Staci's, my legs felt like they'd been plunged in ice water. If I hadn't been sitting down, I might've fallen."

"You're saying you did know, but you chose not to tell me. Why?" he said accusingly.

Hannah took a deep breath and let it out. "I should have. I know I should have. But I was afraid, afraid that if you knew that my father had ruined your life, you wouldn't want to see me anymore. Because every time you saw me, you'd be reminded of him and what he did to you. To both of you."

"That doesn't speak well of your opinion of me, does it?" Silence hung between them.

"I held back because I didn't want to hurt you. That you have to believe."

Donald looked down at their clasped hands. "How is your mother holding up?"

Grateful for a change of topic, Hannah said, "The police have informed her there will be no charges filed against her, that she killed her attacker in self-defense. To me privately, she called it an honor killing, for what he'd done to me as a child. She's still shaken up, but because she felt killing him was the right thing to do, she sleeps pretty well. I don't, though."

"Because he dredged up memories of what he'd done to you, and that he was about to do it again?"

"No. Because of you, of my not telling you. You may not feel pain, Donald, but I do. It's emotional for me, and the guilt keeps me up nights. I haven't eaten, haven't been able to go back to the office— Emily's a saint, and Frank's a godsend—but when I do finally get to sleep, I relive that night and wake up in a cold sweat. And please believe me when I tell you I was going to tell you about—him—after your welcome home dinner. Mom and Emily shamed me into making a clean breast of it. But of course, by then it was too late."

"I'm sorry, Hannah."

She waited a moment and brought his hand to her lips. "I know what you brought to my house that day," she said, her voice barely a whisper.

"I wasn't sure you did."

"I found the box on the floor afterward and gave it to the EMT to place with your personal effects."

"Did you open it?"

"No. I didn't have the right."

"Oh."

"It's up to you to open it; that is, if you still intend to."

"Hannah, look at me. I could be in a chair the rest of my life. Could you deal with that?"

"Donald, I fell in love with your heart, not your legs."

"But you do know what that would entail for you, right? Changing my catheters, emptying my ostomy bag? And me never able to function sexually anymore? I wouldn't wish that on anyone, least of all you."

She frowned. "Donald, please don't play the woe-is-me card, okay? I hope, I pray you'll recover, of course I do, but if you don't, I'll still be by your side, always." She took a halting breath. "I will, that is, if you still want me after what I've done to betray your trust."

Donald took a deep breath and told her to open his bedstand drawer. She handed him the box, and he opened it to reveal the diamond solitaire inside. "Hannah, I was going to take a knee before I offered you this." He chuckled wryly. "I can't now, but the question's still the same: Hannah Soong, will you marry me?"

"Of course, I'll marry you."

He placed the ring on her finger, and she kissed him. Her lips were soft, her breath sweet.

"Will you do me a favor?" he asked.

"Whatever you want."

"Would you slide into bed with me?"

Hannah took off her shoes and climbed into the bed. When the nurse came in that evening to check on her patient, she saw the two of them, sound asleep, he on his back, she on her right side, with her left arm across his waist. The nurse saw the sparkle of the ring on the woman's finger. "All's right with the world," she said, smiling, as she turned out the light and left.

The day that Donald found he could feel his toes, he let out a whoop that brought the nurse immediately to his side. Over time, and with the therapist Joe's help, he found he could finally use the bathroom. He told the therapist he never wanted to see another Foley catheter as long as he lived, and Joe assured him he probably wouldn't have to. He also regained bowel function, which he marked as a red-letter day on the calendar.

Donald struggled daily to regain use of his legs. Joe, apprised of the date he and Hannah had set for their wedding, advised him he would still be confined to the wheelchair. Donald smiled and shrugged. "I accept that. My martyrdom days are over," he said.

"Do you remember my telling you about Clyde Applegate?" Hannah asked during one of her daily visits. Donald admitted he didn't. "He owns the sternwheel replica *River Belle*. I was his attorney at the closing, and he loves me. According to maritime law, as a licensed captain he can marry us on the boat."

"Uh huh. It's docked in Point, right?"

"Across the canal from the fishing boats."

"You actually want to charter a giant riverboat; am I hearing you right?"

"I do. And Lou said he'd gather some of his old bandmates to provide the music, as his gift to us."

"Good old Lou. I suppose I'll have to ask Popeye to be my best man."

"You don't have to," Hannah said, laughing. "But he'll kill you if you don't. Emily has already agreed to be my maid of honor. And Mom will give me away."

"Just so I get this straight. Did you say you *want* to charter the boat, or you *did* already?"

She gave him a guilty smile. "Done deal. After the ceremony, Clyde will take us all for a cruise on the Manasquan River, and a good time will be had by all."

Donald considered. "I'd have a tough time negotiating the altar stairs at the church, that's for sure. I assume the boat's ballroom, if that's what you call it, is flat."

"It is."

"Should I ask if we have a guest list?"

"Do we have a guest list?" She pulled a sheet of paper from her purse and handed it to him. "Do we have a guest list?"

Epilogue

The temperature and humidity on the day of the wedding were unseasonably mild for late August. The sky was bright blue, with no summertime haze to obscure it. A breeze wafted over and through the large open windows of the *River Belle*.

Frank drove Donald to the Point Pleasant dock in Moby Duck. His wedding gift, he said, would be to install hand controls in the classic Mercury sedan. He pulled the wheelchair out of the back and Donald hoisted himself into it. A wide gangplank provided easy access to the boat, where Captain Applegate greeted them. He was a tall, burly man with a full head of dark brown hair, kind eyes, and a wide grin. He shook their hands and confessed that this would be his first shipboard wedding. "I'm probably as nervous as you are," he said to Donald, who told him they were in it together.

The ballroom was set up with steam tables on the port and starboard sides, currently empty, and rows of upholstered folding chairs. A flowered arch hung from the forward overhead.

Inside, they greeted Lou Parisi and his five-piece band, which he called Smooth Sailin'. "I got Audra to join us," Lou said, introducing a petite and pretty brunette who greeted them with a shy smile. "She was one of my students years ago, and we've kept in touch. Audra has a voice like an angel. Perfect for you know what."

The two men did know what; they'd planned the song list with Lou days before.

"You guys are looking sharp in your matching tuxes," Lou said. "Like a pair of penguins. Who's going to sit on the egg while the other one fishes?"

Audra smiled and shook her head. "He was nutty in music class, too. Which is another reason we adored him."

The guests, some thirty in all, arrived: Donald's parents came with Emily's, with whom they'd bonded immediately; Donald's friends from the college, including the dean; most of the cast and crew from *Pippin,* along with their choreographer Etta Pourmel; and, looking quite lovely, having shed her black uniform for a green-and-white-patterned sundress, Cindy from the Office Lounge.

"Don't you clean up nice," joked Frank when she walked aboard the boat.

"More than I can say for you," she jibed back. She leaned over and kissed Donald on the cheek. "Thanks for inviting me, you two. It means a lot."

"You mean a lot to us," Donald said.

A black Lincoln limousine arrived at dockside. Daisy Soong got out first, followed by Emily, who helped Hannah emerge, stunning in a knee-length, cream-colored sheath. Frank looked out the window, whose sill was too high for Donald, and said, "Hannah looks like a butterfly coming out of her cocoon. You are one lucky duck, Ducks."

"I don't think you've done so badly yourself, Pops."

"That's why I'm not jealous of you." Emily wore a matching sheath in pale green that she'd bought when Hannah bought hers. It made a perfect complement to her eyes.

Frank wheeled Donald to the forward end of the boat and turned his chair to the bulkhead. "Bad luck to see the bride before the wedding," he quipped.

Lou's band struck a chord, and the guests settled into their chairs. Clyde Applegate, uncomfortable in a white tuxedo jacket, took his place, and Frank turned Donald around to see his bride.

Lou took to the keyboard to play the hauntingly beautiful strains of "Any Dream Will Do," from *Joseph and the Amazing Technicolor Dreamcoat.* Emily walked down the aisle, carrying a bouquet of daisies as a tribute to Hannah's mother. She took her place to Clyde's right, opposite Frank and Donald. Then all eyes turned to see Daisy Soong slowly escorting her daughter down the aisle to her place next to the groom.

When they arrived before the ship's captain, Daisy kissed Hannah and winked at Donald before accepting the bouquet from Emily and taking her seat. The O'Neils sat alongside her, and the Greenes took the front row across the aisle. Hannah handed her bouquet of white roses to Emily as Donald pivoted his chair. She reached down to hold Donald's hand.

They'd decided not to write their own vows, instead opting for the traditional "I take thee ..." They had already made their vows in private two days before.

"Folks, I'm not comfortable saying Dearly beloved," Clyde boomed in his deep baritone, "so I'll just say welcome everyone to the *River Belle* and the wedding of Hannah Soong and Donald Greene. I hope that's all right with you all." Smiles and nods greeted him, which considerably eased his nervousness. He conducted the ceremony flawlessly, and he couldn't have been more relieved when, after the rings were exchanged, he turned the couple toward their guests and said, "Ladies and gentlemen, it is my privilege to introduce to you for the first time, Mr. and Mrs. Donald Greene."

As the guests stood and applauded, Beth Greene whispered to her husband, "That's Dr. and Mrs."

Pete quietly shushed her. "Hannah has her juris doctori, kiddo. Would you prefer he introduced them as Dr. and Dr.?"

She smiled and admitted she was being foolish.

Clyde shook Donald's hand and kissed Hannah on her cheek and announced to the guests, "Please feel free to come up and greet the new bride and groom. Now, if you'll excuse me, I have a ship to run."

As the guests formed a line to offer their congratulations, a low rumble indicated that the twin diesels had come to life. Moments later, the deck hands released the dock lines and the *River Belle* eased into the canal, bound for the calm waters of the Manasquan River. Meanwhile, the caterers set up the steam tables as others cleared the front rows of chairs to make room for a dance floor and set a table under the flowered archway for the bridal party. The other chairs they arranged around folding tables.

Lou took the microphone and introduced himself and his band, making sure to highlight their songbird, Audra, "who you'll be hearing from soon, I promise."

Smoothly assuming his emcee duties, Lou said, "Obviously, this wedding is a little different from what you might be used to, so we're going to alter the traditional dances a little." With a sly grin, he said, "Normally, the bride and groom get the first dance. But Don decided to sit this one out."

Silence fell upon the room like a shroud.; until the guests heard the bridal party laughing out loud and saw Donald give Lou thumbs up. Then the guests laughed along with them, although some with teary eyes.

"Which means, the honor of dancing with the bride falls to the best man, Frank 'Popeye' Populski."

Frank escorted Hannah to the floor, and they danced to Audra's rendition of "That's What Friends Are For." When it ended, to applause, Lou announced that Frank originally wanted "Another One Bites the Dust," but Donald overruled him. This was greeted by more laughter. Then he said it was time for the mother of the bride to dance with her daughter. Frank surrendered her and offered Hannah's hand to Daisy, and they danced to "The Wind Beneath My Wings," again beautifully vocalized by Audra.

They finished to more applause, and Lou formally introduced Donald's parents, Beth and Pete Greene. "Pete has a new daughter now, so we're going to ask him to stand up and dance with Hannah next."

Pete was surprised but happy to take Hannah's hand, and they danced as Lou sang, "You Are My Special Angel." Donald looked over at his own mother and Hannah's, who stood side by side, smiling, with their arms around each other's waists.

Champagne flutes were filled all around, and Lou declared it was time for the best man's toast. Attention focused on Frank, standing behind the bridal table alongside Donald.

"As most of you know, one of our favorite Broadway musicals, Donald's and mine, is *Pippin,* which opened on Broadway in the early '70s and took home a ton of Tony awards. Our high school put it on when we were students, and this year my colleagues and I—Lou, Etta, Emily, and a fantastic cast, most of whom are sharing the day with us—staged it for the paying public in the Ocean County College theater. For those who might not be familiar with the story, it's about a young man who wants nothing more than for his life to have some profound meaning. After one frustration is followed by another, he finally finds what he's looking for in the arms of a good woman." He paused and scanned the faces of the guests. "I don't think it's a stretch to compare my lifelong friend here to Pippin. Let me explain. Donald first found success as a platoon leader in a war zone; he found further success in achieving his Ph.D.; and then he found success teaching, where he made a difference in a lot of other people's lives. But Donald, like Pippin, was still frustrated; he was emotionally adrift. Adrift, that is, until he met this beautiful woman who steered him on the proper course. The course that led them both to this place and this time." He paused to scan the room, as good teachers do, before continuing.

"You've all heard the expression that getting married means tying the knot. It's an obvious metaphor, but in the finale of the play, Pippin really defines it. And I know that Hannah and Donald will agree when Pippin says, 'If I'm never tied to anything, I'll never be free.' Here's to Hannah and Donald, as they celebrate their first day of being free!"

Cheers erupted from the guests, and Frank grinned self-consciously before lifting his glass to lead the others.

After the toast, Lou announced that the best man deserved a spotlight dance for himself and the maid of honor. As they approached the floor, the band struck up "How Much Is That Doggie in the Window?" Laughter ensued as Frank and Emily stumbled. Lou cut the band short, and joked, "No, no, not *that* Patti Page song; the *other* one!" And they segued smoothly into "Allegheny Moon."

"Should we tell them?" murmured Frank in Emily's ear as they danced.

"Don't you dare," she whispered back. "This is their day. Hannah has no idea; I haven't even worn it to the office yet."

"Don't wait too long; I might change my mind."

Emily chuckled. "Fat chance of that. You know you can't do better than me. Except maybe Hannah, but she's off the market now." She added, "Did Donald tell you that Hannah's mom found them a ranch house in Point Borough?"

"No; we've been kind of busy doing other things."

"It's a good-sized ranch, comes with a ramp. For their wedding gift, I'm hiring an electrician to run a line in the garage for Moby Duck."

"Let's hope he doesn't need the ramp all that much longer."

"Have faith, sweetheart, have faith."

The buffet dinner and cruise up the river and back proved delightful, with the consensus declaring it the best of weddings, ever. As the *River Belle* returned to her dock, and the celebration neared its completion, Lou announced the bouquet toss, and the single girls, most from the cast of the play, formed a knot on the floor, all of them ready to duck the dreaded bouquet. "You too," Hannah said to Emily. "You're single."

Emily acquiesced and joined the others, and Hannah shocked her when, instead of tossing the bouquet on Lou's count of one, two, three, with a broad smile she turned around and placed it in Emily's hands. The other girls applauded, and some exaggeratedly wiped looks of relief from their faces.

"You knew?" Emily asked.

"I saw the indentation the ring left on your finger. You can't hide it from me, Emily." Then Hannah wrapped her in her arms.

Emily looked up and grinned at the stunned look on Frank's face.

"Don't even think of leaving yet, folks," Lou announced to the guests. "There's one more thing to do before we close out the festivities. Would you all please clear the floor for one final, one very special dance?"

On cue, Donald wheeled his chair onto the dance floor alongside Hannah. She perched herself sideways across his lap, legs draped over the arm of his chair, and her arm looped around his neck. "Just like we rehearsed, right?" she whispered, and he told her he had the moves down pat.

To applause from all, Lou cued the band and he and Audra together sang, "Save the Last Dance for Me."

And on the middle of the floor, Donald and Hannah danced.

About the Author

Stephen M. DeBock's first writing award came at age 17, when a 25-word essay, written in blank verse, earned him a fishing trip to Alaska. Entering the Marine Corps a month later, he was assigned to Washington, DC, where he served in the Presidential Honor Guard. An article on his experiences appeared in American Heritage Magazine.

Following his discharge, Steve worked days, went to college nights, and spent weekends earning a private pilot's license. His writing has been published twice in AOPA Pilot Magazine.

A career teacher, Steve was honored by the State of New Jersey for his work in consumer/media education and had a curriculum he devised published in a manual distributed to school libraries throughout the state.

For three years, Steve and his wife Joy lived aboard a 42-foot trawler yacht. An article on their final summer cruise appeared in Living Aboard Magazine. (A photo of their home afloat is on his Facebook Author Page.)

Steve is a member of the International Thriller Writers Organization and the Central Pennsylvania Writers Organization. He and his wife live in Hershey.

FACEBOOK: https://www.facebook.com/Stephen-M-De-Bock-295034173887998